Q-SHIP
CHAMELEON

BOOK FOUR
OF THE CASTLE FEDERATION SERIES

Q-SHIP CHAMELEON

BOOK FOUR
OF THE CASTLE FEDERATION SERIES

GLYNN STEWART

**FAOLAN'S PEN
PUBLISHING**

faolanspen.com

All rights reserved. For information about permission to reproduce selections from this book, contact the publisher at info@faolanspen.com or Faolan's Pen Publishing Inc., 22 King St. S, Suite 300, Waterloo, Ontario N2J 1N8, Canada.

This is a work of fiction. All the characters and events portrayed in this book are fictional, and any resemblance to any persons living or dead is purely coincidental.

This edition published in 2018 by:

Faolan's Pen Publishing Inc.

22 King St. S, Suite 300

Waterloo, Ontario

N2J 1N8 Canada

ISBN-13: 978-1-988035-52-9 (print)

A record of this book is available from Library and Archives Canada.

Printed in the United States of America

1 2 3 4 5 6 7 8 9 10

First edition

First printing: October 2016

Illustration © 2016 Tom Edwards

TomEdwardsDesign.com

Faolan's Pen Publishing logo is a trademark of Faolan's Pen Publishing Inc.

Read more books from Glynn Stewart at faolanspen.com

1

CAPTAIN KYLE ROBERTS of the Castle Federation Space Navy paused in the transfer tube to take one last look at *Avalon*. He'd commanded the big carrier for four months and ten days and was now handing her back into the hands of the same yards he'd received her from.

Despite her immense bulk, battle damage was clearly visible on her outer hull. They'd covered the most egregious of holes before making the two-week flight home from the front, but given the amount of damage the supercarrier had taken, many smaller ones were still visible. It would be months before the ship could fight again, but she'd done her builders proud in managing to come home at all.

The other man sharing the transit tube with the immense redhaired Captain coughed slightly.

"I hate to rush you, sir, but we are the last ones off and the yard wants to commence the atmosphere purge immediately," Fleet

Commander James Anderson, no longer his executive officer as of twenty minutes earlier, told him. The slim man shared his former Captain's height and dark red hair but lacked the senior officer's sheer bulk.

"They completed the life-form scan?" Kyle asked softly. Last he'd checked, there were three cats officially assigned to the carrier and *they* wouldn't necessarily follow orders to leave.

"They have," Anderson confirmed. "Thermals and internal scanners show nothing aboard; they could probably skip the purge."

Part of the purpose of removing the entire atmosphere from the warship was to deal with the inevitable rats and cockroaches and other vermin that inevitably ended up aboard any human spaceship. It was part of any ship's annual maintenance—the maintenance Kyle's ship was eight months early for.

Hopefully concealing his misgivings from Anderson, Kyle nodded and continued down the tube. His neural implant was still linked into *Avalon*'s command net, and the ship calmly informed him as it continued shutting down system after system.

Reaching the end of the tube, Kyle sent one final series of commands to his ship to finish shutting down *everything,* and then handed over control to *Merlin Four*'s central systems. The sudden silence in his head gave him pause: the ceremonies had been almost half an hour earlier, but *now* was when he truly ceased to be *Avalon*'s Captain.

"Where are you being sent?" he asked his former XO as they stepped into the station itself, both officers trading salutes with the Marines guarding the access. With *Avalon* estimated to be in repairs for as long as she'd been in *service,* a Federation at war couldn't afford to let her crew sit around waiting for her to deploy again.

"*Alexander,* as her senior tactical officer," Anderson replied. "She's one of the new *Conqueror*-class battlecruisers—I'm pretty sure *everyone* thinks I need more seasoning before giving me my third circle!"

Kyle nodded silently. *He'd* recommended that Anderson pick up the third gold circle of a Senior Fleet Commander and be given the executive officer slot on an older, smaller ship. While experience as a department head on the Castle Federation's newest battlecruisers wouldn't hurt the junior man, the lack of promotion was telling as to the weight *Kyle's* recommendations were getting.

"Yourself?" his former XO asked. "Which ship are they giving you?"

The big Captain smiled mirthlessly.

"You'll recall that I got the battle group ripped to pieces," he said quietly. "I don't know if I'm getting a new command. My only orders are to meet Admiral Kane in an office in the transient officers' section of the station. Where I go from there?" He shrugged. Vice Admiral Mohammed Kane was the head of the Castle Federation's Joint Department of Personnel, and Kyle was a little surprised to be meeting with the man in person. "I will go where the Federation sends me."

"Anyone else wouldn't have done nearly as well," Anderson said confidently. "They'll have a command deck waiting for you, boss. They'd be mad not to."

"I appreciate the vote of confidence, James," Kyle told him. "But we both know the Navy isn't always the most...logical of institutions."

Stopping at the bank of elevators that would carry each of them to their destinations, Anderson drew himself up to attention and saluted crisply.

"You'll see, sir," he said, still voicing a confidence Kyle didn't share. "Good luck."

"*Alexander's* tactical department doesn't know how lucky they are," Kyle replied. "Good luck, Commander Anderson."

———

KYLE'S ELEVATOR stopped at the level for transient officers' quarters aboard *Merlin Four*—a space where officers between ships could lay their heads and use the offices to do their admin work. Before he could leave the plain metal box to head to his appointment, however, a strange man barged into the elevator and tapped a trio of commands into the console.

"That was my stop," Kyle objected, stepping forward to lean over the man. The stranger was a bald older man with a gauzy white goatee and faint liver spots, significantly shorter and skinnier than the immense Navy Captain.

"It was," he agreed with Kyle calmly. "Of course, there were *also* three well-paid young men waiting to kill you in what I'm sure would have been very convincingly a mugging gone wrong. So, would you rather be late for your appointment with Admiral Kane, Captain Roberts, or never make it?"

"I...find that difficult to believe," Kyle said slowly. He didn't, sadly. One of the officers assigned to *Avalon* when she'd left Castle had *also* tried to kill him. He was also aware he had enemies, even if he hadn't expected them to try and kill them here.

"I'll deliver you to Admiral Kane intact, Captain; don't you worry," the stranger told him. The commands he'd punched into the elevator appeared to be moving the vehicle—a pod with far more travel options than the simple title of *elevator* suggested—to a stop Kyle hadn't known existed. "But I also need a few minutes of your time for a brief I can't give you on the record."

"On the record? Who *are* you?" Kyle demanded.

"You can call me Mister Glass," Glass replied. "I'm with Federation Intelligence, Covert Ops Division. Aside from anything else, we owe you more of an explanation than Kane will be able to give you."

"An explanation for *what*?" the Captain asked, feeling more than a little lost in the conversation.

Glass sighed and gestured out the door as the elevator stopped again.

"This access isn't available to anyone with normal routing privileges," he said, avoiding the question. "We're closer to the Admiral's office and you were early. Give me ten minutes of your time, Captain Roberts. I won't say you won't regret it—I can't promise that—but it will be informative."

Kyle looked at the man for a long moment, instructing his neural implant to try to confirm anything about the stranger. Linked into the station's systems, his implant *should* be able to identify any member of the Federation armed forces, though a Covert Ops officer would likely not show up.

Instead of a name, a rank, or indeed *any* actual information, his implant brought up only an authentication code showing that it *did* recognize Glass, along with a note that Navy officers should provide the man with any requested assistance.

If the man was telling the truth, he might have just saved Kyle's life —and if nothing else, the evidence Kyle had was that Glass was exactly what he said he was.

"Lead on, Mister Glass," he instructed with a sigh.

———

GLASS LED the way to one of the offices in a row full of them. Nothing distinguished this office from the other twelve in the corridor other than that it opened to a silent command from the intelligence agent's neural implant and let them in.

With over ten years in the Castle Federation's military, Kyle was thoroughly familiar with the standard layout of the office: one semicomfortable swivel chair behind the plain metal desk and two uncomfortable folding chairs in front of it. One wall was a screen, easily linked to a neural implant or a tablet. The other was some form of decoration; on *Merlin Four*, all of them had the formal seal of the Castle Federation stenciled onto the wall, a stylized castle inside a circle of fourteen stars.

"Take a seat, Captain," Glass told him as he grabbed the swivel chair and rolled it out so the desk wasn't between them. "I contacted Admiral Kane on our way over, he'll meet us here in twenty minutes."

Surprised that the head of the Navy's personnel would adjust his plans at anyone's request, Kyle looked at the other man askance as he took a seat. Glass might be presenting himself as "just" a Covert Ops agent, but there was definitely more going on.

"I'll start with the simple," the spy continued. "As I suspect you've worked out, you're not getting a ship. What you may *not* have realized is that you're not getting *Avalon* back when she's repaired, either. You have been unofficially beached."

Kyle swallowed hard. He'd screwed up in the Huī Xing system— faced with a prison camp containing over a hundred thousand Alliance prisoners of war, he'd changed the plan and attacked the system rather than simply acting as a distraction. He'd *freed* the POWs, but *Avalon*, scheduled for six months of repairs, was the most intact unit of the four-ship battle group he'd taken in.

"I didn't expect the fallout from Huī Xing to be that bad," he said quietly.

"It isn't," Glass replied. "That's the explanation I'm going to give you that Kane can't: *he* has to tell you we think you'd be more valuable in a testing or educational role. *I* can tell you that's bullshit.

"The Joint Chiefs are frankly impressed with what you did, and you handed us one *hell* of a diplomatic coup when it comes to dealing with the rest of the Alliance. You're nowhere near ready for your first star, but in a *rational* universe, you'd be taking command of *Alexander* or *Paradiso* and heading back out to the front."

Paradiso was a *Sanctuary*-class supercarrier, *Avalon*'s slightly newer sister that Kyle recalled as being due to commission in just a few weeks. Despite Huī Xing, the older man seemed to think that Kyle still belonged in command of one of the Federation's best ships. If the Joint Chiefs agreed with him, then why…

"The *problem*, Captain Roberts, is that despite his best efforts, Senator Joseph Randall hasn't found any way to get his son out of prison, and he blames you," Glass said bluntly. "Castle's Senator, for all his many and grotesque flaws, is also proving to be one of the best wartime industrial leaders the Federation has ever seen. He knows how to talk to our industrial people and where the bodies are buried— some of the quiet estimates I've seen are that Randall's involvement alone has boosted our war materiel production by at *least* ten percent."

And Kyle Roberts had all but personally put said son, James Randall, behind bars for rape, theft, and treason.

Theoretically, the Castle Federation's thirteen-person Senate was a co-equal executive. In practice, the Senator for Castle was just a bit more equal than others. Combined with the kind of impact on the war effort that Glass was talking about, Randall could get away with a *lot*.

"The fact that he outright demanded you be beached is going to bite him in the ass," the spy noted, "but for the moment, bluntly, the Joint Chiefs have chosen the best wartime leader we've ever had over one Navy Captain, however competent.

"I presume, though I have no evidence, as there are some *very* skilled middlemen involved, that Randall hired the gentlemen who planned on prematurely ending your career," he continued. "You have earned the undying hatred of the most powerful man in the Castle Federation—arguably the second most powerful man in the Alliance."

No elected official, after all, could ever compare to the direct power wielded by the Imperator of Castle's largest ally, the Coraline Imperium.

"So I'm...what, just done?" Kyle asked. Glass was very calm as he laid out the destruction of Kyle's career because he'd seen a criminal arrested and punished.

"No," the spy disagreed. "Kane has several offers he intends to lay before you—the situation is enough of a mess that you get your choice of assignment...so long as it isn't a starship command."

"I was a starfighter pilot," Kyle said slowly. "I sacrificed even my *ability* to do that to the service." A near miss had left him with a radiation-induced cased of neural scarification induced implant degradation, NSIID. He'd gone from the top point two percent of the human race in his ability to interface with computers through his neural implant to "above average."

"I took a transfer so I could keep fighting," he continued, getting angrier as he spoke. He *could* yell at Glass since the man hadn't given him a rank. He couldn't yell at Vice Admiral Kane. "I've fought well —*damn* well, even if Huī Xing was Pyrrhic at best. This is what the Navy gives me in exchange? Beached without trial, without appeal?"

"It's a stinking heap of bullshit and I won't tell you otherwise," Glass said flatly. "But while I don't like it any better than you do, it's hard to argue with the Joint Chief's logic. Randall's contributions could easily give us an extra carrier by December. You're good, Kyle, but I'm not sure you're an extra-carrier-in-the-line-of-battle good."

"So, other than giving me a chance to get angry before I talk to the Admiral, was there a *reason* for this conversation?" Kyle demanded.

"Yes. Kane will have his options for you, but as I said, none of them are starship commands," the spy said. "*I* have another option."

"And it's a starship command?" Kyle asked carefully, trying not to let his anger lead him into an instant yes.

"I can't say more, not yet," Glass told him, "but yes. It's a critical mission, one that could turn the tide of the war. It's black, it's covert, I need the best damn warship commander I can find and I don't answer to the Joint Chiefs."

Kyle thought about it for a moment. It was true there was probably value he could provide at a desk job, but he was a *combat* officer.

"I'm in," he said flatly.

"Listen to Kane's offers before you make up your mind," Glass told him. "But he knows I'm making this one as well. If you're still sure once you've spoken to him, tell him you're taking my offer."

An admittance chime buzzed.

"And that's my cue to leave, and the good Admiral's turn to pitch," the spy said calmly. "Hear him out, Captain, but I'll be honest: I expect to be seeing you shortly."

2

Castle System
11:10 April 25, 2736 Earth Standard Meridian Date/Time
Orbital Dry Dock Merlin Four

VICE ADMIRAL MOHAMMED KANE was a tall man clad in a perfectly turned-out black Castle Federation Space Navy uniform and a plain black turban. The last time Kyle had seen him, his skin had been tanned dark by the sun, but in the intervening months, that had faded to an almost sickly pallor.

He passed Glass as he stepped through the door, exchanging an uninterpretable glance with the smaller man.

"Somehow, I have the feeling that Glass has stolen much of my thunder," the head of Castle's Joint Department of Space Personnel told Kyle, taking the chair behind the desk and laying a tablet on it.

"Is that actually his name?" Kyle asked, buying himself time to regain some control of his temper as much as anything else.

"No," Kane confirmed Kyle's suspicion. "It is the third I've known him by, and I don't entirely believe the *Federation* knows his real name.

All I can tell you is that he speaks for the highest levels of our intelligence apparatus."

"So, what he told me was true?"

Kane sighed.

"I don't know for certain what he told you," he admitted. "I can guess, though I can neither confirm nor deny any of it. Glass's conversation was off the record. Ours is not. Do you understand me, Captain Roberts?"

The Admiral's tone was apologetic, but there was also no mistaking the command.

"I guess, sir," Kyle allowed with a slow nod. "Interrupted as we were, this is your meeting. What did you need from me?"

"With *Avalon* laid up, you're at loose ends and the Federation would like to put you where we think you can do the most good," Kane explained.

"And you're going to tell me that's not on the bridge of a warship?" the junior man asked.

Kane sighed again.

"We can argue the logic until the heat death of the universe," he pointed out. "You know some of the background details, but the truth is that a purely administrative position is one of the big checks you're missing to make flag rank."

That stopped Kyle in his tracks.

"I've been a Captain for less than a year," he pointed out. "I've been in the *Navy*, as opposed to the Space Force, for barely more than that. It's a little early for that, isn't it?"

"Yes," the other man agreed calmly. "But not too early for us to be considering it as your career progresses. We are at war and war has an...unfortunate accelerating factor on military ranks. I don't expect to be pinning a star on you this year, Captain—but I would be unsurprised to be doing so *next* year.

"An educational, administrative, or technical command would fill a noticeable gap in your record," he continued, "and help soothe the opinions of those who see the Stellar Fox as a glory hound."

"I *hate* that nickname," Kyle grumped. "And I'd happily trade glory just to have Michael Stanford back, or to not have brought home two crippled ships in six months. *No one* wants glory, sir."

Michael Stanford had been *Avalon*'s CAG and his Captain's strong right arm and friend. He'd died at Huī Xing because his Captain hadn't been good enough.

"I agree," the Admiral said quietly. "But, frankly, *you* need time away from a combat assignment. Time with ready access to a counselor and no *new* memories and losses."

"We don't have time for that," Kyle objected. "And Captain Solace is still with Seventh Fleet, for that matter. I don't think we *have* enough shrinks for if my girlfriend dies on the front and I'm flying a *desk*, sir."

The room was silent for a long moment, and then Kane chuckled softly.

"I see Glass got you more than a little riled up," he noted. "I *do*, for the record, know probably about as much about his offer as you do, but I would appreciate it, *Captain*, if you at least let me explain what the Federation wants you to do before you take a dive into the black."

"Yes, sir. Sorry, sir."

"We see two places that you could have an outsized impact on the war effort," the Admiral noted. "My own suggestion, my biases being what they are, is to send you to the Academy. We're trying to rush our cadets through what's supposed to be a three-year program—even *with* neural implants—in eighteen months. A top-tier tactician is *exactly* what they need, someone who's seen combat in *this* war and won't forget things have changed.

"Your knowledge has also been requested by JD-Tech's testing and oversight committees," he continued. "We'd want you to review early- and late-stage planning and development for real-world applications. We're trying to consolidate twenty years of military R&D by four major and two dozen-plus minor powers into a new generation of standard-ized weapons and systems. Again, someone who's seen combat in this war would have a disproportionate value to those programs."

"Why me?" Kyle asked. The Joint Department of Technology ran all of the Federation's military research and development—and its testing and oversight committees had to sign off before anything went into service. It was a position a lot of officers would give their left arm for. "We've seen a lot of action this last year. Any of those officers would do for that."

"Yes," Kane admitted. "The same tactical instinct that makes me want you for the Academy would have real value to the design committees, but we have other officers we can send for that. Other officers who can train our cadets. You'd be damned good at both jobs, and it's your call. With the background crap going on, that's the least I can do."

"But if I take any of these jobs," the Captain said quietly, "I don't get *Avalon* back when she's repaired, do I?"

"No."

"And what *do* you know of the op Glass wants me for?"

"That he has a ship and needs a Captain," Kane replied. "It may change the course of the war...or it may do nothing but get people killed. It's that kind of black-ops affair, Captain Roberts."

"But it's my only choice if I want a command?"

The tall Admiral sighed again but nodded.

"Yes. I can't give you a ship—but the nature of Glass's job protects him from...high-level disapproval."

Kyle shrugged.

"I'm a combat officer, sir," he told Kane. "I'm no glory hound—I don't think, anyway—but I can do better for the Federation and the Alliance on a command deck than behind a desk."

"I'll let Glass know," the Admiral said after a long moment.

3

Castle System
17:30 April 25, 2736 Earth Standard Meridian Date/Time
Orbital Dry Dock Merlin Four

MERLIN FOUR WAS PRIMARILY a military station, one of the several central hub stations serving the shipyards and dry docks orbiting Castle. Given the scale of the station—each of its six dry docks was almost two kilometers long—there were a *lot* of military personnel aboard, which had inevitably required a civilian presence to support them.

The core of that presence was the promenade, a two-tiered mall located as far away from anything important as could be arranged. The better restaurants were reserved up to a month in advance, but Kyle wasn't above leaning on his fame as the "Stellar Fox" to get a table once he discovered that Senior Fleet Commander Kelly Mason, his one-time subordinate and the late Michael Stanford's girlfriend, was going to be on the station.

The small satchel the big officer carried through the crowds felt a *lot* heavier than it actually was. Technically, Kyle wasn't supposed to have it. While Stanford had arranged for the samples to be taken, he'd never actually formally recorded his intentions.

Since both his doctor and his Captain had known about them, however, they'd quietly arranged for them to end up in Kyle's care so he could deliver them to Kelly Mason—the only woman in the galaxy for whom Michael Stanford might have had sperm samples put aside.

The crowd was dense and mobile, a sense of life and energy that energized the big man. The solitude of command clashed with his base nature, and it was good to be surrounded by people who didn't look to him as their master after the Gods.

His size and bulk meant that most people shifted out of his way unconsciously and even the densest crowd was easy to pass through, allowing him to cross the promenade toward his destination without issue until someone bodily slammed into him.

Kyle stumbled backward and was suddenly aware of another man, almost as large as he was, with a *very* ugly-looking knife in his hand.

"Your wallet and the bag, now, or I gut you," the mugger snarled.

"I'm with the Navy," Kyle said calmly. "I don't carry a wallet on *Merlin Four*—and the bag is the last thing a dead friend of mine left for his girl and you don't *want* it."

The knife jabbed at him, a warning that came well short of touching him.

"Not playing, Navy boy. The bag and any money you got."

"Not happening," Kyle replied, trying to hold the mugger's gaze. "The bag is bio samples, you twit."

"Open it," he gestured with the knife. "Prove it."

"It was sealed by medical professionals and should only be *opened* by them or the samples could be ruined," Kyle snapped. "Just...go. I've got nothing for you."

Something in the mugger's eyes finally clicked with Glass's original warning—that someone had been waiting to kill him and make it look like a mugging. He didn't look *nearly* disappointed enough, and any *sane* mugger would have vacated as soon as Kyle refused to be intimidated.

Kyle wasn't a martial artist or *any* kind of hand-to-hand fighter, but he *was* a massive man who worked out religiously. As the knife stabbed toward his chest, he punched his attacker in the face. At least one tooth shattered under the impact and the stranger stumbled backward, spitting blood.

"Oh, you'll regret that," he snapped. "Take him!"

The sight of the knife had sent the crowd scurrying away, but two other men had stayed close enough that they lunged in to grab Kyle's arms.

He flung the first one forward, whatever plan or tactic they were using insufficient to deal with how strong he was. The *second* one, however, took a grip that accounted for that—and his attempt to use brute force to fling the man away instead crumpled him to the ground in excruciating pain.

He kept enough presence of mind to *place* the bag of precious samples on the metal floor, freeing his hand to try to defend himself as the first assassin came at him with the knife.

The one he'd flung aside grabbed his arm again as Kyle tried to defend himself, moments too late to stop the big officer from knocking the knife to the ground. The blade flashed along his skin, the fabric of his uniform jacket and emergency shipsuit splitting under the ultra-sharp blade, and blood spattered to the ground.

Shouts sounded from behind him and the sound of running feet echoed as Kyle found himself staring down the barrel of a Navy-issue pistol.

"Out of time," the thug snarled—then his head *exploded* as three rapid gunshots echoed through the promenade. The corpse crumpled to the ground to reveal the old man who'd introduced himself as "Mister Glass" holding the same type of gun.

"I really can't complain," the spy said grumpily, "but you'd think professionals would *talk* less."

———

BY THE TIME Kyle had been rushed to a nearby clinic under escort by Castle Federation Military Police, had the gash in his arm cleaned and stitched up and given a statement, his dinner appointment was over an hour in the past.

Once the MPs had filtered out, however, Glass dropped into the chair next to his bed and looked at him levelly.

"You gonna live?"

"It's a five-centimeter cut that barely made it through the skin," Kyle pointed out. "I don't think that was *ever* in question. The *gun* was going to be a problem, though. Thanks."

"I was in the area," Glass said, his tone somewhat apologetic. "I'd passed the details of those three onto the station MPs, but I underestimated their ability to stay under the radar. I apologize, Captain."

"You also saved my life. Apology accepted."

"Good." The spy smiled. For a moment, he looked like someone's friendly grandfather—except for his eyes, which remained utterly flat. "I also took the liberty of informing Senior Fleet Commander Mason of your travails. She is waiting outside for the conversation you promised her—one I don't envy you, Captain."

"Thank you again," Kyle said honestly.

"From the sounds of it, you'll be out of here tonight," Glass concluded. "In the morning, meet me at shuttle bay Seven-Delta at oh eight hundred. We're going to take a field trip."

With that, the old spy left the room, almost immediately replaced by the voluptuous blonde form of Kyle's first executive officer, Kelly Mason.

"I'm mourning enough people, Roberts," she said sharply as she took the seat Glass had vacated. "Could you *try* not to get killed at *home*?"

"Working on it," he told her. "I assure you, Senior Fleet Commander, *not dying* is high on my list of priorities."

Mason nodded sharply, inhaling deeply.

"I saw the reports from Huī Xing," she told him. "The smart ones are calling you a hero again. The rest… Well, you know you have detractors here, right?"

"Yes. It's why I'm heading back out there as fast as I can," he replied.

"You have a command?" she asked, surprised. "Rumor mill was that you were heading to a desk for 'seasoning', whatever that means."

"It's complicated and I don't know the details yet, but I'm definitely heading back out," Kyle told her, being vague about even the details he had.

"I'm sorry about Michael," he continued. "I should have done better, done something—*anything*—different."

"And left a hundred thousand people to rot?" she asked quietly. "Michael wouldn't have *let* you."

"He generally did a good job of recognizing when my head was up my ass," Kyle admitted. "I miss him. A lot."

"Yeah."

Kyle dug through the pile of his effects they'd left next to him and found the satchel from *Avalon*'s doctor.

"Here," he passed it to her. "Technically, Michael had no formal statement of what was to happen to these, but when both your doctor and your Captain *know* your plan, these things happen anyway."

Mason studied the bag for a moment, inhaling sharply as her neural implant picked up the ID tag that was keyed to her implant codes.

"We'd talked about this," she whispered. "I...I assumed he'd died before he could put samples aside."

"According to the doctor, he had them prepped just before we arrived in Huī Xing," Kyle told her. "I don't know if you'll want to use them with him passed, but...I *know* he would have wanted you to have them. To have that option, no matter what."

Mason was blinking back tears now, and Kyle ignored the stupid hospital gown they'd given him to wrap her in his arms.

Michael Stanford had been a comrade-in-arms and a friend. He *deserved* to be mourned.

4

Castle System
08:00 April 26, 2736 Earth Standard Meridian Date/Time
Shuttle DXC-5523

HAVING SPENT his entire adult life in the Federation's military, Kyle arrived at the shuttle bay Glass had asked to meet him at exactly on time. It was one of the smaller docking bays on *Merlin Four*, a secured single-shuttle bay used for VIP transit, according to the directory.

Two men in casual civilian clothing leaned against the wall by the hatch to the bay, attempting to look casual. The sharp precision with which their eyes tracked every individual moving down the corridor toward and past them gave the lie to that illusion.

As he approached the door, Kyle felt his implant buzz—a purely mental sensation—as one of the two guards pinged him for authorization and identification. He extended a limited access to his systems, one that would allow the guard to confirm who he was and why he was there without accessing any of the confidential data or personal memories also stored in his implant.

"Proceed," a voice sounded in his head, and he stepped through the door. To anyone outside, it would have looked like he'd casually walked through the door, but Kyle had still passed a high-tier security check before the guard had unlocked it.

Covert ops was entirely outside his experience, but he could still recognize a slick job when he saw it.

The ship inside the bay was a surprise. He'd been expecting an orbital runabout, one of the small craft used to transfer people between ships without ever leaving orbit or landing on a planet. Instead, he found himself looking at the significantly *larger* shape of an interplanetary shuttle, barely smaller than a Marine assault shuttle.

"I presumed you'd want to fly us yourself," Glass told him, the gaunt man emerging from behind the corner of the spacecraft and wiping his hands with a cloth. "She's fully fueled and the maintenance crew checked out her zero-point cell this morning. Should be good to go."

"Where are we heading?" Kyle asked.

"Gawain," the spy replied. "I'll give you more detailed coordinates once we're close. There's more out there than cloudscoops and the Reserve Fleet stations."

Gawain was the Castle system's largest gas giant, anchor to the cloudscoops that fed the system's rapacious demand for hydrogen, and to the stations that had un-mothballed the ships of the Castle Reserve Flotilla, the Federation's insurance policy against the very war they were now fighting.

Kyle's understanding was that the Reserve Flotilla stations had been mostly decommissioned now that the ships from the Castle system, at least, had been reactivated and deployed. The Terran Commonwealth had demonstrated that they were *extremely* vulnerable in an attack on the system a few months before.

"That's twelve hours away, even in this bird," he pointed out.

"Then I suggest you start your preflight," Glass told him, tossing the cloth he'd cleaned his hands with in a nearby bin—had the frail-looking spy actually disconnected the fuel line *himself?*

————

THE SHUTTLE WOULD HAVE BEEN a far clunkier beast than a Marine assault shuttle in an atmosphere, but in deep space, she was a joy to fly. Once clear of the orbital structures around Castle, Kyle got clearance from orbital control to go to full power and lit up her engines.

As the zero-point energy cell fed antimatter to the thrusters, a suite of mass manipulators flared to life. Several created a gravity field that exactly countered the acceleration. Others decreased the mass of the shuttle, while still others increased the mass of the thrust blasting out the thruster nozzles.

Once at full power, the shuttle accelerated toward the two-light-hour-distant gas giant at a tad under five hundred gravities. He checked the course was clear out to the limits of the small craft's radar and passive thermal scans, and then leaned back in his chair, reducing his link to the ship to a background data update.

"ETA is just after twenty hundred hours," he told Glass.

The other man had his eyes closed but opened them slowly as Kyle spoke.

"Good," he announced. "They'll be expecting us. I'm going to grab a coffee—the galley is fully stocked. Want anything?"

"More details on what I've signed up for?" Kyle asked.

"Be patient, Captain," Glass replied. "I'll brief you before we arrive; I just want some more empty space between us and anyone who might get curious."

The spy disappeared, leaving the Captain shaking his head at the controls as he studied the network of space stations he was still flying through.

Castle wasn't the single wealthiest world in the Alliance of Free Stars; that distinction went to Phoenix, the largest of the three habitable planets in the system of the same name, and capital of the Star Kingdom of Phoenix. It was still the *second* wealthiest, and the smelters, habitats and microgravity factories formed an immense, entirely artificial ring around the world.

Ten warships, over a tenth of the Federation's peacetime fleet and a massive commitment even with the Reserve deployed, stood guard over that ring, backed by an additional five *thousand* starfighters based in orbiting platforms.

Once they were clear of the densest core of the orbital infrastructure, the flight quieted down, but it was still a busy region of space, with hundreds of sublight ships arriving or leaving in any given minute. While Kyle didn't need to have his hands on the controls at every moment, he also couldn't leave the cockpit or ignore the data feeding to his implant.

At five hundred gravities, however, they eventually left everything else behind. While there was other traffic moving to and from Gawain along the direct path, the rest of the traffic was big tanker ships, mostly automated vessels moving at fifty gravities. Fifty gravities was Tier One acceleration, the first "plateau" in the efficiency of the combination of antimatter engines and mass manipulators. Tier One was immensely efficient, if too slow for most military needs.

Kyle checked the course he'd laid in and made sure it was clear of the corridor used by the tankers, then went to join Glass in the galley.

"We're clear of Castle's orbital traffic," he told the spy as he grabbed a coffee cup of his own from the galley's automated systems. "ETA's unchanged."

"And sensors show the nearest ship is over two light-seconds away," Glass confirmed. "I just deployed a drone to orbit us and sweep for stray radio signals. It won't help if someone has snuck a Q-Com-equipped bug aboard, but those are sizable and we swept this ship barely an hour before launch."

"That's…a little paranoid, isn't it?" Kyle asked slowly. The smallest Q-Com he'd ever seen had contained its quantum-entangled particles in a box roughly the size of a briefcase. He didn't think they *came* small enough to be used as an eavesdropping device.

"It is," Glass agreed, "but we absolutely *cannot* afford for any information on this operation to leak back to the Commonwealth; do you understand me, Captain Roberts?"

Kyle nodded slowly. The Terran Commonwealth was the largest and most powerful human nation in history. He had no illusions about how deeply they had probably infiltrated the central world of the Alliance's most powerful member.

"If they don't know it was us, Operation Blue Sunbeam could

change the course of the war," the spy noted. "If they learn it was us, it'll have been a giant waste of everyone's time."

"Blue Sunbeam?"

"We randomly generate operational code names," Glass explained with a pained smile. "It doesn't result in particularly impressive names, but it means that the names don't give any clues to our objective."

"Which is?"

Glass sighed and nodded.

"Everything checks out as clean as I can be certain of," he told Kyle. "Our objective, Captain Roberts, is to attempt to turn the tide of the war with a deep raid into Terran space, attacking their core ship-building complex and attempting to blame someone *else* for it."

Kyle looked at him in shock.

"You're a smart man, Captain Roberts," the spy noted. "You've done the math: The Terran Commonwealth has over three hundred star systems. The Alliance has less than a hundred. On a functionally peacetime footing, the Commonwealth produces more warships a year than we do. Our crews are more experienced, our training is better, we currently have a slight but clear tech edge…but if the Commonwealth ever *truly* went to war, they could provide Walkingstick with the ships to swamp us with sheer numbers."

Fleet Admiral James Calvin Walkingstick was the current bogey man of the Alliance, charged as Marshal of the Rimward Marches by the Commonwealth—a charge that meant he was expected to bring those systems *into* the Commonwealth. Systems that happened to coincide with the Castle Federation and its allies.

"We can win battles and push them back. We've held our own so far in this seesawing disaster of a war. But we can't win. Our best hope is a peace treaty that returns us to status quo—and all the last one of those bought us was time to raise another generation in the shadow of conquest."

Kyle sighed and took a gulp of coffee.

"I see the appeal," he admitted. His own father had survived the last war only to eventually commit suicide from PTSD so extreme, even twenty-eighth-century medicine couldn't help. Two generations of Castle's young men and women had gone to war to stay free from Terra. Ending the war with an outright victory could prevent that from happening—even if Kyle couldn't see a way that would be even remotely *possible*.

"They'll identify any ship we take on a deep raid, though," he pointed out after a moment. "Even our *starfighters* would be enough of a hint. All us attacking a core world would achieve would be to put them on a true total war footing."

"Before Seventh Fleet's Marines joined you in Alizon, they stopped in the Kaber system to deal with a pirate attack," Glass explained. "Any record outside those Marines' heads shows that there were two pirate ships, both glorified freighters with strapped-on mass drivers and some junk second-generation starfighters.

"The *third* ship was erased from every record Federation Intelligence could find. She was a Commonwealth Q-ship, a *Blackbeard*-class like the vessel you took out in the Hessian System. Thanks to Brigadier Hammond, we took her intact. We don't know how she ended up in pirate hands…but we suspect the Commonwealth knows she *did*.

"And, so far as Alliance Joint Intelligence can tell, they *don't* know we captured her," he concluded. "We've assembled a fighter group of Stellar League sixth-generation starfighters and have a plan to acquire munitions and supplies to make the Commonwealth think the League is backing us.

"The Stellar League is in an unusually unified state at the moment, and a Commonwealth punitive expedition could kick off a bigger war than Terra may think," Glass said. "We *need* that distraction, Captain Roberts."

The Stellar League was the second-largest polity in human space, but it was also notoriously disorganized. The overarching government of the League was politely described as "anemic" and its member systems acted as independent states as often as not—and seemed to make a hobby out of minor wars with each other. Wars that often either spilled directly into Commonwealth space or whose losers turned pirate in Commonwealth space.

If they could make the Commonwealth think their attack was yet another raid by League mercenaries, the so-called *condottieri*, then the

Terrans might well engage in one of the semi-regular expeditions to burn out the source of pirates in League space. They couldn't *conquer* the League—its systems were too advanced and too numerous for an easy war—but it was disorganized enough normally that they could eliminate a specific pirate base and punish the home system without *too* much trouble.

But the League's weak central government had been taken over recently by a *condottieri* Admiral, Kaleb Periklos, who now styled himself "Dictator of the Stellar League." He would see a Commonwealth expedition as a challenge to his authority. If the League pushed back, they might push the Commonwealth into a two-front war—and *that* would finally be something resembling an even match.

"And I'm to command this Q-ship," Kyle concluded.

"Indeed," Glass confirmed. "If you back out now, Captain, well… we'll need to keep you out of communication until the operation actually goes off. We trust you, but that's a risk we can't take."

"That won't be necessary," Kyle told him calmly. "Though I do want to see this ship."

5

Castle System
20:00 April 26, 2736 Earth Standard Meridian Date/Time
Secret Castle Federation Intelligence Shipyard Facility Redoubt,
    Gawain Orbit

FOR EASE OF SUPPLY, security, and mutual support, the cloudscoops that extracted hydrogen from Gawain's upper atmosphere were clustered together into an area roughly the size of a normal habitable world. The Castle Reserve Flotilla station was in a trailing orbit, but one that generally kept it aligned with the extraction infrastructure for everyone's convenience.

The final coordinates Glass gave Kyle were on the opposite side of the massive gas giant from all of that activity, and the Captain saw nothing on his sensors as he brought the shuttle closer to the coordinates.

"There's nothing here," he pointed out aloud.

"Check your elevation," Glass replied. "We're still about a thousand kilometers too high."

"That puts us *in* the atmosphere," Kyle objected.

"Yes," the spy agreed. "Hides the facility from prying eyes. There *is* a beacon, though. You should be picking it up about now."

It was almost two minutes later, sweeping across the planet at several dozen kilometers a second, before Kyle actually picked up the beacon. It wasn't transmitting any warnings or information, simply a six-digit number on repeat.

Shaking his head at the intelligence agency's paranoia, he dove the shuttle into Gawain's upper atmosphere under the beacon. The upper layers of the massive planet weren't *too* dangerous, but they did reduce his sensor visibility to a hundred kilometers at most.

He'd made it halfway down to the coordinates when *something* ripped into that limited visibility, rapidly resolving into a Falcon starfighter that trained its main weapon—the positron lance that fired a beam of pure antimatter from a modified zero-point cell—on the suddenly fragile-feeling shuttle.

"Unidentified shuttlecraft, this is a secured no-fly zone," the fighter transmitted. "Flying down here is also bloody stupid, so I assume you have a reason to be here. Transmit authentication codes or head back to the surface *now*."

Glass leaned forward across the console and tapped a command.

"Redoubt Security Flight, authentication is Gamma Kappa One Charlie Zulu Seven Seven Niner. Countersign: Excelsior. Confirm authenticate."

"We confirm authentication, Agent," the fighter's crew replied immediately. "Lights are on for the scenic tour. Captain Rondell says, and I quote, 'Don't rush on my account; let Roberts see his new toy.'"

Their escort's voice shifted into a quavering imitation of an old man for the last bit.

"Received and understood, Redoubt flight," Glass told them. "We're continuing on down."

The starfighter flipped away and disappeared into the clouds. Unlike Kyle, the other pilot was clearly *very* comfortable flying in the gas giant's atmosphere.

"There are carefully calibrated sensor buoys scattered through the atmosphere here," Glass explained at Kyle's surprised look. "Flight

Commander Macready has a *lot* better visibility than you do—its not just that he's more familiar with this pea soup.

"And here we are," he concluded, gesturing toward the sensor display, now showing a large artificial structure orbiting *inside* Gawain's atmosphere. As they grew closer and Kyle slowed the shuttle's velocity more, they entered a region of clearly artificial lower-density atmosphere, allowing a clearer view of the station.

The *Redoubt* was built around a single construction and refit slip. The slip itself was a collection of girders and scaffolding five hundred meters across and a kilometer long, not quite large enough to contain a modern warship but large enough for most needs. A quarter-kilometer disk of a space station capped one end, presumably home to the *Redoubt's* staff and starfighters. A scattering of smaller platforms that Kyle recognized as automated lance and missile batteries traced circles around the entire complex, as did a trio of Falcon starfighters.

They'd clearly passed whatever security checks they needed to get this far, as none of the defenses reacted to them, but as they drew closer to the slip, a series of immense floodlights switched on and highlighted the ship resting in the middle of the slip.

No one looking at her would have thought she was a warship. Warships were usually long lines and sharp edges, designed to both provide a reduced target when approaching an enemy and to focus vast quantities of firepower on specific points.

This ship was the almost-perfect sphere of a civilian ship, a little over four hundred meters in diameter and painted in soothing tones of blue. This close, with the shuttle's sensors to hand and *knowing* what he was looking at, Kyle could pick out the panels that concealed lasers and positron lances. The bands of differing colors were well designed to help conceal the panels from a visual inspection.

The last time he'd encountered a Commonwealth Q-ship, it had blown a space station occupied by over forty thousand souls to pieces. Calm and innocent as this one looked, he couldn't help but shiver looking at her while knowing what she was.

"What's her name?" he asked aloud.

"She has the ability to change transponders and the name on the hull with ease," Glass said quietly. "She was *Christopher Lee* in

Commonwealth service. Once we fully recommissioned her in our service, we decided to rename her *Chameleon*."

———

EXITING THE SHUTTLE, Kyle and Glass were met by a squat, heavily overweight man with stark-white hair. He wore the blue-piped black jacket-and-shipsuit uniform of a Castle Federation Space Navy officer with the golden planet of a full Captain.

"Welcome to the *Redoubt*, Captain Roberts, Agent Glass," he greeted them in a quavering voice. "I am Captain Isaac Rondell and I lead the Navy staff that run this installation."

Age, weight, and war wounds had clearly taken their impact on Captain Rondell, but he moved with confidence if not speed or power as he gestured for them to follow him.

"We've been working on *Chameleon* since she was dragged in from Kaber two months ago," he continued as he led the way down the sterile corridors of the station. "The Commonwealth built her class well, but the pirates who'd been flying her had no clue how to maintain her equipment."

"Is her armament intact?" Kyle asked. "I had the misfortune of seeing one of these at close range in Hessian."

"*Ian Fleming*, our intelligence suggests," Rondell agreed. "*Chameleon* is a later ship and the Blackbeards were each custom-built, from what we can tell. *Fleming* had no capital missile launchers, but *Chameleon* has six. The other armament is much the same: four half-megaton-per-second positron lances, a dozen fighter missile launchers and a suite of defensive lances and lasers."

"It's not much, but I've seen what it can do," Kyle said softly, memories of a disintegrating space station fresh in his mind. "Curious, though—is she more obviously a warship on the inside?"

"In places," the man charged with recommissioning the ship replied. "She has a complete false interior that looks like her original merchant-ship class. Her weapons and military systems are hidden in what would have been the cargo hold. She still has much of that merchant-ship's cargo capacity, allowing you to haul a *lot* of missiles if you can find them, but the inefficiencies inherent in her design reduce it significantly."

"What about crew?"

"We've been quietly recruiting personnel from Home Fleet since the ship arrived," Rondell answered. "There are a few slots open where we'll want to lean on your contacts and knowledge as well. Your new exec has been helping us put everything together; she should be able to fill you in momentarily. Ah, here we are."

"Here" turned out to be a hatch off the corridor that looked identical to every other hatch Kyle had seen on Federation space stations, though this one had a small plaque stating it was a conference room.

Rondell opened the door and led them into the room, which was currently occupied by a single, familiar-looking, woman with dark hair and skin. She wore the same uniform as Kyle or Rondell, though her collar carried the three gold circles of a Senior Fleet Commander.

Kyle was still trying to place why she was familiar when she met his gaze frankly.

"You!" she half-snarled. Her glare switched to Glass instantly. "Sir, I'm afraid I must resign from my involvement in this project. I refuse to work under Captain Roberts's command."

The room was silent.

"Commander Sanchez, I don't understand," Glass admitted. "You are aware that resigning from Operation Blue Sunbeam at this point will require you to enter communication isolation for at least six months, yes?"

"I don't care," she snapped. "I refuse to work under the man who killed my sister."

———

It still took Kyle a moment to realize who she had to be, and then he sighed aloud. Senior Fleet Commander *Judy* Sanchez had been chief of staff to the first Admiral he'd served under—and she'd led a mutiny with the intent of killing Kyle himself.

While no one had ever officially admitted it, his understanding was that she'd been sent after him by Senator Randall.

"Your sister was Judy Sanchez?" he asked aloud to confirm his thought.

"She was. Until you killed her."

Technically, Kyle reflected, Judy Sanchez had been killed by one of his Marines. But even he would call that a technicality.

"Judy Sanchez mutinied in the face of the enemy," he said quietly. "She attempted to assassinate me, personally, and, per the last estimate I saw, committed no less than four separate *types* of treason.

"We also tried to take her alive," he concluded. "I didn't choose your sister's fate, Commander. *She did.*"

"You think I don't know that?" Sanchez demanded. "I don't know why she did it, but I know you think you had no choice. Don't know if you did or not. But she was my *sister.*"

She turned her gaze back to Glass.

"Sir, I did not realize that Roberts would be commanding this mission or I would have already withdrawn," she said flatly. "I would not be able to separate my personal feelings from the performance of the mission. My remaining on the mission would compromise our efficiency and objectives.

"I will prepare a summary of *Chameleon*'s status for the Captain to review and then I will retire to my quarters and wait for further orders."

Sanchez snapped a perfect salute to Rondell and Glass, then walked stiffly out of the conference room.

The three men remained silent for several seconds.

"I was not aware that Sanchez had a sister," Kyle said quietly. "I can't blame her."

"Neither can I, though that leaves us with a massive gap in your roster," Rondell admitted. "We already needed a CAG and a tactical officer for you. I guess we now need an executive officer as well."

"Let me dig into my contacts," *Chameleon*'s Captain-designate replied. "Is there anything *else* I need to keep in mind right off the bat?"

"*Chameleon* has almost no munitions aboard, and while the launchers can handle ours, it would undermine the point of the mission to use Federation weapons," Glass said after a moment's hesitation. "The pirates who stole her from the Terrans apparently sold off most of her munitions stockpile—she only has one missile per launcher.

"We've got a bit more ammunition for the starfighters, but the birds are...well, they're crap," the spy admitted. "League sixth-gen birds are closer to our fifth."

"Great," Kyle half-groaned. "Please tell me we have a plan for getting *some* missiles before we go all the way to the heart of the Commonwealth?"

"We do," Glass confirmed. "But, like most aspects of this operation, we're keeping it under wraps. I'll brief you once we've left the Castle system."

"Are you really arguing that I don't need to know that?" Kyle demanded.

"No, I'm saying you don't need to know it *yet*," the spy replied. "And certainly, for example"—he gestured at the third man in the room—"Captain *Rondell* doesn't need to know.

"It's a covert op, Captain. You're going to have to get used to a bit more compartmentalization and secrecy than you're used to. I'd apologize...but we don't have a choice.

"Terra *cannot* learn what we're doing."

6

Castle System
09:00 April 28, 2736 Earth Standard Meridian Date/Time
Castle Orbit, Station Navy Prime

"WHAT'S the plan looking like for today, Marco?" Wing Commander Russell Rokos asked his minder. The stocky fighter pilot was *trying* to put a good face on things, but he *hated* the ringside circus his involvement in the mass rescue at Huī Xing had stuck him in.

Roberts was stuck with the burden of the pyrrhic victory that had followed, but Russell had led the fighter escort that had covered the escape of over a hundred thousand prisoners of war. When those prisoners had started talking to their command structures, governments, and *families*, Russell Rokos had been available for them to make a hero.

"The ambassador for the Renaissance Trade Factor has invited you to a dinner in your honor at the embassy," Lieutenant Marco Belmonte replied. The tall and slim public relations officer was a stark contrast to Russell's own stocky shoulders and average height. "That is at thirteen hundred hours Earth Standard, seven PM New Cardiff time. You're also on schedule to speak to the flight school entry class at twenty hundred ESM.

"We have a shuttle scheduled for your trip down and back up," he continued. "Everything should run smoothly."

Russell sighed and nodded.

"Any idea if I have a chance of *ever* getting back into a starfighter?" he asked.

"Eventually, I would assume your chances are one hundred percent," Belmonte replied calmly. "Though you must realize this is *also* valuable to the war effort."

"I *realize* that," the big man grouched. "I just don't *like* it."

His thoughts were interrupted by a ping in his neural implant informing him he'd received a message from one of the people he'd listed as "High Priority—Always Interrupt."

He absorbed the message, then turned his attention back to Belmonte. As he was a starfighter pilot, Russell's interfacing capability with the implants everyone had was well over the ninety-ninth percentile. Belmonte clearly hadn't even noticed his moment of distraction.

"Captain Roberts wants to meet with me today," he told Belmonte. "I presume before we make nice with the Factor's ambassador works best?"

The PR officer took a moment to adjust to the sudden shift in subject, but nodded gamely as he caught up.

"Indeed. If the Captain is aboard Navy Prime, I can have a booking for breakfast for the two of you in the deck two-thirty-six officers' lounge for ten hundred hours?"

"Do it," Russell ordered. Sometimes, it was convenient to have a minion.

———

NAVY PRIME WAS the centerpiece of Castle's defenses and the centerpiece of the Castle Federation's war effort against the Terran Commonwealth. It was a sphere a kilometer in diameter, its surface encrusted with missile launchers, fighter bays, positron lances and defensive lasers.

Its *real* value, however, lay in the hundreds of decks of administrative offices, thousands of cubic meters of hyper-dense computing circuits, and its links to the heavily defended Q-Com switchboard station that orbited one hundred kilometers behind it. From Navy Prime, the Federation Joint Chiefs of Staff ran the war effort—with a support staff measured in the tens of thousands.

There were no civilian promenades or restaurants aboard Navy Prime. Even more than the shipyard complexes it shared its orbit with, Prime was a purely military facility. There were, however, hundreds of mess halls and officers' lounges.

Each lounge had their own reputations and specialties and the best often booked up weeks in advance. The 236 officers' lounge wasn't *the* best place on the station for breakfast—but it was in the top ten, and Belmonte had managed to grab a table for two on an hour's notice.

Russell was impressed.

He waved Roberts over to the table as he spotted the big Captain entering the lounge, rising to greet the other man with a firm handshake.

Russell shared his ex-Captain's immense build but lacked about fifteen centimeters of height versus the immense officer.

"I have a slew of diplomatic bullshit to get through later today," he told his former Captain. "I have a *lot* more sympathy for your tour as the 'Stellar Fox' now than I ever thought I would!"

"Oh, dear *Gods,* does it suck," Roberts agreed fervently. "I can see the *value,* but that does not mean that most of us enjoy it. I'm glad to see you made it back in one piece with them all, though."

"Wasn't fun," Russell replied. "Those ships were *not* designed for the number of people we had crammed into them. Even the Marine transports *stank* by the time we made it to Alizon."

"Didn't have a choice. Those were the ships we had."

"So those were the ships we used," the Wing Commander confirmed. "What do you need, skipper?"

"I'm not your skipper right now, Russell," Roberts pointed out. "I don't, officially, even have a command."

That "officially" spoke volumes, though, and Russell perked up.

"So, what do you need?"

"A CAG," the Captain replied. "One able to go on a mission without leaving someone else in the lurch. A black mission. One that will never officially have happened."

"How'd *you* get tied up in something that black?" Russell asked quietly, glancing around to be sure no one was overhearing them. Navy Prime's officers' lounges were designed for this kind of conversation, though, with high-backed booths and strategically positioned white noise generators.

"It was that or a desk," Kyle Roberts explained cheerfully. "It won't be an easy op, Commander," he continued. "I can't tell you much, but I can warn you that you won't be flying Falcons, and you'll be taking on an already-existing wing."

"Can you get me out of the PR grind?" Russell asked.

"I checked in on that before I even called you," his old Captain said with a chuckle. "If you're in, we'll scoop you out of that in about forty-eight hours."

"You should have *led* with that," the CAG replied. "I'm in."

———

EXITING THE LOUNGE AFTER BREAKFAST, Kyle found himself immediately flanked by the two women in black, unmarked shipsuits who'd accompanied him from the *Redoubt*. While the black-ops troopers were present for his security, he was sure they were *also* there to make sure he didn't break the confidentiality agreements he'd made.

"Please tell me you two ate," he asked them as they headed to his next meeting.

"The lounge is familiar with bodyguards," the senior of the two women said calmly. "They brought us breakfast."

Outside of Navy facilities, Kyle had a Marine protective detail. He didn't normally have Marine bodyguards inside Navy stations or aboard ship, but he would have changed that policy on his own even if Glass hadn't imposed the pair of black-clad Amazons on him. Getting stabbed wasn't something he wanted to get used to.

"Good," he told the troopers. "We've still got a busy time ahead of us and I wouldn't want either of the badass women they assigned to guard me deciding they need to eat a passerby for sustenance."

That got a smirk out of both of them—and a thorough double-take from a Navy Lieutenant Commander heading the opposite direction.

"We're meeting Mason at the deck one-seven-five shuttle bay," he reminded them. "Let's get moving."

———

Mason looked better than she had even a few days before, though part of that might be that Kyle hadn't just got himself *stabbed* before meeting up with her. She looked *much* more relaxed as they met over coffee at another officers' lounge.

"Did you decide what you're doing with that package?" Kyle asked her.

"Not yet," she admitted. "Knowing…knowing that he was thinking of that possibility, of us. It helps. I've had the samples stored ground-side in a proper facility. They'll be there when I decide." She smiled sadly. "It's almost as though *he'll* be there when I decide."

"He wouldn't have wanted you to rush the decision," he told her. "You know that."

"I do," Mason agreed. She glanced at the two bodyguards at the next table over. "I'm guessing that this isn't entirely a social call, what with the shadows and all."

"I'd have Marines if I didn't have them after what happened the other day," Kyle admitted. "But yeah, I'm after more than a coffee."

"What do you need?" she asked.

"I have a command," he told her quietly. "It's all hush-hush, cloak-and-dagger crap, but I have a command. I need an XO, one I can trust. You were the first to come to mind."

Kelly Mason paused, silent in thought for a long moment.

"I've only been on *Sunset* for six months," she said quietly. "Leaving them in the lurch wouldn't feel right. I'm guessing this is volunteer-only?"

"Yeah," Kyle admitted, wracking his brain for arguments.

"Then I don't," she said simply. "I can't leave my ship in the lurch just because you ask, Kyle. Holding her together is my job, after all."

"I hate to say any ship is more or less important than any other," he replied, "but *Sunset* is a Home Fleet cruiser. We're…we're going back to the front, I can't say more than that, but this mission is a lot more important than holding down the fort here!

"Plus"—he glanced over at the bodyguards—"I'm only so sure I can trust even our Intelligence people. I'm walking into a snake pit, Kelly, and I'm bringing half of the snakes with me. I need someone I can trust at my right hand."

She was shaking her head as he spoke.

"I can't, Kyle. You're going to walk into the heart of the fire—it's what you do! You've walked out every time before, but I can't be sure you'll walk out this time. And, well." She shrugged helplessly. "If I walk in there with you and *don't* walk out, then I never get to decide about Michael's child.

"The Navy will still send me to war sooner or later," she continued. "And I'll go. But I'm not sticking into my head into the fire next to you, Kyle. I'm sorry, but I'm not."

He sighed.

"Fair enough, I suppose," he allowed. "It's not like we can order you to volunteer."

"If you got JD-Personnel to sign off, they could order me to go, but I'm not volunteering. Anything else I can do to help, I will, but I'm not going with you," she said, her tone final.

"Got a suggestion for a tactical officer?" he said hopefully, mostly joking. His own list for that role was nonexistent, but he was hoping Glass or Rondell would come up with someone.

"I do, actually," she said after a moment's thought. "Our ATO"—assistant tactical officer—"is due for her second gold circle. She's the type that might be brilliant but hasn't had a chance to show it yet. Even if she isn't, she's damn capable and looking for a role where she can earn herself some…attention."

"What's her name?"

"Jenny Taylor," Mason told him. "She doesn't know it yet, but she's getting bumped to Commander the moment we *have* another ship to put her on. She'll volunteer—and twice as fast if I tell her the Stellar Fox is in command."

"I don't have a lot of options," Kyle admitted. "Talk to her and let me know."

———

TAKING over one of the designated "hotel" offices left empty for officers passing through the Navy's HQ to use, Kyle waited impatiently while his escort checked that the communications linkage was clear of bugs and monitoring programs.

"You're clean," she reported.

"Thank you." He linked his implant into the setup and flipped a video channel onto the wallscreen.

One of Navy Prime's ubiquitous Junior Lieutenants popped up on the screen.

"Navy Prime Off-Station Communications; please authenticate ID and state your request," she said calmly.

"This is Captain Kyle Roberts," he told her while simultaneously flashing his ID code from his implant. "I need access to a Q-Com channel for a self-directed connection, please."

"Understood, Captain Roberts. Connecting you in to the Q-Com and switching you over."

The earnest young woman disappeared, replaced by an interface screen that Kyle was only partially familiar with. Fortunately, his implant had the instructions, and he followed those quickly as he input the code to connect him with Glass at the *Redoubt*.

"Captain Roberts, how are you making out?" the old man asked as he appeared on the viewscreen.

"Not bad," Kyle replied. "Rokos has signed on as CAG. Mason wasn't interested, but she found us a tactical officer. I've got a few people I can reach out to fill the XO slot still, but I'm wondering if Rondell came up with anyone."

"He did," Glass told him. "The ATO from Rondell's last ship is just finishing up a round of medical leave. Maxim Chownyk is the man's name; he was XO on *Corona* last. Barely made it off the battleship alive."

"How's his mental?" Kyle asked carefully. *Corona* had been Vice Admiral Tobin's flagship before *Avalon*—and Tobin had ended up on medical relief while flying his flag from Kyle's ship.

"Not perfect, according to his shrink," the spy admitted, "but he's itching to get back into action and volunteered. You'll meet him on the *Redoubt*, unless you want to veto him?"

Kyle considered his own list of potential execs, all of whom were already *on* warships somewhere.

"No, I'll take him," he decided. "Anything else?"

"Just one thing," Glass told him. "Your Marine company commander got tied up in paperwork and is still on Castle. It would save time if he can hitch a ride with you. You know him—Lieutenant Major Edvard Hansen."

"Hansen volunteered for this?" Kyle asked. "I'm going to owe the man a beer." He'd already sent Hansen into a few more hells than he liked, but the Marine was *good* at his job.

"Toss him one on the shuttle flight. I want you back on the *Redoubt* as soon as possible. I'll fill you in on details once you're back, but it looks like we're going to need to accelerate our launch."

7

Castle System
16:00 April 28, 2736 Earth Standard Meridian Date/Time
Chameleon, *Gawain Orbit*

WING COMMANDER RUSSELL ROKOS regarded with scant favor the starfighters neatly stacked along *Chameleon*'s flight deck. He'd been flying the Federation's new Falcon starfighters since their first major deployment aboard *Avalon*'s predecessor ship.

The Falcon was a seventh-generation starfighter and generally regarded as one of the best seventh-generation birds so far.

The Cataphract that the Stellar League had put into commission fifteen years ago was...not so well regarded. It was a sixteen-meter-long cylinder, four and a half meters in diameter, with a lance along the spine and launchers that basically dropped missiles into space and let them fend for themselves.

Its engines sucked, pulling fifty gravities less than a Falcon. Its electromagnetic deflectors sucked. Its positron lance sucked, barely sixty percent of the strength of the Falcon's weapon.

"I don't suppose we snuck any upgrades into these?" he asked plaintively, studying the ships.

"Some," his newest headache, Flight Commander Laura Cavendish, replied. The black-ops squadron leader studied the starfighters without any more positive of an eye. "Only what Intel said we could justify pirates having, though. Engines and mass manipulators got rated for *modern* third-tier acceleration, so closer to five hundred gees, not four-fifty. Deflectors are tougher than we could honestly justify, stacked up to the Falcon's standard."

"Weapons?" he asked hopefully.

"Same lance," she admitted. "Our targeting package, which helps more than you'd think. The launchers are a type you won't find on our birds, though. Better in a lot of ways."

"Oh?" Russell asked. There wasn't much he'd expect the League to have done *better* than the Federation.

"Cycles slower, but the magazine and the launchers can take *anything*," Cavendish told him. The dark-haired woman eyed the fighters with a cold smile. "The guys we got the sample from had them all intermixed in the magazines—the performance parameters are *close*, but if you've got one of our Starfires in one launcher and a League Sarissa in the other..." She chuckled. It wasn't a pleasant sound. "I don't recommend it."

"But they let us use whatever ammunition we can get our hands on and break the security codes on," Russell said. That would come in handy.

"Exactly."

The Wing Commander studied his deck carefully. Thirty-two of the starfighters were painted in the standard dark gray the Commonwealth used for all of their small craft. Eight, however, had been coated in a shimmering black material.

"I'm guessing the black ships are yours?" he asked Cavendish.

"Yeah," she confirmed. "The coating is radar-absorbent and we built cold-gas thrusters into ours. They're not *particularly* stealthy, but it can give us a nice surprise every now and then."

From Cavendish's comments, Russell suspected that the stolen pirate fighters weren't *nearly* as new to her pilots and crews as they were to his people.

Just what *had* they been up to before they were assigned to *Chameleon*?

———

Lieutenant Major Edvard Hanson didn't exactly *mind* flying. The lanky, dark-haired Marine spent the vast majority of his time aboard spaceships of one stripe or another, but…somehow, shuttle flights were different.

Assault landings and so forth were one thing, but a twelve-hour flight trapped in a barely armored tin can left the Marine *very* aware of the emptiness of the void outside. He was *ecstatic* to finally reach *Redoubt* and board *Chameleon*—actual *ships* had internal bulkheads, armored baffles, and emergency airlocks in the case of a breach. Shuttles didn't.

By the time he carried his duffel into the barracks aboard *Chameleon* —hidden away in the extremely utilitarian portion of the ship not meant to be seen by inspectors—he was in a spectacularly foul mood.

"Who's the new guy?" someone bellowed as he entered the central area and glanced around.

The Commonwealth used much the same structure for the Marine bays as the Federation did, with a central mess hall cum gym cum gathering area with multiple "wings" of rooms heading off, one for each platoon's berths and one for the officers' quarters.

The original bellower stood up, drawing attention to himself amidst the gathered collection of Marines. Edvard's practiced eye picked out the different collections of people, almost but *not* quite breaking down by platoon.

One platoon had come from *Avalon*. *They* recognized him and were leaning back to watch the show. A second was the Intel black-ops people, their shipsuit uniform bases lacking the green piping of the rest of the men and women in the room. They might not have recognized Edvard, but they saw that *Avalon*'s platoon had.

The last platoon, according to his files, was a collection of squads cut free from various Home Fleet units—and he knew *damned* well they wouldn't have sent the best.

"Well?" the big thug demanded, closing with him. Edvard realized his duffel was covering his rank insignia and made the instant decision to leave it there. "Who are you, new guy? A Marine? Or did somebody mess up and send us a stripper? You're too pretty to be a Marine."

"And who are you?" Edvard asked calmly. The other man had half a dozen centimeters on his own height and, unlike the officer, was *not* built like a beanpole.

"I'm Sergeant Rothwell," the brick wall replied. "A name you should remember, new guy. *Nobody* messes with Rothwell, lesson you should learn *fast*."

"Is it?" the officer said slowly, glancing around the room. "And if I suggest that perhaps you should tone down your welcome to newcomers, Sergeant, what happens then?"

That clearly hadn't been what Rothwell was expecting, and his face flashed white with anger. Edvard ran through his mental checklist and wondered how this bully had ever made Sergeant.

He went to drop his duffel bag and end the game, but Rothwell was already moving. For a big guy, he was *fast*—but not fast *enough*.

Before the Sergeant managed to reach Edvard, however, there was a blur of motion. A petite young woman with short-cropped copper hair had been sitting at one of the tables next to where the confrontation had been taking place—and she was up and in Rothwell's way in a burst of impossible speed.

The next thing anyone knew, Rothwell was on the ground and the woman in the unmarked shipsuit was saluting Edvard.

"Welcome aboard *Chameleon*, Lieutenant Major," she said crisply.

He didn't need his implants to identify her. While every Marine had a degree of chemical and cybernetic enhancement in addition to the neural implants every citizen and soldier had, only the heavily augmented black-ops troopers could move *that* fast.

"Lieutenant Sandra Riley," he greeted the commander of his black-ops platoon. "Thanks for the assist."

Giving her a nod, he stepped over to Sergeant Rothwell and slung his duffel onto the floor, unveiling his insignia at last.

"Caleb Rothwell," he said harshly, pulling the man's name from his implant files on the entire company. "*ATTEN-HUT!*"

The big man struggled to his feet and saluted carefully.

"Sir! Apologies, sir! Didn't recognize you."

"Striking an officer is a capital offense, regardless of whether or not you recognized him," Riley put in from behind Edvard, and he concealed a smile as the black-ops officer dropped *instantly* into *bad cop*.

"That would require him to have actually reached me, Lieutenant Riley," Edvard pointed out. "Or to have struck me, which, frankly, I don't believe Mister Rothwell would have managed in any case. I think we can skip the firing squad, don't you, Sergeant?"

"Sir! Yes, sir!" the noncom said desperately.

"Of course, you did *attempt* to strike me," Edvard continued calmly. "And your attempt at hazing would have been unacceptable regardless. Your stripes, please."

Rothwell swallowed hard and hesitated.

"Your *stripes*, *Private First Class* Rothwell," the company commander snapped.

Hesitation had just cost the man another rank, something he seemed to realize as he removed his Sergeant's stripes and held them out to Edvard.

"Prove you gave me a bad first impression and you'll get these back by the time we're home," Edvard told him. "Prove my first impression was *right* and I'll drum you out of the service. Are we understood, Mister Rothwell?"

"Sir! Yes, sir!" the big man barked, but Edvard recognized the look in the man's eyes.

He'd locked in his command of the company—but he couldn't expect the demoted Rothwell to forget how anytime soon.

8

Castle System
12:00 April 29, 2736 Earth Standard Meridian Date/Time
Chameleon

THE "MERCHANT SHIP" component of *Chameleon* was fully functional in most ways, and though most of her actual working spaces were concealed outside that false front, the best conference room space aboard the ship was inside.

Kyle stood at the center of the semicircular room, watching Lieutenant Major Edvard Hansen, the lanky commander of *Chameleon*'s single company of Marines, chivy the last straggler into the room before sealing the door.

With the exception of Glass, standing next to him at the podium, the men and women in the room were now under his command—and he knew far too few of them. Rokos sat at the back with his four Space Force Flight Commanders. A fifth Flight Commander sat with the rest of the black-ops contingent near the front: Glass had assigned a platoon of ground forces and a squadron of starfighter crews from Intelligence's Special Forces teams to the mission.

Kyle knew *none* of the black-ops people, and they made him uncomfortable. Nonetheless, it was Glass's mission in many ways, so he'd let it stand. With Rokos and Hansen in command of the two groups, he was confident they couldn't cause too much trouble.

His new executive officer sat in the middle at the front, looking like he was ready to spring into action, fight-or-flight reflex engaged. Chownyk had apparently partially rejected regeneration treatments and both of his legs and an arm were now artificial, but the surgeons had done a good job, and even knowing, Kyle couldn't tell.

Next to the shaven-headed Senior Fleet Commander sat newly promoted Fleet Commander Jennifer Taylor. Unlike Chownyk, the woman with the shoulder-length blond braid sat perfectly still, almost creepily so.

His navigator and chief engineer had been selected by Rondell. Lieutenant Commander Tai Lau was an androgynous officer with dark skin and a pronounced epicanthic fold. Silver highlights on their forehead marked contact points for implants beyond the standard neural network—Lau's record noted them as a semi-augmented hermaphrodite, one of the Federation's pseudo-transhuman minority.

His chief engineer was a small sandy-haired man who seemed content to let everyone else do the talking. If Kyle hadn't known better, he'd have guessed the man as a nonentity—except that Kyle knew that Javed Ajam had been the lead engineer on converting *Chameleon* to Castle's service.

"All right, people," Kyle declared, drawing everyone's attention to him. A scattering of junior officers around each of the seniors filled up the room, though he still only had about a third of *Chameleon*'s officers present.

"First, I want to thank all of you for volunteering for this operation," he told them. "None of you have more than the vaguest of what we're about, and you've signed on trusting the officers who asked you. We appreciate it.

"That said, Mister Glass is about to brief you on the high level of Operation Blue Sunbeam," Kyle continued. "Once that briefing is complete, you will have one final opportunity to back out. Unfortunately, that will come with significant communication restrictions until the operation is complete. If there's anyone you want to talk to in the next six months without it going through censors, I suggest you leave now."

He was unsurprised when none took him up on that, and stepped back, gesturing for Glass to take over the briefing.

The old spy stepped up to the podium and eyed the crowd.

"As I'm sure you've all realized, *Chameleon* is an unusual vessel," he said. "For those of you who *don't* recognize her, she's a Commonwealth-built *Blackbeard*-class Q-ship, built on a *Troubadour*-J freighter hull. The various iterations of the Troubadour design are common even in Alliance space, and are *extremely* common in Commonwealth space.

"This means she's a ship that can go deep into Terran space without being noticed," Glass continued. "She has a suite of civilian and paramilitary ID codes, though using any of them around Terran intelligence could potentially blow our cover.

"However, the Commonwealth does not realize we captured her. We have assets that have dug into this, and *they* believe she's still in pirate hands. We are not," he admitted, "entirely sure how she ended up *in* pirate hands, but no one knows *we* have her.

"We have a line on munitions and intelligence from a contact in the Stellar League," Glass noted. "Blue Sunbeam will take us into the League, from where we will strike into the heart of the Commonwealth: the core worlds that fuel their industry and military machine.

"I will explain more details as they become relevant," the spy concluded, "but the key objective of Operation Blue Sunbeam is to trigger a Commonwealth punitive expedition into the Stellar League— an expedition the League's new Dictator will be forced to respond to.

"Our mission is nothing less than to force the Commonwealth into a two-front war."

———

KYLE'S OFFICE aboard *Chameleon* was outside the false front and suffered noticeably for it. There was no decoration, the chairs were uncomfortable and the walls were plain metal—but the communications system and wallscreens worked, so he could live with it.

Especially once his beer fridge was installed in the corner.

He slid a beer across the desk to Glass and considered the spy for a long moment.

"If you're planning on dealing out the details in penny packets, I'm assuming you're planning on coming with us?" he asked carefully. The concept of having each piece of the mission doled on a bit-by-bit basis wasn't appealing, but it *was* a covert mission.

"I am," Glass confirmed. "There's a lot of moving parts to this, and a lot of details are classified at the highest levels. I'm the only one who knows everything, and I don't plan on changing that. No offense, Captain, but I've been building this op and the contacts for it as a potential plan for ten years. I *need* to see it go off."

"We weren't at war ten years ago," Kyle pointed out.

"We knew it was coming," the spy countered. "*Everybody* knew it was coming. The Commonwealth believes humanity must be reunified under Terran guidance—so long as *that* principle of their culture is unbroken, Terra *will* attack anyone who does not kneel."

"And I don't think we've ever known how to kneel," the Captain admitted. "My understanding was that *I* would be in command."

"You are," Glass told him. "I run the op. You command *Chameleon*. I'm not qualified to command a capital ship."

"Then I damn well better *be* in command," Kyle told the older man bluntly. When he'd commanded *Avalon* and Vice Admiral Tobin had taken them out as a one-ship battle group, there'd been *problems*.

"You give the briefings and the objectives, but *I* decide how we carry them out," he continued. "We can't have a divided chain of command in combat, do you understand?"

"Completely, Captain," Glass agreed. "I will keep you informed as it becomes necessary, but understand that much of the information that enabled this mission could get our agents in the Commonwealth identified and killed if the Terrans knew we had it. My obligation to *them* is to hold the data close to my chest. I trust you as much as I trust anyone, Captain, but I'm afraid you must allow me my paranoia."

Glass's tone made the words an order. He clearly intended to cooperate—but *his* way.

"All right, Mister Glass," Kyle allowed. If nothing else, he'd confirmed that Hansen's Marines had all come from *Avalon*. If the spy went too far out of line, well, that gave him *options*.

He raised the beer.

"To the Alliance, then," he toasted.

"And damnation to our enemies."

9

Under Alcubierre Drive outside Castle System
15:00 April 30, 2736 Earth Standard Meridian Date/Time
Chameleon

IT WAS a point of pride among many Navy officers that they didn't actually *need* the consoles and displays that made up a warship's bridge. The vast majority of their work took place in cyberspace via their neural implants and the ship's computers. The displays were an augmentation to that, handy to have but not a necessity.

Kyle and the bridge crew of *Chameleon* were getting to test that theory. The ship's Terran designers had considered the possibility of needing to fool boarders, so the public areas of the ship were an exact clone of the *Troubadour*-type freighter she been built to resemble. This meant her bridge was very much a *civilian* one. One big display, not dozens of little ones. Seats enough for the core officers, but no space for the immediate department sections they'd have around them on a warship.

Those department sections still existed, but *Chameleon*'s design had

55

relegated them to a support bridge in the hidden sections of the ship. In theory, they were just as linked into the network as they would be in their usual location, but only time would tell if there was a reduction in efficiency from it.

Kyle personally suspected that the designers were correct when they said there was no change in communication time or efficiency from the *technology* side. He also suspected that they'd see a reduction in efficiency regardless, just from the teams not being able to see their officers' faces.

"Commander Lau," he said aloud to his new Navigator. "How are we bearing?"

"Running clean, sir," the officer replied quietly. "Ten minutes to Alcubierre safe zone. Destination?"

"Good question," Kyle told them with a broad grin. Lau responded with the tiniest hint of a smile, but there was a sign of hope there. "Let me ask Mister Glass."

Opening a channel through his implant he pinged the spy.

"Glass."

"We're ten minutes from FTL," Kyle thought at the man. "Is this the appropriate time to tell us where we're going, or do you still want to wait?"

Glass's chuckle came across the link clearly.

"Our destination is the New Edmonton System," he replied. "Though I'm sure it's irrelevant at the moment, we'll be dropping out in the outer system, at McMurray's trailing Trojans."

"That's…a hundred and sixty light-years from here," Kyle noted. Ten days for them to accelerate up to their maximum ten-light-years-per-day pseudo-velocity, ten days to decelerate and six days at maximum speed. "Long trip. We have the supplies for it, don't we?"

"We do," Kyle admitted. *Supplies* weren't the main concern for a long trip. Zero point cells would pump out energy forever, so far as humanity could tell, and the Alcubierre-Stetson drive didn't require fuel, just power. Food, water and air were the issues, and the recycling capabilities of a warship were…disturbing in their efficiency.

Chameleon had those same recyclers and was better stocked than most warships. It would be ninety days—almost three months—before they had to go to the recycled protein bars that *inevitably* reduced crew morale.

"We'll set the course," he promised. "I'm not sure a Federation starship has *ever* taken that long a voyage in a single jump."

Their course would take them through thirty light-years of space belonging to the Alliance of Free Stars and then a hundred and ten light-years of the Commonwealth before entering the Stellar League.

"Few ships have," Glass admitted. "But there is more to this mission than meets the eye, Captain. Testing our strike distance…that's another, if small, part of it."

Dropping the mental channel, Kyle turned his attention back to Lau.

"Set your course for the New Edmonton System," he ordered the Lieutenant Commander. "Let me know if there are any problems."

"Shouldn't be," Lau said quietly, their eyes glazing slightly as they dove back into their systems. Running the calculations for a one-point-five-*quadrillion*-kilometer jump wasn't exactly straightforward, and Kyle left the navigator to it as they checked in on the gravity fields.

Minutes ticked by as the Q-ship accelerated farther and farther from Castle and Gawain. Finally, Lau turned to check back in with Kyle.

"Course for New Edmonton complete," they noted. "We are outside all detectable gravitational interferences and prepared to warp space on your command."

"Carry on at your discretion, Commander," Kyle ordered.

He was linked into the neural net and noted that Lau confirmed the readiness of the ship's class one mass manipulators—the massive exotic-matter devices that created the Alcubierre effect and made up half of the ship's cost—with engineering via implant instead of aloud.

"Interior Stetson online," Lau announced softly.

The image of the world outside in Kyle's implant faded behind a strange glaze, an energy field taking form that would protect the ship from the terrific energies contained inside the Alcubierre bubble.

"Exterior online. Singularities forming."

The navigator's voice was clipped and quiet, and Kyle was used to longer reports on the process—though Lau's certainly contained all of the *information* he required.

A second haze appeared farther out from the ship, protecting the Castle system from the immense force of the four singularities *Chameleon*'s mass manipulators had forced into existence. They twisted his view of space, slowly warping space-time to create the bubble predicted so many years before.

Then reality vanished, an almost-instantaneous flicker before a computer-generated image dropped into its place. The view from a ship under Alcubierre-Stetson drive wasn't particularly *useful*, so the computers assessed what a human eye would theoretically see at their pseudo-velocity in the absence of relativistic distortion and put that on screen.

"We are underway. Running clean."

"Thank you, Commander," Kyle told Lau, glancing around the bridge. "You have the watch, Commander Lau. Let me know if we have any problems."

———

RANK HATH ITS PRIVILEGES. In the case where two significant others were both capital-ship commanders in the Castle Federation Space Navy, those privileges included being able to co-opt a few of their respective ships' Q-Com links to talk to each other.

Everything Kyle or Captain Mira Solace said was encoded and fed into a subsection of the block of quantum-entangled particles at the heart of each ship's communications array. A matching section in a station back in orbit of Castle changed simultaneously, and then the switchboard station's routing computers connected it to the particles linked to the other ship.

The quantum entanglement communicators and their associated switchboard stations represented mankind's mastery of one of the great mysteries of the universe—and unlike many of its other uses, Kyle didn't regard using it to talk to Mira as an abuse of said mastery.

"We're on our way," he told her. "I can't say much more than that, obviously, but everything is moving according to plan."

"Wish I could say the same," Mira replied. The elegantly tall black woman looked tired. "The reinforcements the Terrans have rushed in aren't enough to take on Seventh Fleet, but they are enough to keep us watching over our shoulders and making showy appearances to keep the locals happy. The Admiral has a plan, but, well, I'm pretty sure Walkingstick does too."

"And no plan survives contact with the enemy," Kyle agreed. "How's *Camerone*?"

Camerone was the flagship of Seventh Fleet and the battlecruiser his then-executive officer had inherited when Miriam Alstairs had been promoted to command the Fleet. Both of them had done a decent job of ignoring their attraction *until* she'd no longer been under his command.

They'd made up for as much time as they could until the war dragged Kyle home and left Mira at the front.

"Solid," she said after a moment's thought. "Getting a bit worn, for reasons that, well, I can't really say."

There were probably no censors listening in on their conversation— but that was because it was a safe assumption that two capital ship commanders could censor themselves. Given the nature of both of their missions, the conversation was still recorded and could be reviewed if there were questions later.

Kyle was quite certain that *Camerone*—and the rest of Seventh Fleet, for that matter—had been running around from system to system in the area they'd liberated from the Commonwealth, seeing off any intrusion before it became a real threat. It would be exhausting, emotionally draining work with no clear end point—and Mira could no more tell him that was what was going on than she could tell him which system *Camerone* was currently in.

He hadn't even been able to tell her the *name* of his own ship. The gaps in their conversation were almost more noticeable than what they *could* talk about.

"Did you manage to see your son while you were in Castle?" Mira asked.

"This op came up so fast, I didn't even set foot on the planet, let alone see Lisa or Jake," he admitted. Jacob Kerensky was his son, not quite twelve years old, with his high-school sweetheart Lisa. Jacob had been an accident he had responded to in the worst way possible, and he hadn't spoken to either of them for the first eleven years of Jacob's life—for all that the pair had lived with Kyle's mother and received the highest child support the Federation's military would let him pay.

"His birthday's coming up in six weeks," he continued with a sigh. "I guess after the last eleven, my absence won't be strange, but…still would rather have made it."

"I look forward to meeting him someday," Mira told him with a smile. "I'm sure he'll understand, Kyle."

"He understands my being away in the military better than he understands why I was gone for so long before," Kyle admitted. A twelve-year-old, after all, couldn't be expected to understand that he had one of the worst fathers in the Federation.

"Give it time," she replied.

"*Lisa* gets it," he said thankfully. "Don't know how she ever forgave me, but she seems to have. But Jake… The only way to really fix that is to be there. And I can't do that until the war is over."

Though he supposed, now that it was too late to impact his decision, that the ability to spend time with his son should have been a selling point to the desk job Kane had offered him.

"This mission is going to be long," he admitted. "I don't know when I'll be back. *You* need to be careful," he admonished Mira. "No fighting like me. *No one* should fight like me. Not after Huī Xing."

"Nobody in the *Alliance* thinks you messed up at Huī Xing except you, Kyle," Mira told him. "Everyone else is too busy being stunned at one of the largest POW rescues of the last couple centuries. The Terrans won't know what hit them once we're done with them!"

Kyle returned her predatory grin.

"No," he agreed. "They won't."

10

Deep Space
09:00 May 5, 2736 Earth Standard Meridian Date/Time
Chameleon

RUSSELL ROKOS HAD A HEADACHE, and approximately sixty percent of it was due to the normally-cheerful young man sitting on the other side of his desk. Flight Commander Zhong Li, despite his name, had the darkest skin color Russell had ever seen on a human, with the epicanthic-folded eyes of his Chinese family.

So far in the week Russell had known him, the squadron leader's teeth were usually flashing startling white in a wide smile as he told some joke or another, or simply in a brilliant grin at the general absurdity and wonder of life.

Right now, however, Li's lips were pursed tightly enough to visibly pale as the younger officer considered his words carefully.

"Well?" Russell asked gruffly. "You asked to see me, Flight Commander. And you seem *pissed*, so perhaps you can tell me what's going on?"

"It's the black-ops squadron," Li finally admitted. "They're…" He sighed. "Throwing their weight around? I'm not sure how to describe it, sir. One of them yanked two maintenance crews off one of my birds to have them refinish a *scratch* in their anti-radar coating.

"My pilot was standing *right there*," he noted. "They didn't *quite* threaten her when she objected—but they were pretty damned close to the line."

The Wing Commander sighed. He'd been afraid of that. The black-ops squadron had clearly been doing *something* on their own, without having to interact with regular Space Force crews, before being assigned to *Chameleon*. Whatever that something was, it led Russell to doubt the supposed lack of other Q-ships in the Federation's service.

"Anything else?" he asked carefully. "I can only drop so many bricks on them for that."

"It's a lot of little…*shit*, sir," Li snapped. "They're constantly harassing my people. Nothing significant, just 'joking' and the like. I'm not sure my people are going to take it for much longer, and if someone takes a swing…"

"We'll have a much bigger problem," Russell confirmed. "What about the Chiefs?" he asked. His Chief and Senior Chief Petty Officers should know better than to let this kind of crap continue.

"They either grab the teams without a Chief or lean on the couple who either worked with them before or are scared of them," the junior man replied. "It doesn't *feel* like they're being careful, but…"

"But these are the kind of guys who end up in black-ops squadrons," the Wing Commander said flatly. "The next time you see something, Li, ping me—*immediately.* Understand?"

"Yes, sir."

Technically, Li was on par with Flight Commander Cavendish, but in practice…on an Intelligence ship, the black-ops Flight Commander was more equal than others.

But no matter what she thought, she reported to Russell and was part of his Wing.

He might need to remind her of that.

———

IN THE END, Li didn't need to ping Russell at all. His own first squadron leader had insisted that all of the flight crews be thoroughly familiar with and review the maintenance of their starfighters. Russell had taken it a bit further than most since he *enjoyed* occasionally getting his hands dirty by directly helping with the maintenance of his ship.

That meant he was unidentifiable, head and shoulders inside the access panel to his Cataphract's electronic warfare systems, rearranging blocks of molecular circuitry to see whether he could squeeze in another tower, when Cavendish loudly interrupted the team working on the starfighter next to his.

"Chief Peyton," she snapped loudly. "I need your team to check over my bird. I'm seeing a drift in the targeting radar alignment."

"We're in the middle of a diagnostic run on Flight Lieutenant Petrov's mass manipulators," Russell heard Chief Petty Officer Lyle Peyton object.

"I'm sorry, Chief, I thought I was giving you an *order*," Cavendish replied. "Shut it down and get to my bird *now*."

With a sigh, Russell dropped back out of his starfighter and ducked under the nine-meter-tall spacecraft.

"Commander Cavendish," he greeted her politely. "What is going on here?"

The woman looked at him in surprise.

"As soon as Peyton is done being insubordinate, he's going to be checking into my starfighter. Why?"

"Given that Flight Lieutenant Petrov's starfighter is on the maintenance schedule for Peyton's team for today and yours is not, that was my question for you," Russell said mildly. "Does your starfighter have an antimatter leak? Has one of our zero-point cells somehow turned on in storage and the security of the ship is threatened?"

"No," Cavendish said slowly.

"Then you don't have an emergency worth disrupting the schedule that the Chiefs carefully put together, Commander," he told her mildly. "Carry on, Chief Peyton."

"What in Endless Void are you *smoking*?" Cavendish hissed. "You want him to waste his time on one of your second-tier pilots' ships? My squadron has priority for repairs on this deck!"

"No, it doesn't," Russell replied. "Certainly, I didn't sign off on you having special priority."

"We both know my squadron will bear the brunt of the real work," she told him. "My people could run rings around *any* of the other squads."

He hadn't been *planning* on having this out in the middle of the flight deck, especially not with Chief Peyton and his maintenance team right there trying to be invisible.

"Two of those squadrons have been in action with me since the beginning of the war," he said quietly. "I've seen them fly, I've seen them fight. I trust them. I *don't* trust your people's skills, and your current attitude is aggravating that situation.

"This is *my* flight deck, Commander Cavendish," he reminded her. "*I* signed off on the maintenance schedule. There is no special priority in it for anyone, and *there will never be*.

"Now apologize to Chief Peyton for your unjustified accusation of insubordination."

She stared at him for a long moment.

"By the Stars, you're serious," she snapped. "Are you mad?"

"I am the commanding officer of this fighter wing and you answer to me," Russell said, the control on his temper slipping slightly. "You've interfered with Chief Peyton's work and falsely accused him."

"I don't answer to you. I answer to Glass," Cavendish told him, "And trust me, he will hear about this!"

"You answer to Glass?" the Wing Commander ground out. That was *not* how the chain of command on this ship was supposed to work —and if it was, he wanted off! He knew *damn* well what *Roberts* would think of that theory.

He held out his hand.

"Insignia, please," he said flatly.

"What?!"

"Glass is a civilian. If you answer to him, *you* are a civilian, and impersonating an officer is a criminal offense," Russell told her calmly, twisting his anger into a flicker of a righteous smile. "You have two choices: either you are *Commander* Cavendish, and you answer to *me,* or you are *Miss* Cavendish, and you are not flying a starfighter from my deck.

"Choose." His hand was still outstretched and her gaze focused on it. He was quite proud that there was no waver in his palm. "*Now.*"

There was a long moment where he truly wasn't sure what the dark-haired woman in the unpiped uniform was going to do, then she inhaled sharply and nodded.

"Chief Peyton, I apologize for my hasty comments," she ground out slowly. "I will…make sure my request is added to the maintenance schedule for before we arrive in New Edmonton."

"Was that so hard?" Russell asked, knowing it was probably too much of a twist as he said it.

"Eternal Stars, Rokos, you win," she snapped. "I'll talk to my people; we'll respect your damn schedule. Just…let it go."

"Carry on, Commander Cavendish."

————

AFTER THE FIRST WEEK, Kyle had settled into a routine of having dinner each evening with Chownyk and Taylor. Both were junior for their roles, and it let them bring up their concerns in a less formal setting than his office.

Tonight was the second time Glass had joined them, and Kyle noted that the spy's presence put both of his junior officers on edge—though he would admit it could also be the food. As a matter of principle, he never ate anything different from what was being prepared in the regular officers' mess. This time, they were trying for Tau Ceti cuisine—described as the result of a French father and Indian mother arguing over what to feed the children—and the cooks hadn't got it *quite* right.

"My biggest concern remains our magazine levels," Taylor told him as they finally gave up on their meals, a mix of flavors that might have worked in different proportions, and Kyle gestured for the stewards to bring in dessert. "We only have three missiles for each of the Javelin launchers, and a grand total of *six* for the capital ship launchers."

"The pirates who stole her from the Terrans sold everything that wasn't nailed down," Glass admitted. "We couldn't risk using missiles from our own stockpiles—even a single dud could be traced back to having been in our possession by Commonwealth Intelligence after the fact and undermine the entire operation."

"I hope we have a *plan* for that?" she asked, somewhat acidly. Were Glass a superior officer, Kyle would have yanked her up short—but he was a *civilian*, and one that was playing his cards too close to his chest for Kyle's liking.

"Of course we do," Glass confirmed affably, proceeding to sip his wine rather than explaining further. Realizing more was expected of him, he shrugged. "We made sure that we had fighter munitions, and since *those* are League manufacture, the Terrans won't have the data to trace them back to us. They'll have *far* too good an idea of where exactly any Commonwealth weapons went missing."

"A little more detail would be handy," Chownyk murmured. "It's hard for us to plan tactics and strategies in a vacuum."

"Even under Alcubierre drive, twenty light-years from anywhere, there is no guarantee that this ship is entirely secure," the spy said calmly. "A spy could have hidden a Q-Com relay aboard without it being detected."

"This crew was double- and triple-checked," Kyle objected. "You do them a disservice, Mister Glass."

"Perhaps," Glass allowed. "But a secret held by one man cannot be spilled. Every person who knows the details increases the odds.

"Besides," he shrugged, "it's not like your people are doing everything to inspire my confidence, Captain. I'm hearing a lot of complaints from my people on the flight deck."

"'Your people', Mister Glass?" Kyle said mildly. "I wasn't aware you *had* any staff with you."

"You know what I mean, Captain Roberts," Glass said flatly. "The black-ops people are mine, regardless of what you think, and they do *not* appreciate the way they are being handled."

"Mister Glass, who is in command of this ship?"

"What? You are," the spy replied.

"I thought so," Kyle said. "So, *why are you interfering*? Regardless of the branch of the personnel under my command, they are under *my* command. The black-ops squadron on *my* flight deck was interfering with the proper operation of the deck, and Commander Rokos handled the matter."

"We are going to *need* those people at their best, Captain," Glass replied. "Harassing them is not going to help."

"Wing Commander Rokos has been far more patient with Cavendish and her people than I would have been," Kyle told him mildly. "I'd have grounded at least one of them by now, assuming I hadn't thrown any of them in the brig."

"They're black ops, Captain. They're *worth* some coddling."

"I've flown with Commander Rokos," Kyle replied. "I *know* what he and his people are worth—Cavendish and her team could be Gods made flesh and they wouldn't be able to outfly the squadrons we brought over from *Avalon*.

"Regardless, when you assigned them to this ship, you placed them under Rokos's and my command. They will follow our orders and operate under the rules of Rokos's deck, or they will not fly off that deck."

Kyle held up a hand before Glass could say anything more.

"You told me I commanded this ship," he reminded the spy. "So I will command her."

"Very well," Glass said with a sigh, leaning back in his chair with his wineglass. "I just hope your command doesn't cause us more problems than it might solve."

11

CHAMELEON HADN'T BEEN BUILT by the Castle Federation, which meant it lacked many of the amenities a Federation warship would have included by default. The lack that Lieutenant Major Edvard Hansen felt the most keenly, however, was the atrium.

Every Federation warship had at least a small artificial island of greenery buried somewhere near its heart. While the designers swore the greenery was an essential part of the life support system, the young Marine figured it was about two-thirds tradition and one-third the religious preferences of the crews.

He wasn't entirely sure how the Reformation Wiccans aboard—like the Captain and the new XO—were handling the lack of green space. While Christianity was firmly the second-largest religion in the *Federation*, it kept trading the place of second largest on *Castle* with the

Wiccans, which probably resulted in their desires having a disproportionate impact on the design of Castle warships.

Edvard himself, though, was a member of the single largest religious grouping in the Federation—the largest in the Alliance of Free Stars and in the top four in the Commonwealth, as he understood—the Stellar Spiritualists.

A disorganized, "come as ye are, leave as ye will", half-secular awe at the universe, half-semi-agnostic worships of stars-as-divine path, the Spiritualists nonetheless had been *very* successful spreading their word over the last five or six hundred years.

Like Wiccans, they preferred to worship in natural settings under the stars. In the absence of atriums or observation decks, however, they made do. Edvard wasn't sure who exactly had set up the spare storeroom near the Marine barracks with the wallscreen of the stars and the half-dozen potted plants as an approximation of the usual shrine, but he appreciated it nonetheless.

His quiet was interrupted, however, when Lieutenant Sandra Riley threw the door open and looked down at him with a sigh of relief.

"Oh, thank the Stars you're here," she told him. "First place I checked, too."

"'Sorry for interrupting, sir,'" he replied dryly. "'We have an emergency, sir.' Any chance these sound like they should be familiar?"

"Sorry for interrupting; we have a fucking emergency," Riley snapped, and tossed him a weapon.

He caught it instinctively, only then realizing she'd been carrying two weapons in her off hand. Years of practice had him checking the weapon, instantly identifying it as a military police electron laser stungun.

"What's going on?" he asked, suddenly serious and mildly afraid.

"One of my boys and two of yours have gone missing," Riley said harshly, gesturing for him to follow her.

Gunnery Sergeant Jonas Ramirez, Edvard's strong right hand since before he'd joined Seventh Fleet and then followed Roberts to this sideshow, waited outside. The shadow-skinned wiry man held a third stungun, but he'd *also* slung an assault shotgun over his back.

"Who're we missing, Gunny?" he asked quickly.

"Rothwell and Carter," Ramirez replied instantly. "Neither are from our last company. Carter's young and pretty, naïve as fresh milk too."

"Fuck. Yours, Riley?"

"Ivan Conner," she said flatly. "Gambler, petty smuggler, the usual source of porn and harmless vice for my team. A perennial problem child, but never caught red-handed and never into *real* trouble."

"Familiar with the type," Edvard noted. "How missing are we talking?"

"They left the barracks together an hour ago," Ramirez explained. "Didn't say where they were going. Could be a card game, could be a tryst…"

"But this ship's systems were set up by paranoids and we didn't see a reason to change that," Riley said grimly. "Internal systems ping everyone's implants every fifteen minutes. One missed ping doesn't flag anything. *Two* does."

"And why did *I* not get this alert?"

"Because Glass wouldn't trust his own mother to serve him milk and cookies," Riley said in an exasperated tone. "Of course, *I* don't have the authority to jack into the internal security sensors and sweep the cameras for them."

"I do," Edvard said grimly, already halfway through that process.

He never finished it. He was bringing up the artificial stupid daemon he'd use to run the sweep when a message hit his personal comm code like a ton of bricks.

"It's Rothwell. Deck six, sector twelve. Son of a bitch fu—"

The message cut off in a squeal of jamming, but the recently demoted noncom had told Edvard everything he needed to know.

Ramirez and Riley were only steps behind him as he took off running.

———

DECK SIX, sector twelve was buried deep in the concealed "warship" components of *Chameleon*, a storage bay that would, eventually, contain the components that would allow her to manufacture replacement missiles, provided a supply of raw rock.

Since *Chameleon* didn't *have* any of those components, the entire sector was currently empty. Corridors were on minimum lighting and doors were shut. Maintenance bots kept there from being enough dust to track anyone, but Edvard didn't need to resort to anything *quite* so traditional.

The Castle Federation assumed that their Marines would spend most of their battles wrapped in the heavy armor the Federation had built for them—but not *all* of their battles. Edvard had nowhere near the level of genetic or cybernetic augmentation that, say, Riley had, but he was even less vanilla human than a Navy officer.

Most usefully right now, he could see thermal signatures without any additional gear—which meant that from this close, he knew *exactly* where their three lost sheep had ended up. All three appeared to be alive, too, which was better than he'd expected.

"That way," he silently sent to the other two over their implants while he gestured to the specific door. "On three."

Three fingers folded down in sequence, and then he overrode the door and forced it open.

Ramirez was through first, cutting in front of both officers before they could object. There was a blur of motion and then the wiry NCO was skidding across the floor with no one knowing quite what had happened.

"Drop the weapon, Conner," Edvard barked, charging into the room after his noncom and registering the pistol in the soldier's hand.

Years of training allowed him to process the scene in moments. Rothwell was slumped against the wall, maintaining pressure on a gut shot. The wound wouldn't *kill* him, not with the nanites running in any Federation citizen's system, but letting go of it would be a *bad* idea.

Private First Class India Carter wasn't in much better shape. It didn't look like she'd been shot, but the way she was crumpled on the floor suggested that she'd broken at least one limb. She was looking at *both* of the men in the room with a death glare that Edvard was perfectly happy not to have directed at him.

Conner had been in the middle of the room, quite probably threatening both of the Marines with the gun, when the door opened—but had met Ramirez before the Gunny was a full meter inside the door.

The black-ops trooper was still turning with the throw that had deflected the first Marine.

But his gun was turning *toward* Edvard, and his training kicked into full gear as the threat fully registered. Time stayed in the strangely slowed state of adrenaline-fueled action and he charged into Conner's arm, throwing his full weight against the cyborg's single arm.

From the somewhat-less-redacted briefing Edvard had received on the black-ops troopers assigned to his command, Conner's arm was as much metal as it was flesh and blood. Ninety kilos of *pissed* Marine officer was more than even that could resist.

The gun went flying, but Conner's other hand flashed around, driving for Edvard's throat. The cyborg was *fast*—but so was Edvard.

He smacked aside the fist and then ducked under the half-wild haymaker the other man used to recover from the original impact. Edvard blocked a second strike and kicked out at Conner's leg, trying to bring the man down.

Conner yanked his leg back *just* enough to avoid the blow, using the momentum to launch a series of strikes that pushed Edvard back. The Lieutenant Major had been fast and strong *before* the Marine physicians had their way with him—but he couldn't match the cyborg coming at him.

"Edvard, down!" Riley snapped.

He dropped. He saw a moment of realization flash into Conner's eyes as the black-ops trooper realized just how badly he'd screwed up.

Then the electron laser of a full-power stungun flashed across the room like the wrath of an angry god. Thousands of volts transferred into the man's chest and he exploded backward, flesh and circuitry alike flashing to vapor as the overcharged beam tore through him.

"Dammit, Conner," Riley said quietly. "You *know* these things only work on us at lethal."

12

Deep Space
23:00 May 20, 2736 Earth Standard Meridian Date/Time
Chameleon

"All right, Rothwell. What in Endless Void *happened*?" Edvard demanded.

With Carter in the infirmary and Conner in the *morgue*, the big ex-Sergeant was his only chance of getting an explanation of just *why* one of Lieutenant Riley's men was now an electrocuted corpse. To be fair, Rothwell belonged in the infirmary, but he'd been patched up enough for this conversation—and unlike Carter, he could currently *walk*.

Ramirez had dragged Rothwell into the office and was standing directly behind the Marine, somehow managing to loom despite being barely two thirds the other man's height. Riley had taken over the only chair other than Edvard's in the room.

"It was supposed to be a poker game," Rothwell said with a sigh. "Conner was trying to play me, I was trying to play him, I brought

Carter along to make him feel comfortable. She's not a bad poker player, but she was playing honestly and we...weren't."

"And this led to multiple broken limbs, a gut shot and a dead man how?" Edvard said sharply.

"Didn't realize until too late that Conner was after more than money out of Carter," the ex-Sergeant admitted. "I let him run her out of cash to get him confident—I was *planning* on getting her most of it back in the process of cleaning Conner out—but then he talked her into putting, well, sleeping with him in the pot."

"Void," Riley whispered. "That shit..."

"I may be an asshole, but I'm not one hundred percent a dick. I wasn't having *any* of that," the Marine told them. "So, I...cheated the next hand in Carter's favor. I don't even think he *caught* me, but he was *not* accepting losing that hand."

"If he wanted in her pants that badly, he should have tried flowers," Edvard said grimly. "I take it things went poorly from there?"

"Conner pulled a gun, Carter kicked him in the nuts, I tried to separate them and got shot," Rothwell said calmly. "That's when I pinged you."

"What about the jamming?" Edvard asked.

"Gambling is against the Articles," the Marine said calmly. "So, we had a small jammer covering us to keep our implants off the ship's net. I killed it to ping you, and then he triggered another one I couldn't see."

"All right," Edvard allowed, glancing at Riley. Her expression suggested there was more she had to say but not in front of Rothwell.

"You understand that you fucked up royally, right?" he demanded of the Marine.

"Figured that out about when Conner tried to rape the kid, yeah. I'm an asshole, but *that's* too far."

"On the other hand, you called it in when you *did* realize that things had gone too far," Edvard allowed. "Are you prepared to accept administrative punishment, or do I need to bump this to Captain Roberts?"

Rothwell straightened to attention, his eyes straight ahead.

"Administrative punishment, sir," he said crisply.

Edvard glanced at Ramirez, who gave him the tiniest of nods—a sign to go at least a little easy.

"Gunnery Sergeant Ramirez, note for the record that Private First Class Rothwell is restricted to quarters and company exercises for one week," he said calmly. "Also note that Private Rothwell is docked one month's pay.

"No disciplinary note is to be made to Private Rothwell's file," he finished. The five ranks he'd slashed the man for attempting assault on an officer would be enough of a black mark on the man's career.

"Do you understand your punishment, Private Rothwell?"

"I do, sir," the big Marine confirmed. He still looked *pissed* at Edvard, but at least he seemed to know where the line lay.

"Gunny Ramirez, escort Private Rothwell back to the infirmary, please."

———

ONCE THE DOOR slid shut on the Gunny and his prisoner, Riley made a loud sound of disgust.

"One of my men dead, and not even because we have a spy or a traitor," she snarled. "Just because the *idiot* was a throwback who somehow thought he could get away with blackmailing and threatening someone into sex. Endless Star-swallowing *Void*."

"This is going to be a problem," Edvard told her. "Your platoon is already getting on the nerves of the rest of the company. Once word of this spreads, we're going to have fights—and your people are immune to *stunners*?"

"They are," she confirmed. "And, since you'd figure it out pretty quickly anyway after Conner's stunt, we also have internal short-range jammers. Any of my people who want to go dark on the ship's systems can."

"I hope you can understand my lack of enthusiasm for *that*," the Lieutenant Major told her. "Your people *better* be worth the Voids-cursed hassle, Riley. Augments or no augments, they're no better than mine in battle armor."

"Until this war started, they might have been," Riley replied. "We had a *lot* more action during the peace than your Marines did. But you're right; my people's best use is when we're *out* of armor."

"Right now, Lieutenant, I'm frankly concerned about their *reliability* as much as their effectiveness. How much of a problem are they going to be?"

"Less than they have been," she said flatly. "Inserting a black-ops platoon into a Marine company was never going to be easy, so I was *expecting* friction and didn't step on it. Now, though..."

"It stops, Lieutenant Riley," Edvard told her. "I'm not going to presume innocence on the part of Marines, but we *cannot* have any more of this kind of bullshit. I can't afford to cut the company strength by a dozen troopers, but by the Stars, I *will* throw every idiot who gets into a fight in the brig regardless."

"You're in command, sir," she agreed. "My *idiots* will follow my orders, and I'll follow yours. My noncoms and I will crack down on the attitude problem. Regardless of their barracks issues, though, my men *will* fight and *will* follow the plan in action," she concluded. "They're some of the best we have."

"Some of my Marines have been with me since the *Ansem Gulf* Incident," Edvard pointed out. "I've walked into six different kinds of hell with them. There's no one on this ship that isn't among the best we have—you may want to remind your people of that."

13

KYLE SAT in the command chair at the center of *Chameleon*'s bridge, watching the streams of data running through his implant with a practiced mental eye. He was surprised by how much he missed the physical backup screens that allowed old-fashioned situational awareness to kick in, but the neural feeds were *almost* as effective.

Seconds ticked away as the Q-ship's icon approached the marker in his datafeed where she would exit Alcubierre drive, and Kyle did his best to look as relaxed and cheerful as always. Glass was still playing his cards close to his chest, and *Chameleon*'s Captain wasn't certain what he'd meet in the New Edmonton System.

It was possible his people would be going into battle, and the *last* time he'd commanded a battle, a lot of people had died. Even in his own head, he couldn't argue much with the general assessment of his peers and superiors that he hadn't actively screwed up at Huī Xing, but he still felt there had to be something he could have done *better*.

"Alcubierre emergence ninety seconds," Lau reported. "On target."

"Taylor? Rokos? Ready?" Kyle asked.

"Active sensors are locked down to avoid drawing attention," his tactical officer reported. "Lance source cells spun up; our one missile salvo is prepped and in the launchers. Deflectors are ready to come up at civilian radiation protection level. *Chameleon* is ready for whatever you need, sir."

"Birds are locked and loaded," Rokos reported once Taylor was done. "Five squadrons of glorified showboats ready to go on your order."

"Thank you," Kyle replied. "Taylor—who are we today, anyway?" he asked with a chuckle.

"We're the Centauri-registry freighter *Golden Moonlight*, sir," she replied swiftly. There was no point in flying a Q-ship if they were going to arrive in every system flashing their Federation ID codes, after all.

"Emergence ten seconds."

Kyle waited.

Exiting the warp bubble created by the Alcubierre-Stetson drive was always sudden. One moment, all of reality around you was torn to incoherent shreds by the gravity wells that created your bubble of space-time. The next, reality snapped back into place with a suddenness the human mind couldn't *quite* comprehend.

In the center of the screen was an immense gas giant, one of the largest Kyle had ever seen. A super-Jovian, on the edge of becoming a brown dwarf: McMurray, source of hydrogen and rare gasses for half of the Stellar League.

"What am I looking at?" Kyle asked, watching as Taylor's team started dropping icons onto his screen.

"That's...a *lot* of extraction infrastructure," the tactical officer noted slowly. "I'm reading...at least fifteen hundred cloudscoops. Twenty-four central processing stations. *Thousands* of prospecting ships. I've never seen anything like it."

That was almost five times the processing infrastructure around Gawain, which represented the largest hydrogen extraction facility in the Federation and one of the biggest in the Alliance.

"I'm not reading any defenses," she said quietly.

"They're there, Commander," Glass said softly, the spy stepping onto the bridge with a confident stride. "The League makes a hobby of war in a way that makes no sense to most of us. While their internal wars are fought by specific rules, they don't expect anyone *else* to fight by them.

"The McMurray production stations are guarded by mercenary pilots who've seen more battles than anyone else outside of a war," he continued. "Their gear isn't quite as good as ours, but it's better than the Terrans' current starfighters."

Both the Commonwealth and the League were flying sixth-generation starfighters versus the *seventh*-generation spacecraft the Alliance now had deployed across their entire fleet. The Cataphract-type League starfighters Rokos's people were flying were late fifth-generation birds, replaced in most League service by the Hoplite type.

Inferior to the Falcons or not, in the hands of the League's mercenary *condottieri* pilots and crews, the Hoplite was a dangerous, dangerous starfighter.

"Where are we headed, Mister Glass?" Kyle asked the spy, managing to *not* sound utterly frustrated with the man.

"*Chameleon* wants to head to high orbit, near the Nexen Cloud in the third ring," Glass told him. "The Cloud sticks out to scanners, so it's a common waiting ground for ships negotiating refueling status. I'd suggest you do so from there, but I will be taking a shuttle into one of the processing stations to meet with my black-market contact."

"I will accompany you," Kyle decided. He'd been kept in the dark on the nature of this mission for too long.

"That would be...unwise," the spy said slowly. "Shouldn't you remain with your ship?"

"I need to be fully informed on our missions, Mister Glass," Kyle replied. "Commander Chownyk is perfectly capable of negotiating our resupply."

Glass looked like he was going to argue for a long moment, then sighed and shook his head.

"I'm not going to win this," he acknowledged aloud. "I presume you have something *other* than a uniform to wear?"

―――――

GIVEN *CHAMELEON'S* COVERT STATUS, Kyle actually had multiple civilian outfits aboard. With modern computer technology for image substitution, there was no need for him to be out of uniform under normal circumstances, and the full-body shipsuit that resembled a turtleneck and slacks at a distance was a relatively standard garment galaxy-wide.

He'd switched out in this case for a slightly differently cut shipsuit in dark blue instead of military black, and strapped a shoulder holster under a black leather jacket.

Glass looked him over as they met in the shuttle bay and nodded approval. The spy wore the same plain civilian suit he'd always worn, though Kyle knew from the ship's safety systems that he wore a thin shipsuit *under* the black suit.

Lieutenant Riley and the two black-ops troopers that were joining them were in a mix of shipsuit styles and jackets closer to Kyle's array than Glass's. All three carried slung stubby carbines, not a model *Chameleon's* Captain was familiar with.

"They're okay with us hauling that kind of hardware?" he asked, indicating the guns with a jerk of his head.

"Not in most places," Riley said with a grin. "But the New Edmonton processing stations have a *reputation*. No one is going unarmed here."

"Station Seven is *not*, despite what Riley implies, a lawless hell-hole," Glass pointed out. "It is, however, notably lacking in what even the League would regard as sensible gun laws. Riley's guns will be fine.

"We have no enemies here," he continued, "but there are people here who will try and rob us without personal rancor. Outside of my contact, no one here knows that we are Federation. Keep it that way."

"We're off the freighter *Golden Moonlight*," Kyle reminded them as he stepped into the shuttle, his implants linking in to the small space-craft's computers and artificial intelligences. "Looking for cargo while my XO negotiates fuel and food?"

"Exactly," Glass confirmed with a small smile. "We may make a useful spy out of you yet, Captain Roberts."

Kyle settled into the control chair and flashed the older man a grin.

"If you're going to insult me like that, I suggest everyone strap in," he ordered.

———

Local space around McMurray was *crowded* by space standards, and there was no planetary-system-wide traffic control. All Kyle could do was keep a careful eye on the vectors of everything around him and make sure that his own course kept him well clear of those vectors.

The shuttle's AIs handled most of the straight number-crunching involved in that, however, and he had more than enough attention to spare to take in the view.

McMurray was a gorgeous world, even by the breathtaking stan-dards of super-Jovian gas giants, with whorls of blue and green cutting across a mostly red base. It lacked moons but had seven rings of varying consistency—the Nexen Cloud representing a portion of the fifth ring that was densely filled with rocks and debris, making it harder to detect anything in its shadow.

The rings added to both the navigation hazard and the lightshow, sunlight from New Edmonton glittering off the ice and metal that made them up.

The processing stations that orbited the planet in a carefully measured circles sat just inside the innermost ring. In a way, they and their cloudscoops formed an eighth, man-made ring around the planet. Each processing station consumed the gas from over a hundred cloud-scoops and hundreds of prospecting ships diving through the outer atmosphere.

The stations were fragile-looking things, especially compared to the more military structures that Kyle was familiar with. Massive fuel storage tanks that looked like—and functionally *were*—glorified balloons hung from kilometer-long struts, with dozens of pipes dragging the unmixed gasses and fluids away to the refining plants that turned it into saleable product.

A single spherical Alcubierre-capable tanker nestled against one end of the station, and two cylindrical sublight ships were linked in along the way. As they grew closer, Kyle's passive sensors finally picked up the defenders: a dozen Hoplite-type fighters maintained lazily varying orbits above the platform, watching for any kind of threat.

The system quietly pinged him to inform him that Processing Station Six's space traffic control was requesting a data handshake. No one was *verbally* reaching out to him, but the data systems were talking to him.

He authorized the handshake and linked in to the STC. A new course flashed up on his systems and he dropped the shuttle into it, arcing the spacecraft toward the designated docking bay.

None of the Hoplites paid *any* attention to him, their *condottieri* pilots clearly having dismissed the unarmed ship as a non-threat—a piece of overconfidence that could have easily destroyed the station. Small or not, the shuttle was capable of over four hundred gravities and contained a zero-point cell producing a small but constant stream of pure antimatter when active. That antimatter fueled its engines, fed into a secondary power generation system—and filled capacitors to make sure those systems continued working.

Rammed into one of the gas balloons or the core of the station, the shuttle would turn Processing Station Six into a massive and expensive fireball.

Of course, Kyle had no intention of doing any such thing, but the lack of concern was disconcerting.

10:35 May 26, 2736 ESMDT
McMurray Processing Station Six

As KYLE SETTLED the shuttle down on the floor of the docking bay, Glass gestured for Riley and her troopers to join them.

"We are meeting a man named Kamil Ostrowski," he told them. "Despite being in the League, he was born on Old Earth, in Poland of all places."

Kyle was relatively sure he wasn't the only one drawing a blank on where *that* was.

"He's very high up in one of the organized crime families that are woven throughout the Commonwealth and the League," the spy continued. "I'm relatively sure his *Bratva* family have fingers into Alliance space as well, but *Pakhan* Ostrowski works in the League and has fingers all the way back to his homeworld."

"If he knows who we are, are we sure he's okay with selling out Terra?" Kyle asked.

"Ostrowski was caught by Commonwealth Internal Security twenty-three standard years ago and sentenced to a *very* long time in prison," Glass said with a wicked smile. "He escaped, but his biometrics are on too many lists. Even with his resources, he can't go into Commonwealth space for very long. He *hates* the Commonwealth and is perfectly happy to sell them out for money. Speaking of which, Riley?"

The black-ops Lieutenant hefted a briefcase.

"I'm guessing this is for him?"

"That's a good chunk of the price of a starship in bearer bonds. Be a *bit* more careful with it, please," Glass said plaintively.

Riley looked thoughtful.

"I'm not sure about that," she pointed out. "Were I *actually* the mercenary thug I'm dressed like, you would *not* have told me that."

"Fine," Glass allowed. "Roberts—you're the ship captain, but don't use your first name. While no one is likely to recognize you by face, even here they've probably heard of the Stellar Fox."

————

THE INTERIOR of the station was almost reassuring to Kyle. From the lackadaisical attitude of the security fighters and the frail-looking exterior, he'd wondered if the inside would show a similar failure of concern or structure.

Instead, the hallways and corridors Glass led them through could have been on any modern space station anywhere in the Federation or its allies. Panels along the walls provided a diffuse-but-bright light. Doors had implant-authorized locks. Restaurants and stores hawked their wares.

Security was rarer—but noticeably more heavily armed where they were present—than it would have been on a Federation station, but otherwise, the crowd with its mind-boggling variety of people and clothes could have been right back in orbit of Castle.

Glass led them through the station with the confidence of someone who had either been there before or had a *very* up-to-date map in their implant. Dodging crowds and missing main commercial concourses for side corridors, he finally led them to a door that looked no different from any other they'd passed and paused.

"Watch your manners," he said crisply. "Show *Pakhan* Ostrowski respect."

The old man then rapped twice on the door, waited a moment, and then rapped three times. An old but simple identification trick, though one that Kyle presumed was followed by some kind of implant inter-rogation.

The door slid open and the spy led the way into a lushly decorated lobby. Thick carpet cushioned their shoes and gorgeously detailed massive couches laid out a square around a holographic fire in the middle of the room. Bookshelves covered every wall, though Kyle presumed at least some had to do double duty as concealed doors.

Two men in heavy combat vests, about as damage-resistant as unpowered armor *got*, stepped up to flank the Federation party, massive shotguns drifting gently to cover everyone.

"Weapons. Now," the man on the right said in thickly accented English.

"Hand them over," Kyle ordered before Glass could speak, removing his own sidearm and offering it to the bodyguard. He hadn't really dealt with criminals in his life, but he doubted that insisting on hanging on to their guns counted as "respect."

The one guard collected their weapons, gracelessly surrendered by the black-ops team, while the other ran a scanner over them. He looked…unenthused.

"Watching," the speaker grunted at Riley. "Implants won't save you."

"Please, Ivan," a new speaker said calmly. "Our guests did not fly the length and breadth of Terran space to start a fight. Come in, come in."

The Federation party obeyed, Kyle surreptitiously studying the man in the couch on the other side of the holographic fire. *Pakhan* Kamil Ostrowski was a large man, only a little smaller than Kyle himself, his graying hair cropped short to his scalp. He looked to have been massively muscular once but now carried an immense gut.

Somehow, Kyle doubted that the extra weight would stop the crime boss moving as fast as he needed to if threatened. For now, Ostrowski was smiling as he gestured them to seats.

"It's Glass this time, right?" he asked Glass genially. "I always forget with you spies."

"You remember correctly," the old spy replied calmly. "And I doubt you ever forget unintentionally."

Ostrowski laughed and gestured to the couches again.

"Please, sit, you're stretching my neck," he told them.

Kyle gingerly took a seat, suspecting that the couch cost about as much as the shuttle they'd arrived on.

"We had a deal, Ostrowski," Glass reminded him. "I have the money. Do you have what I asked for?"

"I do," the crime lord replied. "But so fast to business! We should drink, have some scones—Maria!"

A young blonde woman materialized *through* one of the bookshelves, one Kyle now realized was an *extremely* high-fidelity hologram, carrying a tray of small cakes and shot glasses of clear liquid.

"Drink, eat," Ostrowski commanded, grabbing a scone and a shot himself. "It is all safe—what kind of man would poison his guests?!"

Glass sighed and obeyed, and Kyle followed suit.

"I found what you wanted," the crime boss finally noted. "There's a depot in the Aurelius System, used to support patrols along the border with the League. They'll have munitions, fuel, food, everything you can need. I even, kind soul that I am, have their patrol schedule for the next two months so you can strike when they are undefended."

"Thank you," the spy replied, gesturing for Riley to pass over the briefcase. The crime boss gestured for the girl to check it. Despite appearing to be the server, Maria had the case opened and the bonds flipped through in a second.

"Exactly as agreed," she said calmly, then disappeared back through the bookshelf with the case.

"I believe that concludes our arrangement," Glass said. "The data?"

Ostrowski removed a small disk from his pocket and tossed it to Riley.

"If you have more of that money," he said lazily, "I *may* have found something *else* of interest to you. Two things, in fact. Each worth what you paid for the depot," he finished, his voice suddenly sharp.

"I don't have that kind of discretion, *Pakhan*," Glass said respectfully. "I could perhaps offer as much again, but no more."

"We both know that's a lie, Mister Glass. One and three quarters."

"One and a third. And only because you've always come through before."

Ostrowski smiled. It was a *very* predatory expression, one that made Kyle very glad he had three black-ops cyborgs in the room with them.

"One and a half, then," he suggested. "Roughly. Call it an even trillion of your stellars."

Kyle couldn't conceal a wince. That was a chunk of the cost of a starship and a not-insignificant fraction of a percent of a star system's GDP. Just how much money was changing hands in this quiet little meeting? And for that matter, how much did Glass have available to spend?

This time, instead of a briefcase full of bearer bonds, Glass removed a single data disk from inside his suit jacket. He tapped a finger on it, linking the disk to his implant and loading something into it, then passed it over to Ostrowski.

"There are seven account numbers and access authorizations on there," the spy said calmly. "All told, they add up to one hundred billion Commonwealth dollars: one trillion Federation stellars."

"I will trust you, Mister Glass," the crime boss told him, taking the disk. "You know the consequences of lying to me.

"Your first piece of information, and Maria will provide me a file of details in a moment, is that the Commonwealth has finally begun forward deployment of a seventh-generation starfighter: the Katana type. I'm not certain on what the specifications mean, but we have them. You should not encounter them at Aurelius, as Walkingstick has claimed the entire first production run for the Rimward marches."

Kyle managed not to swear aloud. They'd known their one-on-one fighter superiority couldn't last forever, so they'd been leveraging it as hard as they could. If that intel didn't make it back in time, more than a few Alliance ops could run into an unexpected buzzsaw.

"Secondly, the Commonwealth has been developing an entirely new *type* of starfighter," Ostrowski continued. "Several, from what I can tell. An eighth generation of starfighter, but also something entirely new.

"I don't know what they are thinking, but I *do* know that the specifications, plans, test results and prototypes are all scheduled for delivery to the Terran Commonwealth research and development center at Tau Ceti on June tenth.

"All of the information my network has on both of these items is on this disk," he finished, gesturing to where Maria had emerged once again, this time holding a single small disk identical to the one Ostrowski had given them himself.

"It is always a pleasure to do business with a professional," he noted to Glass. "And I must confess that, quiet as he has been, it has *also* been a pleasure to meet Captain Roberts. It is rare that one sits in the presence of a living legend."

Kyle sighed.

"I am no legend, sir," he said quietly. "Just one man."

"One man," Ostrowski agreed, chuckling. "One man that Walkingstick was prepared to trade his entire Twenty-third Fleet to kill. You've made an *impression* on the good Marshal, Captain."

The crime boss smiled.

"I'm a fan of anyone who can piss off the Commonwealth Navy *that* badly."

14

New Edmonton System
14:00 May 26, 2736 Earth Standard Meridian Date/Time
Chameleon

RUSSELL ROKOS STOOD PATIENTLY BEHIND the shoulders of the staff in *Chameleon*'s Primary Flight Control. Unlike the Q-ship's bridge, the flight control center was in the hidden portion of the ship and built to a proper military standard.

It was also a *Terran* military standard, which had required some getting used to. A Federation warship would have used more in terms of individual screens backing up implant feeds, leaving each of the sensor techs working their stations with a unique view and requiring the supervisor to mirror people's feeds to their implant to follow an individual tech's work.

The Commonwealth standard used large screens and shared holograms to make sure that *everyone* knew what everyone else was doing. There were arguments in terms of teamwork, Russell knew, but a number of small things about the layout and design told him that the designers had been more concerned about officers knowing what their subordinates were up to at a glance than intra-team efficiency.

Right now, it was mostly allowing the Wing Commander to track every spacecraft near *Chameleon* with relative ease. Even out in the rings near the Nexen Cloud—an unusually marked concentration of hydrocarbon gasses used as a waypoint—there were a surprising number of them. A dozen prospecting spaceships, barely larger than the four-thousand-ton starfighters of his wing, disappeared and reappeared as they dove through the cloud itself, hunting the same precious radioactive materials that made them hard to see.

Another starship also hovered near the cloud. It made a convenient anchor point for negotiating with the locals for fuel and other supplies. The locals knew that as well, which was why two hundred-and-fifty-meter, three-hundred-thousand-ton gunships orbited just above the Cloud. They seemed to be there as much to play tender to the dozen older Cataphract fighters orbiting with them.

The local mercenary guards seemed content to keep an eye on things from above, however, and Russell's link to Chownyk on the bridge hadn't warned him of any contact from them. He had Li and his Bravo squadron in their birds, ready to deploy if they were required, but Roberts's orders were to keep the fact that they had starfighters under wraps here.

Which is why he was *not* expecting the notification that one of the launch tubes was cycling. *Chameleon* was built around ten-ship squadrons and had the tubes and transfer systems to launch one such squadron every fifteen seconds. With just one Federation eight-ship squadron in the tubes, two were empty—and one of those tubes was now charging to launch.

"Launcher Nine is initiating an unauthorized launch cycle," a tech announced across the mental network linking everyone in the room together, far faster than any of them could speak.

"Override," Russell ordered. "Do *not* let it launch."

"The system is refusing my override," the operator replied, panic edging over his mental voice. "I'm completely locked out on Launcher Nine."

Russell cursed aloud as he linked into the system and hit the fighter launch tube with his own high-priority override—a code that should instantly cut power to the tube as an emergency measure.

The launcher happily continued cycling before sliding open its covering hatch and firing the starfighter it contained into space in a blast of gravitational force.

"Who the hell is in that bird?" the Wing Commander demanded.

"Starfighter is refusing IFF ping," one of his subordinates replied. "Checking who's still aboard." The man swallowed. "It's Echo Actual, sir. All other starfighters are aboard and properly responding."

Chownyk chose that moment to link in to Russell's implant.

"CAG, what's going on?" he demanded. "I thought we were supposed to be hiding our starfighters."

"So did I," Russell replied grimly. "Are the *condottieri* responding at all?"

"No," Chownyk said. "It's your bird, CAG. What do we do?"

"Stand by." He turned to his own people. "Get me a channel to that bird. I don't care if she's replying; just make sure she can hear me."

Despite the surprise and confusion, his staff were still moving competently and without chaos. He had his channel in under a second, a tightbeam radio trained directly on the starfighter.

"Flight Commander Cavendish, you are in violation of our standing orders and your launch is unauthorized. Return to ship *immediately*. That is an order, Commander."

He waited.

"Is she responding?" he demanded after a moment.

"No, sir. She's received the message, though I can't guarantee she's listening to us," the tech replied.

"XO, how long until she's out of lance range?" Russell asked Chownyk grimly.

"Four minutes," the cyborg replied instantly. "If she starts evading, our hit probabilities start dropping off in about two minutes."

"*Void*," Russell spat. "XO, clear one of the secondary lances and paint her with the targeting systems."

"Done," Chownyk said grimly, turning his attention away to snap orders to the bridge crew.

"Channel still ready?" Russell asked to a nod from his staff.

"Commander Cavendish, you are now in violation of a direct order in a potential combat zone," he said flatly. "If you do not turn back in the next thirty seconds, we will shoot you down."

Silence for several seconds, and then she *finally* responded.

"Are you fucking *nuts*, Rokos?" Cavendish snapped. "I'm operating under orders. Get the stick out of your ass and get out of my way."

"The only person authorized to give you orders is *me*," he replied. "The only person able to give you launch authorization is *me*. You also hacked our systems, so you're about two steps *past* mutiny, Commander. You have twenty seconds to turn back."

Silence. Five seconds. Ten.

"XO," Russell said quietly. "Please have Commander Taylor destroy that starfighter when the deadline is up."

"Lance is charged and ready to fire," Taylor informed him, her voice subdued. "Active sensors online, target is locked in."

Then, with less than a *second* to spare, Cavendish finally flipped her bird and began slowing down to return to the carrier.

"*Finally,*" Russell snapped. "Taylor, keep her dialed in the whole way back. If she tries to pull a fast one, fire one warning shot."

"Understood, CAG," Taylor said quietly. Technically, Russell couldn't give her orders—but he was also the only one who could authorize shooting down one of their own birds.

"Have the ship's marshal meet me in the flight deck," he ordered grimly.

———

RUSSELL HAD FORGOTTEN THAT, since *Chameleon* didn't have a military police detachment, it also didn't have the ship's marshal that would command that detachment. In the absence, however, Gunny Ramirez had stepped up to fill the role where needed and he met the CAG on the flight deck with a fire team of four Marines.

In powered battle armor.

"A little excessive, Gunny?" Russell asked, eyeing the five hulking suits of metal and ceramic.

"Lieutenant Riley warned me that the pilots are immune to stungun beams," Ramirez replied, the normally wiry man looming over the CAG's broad but short bulk. "But internal augments can't match armor muscles."

"Fair enough," the CAG allowed, turning to watch as the automated system landed Cavendish's starfighter exactly on its point. For a moment, blasts of supercooled air covered the nine-meter-tall cylindrical craft, then the exit ramp popped out.

Flight Commander Cavendish stormed off the ship like an avenging supernova, charging down the ramp to stop directly in front of Russell. If she noticed Ramirez and his Marines, she gave no sign of it.

"What the *fuck* do you think you're planning?" she snapped. "Glass will *break* you for this stunt—threatening me for following orders?"

"Glass has no authority to give you orders," Russell said mildly. "Once you were seconded to my Wing, you were under my command and, through me, Captain Roberts's command. You *are* familiar with the chain of command, aren't you?"

"You just blew off a contact we'd had scheduled since we left Castle," she told him. "And I don't know if the bastard will agree to meet with us again."

"*Any* flight ops are to be cleared through me and the Captain," he replied. "If Glass had a contact, he should have been working *with* us instead of *against* us."

"You didn't have need to know, Commander. Now, if we're done here, I need to see if I can reach out to our contact and *fix* your fuck-up."

"No," Russell said flatly. "You hacked into this ship's systems and shut down the safety overrides to carry out an unauthorized launch and then defied a return-to-base order. Gunny Ramirez, take Commander Cavendish into custody."

The Marines moved forward to grab the woman, their massive armored forms entirely out of scale with the small officer.

"You can't be serious!"

"Deathly, Commander. Because last I checked, mutiny can still carry the death penalty even if we're not in combat. Take her to the brig, Gunnery Sergeant."

15

New Edmonton System
16:10 May 26, 2736 Earth Standard Meridian Date/Time
Chameleon

KYLE CAREFULLY SETTLED the shuttle back down on *Chameleon*'s deck as he received a feed from Chownyk updating him on the events while he was gone.

"Oh, Gods," he muttered as he considered the fallout that was going to land on his plate as soon as Glass was updated.

"What do you want us to do?" Chownyk asked over the mental link.

"Nothing," Kyle ordered. "You made the right call. I'll deal with Glass."

Inhaling deeply, he rose and joined the spy and their bodyguards as they exited the shuttle. A maintenance crew was waiting to take over the spacecraft behind them, but otherwise the deck was empty.

"Good to be back aboard," Glass declared, patting the suit pocket he'd concealed Ostrowski's data in. "Please let me know as soon as

Commander Cavendish returns from her mission, then we'll need to prepare to move on the Aurelius system."

"I didn't authorize any mission by Cavendish," Kyle said carefully. "Since she's under my command, shouldn't that have been run through me?"

"Technicalities, Captain," the spy snapped. "*I* run this mission, and I needed Cavendish to take care of something you didn't have need to know for."

The spy stopped, turning to stare at Kyle.

"What did your thugs do?" he demanded.

"Flight Commander Cavendish is under arrest for mutiny," Kyle said flatly. "My office, Glass. Now."

"Mutiny? She was operating under my authority!" Glass snarled, ignoring the black-ops troopers and maintenance crew around them.

"We can discuss this in my office, *Mister* Glass, or you can join her in the brig," *Chameleon*'s Captain told him.

GLASS BARELY MANAGED to contain himself until they reached Kyle's office near the bridge, clearly fuming the entire way.

As soon as the door slid closed behind them, he exploded.

"What kind of cluster*fuck* are you *running*, Captain?" he shouted. "This mission was always going to have components you couldn't be fully briefed on. Interfering in my orders is unacceptable—I demand that Cavendish be released and Rokos be relieved *immediately*."

"No," Kyle said quietly, his back to the spy. "Mister Glass, right now I am deciding whether or not you will be joining Commander Cavendish, not whether Commander Rokos was correct."

"What? She had orders and authorization; he was out of line."

"Flight Commander Cavendish and her squadron were placed in *Chameleon*'s fighter wing," Kyle pointed out. "That meant they were under Rokos's command and, through him, mine. *You*, Mister Glass, are not in that chain of command.

"You are, in fact, not in the chain of command of any military personnel aboard *Chameleon*. What you promised *me* was that I would have full command of *Chameleon*—a promise you have now repeatedly broken.

"You are a civilian." Officially, at least, though Glass's habit of failing to *act* like one was making Kyle suspicious. "You have no command authority here—and hence cannot protect Cavendish from the consequences of her obeying orders you had no authority to give. Do you understand me, Mister Glass?"

The office was very quiet for a long moment. The spy looked contemplative, his anger swept away in an instantaneous shift Kyle found mildly creepy.

"I do," Glass said finally. "*My* understanding, Captain Roberts, was that I remained in command of this *mission*."

"You are in *charge* of this mission," Kyle pointed out. "You are not in *command*. Even if you were, you would *still* need to run flight operations by any of your personnel by me and by Commander Rokos. I understand, Glass, that you have been preparing this mission for a while.

"I have accepted a frankly intolerable lack of transparency so far out of that understanding," he continued. "But flight operations without my approval? In *opposition* to standing orders? I command a warship, Mister Glass. I *cannot* permit you to undermine the chain of command. Commander Cavendish's actions were unacceptable and illegal. Her career is over and she could spend the next three decades in military prison for them.

"I can't levy the same punishment on you, and it was *your* bloody stupidity that put *her* in this position. So please, Mister Glass, give me a good Godsdamn reason *why* I should keep trusting you?"

The spy sighed.

"I...apologize, Captain," he said slowly. "It is very easy in my line of work to default to lies, deception, and a lack of trust. Where possible, I prefer to rely on people I have worked with in the past. But I understand your point on chain of command.

"*I* made a mistake," he allowed. "Commander Cavendish, based on that previous relationship, followed my orders. *I* am responsible. But..."

He drew one of the data disks Ostrowski had given him from his suit pocket. "May I, Captain?" he asked, gesturing to the wallscreen.

"Go ahead," Kyle said, his implant authorizing the other man to link in. He was curious what the spy had that he thought could dig him out of *this* hole.

The image of a tactical plot appeared on the screen. A single ship sat in the middle, most of its details included. A *Volcano*-class heavy carrier, it was a sixty-three-million-cubic-meter warship massing twenty million tons, one of the most powerful warships in the Terran Commonwealth Navy. A dusting of icons noted a defensive perimeter of the new Katana-type starfighters, though *much* less data was included on those.

A wedge of new icons appeared. There were almost no details for these, though their speed and vector suggested starfighters. The defending fighters assumed a standard Commonwealth defensive perimeter, stretching out to intercept the inbound ships a million kilometers away from their mothership—far enough out that they would be unable to engage with fighter missiles or positron lances.

Instead, the new starfighters flashed at just over *three* million kilometers, firing missiles from well outside normal starfighter missile range, and then turned their vectors ninety degrees away from the defenders.

The entire exercise was running in accelerated time. Kyle could judge even without the system telling him that the attackers would evade interception. The defending starfighters went after the incoming missiles instead, but *those* disappeared in a wall of jamming far more capable than a starfighter missile should carry.

Fifty starfighters launched one hundred missiles and over half survived to reach the carrier. Despite the massive defenses the mothership carried, half a dozen of the weapons made it through and obliterated the carrier.

"That was the centerpiece of the data Ostrowski had on the Commonwealth's new fighter program," Glass said quietly. "That wasn't a simulation. The missiles were practice warheads, but the flight time, the maneuvers, the ECM...all of that was done in real space."

"I see," Kyle said slowly. "I'm not sure…"

"How this relates to Cavendish?" Glass asked. "It doesn't. It *does* relate to our mission. Target selection was always up to me. If the data on this starfighter and its weaponry is at Tau Ceti, however, I don't see a choice. Do you?"

"No," the Captain admitted. "We need this data."

"This mission is more critical now than I thought," Glass replied. "We still need to deliver a critical blow to the Commonwealth's infrastructure, but we also need to steal this research.

"We'll need to hit Aurelius to acquire Commonwealth munitions," he continued. "We also need to meet up with the contact Cavendish was *supposed* to meet, as he was supposed to provide us with upgrade kits to bring our Cataphracts up to their Delta standard. Some of that work is done already, but we don't have the lance upgrades."

Kyle nodded slowly. Glass was giving him the briefing he *should* have provided when they left Castle.

"We can still reach out to them?"

"We should be able to, yes," the spy allowed. "There's a giant wrench thrown in now, but I'll accept that's at least mostly my fault." He sighed. "That contact won't deal with anyone he hasn't met, which meant it had to be me or Cavendish.

"If you're going to blame someone for not telling you what was going on, blame me," Glass said. "And let Laura out of the damned brig."

The spy seemed to have made a major effort to actually bring Kyle into the loop, so he nodded slowly.

"She's still grounded," he said firmly. "That's Rokos's call, and he needs to *trust* whoever he's taking into battle. After everything she's pulled, orders or not, he can't. *I* wouldn't in his place."

"Fine," Glass agreed. "I'll reach out to my contact as well. I'll let you know what the next step for getting those upgrade kits is."

16

New Edmonton System
23:00 May 26, 2736 Earth Standard Meridian Date/Time
Chameleon

KYLE WAS EYEING the scanners as the sublight "clipper" freighter detached the tube they'd delivered food and other supplies to from *Chameleon* and drifted away under careful gas thrusters. If the interstellar equivalent of a bumboat saw anything unusual in the quantity of foodstuff the Q-ship had bought, her crew was wise enough not to say anything.

They might later, but that was fine. Part of the point of this operation was for the attack to be traced back here, after all.

Technically, Commander Taylor had the watch, but this was the first watch the young woman had *ever* held in a potentially hostile environment. So, Kyle had brought a datapad out into the bridge with him and was pointedly doing paperwork—recording the physical, League-minted coinage he'd just handed over for another month's worth of food, as a matter of fact.

All that was really important was that the Captain, despite being on the bridge, did not have the watch. Fleet Commander Jenny Taylor did, and the blonde officer was doing a *fine* job.

And if she needed backup, her Captain was right there.

When Glass came rushing onto the bridge, Kyle was glad he'd made that choice. The old spy disconcerted *him*; he wasn't leaving his junior officers to deal with the man.

"Ah, Captain, good," Glass said when he spotted him. "Can we speak in private?"

"My office is right here," Kyle agreed genially. He glanced over at Taylor and gave her a quick thumbs-up. If she needed him, she could still buzz him, after all.

She somewhat hesitantly returned the gesture, but she'd been doing fine so far, which gave Kyle a level of confidence as he led Glass into his office.

"What is it?" he asked, taking a seat behind his desk and gesturing the spy to sit.

"I finally made contact with Trickster," Glass said calmly. "They've agreed to meet us, but only on their terms."

"I thought that was basically how things were going to work with your contact," Kyle observed.

"They're being *very* specific and I don't like it," the spy replied. "Before, we were meeting someone in the Nexen Cloud to negotiate a delivery that would have come by one of the clippers in the business of servicing starships.

"Now they want me to physically meet them on his station and, I quote, 'bring the big captain, no one else,'" Glass concluded. "Trickster had people watching us. I don't *trust* Trickster and I don't want to take *Chameleon* all the way to their station."

"Where's their station?" Kyle asked.

"Here in New Edmonton," the spy replied. "The system has an outer ice belt, much like Sol's Kuiper Belt. The station is hidden out there, far away from prying eyes. Trickster is…one of the more notorious League pirates, and for reasons I haven't managed to discover, Dictator Periklos wants them *dead*."

"They personally pissed off the man who took over the League? I'm almost impressed."

"Don't be. Trickster is murderous scum, but they've got the tech we need." Glass shook his head. "The Cataphract-D has better acceleration, better ECM, a more powerful positron lance... You know better than I whether we need those upgrade kits, Captain."

"I'm guessing that Ostrowski's intel says we're running up against Katanas at least in Tau Ceti, if not in Aurelius?" Kyle asked.

"Probably not Aurelius, but one of the production lines is in Tau Ceti," Glass admitted.

"If we send our people up against Katanas in the half-upgraded Cataphracts we have now, when we *have* a better option, we're killing them ourselves," *Chameleon*'s Captain said grimly.

"Tell Trickster we'll make their meeting, then forward the coordinates to Lau's people. And I'll make sure our teeth are sharp when we walk into the spider's den."

07:00 May 27, 2736 ESMDT
New Edmonton Ice Belt

EVEN MORE THAN inner-system asteroid belts, ice belts were far less dense than media liked to portray them. As *Chameleon* approached the coordinates they'd been given, there were no swarms of ice asteroids attempting to chew them up.

There *was* a level of ice "dust" that was actively dangerous to the ship at any significant velocity, but that was why even civilian ships had electromagnetic deflectors and armor. Kyle carefully checked the readouts he was receiving to be sure that their current speed, several thousand kilometers a second, was sustainable without increasing the deflectors to less-civilian levels.

"Where exactly *is* this station?" he wondered aloud. Eight hours of flight had carried them over twenty-two light-minutes farther out from McMurray, far into the uninhabited outskirts of the system.

They were rapidly approaching the coordinates Glass had been given, but there was nothing in the ten light-seconds around them except for half a dozen chunks of ice of various sizes.

"Should be exactly at the coordinates," Glass told him. "Unless Trickster is being a *complete* bastard, anyway."

"Taylor?" Kyle asked. "What are you reading?"

"One of our local ice chunks is right at those coordinates," she reported. "Might be denser than the rest, too. Hard to tell on passives —want me to ping them?"

"No," he said slowly. "Lau, take us in as if we're expecting a docking port on that chunk of rock. Taylor—keep the hatches closed, but spin up the lances and charge the missiles."

"Yes, sir," she replied. Lau kept their attention silently on guiding the big Q-ship in toward the presumed station.

"Two of the other chunks of ice share an orbit with our target," the tactical officer reported as they decelerated toward our destination. "Both are about a hundred thousand klicks away, not on top of them, but…"

"Close enough to mount defensive weapons or starfighters," Kyle finished for her. "Keep an eye on them. For that matter, keep a *lance* targeted on them."

Her grin in reply was predatory.

"Two light-seconds from target, on course for zero-zero," Lau reported shortly.

"Mister Glass, if you'd like to reach out to our friend and see how they feel about guests?"

The spy nodded and closed his eyes, focusing on his implants. Kyle's access to the systems showed him logging into the communications systems and sending a directional radio message forward.

"Response incoming from the target coordinates," Taylor announced.

This was a tightbeam radio signal, one focused directly on *Chameleon* and flagged for Glass. While Kyle *could* view it, he left it to the spy. Their working relationship required some trust to go *both* ways, after all.

Finally, Glass opened his eyes.

"We should be seeing a beacon on Judecca Station shortly," he told them. "That should guide us to a docking port for cargo transfer. Captain Roberts and I are to board the station and meet with Trickster directly; we'll make payment then and they'll begin transfer immediately."

"If they've got decent cargo-handling equipment, we should be able to load the upgrade kits in an hour or less," Kyle noted. "Seems like your friend is playing straight so far."

"Would you object, my dear Captain, if I asked you to keep Commander Rokos's people in their fighters a while longer regardless?"

"I wasn't planning on doing anything else."

17

New Edmonton System
07:35 May 27, 2736 Earth Standard Meridian Date/Time
Judecca Station, Ice Belt

THE CARGO TRANSFER tunnel was almost twenty meters across, clearly designed to not only allow movement of any size cargo pod anyone cared to be using but also complete starfighters. Most fascinating of all, it was carved out of the ice of the asteroid Trickster had buried his space station in. There were supporting beams running through the ice, but those were the only sign of human interference.

Kyle suspected that those "beams" were also heating elements and tracks for cutting lasers. Most likely, any access to Judecca Station was temporary, filled with new ice once it was no longer needed. Keeping the station completely encased in ice would protect it from almost any detection.

He and Glass followed a guide line down the "bottom" of the tunnel toward a tiny-seeming human-sized airlock on the metal hull at the far end. Impressively, the spy was almost as comfortable in zero gravity as Kyle was.

They glided to a careful stop at the personnel airlock, orienting themselves with the safety arrows as the door opened, and then made the inevitably graceless transition into Judecca Station's artificial gravity.

The airlock filled with air and the clear plastic bubbles that had extended from their shipsuits retracted as the clothing's sensors confirmed a breathable atmosphere.

Safe, the inner door slid open to reveal the form of an absolutely immense human being. It looked like he'd been easily two meters tall, taller even than Kyle, and *then* someone had gone to town with cybernetics. Both of the man's legs had been replaced with immense monstrosities of steel and artificial muscles, and armor plating had been attached across his bare chest and upper arms.

He grunted at them and gestured for them to follow him as he turned back into the station.

Unlike the processing stations in McMurray orbit, Judecca Station's corridors did *not* look like they could have been in any other station in the galaxy. Only the floor and inner wall here were metal; the roof and outer wall were uncovered ice.

The lights were dim, only the extra processing included in Kyle's neural implant allowing him to pick up enough light to see clearly. Glass, he suspected, had something closer to the black-ops implants and could probably see in the dark.

Their silent guide led them deeper into the station, into corridors that looked like they *should* have been full of people. The more populated the areas looked like they should be, the dirtier they became. The pristine ice walls of the entrance gave way to steel smeared with rust and dirt—but Kyle noted that all of the mechanical equipment was perfectly maintained.

Air intakes, lights, the security systems. Everything that was related to safety or the functioning of the station was in perfect working order, if occasionally smeared with dirt to make sure it didn't stand out.

"We're getting a show," he sent Glass silently through their implants. "Why would Trickster *want* us to think this place is run down?"

"Because they're completely averse to anyone knowing anything about them," the spy replied. "I'm surprised they want to meet us in person. They don't meet *anyone* in person."

That was not encouraging.

Finally, their guide led them to a large security door and turned back to face them.

"Weapons," he grunted.

Kyle shrugged and surrendered his pistol. He doubted that the gun would make that much of a difference. If they were making it out of here, it was on Glass.

"Enter," the giant ordered.

———

RUSSELL SAT in the command seat of his starfighter and watched the sensor reports being fed to him by *Chameleon* as if his stony gaze would somehow conjure answers. Judecca Station was a well-concealed facility and they could pick out only a handful of details even while *docked* to her.

Her two trailing sisters were surrendering even fewer secrets, and the CAG *itched* to order an active sweep of them. He doubted Chownyk, the man who *had* that authority right now, felt any differently—but unless their new friends decided to open the ball, *Chameleon*'s crew didn't want to dance.

"Are you seeing *any* starfighters?" he asked his gunner quietly. That worthy, in addition to running the Cataphract's missile armament and ECM, was also charged with reviewing sensor data in the command starfighter.

"Nothing, which I don't trust for a second," Flight Lieutenant Rauol Alvarado, a gaunt man with wispy hair and pale skin, replied. "Judecca is armed and those other two ice balls have *at least* missile launchers, or I'll eat my uniform."

"Agreed," he muttered. He brought up the map of the area and overlaid the launch vectors for his squadrons. Alpha was in the launchers right now, with himself and an extra from Echo's black-ops starfighters. Now that they were in place and his shoulder blades were itching, he wished he'd thought to drop those stealthier birds into space somewhere along the way. He wasn't used to *having* starfighters that had a half-decent chance of going unnoticed.

"Listen," he said over the implant network, pulling in his squadron leaders. "While I don't see any reason *why* our new friends might betray us, I don't trust them as far as we can throw them.

"So, *if* they decide to open the party, this is what we'll do…"

———

EDVARD WATCHED CAREFULLY through the pickups on *Chameleon*'s hull as the cargo hatch on the other end of the tunnel slowly slid open. A handful of men and women in closed shipsuits came out, guiding and directing the mostly automated jet-equipped harnesses that moved the ten-meter cubes of standard cargo pods.

All were visibly armed, but it was sidearms and slung submachine guns. Nothing that would be a threat to people in powered battle armor, and yet… He knew that Glass and the Captain were both uncomfortable about this meeting, and those cargo pods could hide an entire *platoon* in full battle armor apiece.

"Riley," he pinged the black-ops platoon commander. "Have your platoon go out and be friendly security," he ordered. "I'm going to have everyone else strap on battle armor, just in case these guys decide not to be friendly."

"Wilco," she replied. "Can I throw one of my squads in armor? Might help make the point, while keeping our numbers down to what they're expecting for a pirate ship."

He hesitated for a moment, but…

"Agreed," he said. "Keep your eyes open; this whole thing is making me twitchy."

"Can't we just jump clear if there's a problem?" she asked. "I thought we'd be far enough out for that?"

Edvard chuckled.

"I have *no* idea," he admitted. "Let me check."

Flipping channels, he raised the bridge.

"Commander Chownyk, how's it looking outside?"

"Quiet enough to make me wonder if this might actually go off without a hitch," the XO admitted. "Though I *swear* there's a bull's-eye painted on my back. Does their cargo look right to you, El-Maj?"

"Specs the CAG gave me say ten cargo pods should have it all, and that's what I'm seeing," Edvard replied. "I hear you on the bull's-eye, though. Are we far enough out to go FTL if there's a problem?"

"Sure, if you want to leave Roberts and Glass behind," Chownyk said with a chuckle of laughter. "I may be half-machine, but I don't think even *I* can be that cold. If things go to hell, what are your odds on extraction?"

Edvard pursed his lips in thought.

"I'm going to have two platoons in battle armor in about a minute," he pointed out. "Add in my HQ section and I've got a hundred and forty suits ready to go punch a hole. I don't like to underestimate anybody, but that station is only big enough for about two thousand people.

"I don't care if every damn one of them has power armor, they don't stand a chance against a company of Castle's damned Marines, sir."

———

DESPITE THE INTENTIONALLY DILAPIDATED STATE OF the rest of Judecca Station, Trickster's office was neat and clean. It could have belonged to any middle manager in human space. A plain wooden desk and a wall turned over to a wallscreen.

It didn't look particularly different from Kyle's own office aboard *Chameleon*.

The occupant of the desk was an...enigma. Trickster wore a hood and a mask painted in a checkerboard of white and black squares. Coupled with a surprisingly androgynous figure, a black suit with a long-sleeved white shirt and white gloves, there was no way to tell if Trickster was a man or woman.

"Come in, come in," they instructed Kyle and Glass, their voice shifting modulations as they spoke, the mask clearly including some kind of electronic filter. "Mister Glass, Captain Roberts, it is my pleasure."

"We're here for our upgrade kits, Trickster," Glass said, his voice impressively level, given the strange harlequin behind the desk.

"I know, I know," the pirate replied. "I hope Jose was not too intimidating. The *assholes* who 'upgraded' him did his neural pathways no favors."

"Jose" presumably was the mountain of a man who'd guided them there. Apparently, his cybernetics hadn't been entirely voluntary.

Glass sighed.

"You clearly want more than your money. What is it?"

"Oh, I want my money," Trickster replied, the modulator not hiding the smile in their voice. "I *also* wanted to actually meet you face to face, Mister Glass. I have attempted to put together the components of your operation, and yet I find myself coming up short. Not many are that skilled, though the presence of a Commonwealth Q-ship does suggest *so many* possibilities."

"And how much will it cost us to keep those possibilities to yourself?" the spy asked.

"Discretion is an assumed part of my business dealings, Glass," the pirate said flatly. "I would not have survived this long were it not. I merely wanted to meet you and Captain Roberts here. He, a legend forged by publicity and media—and you, who would *be* a legend, were the records not sealed. The contrast is…delightful."

Trickster made a "pass it over" gesture.

"Nonetheless, I would like my money."

Glass slid a datastick onto the table.

"Codes and numbers for anonymous accounts with the Bank of Golide Swaziland," he said simply. "The agreed amount."

Golide Swaziland was an independent system the Commonwealth had so far left alone—most likely because even Terra could use a black-market banking system that asked no questions and took no names.

"Good," Trickster replied. "My bank account is satisfied. My curiosity is satisfied. Yours is not, but that is the nature of the game. Your cargo is being loaded, Captain Roberts. I could, perhaps, see my way to providing additional hardware…but I suspect your plan depends on using hardware that can be more easily traced than my goods.

"Jose will escort you back to your ship. While you are on Judecca Station, you are under my protection. I will not wish you luck. We share an enemy but not a cause."

"Thank you," Glass said with a small bow.

The two Federation men rose. As they turned to leave, the door slid open behind them to reveal Jose's immense form. The giant grunted, gestured for them to follow him, and then stopped mid-motion.

He spasmed once, his face contorting in pain. Despite *whatever* had just happened, he began to spin around—moving at a pace that Kyle couldn't follow.

Then his chest exploded, spraying gore and metal everywhere as the armor-piercing grenade that had been fired into the massive cyborg's chest detonated.

18

New Edmonton System
08:10 May 27, 2736 Earth Standard Meridian Date/Time
Chameleon, *Ice Belt*

EDVARD HAD STEPPED out to join Riley's platoon in running security in the cargo bay itself by the time the first pod reached *Chameleon*'s cargo bay. The leader of the armed men escorting the pod gave him what probably passed for a salute among the League's *condottieri.*

"I'm Henry; these are my boys and gals," he said brightly. "We're just longshoremen today, but my folk feel naked without the guns."

"Then you won't mind if we watch you like hawks," Edvard replied. "Edvard. I run security here."

Henry snorted. "And if you ain't *somebody's* Marine, my momma's a virgin. But it ain't *my* business; I leave that kind of game to the boss. Move them on up, boys and gals!" He grinned. "Where do you want them?"

The harnesses included built-in small scale mass manipulators that reduced the mass of the multi-hundred-ton cargo pods to something that could roll on the small wheels included. Edvard gestured for one of the Chiefs charged with handling the cargo bay to take over traffic direction and stepped aside.

Henry moved with him.

"Ship's more than she looks like," he observed. "Cleaner than a few of the hulks I've worked on, too."

"We run a tight ship," Edvard said nonchalantly. "*My* boss has his standards."

"So he does," the pirate allowed. "We have ten pods for you. Each contains four upgrade kits for a Cataphract fighter—and unless I misread the specs, nine-tenths of the mass and volume is a replacement positron lance. Your flyboys are gonna be *happy*."

"I look forward to seeing— "

"*Shit!*" Henry exclaimed, holding up his hand as his eyes glazed slightly, the expression of someone linked in to their implant communicator. "*Son of a fucking Martian.*"

"What the hell?" Edvard demanded, but the pirate spun to look at him.

"You've got more people than you're showing," he said. It wasn't a question. "Battle armor. Weapons. *Marines*. Right?!"

"Maybe…"

"One of the boss's lieutenants just decided that *right fucking now* is the best opportunity he can find to make a play—and he sees your ship as a bonus. You've got a hundred guys swarming this way, half in battle armor."

"I can handle that," Edvard said grimly, sending notes to his platoon leaders.

"Can you pull my boss out?" Henry said flatly. "I got a warning from one of the guys I trust, then I lost coms with the station." He swallowed. "I'm authorized to offer ten million Terran dollars for assistance in this case."

"Let me deal with the boarders first," the Marine said grimly. "But then I have to go in after *my* boss, too."

———

"Launch! Launch! Launch!"

Russell's voice echoed over both the implant network and in the cockpit of his starfighter as he barked the order.

No one was quite sure *what* was going on yet, but they'd lost communications with the Captain and Glass at the same time that Edvard's new friend had lost contact with the station. Whatever the situation was, however, Russell was more confident in their ability to handle it with forty starfighters in space.

A giant's palm slammed him back into his acceleration couch as the Q-ship fired his ship into space. With every mass manipulator on his ship dedicated to counteracting the force, it was *survivable*, but they could only absorb ninety-nine-point-nine percent of the over *twenty thousand* gravities he was subjected to for a fraction of a second.

"Alpha Squadron clear," Flight Commander Churchill reported. "And...accessories."

"I heard that," Russell snapped back at his subordinate. Those "accessories" were his starfighter and the first of the black starfighters from his Echo squadron.

"Second cycle in ten seconds," his deck chief reported. "Clear the airspace, people."

Russell engaged his link with the starfighter. His implant kicked into a new gear, and suddenly he *was* the agile, four-thousand-ton starfighter. A moment's thought brought the antimatter engines to life, moving his ship out of the path of the next wave of starfighters—and bringing his weapons to bear on one of the two defensive platforms trailing Judecca Station.

"CAG, you have incoming missiles," Chownyk reported. "Both stations just launched; I'm reading a dozen capital-ship missiles from each of them. We're trying to clear the gunports, but scans show *someone* mounted explosives on the cargo tunnel.

"If I break free to maneuver, I'll blow a big enough hole in the side that we won't *need* a carrier deck," the XO told him grimly. "Missile defense is in play, but unless someone flies in front of our big guns, this isn't going to be *Chameleon's* fight. I've got one missile salvo; let me know if you see a use for it."

"Will do," Russell said distractedly, studying the incoming missiles and the stations behind them.

"Alpha Squadron, take those lead missiles. Cover *Chameleon*," he ordered. "Bravo squadron, form on me as you emerge, we're going after those launch platforms."

"Wilco," Churchill replied. Moments later, all eight of Alpha Squadron's Cataphracts charged forward at four hundred and eighty gravities—not what the Falcons they were used to could achieve, but still more than the un-upgraded Cataphract was capable of.

Bravo Squadron and two more of Echo's fighters were accelerating to catch up with Russell as he held his own acceleration down, studying the ice-encased weapons platform he'd designated as "Target Alpha".

It was hard to say just how large the actual platform was, with the ice wrapped around it. The entire ice ball was a rough egg two hundred meters long and a hundred and fifty wide, but at least a few meters of that had to be ice.

They were hitting it with active radar now, which wasn't helping as much as he'd like. The pirates had crammed a dozen capital-ship launchers into the thing—even if there was only a meter of ice on each side, the platform wasn't big enough for more than a handful of small lances and maybe two good-sized ones.

The two platforms *had* to be primarily missile bases, which meant that they were a bigger threat to *Chameleon* than his starfighters. Even the Cataphracts were going to eat the stations alive—which meant there had to be starfighters somewhere, as he doubted someone with Trickster's reputation would have missed the shortfall.

His attention was broken by the rippling explosions of failing containment on antimatter warheads. With Target Alpha only eighty thousand kilometers from *Chameleon*—and Target Bravo only a hundred thousand kilometers farther away—Churchill's squadron had *started* in range of the missiles.

The weapons might be smart and maneuverable, but they weren't *that* capable. The salvo from Target Alpha came apart in a series of one-gigaton explosions as they ran into Alpha Squadron's positron lances, and Russell smiled mirthlessly.

He was even less sure of the station's defenses than of its weapons, but at fifty thousand kilometers, his people had a decent chance of burning through its deflectors for a hit. Charlie Squadron was out behind him now, and once Alpha Squadron had finished shredding Target Alpha's missiles, they could move on to Bravo's…

Wait.

"Guns, what the *hell* are Target Bravo's missiles doing?" he demanded of Alvarado.

Even as he was noticing the change in Bravo's missiles' path, so was Target Alpha. The weapons platform had so far been relatively quiet other than launching the missiles, but it sprang to life as Target Bravo's missiles charged *toward* it, not *past* it.

Lasers and defensive positron lances flared to life in flashes of vaporizing ice, but Bravo's commander had timed the change in their missiles' course perfectly—there wasn't enough *time* for Alpha to shoot down all of them.

There *was*, apparently, enough time to fire Alpha's main weapon, though. In the moments before the surviving trio of missiles impacted, a megaton-per-second capital-ship-grade positron lance flared to life, connecting the two platforms with a beam of pure antimatter.

Both platforms vanished in near-simultaneous explosions, vaporized ice and metal flaring out in every direction.

"Well, that'll make things easier," Churchill noted. "I'm guessing some of our friends don't like each other much."

"What the *hell* have we stumbled into the middle of?" Russell asked aloud.

"I don't know," Chownyk interrupted, "but we're not done yet. Judecca Station's weapons aren't online yet, but we're running active pulses and picking—*son of a bitch*."

Everyone's sensors were suddenly overwhelmed with a brilliant flash of Cherenkov radiation as a starship emerged from Alcubierre drive barely two light-seconds away.

———

It took Edvard a moment to realize what he was seeing after the massive door at the other end of the cargo tunnel slid open again. *Something* was moving forward, but it wasn't armored troopers. The incoming *things* were each about a meter high, four-legged—and armed.

"Combat drones!" he finally realized aloud. "Stand by to take them out."

He glanced over at Henry. Trickster's people had joined his in taking cover as they prepared to defend the cargo bay.

"Please tell me those are remote-controlled," he said calmly. Fully autonomous war machines were banned by treaties and agreements dating back to pre-Alcubierre Earth—and the occasional secret project by various governments tended to blow up sufficiently to keep those treaties honored.

"No," the pirate admitted. "Fully self-directed. Supposed to ignore people who are unarmed or wearing a certain badge, but...well, let's just say these ones ended up in a black marketer's inventory for a reason."

"Usually, just the *threat* is enough to get a ship that's being stubborn to surrender," he added. "Boss only actually *used* them once that I know. On the Dictator's people."

"No wonder he hates your guts," Edvard muttered. "Any particular weak points?"

"The override codes?" Henry grunted. "Which I tried ten seconds ago. They've either taken out the three I know or just outright disabled the override. Bastards."

From the sound of it, disabling the overrides turned the drone into an area-denial weapon—they'd probably shoot at *anyone* they saw.

"Great," Edvard replied, watching the distance drop. He doubted the pirates had sent the drones unless they had some way of getting through *Chameleon*'s hull.

"Commander." He raised Chownyk. "How are we doing with those explosives?"

"Chief Radnick says he's just disabled the remote detonators," the XO replied, a distinct tone of relief in his voice. "The pressure detonators are still in place, so we're not going anywhere, but they aren't going to have any luck blasting their way in, either."

"Then I guess we'll have to let them knock," Edvard said calmly. "If the Captain wasn't in there, I wouldn't let them do more."

"You have a plan, El-Maj?"

"Yes, sir."

"Then go get our Captain back."

"Wilco," Edvard replied with a grin, turning his attention back to the cargo tunnel linking the two ships.

The drones were almost to the access to *Chameleon,* and he could see people starting to move in the station itself. At least some were in battle armor, though it didn't look like all or even a majority.

"Door opens in ten seconds," he barked. "Pick your targets. Put down those fucking drones, then assault the station. These bastards have no clue what it means to deal with Castle's *damned* Marines."

A yipping wolf-howl echoed from the speakers on his Marines' battle armor, and then the door slammed open, exposing the incoming robots to their fire.

The robots might be fast and self-directed, but they couldn't scan and target through starship armor. The *Marines,* however, had access to the pickups on the outside of their ship. They'd already picked their targets before Edvard hit the command to open the door...and he had two hundred Marines and black-ops troopers, plus two dozen of Henry's people, targeting barely a hundred drones.

Henry had clearly thought the drones were tough, a credible threat —but Edvard's people were firing tungsten penetrators designed to take down battle armor, and each drone was hit by at least half a dozen of them.

Moments after the door opened, his howling Marines charged over the junkyard that had been the pirates' first wave.

19

New Edmonton System
08:15 May 27, 2736 Earth Standard Meridian Date/Time
Judecca Station, Ice Belt

JOSE BLOCKED the door for a long moment, his shattered corpse still sufficient to stop a spray of bullets from reaching the room. As his immense form finally fell, a security shutter slammed down to seal the room away.

"We're being jammed," Kyle told Glass after an abortive attempt to reach *Chameleon*. "What's going on?" he demanded of Trickster.

The pirate was busy opening a concealed locker in the wall and pulling out weapons.

"They're jamming you because I just shut down Judecca Station's defenses to be safe," they said calmly. "I *think* I managed to ping people I believe are loyal on the defense platforms as well, which *should* stop their weapons being turned on your ship."

"Why my ship?" Kyle demanded.

"Because up until the moment you demonstrated that your ship had at least one fully functioning, military-grade fighter launch tube, no one in this system except me and presumably whoever you met on Station Six knew your ship was a Q-ship," Trickster said flatly. "Which makes her the most valuable prize any pirate can think of."

"Well, except me," they noted after a moment. "I can think of a more valuable prize: my *life* and my *fleet*, which I wouldn't expect to survive a *stupid* attempt to seize a properly crewed Q-ship."

Glass looked vaguely sick, probably realizing that his attempt to have Cavendish contact Trickster quietly had created even more problems than he'd known.

"So, your people are trying to kill us to steal our ship?" the spy asked slowly.

"No," Trickster replied with a bark of laughter. "They're trying to kill me *today* because your ship makes a nice bonus. They're trying to kill me to take over, since they think Periklos will turn a blind eye to our little operation once I'm dead. Which he won't."

The pirate tossed a pair of weapons onto the desk.

"Glass, I *know* you can shoot. Roberts?"

"I'm no Marine, but I can shoot," the big Captain said grimly.

"These are Commonwealth Presidential Protection Detail Anti-Armor Carbines," the pirate noted. "They're recoilless, so watch the fucking vent, but fire the same tungsten penetrator their Marine battle armor rifles use."

Kyle took the carbine and studied it carefully, making sure he was clear of the vent that would spew superheated gas while firing. His shipsuit would absorb *most* of the heat from it, but even with it he suspected firing a battle armor–equivalent weapon was going to get...warm.

"In about a minute, Rainier's men are going to realize that shutter is made of old-style neutronium armor and *nothing* they have is getting through it," the pirate told them. "Unfortunately, the rest of the room is *not*, so they're going to come through the walls."

Trickster kicked over their desk and gestured for them to take cover behind it with them.

"Who's Rainier?"

"Captain of my best ship, the ungrateful bastard," Trickster replied. "Also the only one of my people with the spine to even try this."

"Is his ship here?"

"If it isn't yet, it will be. I hope your people are ready to fight."

"They are," Kyle confirmed. "We were expecting *you* to betray us."

Trickster chuckled.

"I won't deny I thought about it, but the *last* people who tried to betray 'Mister Glass' here ended up with their entire station dropped into a gas giant."

Kyle glanced over at Glass, who shrugged and then pointed.

"They're about to come through there," he said calmly.

The desk was pointed in roughly the right direction, allowing Kyle to train the carbine on the wall the spy had indicated. *He* couldn't see anything, but he knew Glass had a higher level of augmentation than he did.

A few seconds later, his faith in the spy was vindicated as the wall exploded, shards of rock, ice, and metal spraying across the room and slamming into the desk. Despite the furniture's apparent plainness, it clearly had been designed with this exact purpose in mind, as nothing made it through.

"And…*now*," Glass snapped.

Kyle rose over the desk and opened fire along with the other two men, filling the still-steaming hole with hypervelocity penetrators. A man in battle armor appeared to be leading the way, but half a dozen rounds punched clean through his armor and he collapsed to his knees, adding to the debris the explosion had created.

Return fire flared in the smoke, bullets ricocheting off of the desk as Kyle dropped behind it again, firing blindly over the top of it.

Bullets flew both ways for a few seconds, until Trickster attached a cylinder they'd removed from the locker to the top of their carbine, lifted it over the desk and triggered it.

Heat washed over Kyle, even more than the venting gas from the anti-armor carbine, and then the entire room shook as *something* exploded in the tunnel.

Silence followed.

"I only have one more of those," Trickster said conversationally. "Am I safe in presuming your Marines are going to come rescue you?"

"What would your plan be if they weren't?" Kyle asked.

"Escape tunnel, one-man shuttle, suicide charge, wait for pickup," the pirate reeled off instantly. "Since that would involve leaving you and Glass behind and probably destroying your ship, I'm hoping you have an alternative?"

―――――

"I'VE GOT Hoplites on the screen!" Alvarado snapped. "No launchers; they're just opening the hatch and *dumping* them out."

"Old-fashioned pirates," the CAG said grimly. "Please tell me everyone's in space?"

"Everyone's in space," the Lieutenant confirmed.

"All squadrons, listen in," Russell ordered. "Alpha, Charlie, Delta, jump those fighters before they get themselves sorted out. Bravo, Echo, we're going after the ship. Launch missiles as soon as you have a clear shot!"

Fitting his actions to his words, he lined the nose of his Cataphract up with the new freighter. He didn't know how many starfighters the pirates had shoved into her, but every starfighter that was still aboard her when she went up was one they weren't going to have to fight.

Whoever had jumped her in *probably* hadn't been expecting to find the space around Judecca Station swarming with starfighters. As soon as the nose of his bird lined up with the ship, he fired his positron lance, hoping that the ship only had civilian deflectors.

That was clearly not the case, as his antimatter beam was ripped to shreds, its particles scattered around the freighter in a pattern that was almost pretty—but definitely wasn't lethal.

"Missiles away," Alvarado reported calmly. "Clean and running true, flight time…" The man sighed. "Flight time is over two minutes; they're going to get their birds out, boss."

"We'll deal with them" he said grimly. The rest of his two designated squadrons were launching as well. Thirty-two missiles wasn't much of a salvo, especially when spread out like this. "Bravo, Echo—network in for synchronized launches. Empty the magazines and engage their starfighters with lances.

"Everyone else, missiles free. Take down those Hoplites!"

More of the Sarissa starfighter missiles blazed free of his fighters, filling the space around them with the tiny suns of antimatter fire as eighty more missiles blasted into space.

Ten seconds later, another eighty missiles joined them. The Hoplites had started to launch missiles as well, their inferior numbers made up by the fact they carried twice as many launchers as his people.

"I'm reading twenty-four Hoplites," his gunner reported. "I'm not seeing any new launches and the freighter is turning to run. She's got to be armed, right?"

"Not heavily," Russell murmured. "How much firepower do you need to intimidate merchant ships? Ride the missiles, Guns; I'm taking us after their birds."

Part of his mind was watching the entire battle. His people had the pirates outnumbered by almost two to one, but the Hoplite was a superior fighter in every sense: more launchers, a more powerful lance, better engines, better ECM…

But his own ships had been upgraded as much as they could without the League-designed upgrade kits they'd come there to buy. They were faster than the pirates were expecting, with better ECM—and his pilots were veterans of the bloody campaign Seventh Fleet had waged against the Commonwealth earlier that year.

Missiles started to explode as his people's lances and defensive laser suites cut into the incoming fire. The explosions expanded, rippling into secondary explosions that lit up the sky—had the pirates not *dispersed* their salvo?!

They hadn't…but there had also been method to their madness. The explosions of the clusters blinded sensors, forcing his fighters to cease firing for precious seconds—precious seconds in which the *un*-clustered missiles closed thousands of kilometers.

He threw his fighter into a ninety-degree turn, building a vector *away* from where the missiles saw him. It didn't buy him a lot of time...but it bought *enough* for his laser suite to blow the missile apart while it was still a dozen kilometers away.

Not all of his people were as lucky.

Alpha Squadron was closest, and those fractions of a second made all of the difference. Three of Churchill's starfighters disappeared, and the Cataphracts lacked the escape pods the Federation had always built into their craft. Nine of Rokos's people had just died, their bodies vaporized in antimatter fire.

Their own missiles fell on the pirates at the same time. The first salvo, launched at the pirate freighter, arrived first. The ship *did* have some defenses—several suites of antimissile laser turrets opened fire as the missiles closed—but not nearly enough.

Over a dozen of that first salvo made it through, obliterating the pirate ship in a massive fireball that rendered about sixty missiles Russell's people had fired into useless navigational hazards.

There were failsafes for that, though, and he turned his attention back to the Hoplites. Their heavier lances and deflectors meant they outranged his people, but it didn't look like it was going to matter. His people were integrating their ECM, random-walking illusions of an additional hundred starfighters in the space around them—and they'd *still* lost three starfighters.

The Hoplite crews weren't trained in that. Each of them was running their own ECM without integration or coordination, resulting in a hellacious mess...one that the humans guiding the Federation missiles could *see* the individual spheres of.

It wasn't quite as simple as guiding the missiles into the center of those spheres, but the lack of coordination cost the Hoplites a massive amount of their effectiveness—and Russell's people had sent them twelve missiles each.

The remaining pirate salvos killed two more Cataphracts and six more of his people, but not one of the pirate starfighters made it out intact.

———

THE MARINES MADE it over halfway through the cargo tunnel before the pirates even realized they were facing a counterattack. If there had been cover, Edvard's people would have used thrusters and magnet boots to account for the lack of gravity—but since there was no cover to be found, they instead used that lack to launch themselves down the tunnel like miniature spaceships.

Scanners in the battle armor suits fed their data to a carefully linked network, all of it feeding back to the Lieutenants and to Edvard Hansen, who reviewed it in his implant as he charged forward with the rest of his Marines.

"Riley, take your people and hit the left gallery," he ordered, highlighting a section where a group of pirates were carrying tripod-mounted anti-armor rifles, the most likely man-portable gear to threaten his armored Marines.

"Tan, hit the armor contingent, grenades, full auto, sweep them out," he instructed his Alpha platoon commander, highlighting the middle of Judecca Station's cargo bay, where the platoon's worth or so of pirates with actual battle armor had gathered.

"Daniels, clean up in between, prioritize anyone who looks to have anti-armor gear.

"HQ Section, follow me," he finished grimly. "We're punching straight through into the station."

"Do we know where we're going?" someone asked.

"I've got coordinates for the Captain's last known location," Edvard replied. "I figure we start there and shoot our way out. Now go!"

The shooting had already started. The pirates clearly hadn't been expecting Marines, as a number of even their battle armored soldiers carried lower-velocity weapons lacking the penetration to threaten his people.

Enough had real guns that the trip through the cargo tunnel *couldn't* be fast enough for all of his people to survive. Suppressing fire hammered their destination, shattering cargo containers, armor and pirates alike, but their return fire was equally intense and the Marines had no cover.

Flashing alerts appeared on his implant feed, warning him that he was losing people. Edvard's own rifle jerked with a recoil that could easily have thrown him back down the tunnel, walking high-caliber explosive rounds across the room.

A spray of fire from one of the miniguns the armored pirate troopers carried walked across his armor, the bullets shoving him backward even as they failed to penetrate his armor. His suit computer highlighted the source, and Edvard sent a burst of penetrators back at the pirate.

The heavy rounds punched clean through the armor suit, sending the other man crumpling backward just as Edvard *finally* reached Judecca Station's gravity and slammed heavily into the metal flooring.

His neural implant coldly informed him that twenty-three of his people had been wounded or killed in the process of crossing the tunnel, and they'd turned the station's cargo bay into a scene from hell. At least one of the pods had been a fuel container of some kind, and it had managed to get spread around before it ignited.

The pirates who'd gathered to attack *Chameleon* would never attack anyone again. If any of them were still alive, they were choosing to *pretend* to be dead, and Edvard was perfectly willing to let them.

"Tan, secure the cargo bay," he ordered quietly. "If any of them are still alive…keep them that way."

"Daniels, sweep the station perimeter—remember, *some* people on here might still be on our side. Give them a chance to drop their guns before you put them down, but *don't* let anyone with anti-armor gear take a shot.

"Riley, you're with me and the HQ section. Move out!"

––––––

THE STATION WAS A MESS. Without a guide, Edvard's strike force was restricted to guessing corridors and occasionally blasting through floors, a process that met with disturbingly little resistance.

Primarily because everyone they came across was dead.

Charging through Judecca Station felt like sweeping a battlefield for survivors. At some point after their arrival, a significant chunk of the people aboard the station had turned on the rest. Being a *pirate* station, however, *everyone* had been armed and it had turned into a vicious multi-way melee.

A melee that his Marines had arrived too late to change the course of.

The eerie silence of the station eventually faded into the distant sound of gunfire as they approached Captain Roberts's last coordinates. The corridors here were narrower, dirtier—intentionally designed to limit an attacker's approach room.

They were still big enough for battle armor, though, and he pushed on toward the sound of the guns. The platoon's networked computers assessed distance from the volume and Doppler shifts, and warned them as they reached the point of no return.

"You don't lead," Riley told him flatly as he started forward. "You know better."

He made a small acceding gesture. He hadn't *quite* intended to go first...but she was right that he needed to be farther back.

"Go," he ordered softly.

Two of the armored black-ops troopers moved forward, their armor suddenly *much* quieter as they engaged a sound-deadening function his Marines' gear lacked. Cameras in their helmets relayed what they saw back to him and Riley.

Any remnant of the original structure of the space the point men could see was long gone now. Explosives and vibroblades had gutted walls and dug new tunnels through the ice, wrapping around an armored capsule that had clearly been cut open twice—and both entrances collapsed by explosives.

An entire side of the room had now been blasted off, and gunfire echoed into and out of the space. The fire coming from inside was *far* heavier than Edvard would have expected from three people with hand weapons, and there were enough suits of battle armor among the dead scattered through the debris to suggest the attackers had underestimated Trickster's armaments supply.

There weren't many of them left now. From the bodies, they'd started with over a hundred people, a third in battle armor. Now they were down to barely twenty...and Edvard was behind them with over sixty.

"Take them!" he snapped.

More of his people charged out of the tunnels behind the point team. The lead two black-ops troopers opened fire first, carefully targeted bursts cutting down the last few survivors in battle armor and ending any chance the pirates had before the fight truly began.

Gunfire continued to echo out of the capsule once it was over, suppressing fire to keep everyone's heads down.

Despite everything, the jamming was *still* up. While Edvard had contact with his strike force by relayed microbeams, he had no communications with his other platoons that were *hopefully* securing the station.

Instead, he approached as close as he could and brought up the loudspeakers.

"Captain Roberts? It's Lieutenant Major Hansen. We've secured the exterior, if you'd like to stop shooting."

"How do we know it's you?" a quavering voice he recognized as belonging to the spy, Glass.

"Tell Roberts he owes me a beer for saving his ass."

"It's Hansen," Roberts proclaimed. "I'll pay up gladly."

Stepping around and into the field of view, Edvard marveled at the state of the office. It looked like every piece of furniture had been used as cover for an impromptu fort as the room itself had disintegrated around them—and that every piece of furniture had been *built* to use as cover.

Glass was leaning on the dented remains of a bookshelf, breathing heavily as he released the two propped carbines he'd been keeping up the suppressive fire with. Behind him, the massive form of Captain Roberts rose from the ground, supporting a masked stranger.

"I will be fine, Captain Roberts," the stranger said in a voice clearly running through computer modulation. "Lieutenant Major Hansen, are you in contact with any of my people?"

"I left Henry and your cargo team aboard *Chameleon*," Edvard told him. "They didn't have the armor for the fight that was coming. I... haven't encountered anyone else alive who didn't shoot at us."

"Damn," Trickster said mildly. "I owe your people, but I wish I could contact more of *mine*. The jamming?"

"I have two platoons securing the station; they'll take it down once they find it," Edvard promised.

"Thank you, Lieutenant Major, Captain Roberts, Glass," Trickster told them, carefully removing their weight from Roberts. They held out a datastick to Glass. "I believe, Mister Glass, that you can keep this. The payment for your cargo has been rendered in full."

20

New Edmonton System
10:15 May 27, 2736 Earth Standard Meridian Date/Time
Chameleon, *Ice Belt*

"We have a problem, sir," Chownyk reported as Kyle finally reentered his bridge.

Somehow, Kyle was *not* surprised. Today wouldn't be complete without more problems.

"What have we got?" he asked, dropping into the command chair and wincing as he jarred his arm. He hadn't been *badly* wounded, just a gouge across the bicep, but the field dressing Hansen's people had shoved on it had left his arm tender.

If Trickster had been one iota less paranoid, all three of them would have died in that office.

"I've got what looks like a *condottieri* carrier heading our way," his XO explained, flipping Kyle an implant feed and highlighting the ship in question. "She isn't super-modern or super-large, but she's at least forty million cubic meters and heading our way at two hundred gravities. I'd be surprised if she has less than a hundred and fifty fighters aboard."

"ETA?"

"Twelve hours, so she isn't an *immediate* issue," Chownyk replied. "Just something you needed to be aware of."

"Agreed," Kyle told him. "Let me check with our friend."

With the jamming *finally* down, Trickster had remained on the station as one of Hansen's platoons finished sweeping the base for the remaining mutineers. Judecca had had a population of just over eighteen hundred. From the sounds of it, Trickster had less than two hundred people left.

Kyle pinged Glass first.

"We have incoming," he told the spy. "*Condottieri* warship. She's still twelve hours out, but I'm guessing they won't be happy with Trickster."

"Periklos put enough of a bounty on Trickster to buy someone a new starship," Glass said flatly. "God alone knows how he's going to *pay* for it, but that's a good chunk of the annual budget of many of the League's system governments. Trickster can't be here when they get here—and neither can we, Roberts."

"How much of a favor do we owe them?"

"Not that big," the spy replied. "If Trickster wants a ride to another star system and it's not out of our way, their goodwill is probably still going to be worth something going forward, but…"

"Understood," Kyle confirmed. "Let's see what they say."

He linked into the radio channel they were maintaining with Judecca Station.

"Get me Trickster," he ordered the pirate who answered the com.

He was apparently high on the pirate's list of people they were willing to talk to, as their androgynous voice was on the channel less than ten seconds later.

"Roberts. Is this you telling me you're leaving us?"

"Not yet, but pretty quickly," Kyle told them. "There's a *condottieri* carrier headed this way, and the Gods know *Chameleon* can't fight a real warship. And, no offense, I'm not going to try for you."

Enough of his people had died because of the pirate as it was.

"Won't ask you to," Trickster confirmed. "In fact..." They paused. "If you come about ninety-three degrees in the ecliptic and angle up twenty-six and wait about ten minutes, I think I can give you some cover for your withdrawal."

"I'd appreciate it," Kyle admitted with a sigh.

"I owe you, Captain Roberts," the pirate told him. "I'll find a way to repay you, sooner or later."

"I might hold you to that," he replied.

"Just don't rely on it," Trickster said with a chuckle. "I didn't earn my name by keeping *all* my promises, after all. Hit that vector, Captain. And watch for the fireworks."

Shaking his head, Kyle cut the channel and flipped the vector to Lau.

"As soon as Hansen's people are back aboard, set on this course and prepare our Alcubierre jump. Destination is one light-month short of the Aurelius system."

Lau nodded silently, but Kyle was already raising Hansen.

"El-Maj, pull your people off the station," he told the Marine. "We are leaving New Edmonton."

"Understood," Hansen replied. "Should be good to go. Give me five minutes."

"You have three. I don't think the station's going to be here in ten."

"On our way."

———

HANSEN'S PEOPLE didn't make Kyle's three-minute deadline but were still out before the five minutes were up, their shuttle chasing after *Chameleon* as the Q-ship accelerated away on the course Trickster had given them.

With several hundred gravities' more acceleration than its mothership, the shuttle had almost caught up by the time Trickster's ten-minute limit had passed. Kyle turned his attention to Judecca Station, expecting a show.

For a few moments, there was nothing. The shuttle grew nearer. The far-off *condottieri* carrier continued to approach. The ice-wrapped station continued in its orbit, its exterior unmarred by the violence that had swept its interior.

Kyle was watching carefully, so he saw the *blip* as something happened…and then the station broke apart. Five major pieces drifted apart, chunks of metal and ice severed apart by clearly prepositioned explosions.

"Jump?" Lau asked.

"No," he said softly. "Prep the Stetson fields, though. Bring them up as soon as the Marines are aboard."

Seconds ticked by and the assault shuttle charged into the cover of the big starship.

"Marine shuttle inside the safety zone," Chownyk reported.

"Fields up. Singularities on standby," the navigator reported crisply.

"Shouldn't there be *some* kind of light show?" Kyle's XO asked.

"And…*now*," Kyle replied with a grin. On the screen in front of him, strings of antimatter bomblets that had been strung between the chunks of the station lit up, dozens of multi-megaton annihilations lighting up space.

"Go!" he ordered.

The first chunk of station went up in a fifty-gigaton antimatter explosion, and then the New Edmonton system disappeared in the distinctive twist of reality warped beyond tolerance.

A few moments later, the standard computer-generated image of the stars replaced the incomprehensible mess of light the Alcubierre Drive left them with. For obvious reasons, it lacked any updated presentation of Judecca Station.

"We were watching closely," Kyle said softly. "Did we pick up Trickster's ship leaving?"

"There was a ship?" Chownyk asked.

"They weren't going to go up with their space station," the Captain pointed out. "Commander Taylor—did we get anything?"

"Smallest FTL ship I ever saw," she said after a moment. "The chunk closest to us was ice wrapped around a starship about two hundred meters long. Her Alcubierre-Stetson drive lit off with the first explosions. We were less than a light-second away and we barely picked her out."

"So, as far as Dictator Periklos's people are concerned, Trickster's probably dead," Kyle noted. "Probably for the best, for now."

He glanced around his bridge.

"Good work, everyone," he rumbled loudly. "I have to admit to an extra appreciation for your efforts to pull my own personal ass out of the fire."

Chuckles responded, but he continued more somberly.

"We'll sort out a memorial for the Marines and flight crew we lost today before we're too far on our way," he reminded them. "We have a mission to complete, but we won't forget our fallen, either."

TWO HOURS AFTER A COMBAT ENGAGEMENT, the flight deck was a hive of activity. Maintenance teams swept over each fighter in sequence, running system tests, cleaning vents, opening panels, and going through every step of the massive checklists required to be one hundred and ten percent certain no part of the deadly spacecraft had been damaged or misaligned.

While the maintenance crews did their magic, Russell's flight crews were either asleep, recovering from the inevitable adrenaline crash, or getting very drunk. Alcohol was rarely to his taste, and sleep would be a long time coming.

There was, after all, a very quiet section of the hangar that *had* held half of Alpha Squadron's fighters this morning. If there was anything the maintenance staff needed from those four hangars, they were finding it somewhere else and leaving the CAG alone with his thoughts.

It was strange. Russell had lost people under his command before —he'd been a squadron commander at Tranquility when the old *Avalon*'s fighter group had been gutted along with their carrier home. He'd seen fighter wings absolutely *destroyed*—the wing he'd escorted the rescue transports out of Huī Xing which had ended up being most of the surviving starfighters from the entire four-starship *battle group*.

And yet those four empty fighter stalls and the one over in Echo Squadron's section of the Flight Deck hit him harder than any of those losses. He might have lost people *under* his command, but he had never lost people while *in* command.

There was no one else to off-load responsibility onto. No one else who could have been smarter, faster. He'd commanded the entire fighter strike, and he'd lost an eighth of his starfighters and fifteen people doing it.

Intellectually, he knew he'd gone up against starfighters with a terrifying individual superiority at point-blank range with no chance for either side to truly grasp what kind of fight they were getting into. Only losing five fighters against an arguably superior force was a decent job.

Once they'd finished upgrading his ships, combining the D-mod kits and his own people's adjustments, they'd easily have added five hundred tons to the starfighters' mass but almost doubled their lethality. The Hoplites would still have been superior, but not as much.

The problem was that they'd be fighting Katanas, the Terrans' new seventh-generation starfighters. *Those* were going to dance rings around his upgraded Cataphracts, and he didn't see a solution for that.

Turning to leave, he spotted Flight Commander Laura Cavendish standing in front of the empty hangar that had held Echo Six. She wore a plain black shipsuit without insignia—by choice, as she had every right to her *uniform*. She just wasn't cleared to *fly*.

He wasn't sure what impulse carried him over to her, but he wasn't nearly stealthy enough to sneak up on her. Cavendish turned as he was approaching her, and her eyes flashed at the sight of him.

"Are you happy now?" she demanded, gesturing to the empty hangar behind her. "I flew with Carter for five years. Devine and Cole backed her for three. Gone. In,an *instant*. Because *you* got a stick up your ass!"

"I didn't know them," Russell admitted. "But I knew Flight Lieutenants Norma Boveri and Marius Knudsen and their crews more than in passing. I'd served with Flight Lieutenants Mai Nguyen and Felix Baas since before Tranquility. They were friends. And I'd met Nelly and her people.

"Do not *dare* assume that I do not know who they were," he hissed. "And before you accuse *me* of causing their deaths, perhaps you should talk to your boss? Because according to the briefing *I* got, this whole mess was triggered when one of Trickster's captains realized we were a Q-ship.

"Something *no one* in this system was aware of until *you* flew a starfighter without permission," he finished flatly. "I'm the CAG, so if you need to blame someone for their deaths, that's part of my job. But take the time to consider *all* the causes, *Commander*.

"Because that's part of *both* our jobs."

21

Deep Space, Under Alcubierre Drive
18:00 May 29, 2736 Earth Standard Meridian Date/Time
Chameleon

KYLE SHUT down the file on his implant and leaned back in his chair, his eyes closed against the light in his office.

The butcher's bill had been far lower than they had any right to expect. The lack of escape pods on the Cataphracts had taken its toll, but Hansen had only lost twenty-six Marines all told while taking a station with almost two thousand residents.

Tradition put the letter-writing on Hansen and Rokos's subordinate officers as the direct superiors of the deceased. Tradition *also* said that the senior officers be available and willing to assist, all the way up to the ship's Captain.

Kyle was also determined to *know*, not merely have in implant storage but *know*, the names of every man and woman who'd died under his command. The list was already far too long, but unless he resigned his commission today, there was no way to stop it.

With a sigh, he cracked open another beer and took a long swallow. *That* was a thought that had rarely crossed his mind before Huī Xing. He couldn't actually resign, of course. The Federation was at war and everyone was now in for the duration. But…he could request a noncombat posting.

It would be the end of his career. He'd never see another promotion and would *certainly* never see a command again—but he wouldn't have to send more men and women to their deaths. Would know, at least, that *his* screw-ups hadn't caused more deaths.

Nothing *he'd* done could have changed the course of the fight at Judecca Station, though. They'd walked into a trap and fought their way back out of it mostly because their enemy had underestimated them. Whether or not he'd stayed with *Chameleon* wouldn't have changed anything.

Another sigh accompanied another swallow of beer, and he found himself studying the plaque of medals hung on the wall. Two Federation Stars of Heroism, the second-highest award the Castle Federation had for valor. The Tranquility Golden Crescent, that system's *highest* award for valor, awarded for turning back the Commonwealth assault at the start of the war. The Alizon Diamond Nova of Honor, given to him for almost accidentally liberating that system.

His understanding was that he had *more* medals waiting for him if he ever returned to the Huī Xing or Frihet systems. The Coraline Imperium, the second-ranked power in the Alliance, had been making noises about the Imperator wanting to hang some chunk of rock on him *personally* for the rescue in Huī Xing.

Kyle could remember how many people had died for each of those medals, from *Ansem Gulf* all the way to the Battle of Huī Xing. And yet…those pretty pieces of metal demonstrated that at least some people figured that he'd done better in those places than someone else would have.

He finished the beer, his third of the evening, and glared at the medals.

A ping on his implant interrupted his foul mood, informing him that he'd received a recorded message via Q-Com from Mira Solace.

That was…odd. Mira commanded a capital ship; she should have been able to activate a live Q-Com link to *Chameleon*—unless *Camerone* was in an active combat zone.

By the time he had that realization, he already had Mira's message and his lover's image filled the wall screen. She looked…tired. Her uniform was still perfectly turned out, she didn't have a hair out of place, but he knew her well enough now to recognize it in the slump of her shoulders and the cast of her eyes.

"Hi, Kyle," she said quietly. "You're getting a recording because Huī Xing is being considered an active combat zone. Would rather see your face, but the rules are what they are…and they're right in any case.

"Commonwealth hit us twelve hours ago, trying to take out the ships we captured here before they could be repaired. Four cruisers, two carriers—an entire *fleet.*"

She inhaled deeply and then let it go in a long sigh.

"You'll see the formal report soon enough, same as everyone else, so I can actually *tell* you about it," she said. "I don't know where Command got the intel about the bastards' new starfighter, but it saved a lot of lives today.

"They were still flying Scimitars off the cruisers and held back the Katanas to lure us in. With the warning that the Terrans were rushing the new Katanas to Walkingstick's fleets, the Admiral *realized* they hadn't launched the carrier fighters.

"She guessed what they were up to—and she guessed right," Mira continued. "They tried to mousetrap our fighters with the Katanas, but we ran them in on a vector they could pull out on. If we hadn't…" She shuddered. "Our CAGs were expecting to run into Scimitars with even numbers, which is to our benefit. With three quarters of their fighters actually being Katanas, it was bad enough.

"We drove them off, obviously," she said quietly. "But…we've been used to taking Terran starfighters less than seriously. That's going to have to change. The Katana is a *nasty* piece of work, same lance as a Phoenix Templar." She shivered. "It's a fighter-killer, and a *hell* of a lot better at the job than anything else they've built."

Kyle had reviewed the specifications Glass had forwarded back to the Alliance. The Katana *looked* deadlier and sleeker than its purely cylindrical predecessor, trading missile capacity and a significantly increased mass for a hugely increased ECM capability and a single extremely powerful positron lance.

"If we hadn't been expecting it, we might have lost Huī Xing," Mira admitted. "As it was, it was a pretty inconclusive slugfest—we took fighter losses and smashed the crap out of their new birds, but nobody lost starships.

"They were testing the Katanas," she concluded. "I *hate* being Walkingstick's test-bed."

With a shake of her head, she smiled at him.

"I wanted to reach out before the official report started circulating," she told him. "I'm fine and Huī Xing's still ours. It could have been a *lot* worse."

She reached out to touch the camera recording her.

"I know you can't tell me much about where you are and what you're doing," she said. "But I hope it's going as smoothly as we can hope. I miss you."

The message ended, and Kyle considered the wall for a long moment.

That intelligence had fallen into their hands by chance, though Ostrowski had clearly known what it was going to be worth. Just that purchase alone had made their entire mission worthwhile.

Breathing deeply, Kyle clasped his hands and smiled grimly.

Maybe when this was over, he'd take that teaching position Kane had wanted him for and take a quiet few months to overcome his survivor's guilt. Today, however, his ship was four days from the Aurelius system—and despite his doubts and fears, he was in command.

He owed his people his best, not his drunken misery.

———

RUSSELL GESTURED Master Chief Petty Officer Adrianna Hanz to the seat across from his desk. The broad-shouldered, squat woman was frankly ugly—an accident with a superheated hydrogen fuel line early in her career had left the right side of her face a mess of scar tissue—

but she'd come highly recommended by some of the best Space Force noncommissioned officers he knew.

As the senior Space Force noncom aboard, Hanz was the Deck Chief—she ran *everything* shipside for the Space Force, a role that often resulted in the senior NCO giving orders to the junior officers who flew the starfighters and ran the Navy logistics team that supported the deck.

"You've had two days to look over the upgrade kits Trickster sold us," he said cheerfully. "What do you think?"

"That anyone who thinks the League are unsophisticated needs to check their assumptions," Hanz said flatly. "Those kits are *slick*, sir. Upgrading a positron lance is a tricky business, but the kit is literally plug-and-play. The new mass manipulators just clamp onto the hull, which *has* to make tuning them a bitch, but the program they provide works like a charm."

The scarred woman shook her head.

"Even the Cataphract-D is going to come off worse against a Hoplite," she noted, "but it's fifteen hundred tons lighter; what do you expect? The D model splits the difference on the lance power and matches the Hoplite for acceleration and deflectors."

"Biggest shortfall remains two missile launchers to the Hoplite's four and weaker ECM. Our EW *software* is better and makes up a chunk of the difference, but that kit really does turn the Cataphract into an effective sixth-gen combatant."

"I hope so," Russell replied. "We're going to be taking them up against Scimitars shortly—if we're *lucky*. You saw the specs on the Katanas?"

"I did," Hanz confirmed.

"Your opinion?"

"If we run into Katanas, we're fucked. The League hasn't managed to expand the third acceleration plateau any better than anyone else has. Pretty much everyone is pulling five hundred gees now—but the Katana has a *much* heavier lance and stronger deflectors.

"If you can't kill them in the missile pass, they'll shred you in lance range."

"About what I was figuring," Russell agreed. "I want you to take a look over the schematics. If you see *anything* you think I need to know from the technical side of either the Ds or the Katanas, let me know.

"Regardless," he continued, "we need to get started on the upgrade-kit installation. My understanding is that we'll be at our hold point for two days, waiting for a gap in the Terrans' patrol schedule, but that still gives us less than a week to get thirty-five fighters upgraded."

Hanz simply nodded and gestured to the wallscreen.

"May I, sir?" she asked. "I have a full schedule and upgrade plan ready to go if it works for you."

Russell blinked. Okay, *now* he was impressed.

"Show me, Chief."

———

"L'CHAIM!"

Edvard stood off to one side with his platoon Lieutenants as the traditional toast echoed through the central chamber of the Marine barracks. He didn't even know what the toast *meant*—and he doubted any of his Marines or the black-ops troopers did either.

But it was the toast at the wake after they lost brothers- and sisters-in-arms for the Castle Federation Marines—and the black-ops troopers might not *technically* be Marines, but they were born from the same traditions.

A dozen of the men and women in the room were still in casts and bandages, nanotech working away to heal their injuries to clear them for action, but tonight was about those who would never join them again. Twenty-six empty chairs formed a closed circle in the center of the room, facing away from the gathering crowd.

As he was the Marine commanding officer, tradition put Edvard in charge of a rather significant supply of approved beer and liquor, and he'd dipped into it heavily for tonight's wake. While he was sadly certain it wouldn't be the last time they lost people on this mission, it was the *first* time this company had been blooded.

"It's a good group," Riley said aloud. "We've fought and bled together now. Buys a bit of respect both ways with the Marines and my black-ops guys."

"I wish we'd had a better idea of how to use your people's skills," Edvard said quietly. "I don't *see* anywhere they could have done better, but your troopers have enough skills and tools my people don't that it seems almost wasteful to use them as part of the assault force."

"Better than *not* using us," their commander replied. "Judecca didn't exactly have an opportunity for us to stealth in and infiltrate subtly, after all. We're trained for assault, and to be honest, that's what we *do* most of the time—same as the Marines. We just do it in places the Senate doesn't like to admit we had people."

"Setting up to infiltrate you guys would be hard," Edvard noted. "Alcubierre emergence isn't exactly quiet, after all."

"Stealth requires making the bastards see what they expect instead of what's *there*," Riley told him. "With a ship like *Chameleon*, it's easier than it might be. Right IFF code, a cargo shuttle—there's a reason we have some bog-standard Commonwealth-built cargo shuttles aboard— we can pull off a *lot*."

"IFF codes only get us so far when everyone is announcing their arrival by Q-Com, but...that still gives me ideas."

"Good," the Lieutenant replied. "Sometimes, a frontal assault in battle armor is all we've got, sir, but"—she gestured at the circle of chairs—"I *really* don't like it."

"Neither do I, Lieutenant Riley. Neither do I."

———

RUSSELL WOKE up in the middle of the night, to the eerie sensation of knowing *someone* was in his room.

An implant command brought up the lights and he found himself looking directly at Laura Cavendish, less than fifty centimeters from his bed. He even managed to have his hand on the gun in the bed's built-in holster before his brain caught up with the fact that she was naked.

"What are you *doing*, Cavendish?" he demanded, carefully controlling an overly enthused libido and focusing his gaze above her right shoulder instead of her perky but probably not augmented chest. Thankfully, modern nanites came along with the ability to intentionally implement the effects of a cold shower without the shower.

An effect she promptly undermined by grabbing his hand and placing it on her breast.

"I've seen you looking at me," she whispered. "And I want my command back. I think we can make a fair exchange, don't you?"

Russell sighed and reclaimed his hand as swiftly as he could.

"Get dressed, Commander," he ordered flatly. "Firstly, what you are suggesting is a violation of the Articles. Secondly, I don't know *what* you've 'seen', but I'm *married* and you're *not* my type.

"I prefer women I'm less likely to wake up *knifed* by the morning after," he finished dryly. Cavendish remained stubbornly naked, subtly adjusting her position in a way that was giving the nanites in his system the worst workout he remembered them having.

"Commander. Laura," he conceded. "Get dressed and have a seat."

She waited another ten seconds as he silently stared over her shoulder, then sighed and slipped her shipsuit back on.

"What do you *want*?" she demanded.

"To do my job and bring as many of my people home alive as I can," he told her. "To do that, I need to trust the people under my command. *None* of your actions to date suggest that I can trust you—and *this* bullshit doesn't help your case!"

The dark-haired woman was silent for several seconds.

"I've worked for Glass before," she said quietly. "Under his direct command. I don't know why he's trying to convince everyone in this mission that he's a civilian, but he's a Navy Intelligence *Admiral* and in *my* chain of command."

It was as close to an apology as he was likely to actually get, and he gave her a short nod in acknowledgment.

"He still isn't in your chain of command for *this* mission," he pointed out. "*And* you disobeyed orders to return to base until we threatened to fire on you. *And* your stunt is why those pirates jumped at Judecca Station.

"I grounded you for a *reason*, Commander. You need to earn back my trust, and trying to *seduce* me is *not* the way to do it.

"Am I *clear*?"

Somehow, he managed full command voice despite wearing a pair of shorts and sitting upright in his bed. With a swallow of air, Cavendish nodded her understanding.

"Good. Now get out of my quarters," he ordered.

As the outer door to his rooms closed behind her, the CAG sighed and locked it with an implant command. He wasn't surprised to confirm that it *had* been locked; that just hadn't slowed Cavendish down.

No *wonder* the Navy-issue officer's bed came with a built-in holster.

22

Deep Space, One Light-month from Aurelius System
10:00 June 3, 2736 Earth Standard Meridian Date/Time
Chameleon

"STAND BY FOR FIGHTER LAUNCH," Taylor announced into the quiet of *Chameleon*'s bridge. "Fighter wing deploying in thirty seconds."

Everyone aboard the bridge was linked into the same network, but the warning was still useful if someone was focusing on different tasks or, indeed, wasn't involved in the upcoming starfighter test at all.

Kyle was paying attention to the test, but he was *also* reviewing the scans of the old light they were picking up from their target. Everything they saw out of Aurelius right now was a month out of date, but that didn't mean it was valueless.

They now knew, for example, that Ostrowski's information on the layout and position of the seven space stations that made up the depot was completely accurate. Hopefully, the crime lord's data on the defenses and patrols was as accurate.

Chameleon didn't have the firepower to take on a warship except by complete surprise. It would make their life a lot easier if the two-day gap they'd found in the patrol schedule actually existed.

"Fighter launch commencing...now," the tactical officer announced crisply, and Kyle turned his attention back to the matter at hand.

Ten Cataphract-D starfighters shot into space, engines lighting off as soon as they were twenty kilometers clear of the ship and assuming a loose formation heading away from the Q-Ship.

A second flight of ten starfighters followed, then a third...and then a final flight of a mere five spacecraft, a permanent reminder of *Chameleon*'s fighter losses in New Edmonton.

"All fighters are running clean and clear, Commander Rokos," Taylor told the CAG. "I'm reading five hundred gees across the board, no concerns showing in the pulse patterns or exhaust signatures."

"Thank you, Commander," Rokos replied. "Now could I pretty please have some target drones?"

Shaking his head, Kyle made a "go ahead" gesture to Taylor.

"One hundred and sixty-five new playmates heading your way," she told Rokos. "Play rough if you need to, CAG, but remember: that's it, we don't have any more."

"All squadrons, this is the CAG," he announced over the channel as Kyle listened in. "See the spread of toys falling out of the cargo hatch? Give them about two minutes to get clear of *Chameleon*, and then we get to go play.

"I'm designating two for each of you," he continued. "Hunt them down and take them out with the new lances. I have *full* interlocks turned on, but play carefully anyway. This is a *test*; we don't want to lose anyone."

Full interlocks had to be physically activated before the fighter left the flight deck and basically acted as reverse IFF: if the positron lance wasn't pointing at something tagged in the system as a target, it would not fire.

The courses Taylor had programmed into the drones would also help reduce the risk of friendly fire, but they were running a weapons test in the middle of nowhere. Everything they could do to reduce risks was a good thing.

"YOUR ASSESSMENT, COMMANDER?" Kyle asked as they gathered in *Chameleon*'s conference room several hours later.

"I know we prefer to replace the entire starfighter," Rokos noted gruffly, "but those upgrade kits are effective tech. We found a few glitches that Hanz's crews are working through as we speak, but while none of the fighters were glitch-free, all are combat-capable."

"You'd be prepared to back them against Scimitars?"

"The Scimitar was *never* a particularly effective starfighter," the CAG pointed out. "It served well against single systems and second-rate powers who didn't *have* comparable fighter tech. They couldn't go one to one with our old Cobras, let alone the Falcons and the rest of the seventh-gen birds.

"The League, on the other, has its notorious collection of issues. The people at New Athens Arms who designed the Cataphract and the Hoplite actually had more combat hours to analyze for their designs than we did."

The broad-shouldered pilot shrugged.

"In many senses, the Hoplite is a better starfighter than the Cobra, almost closer to our seventh-gen ships. The Cataphract-D is roughly comparable to the Cobra once the upgrades are in—and everyone in my Wing has flown Cobras."

"Good," Kyle concluded. A thought and an unnecessary gesture brought up a three-dimensional hologram of the Aurelius system in the middle of the conference room. With no habitable worlds, nothing even worth the effort of terraforming, the only reason the binary system had ever even been visited was to investigate the Aurelius Pair: two tidally locked *gas giants*, close enough that they were forever exchanging atmosphere.

That had been a sufficient astronomical curiosity to get the system a name and a few initial expeditions. The unspoken hope that perhaps the Pair had created an environment hospitable to human life had been proven rapidly wrong, though one of the shared moons *did* have an atmosphere and the beginning of a thriving bacteria biosphere.

There'd even been a research station above the Pair for about sixty years. It was long gone now, the derelict wreckage dropped into the Pair twenty years ago.

But Aurelius had remained. A central system on the Commonwealth's spinward flank, where the Terrans ran up against the League, the Pair offered a prime opportunity for refueling, and the shared collection of moons included some easily accessible transuranics.

So, the Terran Commonwealth Navy had used the Aurelius Pair as the anchor for a semi-covert supply depot. It wasn't a fleet base, lacking in any ability to refit or repair ships, but it had stockpiles to resupply munitions, food, fuel—anything a ship patrolling the border or entering League space could need.

"The Aurelius system, people," Kyle told them. "I hope everyone's reviewed the files Ostrowski gave us. Officially, it's here to support Navy patrols on their spinward frontier. In practice, this is the main basing facility for every covert and black op the Terrans launch into the League."

"Are they sending a lot of those?" Chownyk asked.

"Enough," Glass replied. "Certainly, Dictator Periklos *claims* that the Commonwealth was funding and arming his enemies to prevent the League getting truly solidified. It would be…consistent. Especially given that *Periklos* was armed and funded by the Commonwealth to remove a planetary government that was being uncooperative to Terran interests.

"The League is big enough and, just barely, unified enough to be too big of a pill for the Committee on Human Unification to set their eyes on just yet," the spy continued. "Periklos increasing that unity, whatever the galaxy thinks of his methods, is the exact opposite of what Terra wants. They've been trying to destabilize the League for a century."

Kyle smiled mirthlessly.

"A history of mutual aggravation our mission is intended to ignite," he admitted to his staff. "The League is as large as the entire Alliance. We have better tech and are better organized, but they're still the second-largest single polity in human space. Adding them to our corner could change the entire course of this war.

"Which brings us back to Aurelius," he continued. "The *condottieri* and pirates know it has to exist, but most of them don't have Ostrowski's data. They've been surprisingly successful at keeping it covert.

"Doing so, however, has required them to keep the warship presence in the system surprisingly light. According to the schedule we've bought, there are warships in the system less than half of the time."

The hologram zoomed in on the Pair at his mental command, highlighting the collections of platforms in high orbit of the two gas giants.

"My main concerned with his data, however, is that it's very clearly *wrong* on the defenses," Kyle said quietly, highlighting four of the twelve platforms and a scattering of satellites. "The data shows two Zion-class fighter defense platforms, hosting a hundred Scimitars between them. Maybe a few missile satellites, but no further defenses.

"CIC has identified *four* Zion-class platforms and about sixty mixed defensive satellites, missile launchers and lance platforms. That's a lot of firepower, people. More than *Chameleon* can handle in a straight-up fight, but we're flying a Q-ship for a reason.

"We have two days before I plan on kicking off the attack. Let's see if we can find a way to get the supplies we need *without* losing anyone."

Before Huī Xing, the brainstorming would have been useful, but he'd have had a plan to start from. Now…now he didn't trust his own plans. The first-strike, shock-and-awe, aggressive tactics he'd used earlier in his career had pulled him into a trap there that had almost got his entire command wiped out.

He still had the instinct, but he didn't trust it. Part of him wanted to go full bore, bluff their way as close as they could under a TCN shipping ID and do to the Zions what another Terran Q-ship had done to the main station in the Hessian system at the start of the war: blow them apart with lances at close range.

If they could pull it off, they'd knock out the main defenses, destroy the control center for the defensive satellites, and launch their assault shuttles and starfighters at point-blank range to secure the rest of the depot.

It would be a *very* "Stellar Fox" plan…but the man who'd once rammed a battleship found himself unable to trust his instincts.

———

THE DOOR to Kyle's office chimed softly, informing him that someone was requesting admission. It was late enough that the ensign who would normally be holding down the door and screening his appointments was gone, sent off to his well-deserved rest from playing Captain's watchdog.

His implant informed him that Mister Glass was outside, holding what looked like a paper bag, of all things. They didn't have a scheduled meeting. Kyle was up late going over the plan they'd put together for the Aurelius system, but he was content with what his staff had put together.

With a thought, he opened the door and waved the spy in.

"Have a seat, Agent Glass," Kyle told the older man with an expansive wave. "What can I do for you?"

"The ship seems oddly quiet tonight," Glass said softly. "I feel like I'm walking through a library. Is this…normal?"

"When we're going into battle? It depends," the Captain replied. "If you think it's too quiet, go visit the flight deck lounge or the Marine barracks. More than enough noise there for anyone!"

"I'll pass," the spy said dryly. "Here. Peace offering."

He opened the paper bag and pulled out two tumblers, a small cooler of ice, and a dusty black bottle.

"This came all the way from Earth, one of six bottles I bought in Scotland a *very* long time ago," the spy said quietly. "It's not the last, and it's been opened before, but I don't share this with a lot of people. You saved my life on Judecca Station."

Glass dropped several ice cubes into each glass and then poured a generous two fingers of amber liquid over them before sliding a glass gently across the table.

Kyle took it carefully, sniffing at the unfamiliar scent.

"I think we both saved each other's lives," he pointed out. "That was very nearly a complete disaster."

"And you and your people got us out of it," Glass replied. He offered his glass to Kyle and they clinked together. *"L'chaim!"*

The amber liquid went down like smooth fire and Kyle coughed.

"Scotch whisky," Glass told him. "Castle's version is evolved from what used to be called 'rye whiskey', quite a different drink after a few hundred years."

"So I see, Agent."

"Please, call me Nick," the spy replied. "It's even my real name, which we both know Glass isn't."

They sipped the whisky in silence for a long moment, Kyle studying the hologram of the Aurelius system.

"I have to ask," he said after a moment. "Trickster said something about dropping a space station into a gas giant? What *happened*?"

Glass chuckled, shaking his head.

"That was a long time ago," he pointed out. "Back when I had hair! The war was barely over; a lot of people in the Commonwealth were surprisingly angry at the Alliance, for all that we really didn't put the screws on as much as some wanted."

The Alliance had forced the Commonwealth back to the status quo as of the opening of the war and demanded that they help repair the systems they'd damaged. It had hardly been a new Treaty of Versailles, but you wouldn't know that from the way the Commonwealth media talked about it even now.

"We were deep into Commonwealth space on an intel-gathering op," Glass continued. "The ship basically *was* a freighter. Half the crew didn't know any of us were spies; we were hauling real, legitimate cargo. And we were recording *everything* we saw with high-powered passive scanners and buying intel from people like Trickster and Ostrowski—I first met them both back then, though neither was as big a deal twenty-odd years ago.

"Trickster was in-system when this went down, which is probably why they remember it so vividly—and yes, they already had the mask and the name then.

"We were dealing with the Tetragrammaton Mob at the time. They had a few facilities scattered around the place, but they wanted to do a physical handover of the data and the payment at a cloudscoop they were running *way* out in the outer system."

The old man shook his head.

"It was, of course, a trap. They'd sold us out to Commonwealth intelligence, and we were ambushed by TCMC commandos." He shivered at an unseen memory. "They make Riley's people look soft and fleshy.

"Half the crew might not have known we were spies, but the *other* half were some of the Federation's best," he continued. "We had our pick of veterans after the war ended, hard men and women who'd forgotten how to do anything else.

"The commandos had machinery. We had *experience*. We got off the station and back onto the ship—much like the mess on Judecca."

He took a large swallow of the whisky, forcing Kyle to wait for a moment.

"Then, well, we had a station full of people who'd betrayed us, and Commonwealth commandos. The Captain was dead, I was left in charge, and we had a small antimissile suite to make sure we could run if we needed to.

"We shot out the stabilizers and *pushed* with the ship as we broke free," he finished simply.

Kyle winced. Normally, the stabilization rockets and mass manipulators aboard a space station were an unneeded safeguard. They might fire once a year or so, mostly to counteract the impact of docking ships. With all of them *gone*, however, an attached ship could easily throw the station into an unstable orbit.

"My understanding is that they got almost everybody off," Glass noted after a moment. "It wasn't a *fast* fall, after all. But they were *far* too busy to chase us after that!"

23

Aurelius System
12:00 June 5, 2736 Earth Standard Meridian Date/Time
Chameleon

THE Q-SHIP EMERGED from Alcubierre-Stetson drive in the normal flash of Cherenkov radiation, at the edge of the zone where the Aurelius Pair's gravity rendered warping space dangerous. Their emergence point had been chosen carefully, with the depot platforms twenty million kilometers away and currently hidden by the closer of the two gas giants.

"Echo Squadron launching," Taylor reported crisply.

The ship shivered slightly as seven of the fighter launch tubes fired, the hatches sliding shut to cover and conceal their presence as more fighters were slid into their place.

With no engines active and their heat sinks running on maximum, Kyle was actually impressed by how hard the black-ops fighters were to detect. They were *visible* from this close, but with their dark coatings and small size, they *should* actually be able to sneak up on the depot.

"Good luck, Flight Lieutenant Tomacino," Kyle told the senior Lieutenant in command of the squadron.

"We'll see you on the other side, Captain," the pilot replied.

As the fighters spilled away solely under the velocity imparted by the launch tubes, Lau silently brought up *Chameleon*'s own engines, accelerating toward the depot at the hundred gravities the Troubadour-J freighter she looked like could manage.

Two and a half hours, though it would probably be a *lot* sooner before they were challenged by the depot's defenders. Those four Zion platforms worried Kyle. If their flight groups deployed, this attack was *over*. A rapid and inglorious retreat back to League space would be their only option—Aurelius wouldn't be vulnerable to this style of attack again.

"Ten minutes until we clear Aurelius 4B and have visual," Chownyk noted from the CIC. "Scanners don't show any probes or satellites covering the blind spot. They should be here; I'm worried about our sensors, Captain."

"Are we talking 'our sensors might not be the best Intelligence could find after all' or 'there's a leftover Terran virus that's intentionally screwing with us'?" Kyle asked with an only somewhat forced grin. "Because I'm not buying either explanation."

His XO was silent for a moment.

"I just can't believe they wouldn't cover the blind spot on the other side of the gas giant," the cyborg pointed out. "It seems…reckless."

"Remember that we are *in* Commonwealth space," Glass pointed out from the uncomfortable observer seat at the back of the bridge. "This is a base whose existence is classified as well. They feel safe here —if Ostrowski hadn't been amenable to large amounts of cash, they should have *been* safe here."

"It's arrogant, XO," Kyle told him. "Not reckless. Are we seeing *any* blips? Or are we fully clear?"

"Nothing," he admitted. "I'm going to sit back here and babysit the analysis computers, though, just in case. It's too easy."

"Please do," *Chameleon*'s Captain confirmed. "I agree: the door is *way* too open."

———

As they rounded the edge of Aurelius 4B, they got their first look at the depot that wasn't a month old. Everything they saw now was still a minute old, but that was practically real time compared to Ostrowski's intelligence or their own light-month-out scans.

Kyle concealed a sigh of relief as their view confirmed the promised lack of any starships. Even their current plan would have been in trouble if there had been a TCN warship present despite the schedule.

Everything else looked much the same as it had a month before. Four Zion platforms orbited in a protective square above the single large station and dozen storage pods that made up the storage depot itself. A single squadron of ten starfighters orbited above them…and Kyle inhaled sharply as the data processed.

The ten ships weren't Scimitars. They were Katanas.

"Confirm those starfighters IDs," he snapped.

"Double-checked, triple-checking now," Chownyk responded from CIC. "Data checks out; the patrol squadron are *definitely* Katanas. Do we abort?"

"No," Kyle replied instantly. They *could* still abort, though it would be obvious what they'd done. "If everything works, Echo will still take them by surprise."

If they didn't, he'd just sentenced twenty-one men and women to death unless he could pull off a miracle.

"No signal from them?" he asked aloud. No one *else* needed to know what was going through his head. They had to trust that the Captain would get them through.

"None yet," Taylor confirmed. "We've been in their line of sight for five minutes; they're late."

"REMFs," Kyle said with a chuckle. "*Terran* REMFs at that. Let me know the instant those starfighters move."

———

They'd been in system for forty-five minutes and in view of the depot for over half an hour before the first response from the Terrans arrived.

"I'm getting a ping for our Q-Com ID codes," Taylor reported. "Nothing else. Just…the automated handshake request. Um." She glanced back at Glass. "Can we use our Terran quantum blocks?"

"We have them for a reason," the spy told her. "The system will mark which ones we use today; we'll have to dump them after this is over. Try not to use too many up."

"Understood," the tactical officer said slowly. "Pinging them with the ID for one of the blocks."

"How do I look?" Kyle asked as he tossed his uniform jacket aside, glancing back at the spy. His shipsuit was unmarked.

"You need the hat," Glass replied. "Terran Merchant Marine Captains are never seen without it in their official capacities. *Ever.*"

With a sigh, Kyle grabbed the high-peaked white cap from where he'd hung it on the end of his chair's arm and settled it neatly on his head. In his opinion, no *sensible* spaceborne organization, military or civilian, would insist on something so useless as a *hat* in space, but despite current appearances, he was *not* a Terran Merchant Marine Captain.

It was five *more* minutes after they'd responded to the Q-Com request before the depot's staff *finally* made contact.

Taylor connected the channel through as soon as it was active, showing an extremely pale-skinned man whose hair had been shaved off in favor of a clearly permanently attached cap of circuitry. He wore the red-sashed black uniform of the Terran Commonwealth Navy with two gold bars at his throat.

"Unidentified civilian ship, this is Commander Roger Lafferty at the Aurelius Navy Depot. You are not on our shipping schedule; please identify yourself and state your reason for approaching the Depot."

Lafferty sounded like this was the most exciting thing that had happened to him in weeks…and he still didn't find it particularly interesting. How many months, Kyle wondered, had the man been stranded at this backwater base?

"Aurelius Depot, this is the registered TMM freighter *Historic Ideal*, Captain John Sheridan commanding," Kyle told the Navy officer. "We have a cargo of munitions and food supplies we were told to deliver here. I didn't even know there *was* anything here!"

"I'm sorry, you're not on our shipping schedule and I can't authenticate you," Lafferty told him in a bored voice. "You're going to need to turn around and leave the system immediately."

"Stand by to fake an engine malfunction," Kyle told Lau via an implant channel, then turned his best obsequious smile back on the depot officer.

"I can transmit you our instructions," he told Lafferty. "I don't understand the problem! We were looking for work in the Corsica system and were offered this job." He paused, injecting a hopefully carefully measured amount of panic and distress into his voice. "Sir, I went a week out of my way to come here at the Navy's request; if I don't get paid for this delivery, I may not make the next note payment on *Ideal*. Please!"

Kyle could *watch* the conflict on the Terran officer's face between the urge to be a petty tyrant and the urge to help a fellow spacer out. It was a shorter struggle than he'd expected from the initial interaction, and Lafferty sighed.

"Look, I'll follow up with Logistics Command and see if I can find your orders," he said finally. "For now, you can maintain your course, but do not approach within one million kilometers of the station without further authorization, or my standing orders give me no choice but to fire on you. Understand?"

"I understand, Commander," Kyle told him. "Thank you, thank you!"

And with the notorious speed—or lack thereof—of Commonwealth Navy Logistics Command, he might just make it all the way *to* that million-kilometer mark. Which was even better than they'd been counting on.

———

RUSSELL ROKOS STOOD in *Chameleon*'s primary flight control center, watching the ship inch toward its destination. He had one squadron, Alpha, in their birds and in the tubes. The rest of his flight crews waited in various lounges and quarters around Flight Deck.

It was always a tough call for the CAG as to *when* to have the rest of the crews mount up. *Chameleon* had just made turnover and was still seventy-five minutes from the depot. At ten million kilometers, Roberts could technically order the launch of the starfighter wing at any moment.

That wasn't the plan and Russell glanced at the icon marking the estimated progress of Echo Squadron. It would be another forty minutes before the *plan* called for them to launch, but the plan hadn't expected Katanas at the facility.

He spotted Cavendish standing at the edge of the room, carefully watching the massive central hologram to see where her people were. He felt a moment of guilt at sending her squadron—hell, even her *starfighter*—into action without her, but it faded quickly.

He still didn't trust her to follow orders in action, and he *needed* to know Echo Squadron was going to do their part today. He *sympathized* with her, but he was still glad he wasn't going to have her at his back with gigaton-range warheads.

Standing in the middle of the room, Russell himself was clearly visible to everyone. After a few moments, Cavendish crossed over to stand next to him.

"You're going to get my people killed," she hissed. "This whole op is suicide at this point!"

"Not your call, Commander," he said levelly. "Not *my* call, either. We came here to do a job and we're going to do it. I would have thought that a black-ops pilot would get that if anyone did."

She glared at him for a moment, then turned her gaze on the hologram.

"I get it," she said slowly. "But you've hung my entire squadron out to dry. Their stealth isn't *that* good—*no* stealth is in space."

"There's a plan," Russell told her. "Tomacino knows it. I know it. The *Captain* knows it—and if anyone can improvise their way out if the plan starts coming apart, it's Roberts."

"So I should just have faith; is that what you're telling me?" she demanded. "I'm not good at that."

"Look to the Stars," he said gently. "I, however, have a battle to fight."

Stepping way from the grounded Flight Commander, he raised his voice.

"All right, people, this is it. Drop 'em and load 'em—I want all squadrons on ready status in five minutes!"

24

Aurelius System
13:30 June 5, 2736 Earth Standard Meridian Date/Time
Chameleon

"ALL SQUADRONS ARE FULLY MANNED, armed and standing by," Rokos reported over the intercom. "We are clear to deploy on your order, Captain."

"Thank you, CAG," Kyle replied, pausing to validate the data on the fighter squadrons. They were carrying a full load of the most advanced Sarissa fighter missiles the League manufactured, a surprisingly capable weapon that he suspected actually had *better* electronic warfare penetrators than the current-generation Alliance or Commonwealth weapons.

Chameleon was decelerating toward a point exactly one million kilometers away from the depot. In about twenty minutes, Taylor would deploy her single salvo of capital-ship missiles as stealthily as possible, ready to fire a time-on-target salvo with Echo Squadron's missiles.

The stealth fighters would come around the far side of Aurelius 4B with enough velocity to give them a million-kilometer range, a surprise launch that, combined with *Chameleon*'s handful of Terran-built Stormwind missiles, should take out the four launch platforms and leave the single squadron of starfighters facing *all* of Rokos's people.

Those were odds at which Kyle was comfortable asking Cataphract-Ds to face down seventh-generation space superiority starfighters.

"Any word from Echo Squadron?" he asked. All of the starfighters had been refitted with Q-Coms equipped with Federation entangled particle blocks before they'd left. It meant the ships could *not* be allowed to fall into Commonwealth hands but...that was true regardless.

"On schedule as of the last pulse," Taylor confirmed. The Q-Com might not be *interceptable*, but its use was detectable at several hundred thousand kilometers if someone was paying attention and had the right sensors. So, instead of a full telemetry feed, *Chameleon* was receiving short text updates, minimizing the amount of time the Q-Com was engaged.

Twenty-five minutes to launch. Forty until the Q-ship could reach the depot.

Timers ticked away both in Kyle's implant feeds and on the screens and holograms around him. So far, despite the wrinkle of facing Katanas instead of Scimitars, everything was proceeding according to plan.

Kyle had barely finished that thought, of course, before everything came apart.

"We've been made!" Flight Lieutenant Tomacino's voice suddenly echoed across the bridge as Echo Squadron linked back in. "There's a flight of Katanas flying a security patrol, and they blundered *right* into us."

With the squadron's stealth broken, full telemetry slammed back into the bridge, holograms and tactical plots updating in real time with the scans from the squadron of starfighters on the other side of the gas giant.

The acting squadron commander hadn't waited for orders to engage. The four Katanas had managed to get within a hundred thousand kilometers before realizing they weren't alone, and twenty-one missiles were already closing the gap at a thousand gravities.

The range was short enough there was no way the Katanas could evade the missiles—but long enough that they launched their own birds. Sixteen Javelin fighter missiles closed on Echo Squadron even as their discoverers died in balls of antimatter fire.

The plan was broken. Without the surprise salvo from Echo Squadron, there was no chance of taking out the launch platforms with missiles; that plan had always relied on the fact that it would take at least five minutes for the squadrons aboard the Zions to go from regular shifts to launching.

But there *were* options, and Kyle was giving orders before he had time to doubt himself.

"Tomacino, abort and break away," he snapped. "Flash them your full drives, but dive into the gas giant. Play ghosts."

"You want bait," the Flight Lieutenant said grimly, the icons of his fighters on the screen bracketed by explosions as they took out the incoming missiles. For all that Kyle knew the experience level of his Space Force pilots better, Cavendish's crews were still veterans, and Javelins without ECM support from their motherships were child's play.

"Bait and a stalking horse," Kyle confirmed. "Keep their eyes looking for you—but *not* at the price of your squadron. Understood?"

"I think so," the pilot replied. He paused for a long moment, the silence making it clear that *he* at least understood the odds at making it out of this with his *entire* squadron. "Make it worth it, Captain."

"I will," he promised, turning back to Taylor.

"Jenny, would a deaf and blind merchant ship have seen those explosions yet?" he asked her distractedly, studying the tactical plot in the hologram.

"Thirty-five-plus gigaton-range explosions?" she asked. Despite her flippant response, she was clearly running the numbers. "Yes," she noted. "A few seconds ago now."

"Link me back to Lafferty," Kyle ordered, replacing the stupid high-peaked cap on his head.

A moment later, the Q-Com channel reopened. This time, Lafferty looked significantly more stressed.

"What?" he snapped.

"We just picked up antimatter explosions," Kyle replied in his best panicked civilian voice. "What's going on, Commander?"

"I don't fucking know," Lafferty told him. "A bunch of pirates just jumped one of our patrols but we've no idea where they came from."

"Pirates?!" Kyle exclaimed. "Sir, *Ideal* is unarmed! We're helpless if there's pirates out here."

"They're not on this side of the planet," the Terran officer told him. "Maintain your current course! The exclusion zone is still in effect; we *will* fire on you if you break it."

The channel cut short and Kyle smiled mirthlessly.

"Do I sound panicked enough to push his exclusion zone?" he said aloud. "Lau, adjust our course. Adjust our acceleration, I want us to swing right *past* the station at about ten thousand klicks with at least a hundred KPS left. Doable?"

"Easy," the navigator replied. "Three-five-minute intercept. One-five to exclusion zone."

Twenty minutes. Kyle would have to stall Lafferty for twenty minutes.

———

THE SQUADRON of starfighters flying overwatch for the depot was moving by the time Kyle was done speaking to Lafferty, all ten ships accelerating toward the site of the short battle at five hundred gravities. As the seconds ticked away and *Chameleon* started accelerating again, two more squadrons of the new starfighters launched from the Zions, taking off after the first one.

Thirty Katanas. *That* was going to be a headache.

Kyle found himself holding his breath, waiting for the second wave of launches. It should take five minutes for the other squadrons to prep and launch—almost the exact amount of time Lau's new course had the Q-ship accelerating before the new turnover point.

No one at the depot even commented on the fact that the freighter was now accelerating toward them on a course that would take it into the zone where he'd been told they would fire. From his own experience, Kyle knew that even the most advanced intelligences and sensors still worked at the guidance of their human masters.

Today, those human masters were focused on trying to find Echo Squadron and getting their starfighters deployed. The "harmless freighter" closing with the depot wasn't a factor in the situation, far from a threat.

Chameleon made turnover, hurtling toward the space station while now decelerating away from them at a hundred and ten gravities: well inside the Q-ship's capabilities, but the kind of fuel consumption a freighter captain would only embrace if utterly terrified.

"Do we deploy missiles, sir?" Taylor asked as they crossed the range where the original plan had them launching.

"Negative," he said quietly. "Load the launchers—capital-ship and fighter missile alike—but keep the hatches closed. What's our lance range against the Zions?"

The range in any given exchange of positron fire was a combination of the strength of the defender's electromagnetic deflectors, the power of the lance, and the actual size of the defender. It was easier for a thirty-meter-wide starfighter's deflectors to generate a miss than for a kilometer-long starship's deflectors to do the same.

"Hundred and fifty thousand kilometers." Taylor paused, swallowing visibly. "Are we going to get *that* close?"

"If they'll let us, Gods, yes," Kyle told her with a wide grin, suddenly feeling comfortable in his bridge again.

"At that range, those defense platforms will *shred* us when they open fire," she pointed out.

"Yes. So, when we shoot the Zions, you'd best not miss," he agreed.

———

THE FEED from Echo Squadron was nerve-wracking. The stealthy starfighters had sacrificed any attempt at concealment to try and open the distance from the Terran ships chasing them. Both groups of ships had much the same acceleration, but Echo had been heading *toward* the depot when the rocket had gone up.

They had time, though. Tomacino was taking his squadron into 4B's atmosphere, a risky stunt that his veterans could handle—but that Kyle was willing to bet the pilots assigned to security at a supply depot on the opposite side of the Commonwealth from the major war weren't up to.

Of course, given that the supply depot security wings had better *starfighters* than they expected, it was possible they had better pilots.

If they did, though, the pilots were better than the *rest* of the crew. It was fully ten minutes after his conversation with Lafferty before anyone seemed to notice that *Chameleon* was now on a course that would cross the one-million-kilometer line the Terran officer had ordered them to stay clear of.

"What are you playing at, Sheridan?" Lafferty demanded as his shaven-headed image reappeared on Kyle's communication screen. "We're projecting your vector to bring you inside the no-fly zone. Break off immediately."

"We've picked up the pirates," Kyle insisted back in a panicked voice, the voice of a man who might well be jumping at ghosts. "They're behind us; we need you to protect us! That's what the Navy's for, damn it, man!"

Seconds ticked by.

"We don't see anything behind you," the Terran officer finally said, his tone sympathetic. "I guarantee you, Captain Sheridan, there are no pirates on this side of the Aurelius Pair. Even at a million kilometers, our starfighters can intercept any threat before they could reach you. You *will* be safe so long as you follow instructions."

It had been eight minutes. He needed to get closer—they were still seven hundred thousand kilometers short of the no-fly zone, let alone lance range. Kyle paused, trying to give the impression of a hesitating Captain while he opened an implant channel to Lau.

"On my mark, give me two hundred gravities deceleration for three seconds, then fake a blowout and kill the engines."

Visibly, he exhaled a sigh as if trying to regain control.

"We will comply," he told Lafferty. "Decelerating now."

He reached to cut the channel and stopped as he *felt* Lau's fake blowout throw the *entire* ship. He didn't *want* to know what his navigator had cooked up with Engineering, but it was convincing to *him*. The Q-ship's acceleration cut to zero and she continued to tremble as loose positrons slammed into the hull, triggering a thousand tiny annihilation explosions.

"My Gods," he swore aloud on the channel. "Our engines are down, Commander," he told Lafferty. "I can't change course."

Without accelerating in any direction, *Chameleon* would blast past the depot at ten thousand kilometers' distance and a velocity of almost nineteen hundred kilometers a second—*well* before the pursuing Katanas reached Echo Squadron.

"We have your vector recorded," the Navy officer said grimly. Kyle wondered where the Commander's senior officer was—Lafferty was at most a shift commander. The depot's defenses should have been commanded by an O-6 Captain or the O-7 Commodore that would be equivalent to a Federation Captain like Kyle. Though if it was a Commonwealth Starfighter Corps O-7, a Wing Colonel, that would explain a lot.

If Lafferty hadn't bothered to wake up his superiors, that would also explain why no more fighter squadrons were in space. The Navy officer running the duty shift would only have the authority to call a full fighter scramble in the case of a direct attack.

"We picked up the explosion," Lafferty continued. "Advise *immediately* once your engines are back online. If you adjust vectors without permission at this point, we will blow you out of space. You *will* be boarded by a Marine contingent as you close.

"This isn't negotiable, Sheridan," he snapped as Kyle started to open his mouth. "I'm sticking my neck out for you; *don't* fuck it up."

"I...understand," Kyle said aloud. "I'll be ready to meet your Marines as they board."

The channel cut and Kyle ran the numbers. Unless it took them far longer than was reasonable to get their Marines into space, they'd board before he was in lance range. Unfortunately for Lafferty, he had a solution for that.

"Lieutenant Major Hansen," he said calmly as he raised the Marine CO. "It looks like the Terrans are going to make work for you sooner than we thought."

25

Aurelius System
13:50 June 5, 2736 Earth Standard Meridian Date/Time
Chameleon

EDVARD SPARED four of his precious seconds to curse out *competent* Terran officers.

His entire company was locked into battle armor and loaded aboard their assault shuttles. He was ready to punch a hundred and eighty of the Castle Federation's finest into the logistics depot—which meant he had *no one* in position to counter a boarding they had no choice but to allow.

"They'll arrive in just over eight minutes," Roberts told him. "We're in lance range in *ten* and launching your boarding shuttles in eleven. I need two minutes, Hansen."

"I'll get them for you," Edvard replied grimly. "Bravo Platoon, disembark ASAP and move to the fake civvie boarding zone. *Hustle*, we're on the clock. Alpha, Charlie—stand by for the assault."

For several seconds, he hesitated, unsure which of the two operations his company was about to launch needed him... If the Terran Marines warned their bases what was coming, the assault would never happen. Everyone would be dead before his shuttles could launch, the battleship-grade lances on the remote controlled platforms would see to that.

"Riley, you're in charge of the assault," he ordered the black-ops Lieutenant as he used his implant to order the shuttle to release the heavy metal bars holding his battle armor in place. "Keep me informed, but the strike is yours."

"Understood," she replied. "Good luck."

"I don't need luck," he said. "I have Castle's *damned* Marines."

She gave him a soft wolf-howl, a quiet version of the CFMC's terrifying battle cry, and dropped the channel.

"Ramirez." Edvard raised his Gunny as he stepped off the shuttle, the ramp closing shut behind him on the people who would now be launching an assault without him. "We have jammers in inventory, right?"

"Of course," the smaller man agreed, falling in beside him as they joined in the briskly moving column of armored Marines. "But we can't jam a Q-Com."

"Don't need to," the Lieutenant Major told his NCO. "We need *two minutes*, Gunny, and the Q-Com is on the shuttle, not in the troopers' armor."

Assuming they were feeling paranoid enough to show up in battle armor. It *probably* wouldn't change how this ended, but battle armor certainly had options that Marines in lighter armor didn't.

"Meet me at the docking bay with the biggest, *nastiest* jammers we have in inventory," he ordered. "And like I said, Gunny, we're on the clock."

———

A NAVY CHIEF Petty Officer was waiting for Edvard when he arrived at the docking bay in the fake-civilian part of the Q-ship.

"Are you greeting them?" the painfully skinny redheaded woman demanded gruffly. "Unless you're shooting before talking, they'll need to see *someone* who looks like ship's crew."

The thought hadn't even crossed Edvard's mind. As usual, an informed noncommissioned officer had found the hole in the plan.

He checked the time. Ninety seconds; the Terran shuttle was accelerating hard to match velocities. They weren't going to quite make it, and it was going to be a *rough* stop for the poor bastards aboard, something Edvard was relying on.

"It's going to have to be me," he agreed, starting to issue the commands for his armor to unlatch. "I can get out of the armor, but I don't have a merchant uniform…"

"Got them," the Chief told him with a smile, producing a white cap and jacket from her carry-all. "So long as you're wearing a shipsuit, we should be good."

Sixty seconds.

Edvard stepped out of his battle armor, ordering the suit to close up and move back out of sight on its own. Grabbing the jacket from the NCO, he glanced back at the Marines moving up.

"This ship has false panels there and there," he ordered, pointing them to the accesses as he spoke. "They'll cover you from standard passives. Get in there and *wait*. We need time more than we need dead Terrans."

Forty seconds. He slapped the cap onto his head and turned back to the Chief.

"How do I look?"

"Like a lazy civvie, it'll do," she replied.

"Who am I supposed to be?"

"XO, Merchant Marine Commander," she told him. "No name on the uniform, use your own—the Captain's probably the only one the Terrans would recognize by *name*."

"Thank you, Chief…"

"Poulson, sir. Becca Poulson," she introduced herself, falling in behind him at a respectful distance as he approached the door.

Twenty seconds. The last of the Marines were out of sight except for Ramirez and two Marines he'd recruited as pack mules. They were each carrying the bulky meter-and-a-half-tall cylinders of high-powered regional jammers.

"Get in the compartments and get those set up," Edvard hissed. "Hold them for my order."

Ten seconds. There was no hesitation on the part of Ramirez and his mules as they bolted into the hidden compartments and sealed them. The Terrans were still fifty kilometers clear, the Q-ship's own hull sufficient to conceal the suits at that range.

A wash of plasma slammed into the armored exterior of the docking bay as the assault shuttle desperately shed kilometers per second of relative velocity. She *still* slammed into the docking port at several hundred meters a second, a speed the shuttle was better designed to handle than the theoretically civilian port was.

Edvard *heard* the metal crunch under the impact, but a quick implant interrogation of the systems showed the port was still fully functional. His momentary impulse to lock it down and claim it was jammed was rendered moot a second later as a series of override codes hit the Terran-built lock and forced it to open instantly.

A four-man fire team swept into *Chameleon* immediately, weapons sweeping the space as the Marines advanced. The Terrans wore light body armor but not the heavy battle armor he'd been afraid of. One of them kept Edvard and Poulson covered as the others moved forward.

After about five seconds, a second wave of Marines entered. A fire team in battle armor escorted a hatchet-faced woman in the green-lapelled black uniform of the Terran Commonwealth Marine Corps into the ship.

"You are not Captain Sheridan," she snapped. "Where is he?"

"I am Commander Hansen," Edvard replied, intentionally dragging out his speech to buy precious seconds. "Captain Sheridan is dealing with the engine failure; he asked me to meet with you. What do you need, ma'am?"

"My teams will examine your engines and bridge," she said bluntly, gesturing more people—these in the plain black utility ship-suits of Navy ratings—off the shuttle. "Any resistance will be met with lethal force. Step aside."

"I can escort your people to the bridge," Edvard offered. Suddenly the guns were focused directly on him, the muzzles suddenly very large.

"I am not fooled, 'Hansen'," the Marine said. "Your ship arrives without proper orders at the same time as these pirates? You are working together. I will find out how and stop you."

Forty seconds to lance range. Edvard was running out of time.

"I'd like to assure you that nothing is further from the truth," he told her while ordering Ramirez to jam transmissions. It would take more than thirty seconds for the shuttle to realize something was wrong—and that would be too late, quantum communicators or no.

"Of course, I can't," Edvard admitted with a mirthless smile as every *non*-quantum communicator inside a thousand kilometers ground to a halt in a blaze of static. The access to the shuttle slammed shut in a faked malfunction, and the dozen Terrans found themselves staring down the weapons of fifty battle armored Federation Marines.

"*Vae victis*," he told the Terran Marine—'Woe to the conquered', the unofficial motto of League *condottieri* who turned pirate. "Lay down your arms or die."

"A half-dozen fighters can't defeat these defenses!" she snapped at him. "*You* should be surrendering, not me!"

Zero seconds, and the Terran officer's face went white as she recognized the distinct, hair-tingling sensation of a powerful positron lance firing nearby.

———

KYLE FELT the Q-ship vibrate under him as the shuttle made contact with brutal force. That couldn't have been pleasant for the people aboard, and it was telling about the level of suspicion at least *some* people were applying to "*Historic Ideal*". If the Marines were buying his spiel, it would have been *far* easier on everyone for them to match velocities and board as *Chameleon* passed the station.

"Hundred seconds to range," Taylor said softly. "Sir, they've trained one of the big lance satellites on us. We have stronger deflectors than they do, but that's a megaton-range beam. It will cut *right* through us."

"Target it with the secondary beams," he ordered. "Those satellites don't have *any* deflectors. In fact, target *every* defensive satellite you can without sacrificing your line on the Zions."

"That won't be many," she warned. "We're only going to have two Zions in our sights at a time, boss—the sequence is only going to take about three seconds to complete, but that's three seconds for someone to hit a button and ruin our day."

While the four main positron lances had *some* flexibility in their emitter angle, it wasn't nearly enough for them to hit all four stations in one salvo. It *was* enough for a three-second rotation to bring all four Zions under *Chameleon*'s guns.

"Hit every one you can," he ordered grimly, checking the time and distance. Thirty seconds. "Charge the lances, stand by the missiles. Clear the hatches at t-minus ten seconds."

His tactical officer nodded absently, her mind and attention now completely locked into her system.

"Lau, as soon as we fire, bring up the engines at maximum deceleration," he ordered. "We need to launch Hansen's shuttles with as little relative velocity as possible.

"Chownyk, watch those satellites," he concluded, glancing at the image of his XO in the Q-ship's CIC. "Flag the ones most likely to hit us for Taylor."

"On it," the XO replied. His attention snapped back to the CIC main hologram as he spoke though, and then he continued in a more urgent tone. "We have fighter launch! I've got another ten Katanas clearing Zion Three."

"Too late," Kyle snapped. "Taylor, take the targets from CIC, drop your missiles on them."

Ten seconds.

"Clearing the hatches," she announced. "Retargeting missiles…"

Several seconds of silence followed, everyone on both the bridge and CIC immersed in the tactical network. This was the window of vulnerability: if someone spotted the weapon hatches opening and made the call to sacrifice their Marines, everyone aboard *Chameleon* would die today.

Then the ship shivered slightly as they crossed an invisible line in space and Taylor opened fire. Four half-megaton-a-second positron lances lit up Kyle's tactical plot, the computer happily drawing them in as white lines for the three quarters of a second they were on target.

It was more than enough. The Zions were at combat readiness, with their deflectors at full power—but they hadn't actually been *expecting* an attack. And certainly not from *Chameleon*.

Two beams of pure antimatter struck each fighter launch station, the deflectors pushing the beams away from the center of the station but not far enough to force a miss. Where the streams of positrons hit, they annihilated regular matter, ripping massive tears through the armor and hull.

One of the beams on the first station hit one of the primary zero-point cells, ripping apart the carefully balanced magnetic tubes that pulled the positrons safely into storage chambers. The stream of positrons was weaker than *Chameleon*'s weapon—but it was starting *inside* the station and didn't cut off after less than a second.

By the time the zero-point cell itself came apart, the station was *gone*.

The second station was luckier. There was no single critical hit to incinerate the entire structure, "just" two beams of pure antimatter that ripped through the station, shattering armor, corridors, weapons and systems. It came apart in large enough pieces that there would be survivors—but it came apart in useless pieces nonetheless.

As the Q-ship slewed in space, maneuvering thrusters firing at full power to spin the four-hundred-meter sphere like a child's toy, the secondary lances opened fire. They were weak compared to those a true warship would carry, but they were still fifty-kiloton-a-second beams—beams that ripped into starfighters and satellites alike with deadly force.

The turn took a fraction under two seconds, and then Chameleon's lances lashed out again. The second pair of Zions was no luckier than the first, both coming apart under the sustained pounding of the Q-ship's main guns.

"Missiles in the air, sweeping the remaining stations with the lances," Taylor reported. "We have incoming starfighters!"

"Rokos!" Kyle snapped. "Alpha strike, go!"

26

Aurelius System
14:05 June 5, 2736 Earth Standard Meridian Date/Time
Chameleon

ACCELERATION SLAMMED Russell back into the seat of his command starfighter with crushing force as *Chameleon* flung the first wave of his ships into space. Ignoring the force as best as he could, he surveyed the situation.

Ten seconds earlier, four Zion-class defensive platforms, ten Katana-class starfighters, and sixty defensive platforms had been orbiting above the Aurelius Logistics Depot. In ten seconds, Taylor's surprise attack had shredded all four Zions and four of the Katanas.

"Katanas are launching," Alvarado reported. "Twenty-four missiles launched on *Chameleon*." He paused. "Five of the satellites have also launched, presumably under the Katanas' control. Thirty *capital* missiles incoming."

"All fighters, target the Katanas and launch two salvos," Rokos ordered. "Alpha, Bravo—stop the fighter missiles. Charlie, Delta—take the satellites' missiles."

He had Alpha Squadron and half of Bravo in space already, forming up around him as he led ten fighters after six. He left the missiles to Alvarado and the other gunners, trusting them to do their jobs, while he brought up the Cataphract's upgraded positron lance and started tracking missiles.

The Katanas clearly hadn't been expecting a fighter screen, their missiles pushing toward the Q-ship in a close echelon that concentrated the limited electronic warfare capabilities of the smaller missiles and protected them from a starship's defenses—but left them vulnerable to the starfighters that could get in close and generate multiple approach angles.

His own people's missiles began to fill space as well, starting with twenty from his first launch, followed by forty more as his second wave of starfighters deployed in time to join in. With ten missiles in space for each Terran starfighter, he dismissed the Katanas and focused on their missiles—they too had a second salvo in space.

"Taylor got the missile satellites before they launched again," Alvarado told him. "Charlie is sweeping after those birds and Delta will follow as they launch."

The whole thing was a close-range mess, with *Chameleon*'s lasers and lances flashing past his ships as they closed on the incoming Javelins. Missile flight times were barely a minute with the velocity *Chameleon* had imparted to them, and just to *add* to the mess, he could see the assault shuttles blasting away from the Q-ship behind him.

He tracked across space, firing the lance in tenth-second bursts as he crossed the likely zones for the incoming missiles. Thirteen more of his starfighters did the same—and the six Katanas did the same against *his* missiles.

Space started to get messy as missiles began to explode. First a handful, and then more and more as the two groups of fighters closed.

The Katana crews weren't the disorganized pirates they'd faced in New Edmonton. Their ECM linked together, defensive and offensive systems alike combining to make a hash of the scanners Russell was using to track their missiles.

The explosions didn't help. Each missile killed erupted in a giga-ton-plus explosion as both their warheads and antimatter fuel ignited, filling the space around them with high-velocity debris and hard rads. Each explosion added its own sphere of natural jamming to the chaos, helping cover their sisters as they closed.

Russell's people were expecting it, accounting for it and generating different sensor angles to see past and through the fireballs. The Katana pilots…were not. They were probably *trained* for it—their training was good—but training was no substitute for the harsh mistress of battle.

The last of the first salvo of incoming fighter missiles came apart well over fifty thousand kilometers short of *Chameleon*, nailed by Alpha Four's defensive laser clusters. Their own first salvo struck home, blasting half of the remaining Katanas apart.

Six had failed to stop twenty missiles. Three stood no chance against forty, and Russell turned his own starfighter back to hunt the remaining missiles heading for *Chameleon*.

"Damn it! They got through!" The panicked voice of Charlie Squadron's commander suddenly echoed in his mental link as a new icon popped up onto the screen: a trio of capital-ship missiles that hadn't been there a moment before and were now in a final lunge toward the Q-ship. "They told them to play dead and let the radiation cloud cover them."

It was a trick Captain Roberts had taught his own people, and Russell had seen used half a dozen times—and at this range, it was devastatingly effective. None of his starfighters could attempt to inter-cept those missiles without endangering *Chameleon* themselves.

It was down to the Q-ship's own defenses, the big ship spinning away from the incoming missiles as she began the terrifying defensive pirouette of a warship in the antimatter age. Lasers and positron lances flashed out in a desperate defense.

Two missiles went down almost simultaneously, Taylor skillfully picking them off moments after they appeared—but creating new radi-ation clouds that hid the last missile as it dove across the last ten thou-sand kilometers.

Chameleon vanished behind the explosion as the warhead closed the final distance…and then reappeared as the radiation faded.

"*Chameleon*, what's your status?" Russell demanded.

"Nailed it three hundred meters from the hull," Taylor responded after a moment. "We're shaken…but we're okay."

"Rokos, those other two squadrons are still hunting Echo," Roberts interrupted. "We've got the station; you know your mission."

"I do," the CAG confirmed grimly.

Search and destroy—and hope like *Void* they made it to Echo Squadron in time.

———

EDVARD HAD many unkind words to say about Terran Marines. That they lacked courage was *not* among them.

The hum of the positron lances firing wasn't much of a distraction, but they tried to use it anyway. The battle-armored Marines opened fire on the squads flanking them as the officer and her first fire team charged at Edvard and Chief Poulson.

He was moving in the same instant they were, shoving the Navy NCO out of the line of fire as he scrambled backward. He didn't even try and draw his own weapon, trusting to his men to put the Terrans down.

Even the four in battle armor weren't carrying anti-armor weapons. Their fire ricocheted off Bravo Platoon's armor—and drew a response from troopers who *were* carrying such weapons.

All eight of the Marines were down by the time their CO reached Edvard, his people realizing that he might want *her* alive.

She was clearly planning to take him hostage, training her sidearm on his unarmored head and opening her mouth to shout a demand for his people to stand down.

If it hadn't already been obvious that, determined as the Terran officer was, she was no veteran, that would have been enough. Edvard's bladed hand caught the pistol barrel, yanking it down as she fired into the floor.

The Terran officer followed her gun downward and slammed full-force into his suddenly rising knee. He felt a rib crack over his knee as she rotated around him and hit the ground, her suddenly broken arm trapped behind her as he pinned her to the floor.

"Congratulations, you just killed your men," he hissed in her ear, giving orders over his implant for Ramirez and Bravo Platoon to seize the shuttle. "A lot of people are going to die today; you didn't need to add to the list."

"Shuttle crew surrendered," Ramirez reported. "Whaddya want us to do with them, boss?"

"Is the shuttle still flyable?" Edvard asked, glancing over at Poulson.

"They didn't lock the controls. I guess they didn't want to lose fingers while I made them unlock them," the Gunny replied.

Edvard pinged Poulson by implant, making sure the Terrans—who *had* to think they were disorganized pirates—didn't hear him.

"Can you fly it?" he asked.

"Yes."

"Poulson, get going with Ramirez," he ordered aloud, accepting her claim at face value. "Leave Morris with the prisoners; I'm not letting the others get all of the loot!"

Sergeant Morris commanded Bravo Platoon's fourth squad. He was moving the Marines, techs and flight crew who'd surrendered off the shuttle before Edvard had even finished speaking.

Ramirez handed Edvard a pair of restraints he used to tie up the wounded Marine.

"You get to live today, miss," he told her.

With that final barb landed, he turned to board their newly stolen shuttle. Despite the act he'd put on—the act that made leaving the Marine officer alive necessary, regardless of any disgust at shooting prisoners or idiots—he wasn't worried about the other two platoons stealing all of the loot.

He *was* worried about sending two platoons against an entire *space station*.

————

THE NEAR MISS had left *Chameleon* feeling more than a little crispy to Kyle's senses. A good portion of the emitters and receivers for their long-range scanners and electronic warfare suite had been vaporized. Nothing that couldn't be fixed, given an average-size nickel-iron asteroid and about thirty-six hours, but enough to make him feel a touch more blind than he preferred.

"Drop a Q-probe to back up our scanners," he ordered Taylor. "With the fighters heading out to pull Echo out of the fire, we need to be seeing clearly."

"That will only leave us eight League-linked probes," she noted. All quantum communicators linked through a switchboard station somewhere to offset the inherently point-to-point nature of the entanglement used. While *Chameleon* had some Castle-linked Q-Com probes in her storage bays, those would be far too easily traced back to the Federation.

Given that a normal deployment could easily see twenty or thirty of the sensor drones scattered around a star system, only having nine —eight, after this—of them available made Kyle as twitchy as it did Taylor.

"They're there to be used," he reminded her. "XO, let's see if we can get the hornet's nest we've kicked over to calm down. I don't supposed Lafferty is still around?"

"He was based on one of the Zions," Chownyk noted after a moment's analysis. "He might be *alive*, but he doesn't have access to a Q-Com anymore."

"That would have been *too* easy," Kyle said cheerfully, studying the screen as the shuttles made their approach to the central station. He was taken aback for a moment to note the Terran shuttle returning with his people, but it turned out he had a message from Hansen explaining that.

Shaking his head, he grinned broadly.

"All right," he said loudly, taking the Terran Merchant Marine cap off and hanging it off his chair at a hopefully rakish angle. "Get me a wide-band, wide-angle transmission at the station."

"You're on."

"Aurelius Station," he greeted his audience in the lazy affected drawl of a *condottieri* captain. "This is Captain Sheridan of *Historic Ideal*. As you may have guessed by now, we are *not* what we appear to be. Given your pathetic lack of defenses, I now claim this system as my own. You will stand down and cooperate with my soldiers, or there will be hell to pay.

"You know the rules of the game: you lose, and *vae victis!*"

He made a cutoff gesture and smiled.

"Let me know if anyone responds. I presume we made sure their starfighters got that?"

"Everybody in the system will get it, dependent on the speed of light," Chownyk promised. "Can't promise anyone is going to listen."

"I can hope," Kyle said, a moment of seriousness slipping through his usual façade. "We just killed almost three thousand people. I'd rather not add to the list if I don't have to."

"Incoming response!"

"Link it to me," Kyle ordered.

A new image appeared on his screen, an older man with gaunt cheeks and graying black hair. Unlike Lafferty, he clearly hadn't bothered to put his full uniform on and was only wearing the black ship-suit—with a single red fake lapel—of the Terran Commonwealth Navy, with the single star of a Commodore.

The Federation had bumped Captain to be the equivalent rank and slipped in Senior Fleet Commander, justifying that an interstellar starship with five thousand people aboard needed an O-7 in command.

"I am Commodore Arkwright, commanding officer of the Aurelius base," he said with a surprisingly amount of calm disdain. "Am I speaking to the pirate Sheridan?"

"Pirate?" Kyle asked in an offended tone. "Is that any way to speak to the man offering you your life?!"

"You may have destroyed our defenders, but your flying junk heaps are no match for the Commonwealth's best," Arkwright told him. "I assure you, 'Captain' Sheridan, you are in no position to threaten my life."

"Your fighters are shiny but your pilots are crap," Kyle replied conversationally. "Mine are veterans of a dozen battles apiece; your glorified rookies stand no chance. Spare their lives, Commodore. Yield."

For a moment, Arkwright looked hesitant, *something* breaking through the contempt on his face. But it was only a moment, and then the sneer returned in full force as he gazed down his long aristocratic nose at Kyle.

"The Commonwealth has never surrendered to pirates," he snapped. "It will not start today."

"Well, then," Kyle replied, concealing his own moment of hope between an equally contemptuous sneer, "give my regards to my boarding troops. You'll be seeing them before I do."

———

"WE ARE HITTING HEAVY RESISTANCE," Riley reported as Edvard's commandeered shuttle blasted toward the station. "Disorganized so far, but they've got at least a company of Marines and they were paying attention to our approach vectors. We haven't hit armor yet, but the bastards have anti-armor gear."

"Send me everything you've got," the Lieutenant Major ordered. "We might be able to get in behind them."

Only one of Bravo platoon's squads had fit in the shuttle, but twenty men in battle armor could put on an impressive show.

"Sending you our locations and every one of the Terrans we've bounced off," the black-ops officer replied. "We're pushing them back so far, but they've got a lot of station to play with. I *think* we pulled decent schematics before they shut down the network in our area."

Edvard nodded absently, forgetting that Riley couldn't see him, as he reviewed the schematics. His first two platoons had hit both of the stations' docking bays, as those were the easiest place to land seven shuttles' worth of Marines.

The resistance they'd run into so far had been unfocused, station security and Marines hitting the attackers from whatever angle they were coming from with whatever gear they had—but the defenders had only learned they were under attack at all a few minutes earlier.

Resistance would stiffen sharply on the routes toward the

command center and engineering. In the Terrans' place, he would have *let* the attackers board and penetrate toward those targets while he got his people into armor.

Even with anti-armor weapons, the Terrans had barely slowed his people down and had thrown away over a hundred lives.

"Tighten up your strikes," he ordered. "We're supposed to be *condottieri*, not thugs. Let's look the part—and it'll focus your firepower when they start throwing armor roadblocks in your way in about three minutes."

"Teach your grandmother to knit," Riley told him genteelly. "Got a plan, boss?"

"There's a lovely little promenade gallery about halfway between your current location and the command center," he noted as he studied the schematics. "Great place for an ambush, but closer to the hull than the command center is."

"If I'm walking into an ambush, I wouldn't mind a counter-trap," she replied.

Edvard smiled and flipped his target coordinates to Poulson.

"One surprise, coming right up."

———

"Hang on!"

In hindsight, Edvard realized that he should have, if nothing else, been watching his shuttle's *velocity* as Poulson flew them at the space station. He realized her intention less than five seconds before the Navy Chief *rammed* the shuttle into the station, still traveling at almost a thousand kilometers a second.

She threw every mass manipulator to offsetting their deceleration, but an equivalent *hundred thousand gravities* could only be reduced so much. Poulson was wrapped in an emergency acceleration pod and the Marines had their battle armor—and Edvard *still* felt like an angry giant had stepped on him.

"Delivered. To. Target," Poulson gasped, heaving deep breaths between words. "Twenty meters that way." She gestured forwards. "Lasers firing…now."

Before Edvard could ask just what *that* meant, the assault shuttle's forward lasers opened fire. Multipurpose weapons, primarily intended to defend against missiles but quite capable of taking down atmospheric fighters or other small spacecraft, tore through the structure of the station like superheated wrecking balls.

"Go! Go! Go!" he ordered, suiting actions to words as the shuttle bay doors slammed open into the slagged mess that *had* been the corridors and rooms between the shuttle and the promenade he'd marked as his destination.

Ramirez grabbed his shoulder, armored gauntlets holding the officer's battle armor in check.

"Pretending to be League or not, you don't lead from the front, sir," he said gently as two fire teams swept past, rifles tracking across the debris and the gallery, looking for targets.

Targets that weren't there.

"Riley, report," Edvard snapped as he entered the promenade he'd expected to find the Terrans in. "Watch for incoming; they're not in the gallery."

"If they're not setting up an ambush there...everybody halt! Prep for ambush close!"

Things were silent on both Edvard's end and hers for several seconds. Then the shooting started and Riley cursed.

"*Fuckers*. Just in time, sir," she told him. "First squad, suppressive fire. Second squad, pull back and join the line."

Edvard waited patiently for her to have time for him again.

"They had ambushes prepped in the side corridors, but somebody panicked when we halted," she told him. "No losses, but I'm pulling my horns in to cover our asses. Not sure, but we could be facing half a company or more. We're not advancing, sir."

"We can swing around and take them from the rear," Edvard offered, studying the map. He could, but...

"We'll be fine," Riley replied. "I know I have a cute ass, but I don't need it hauled out of the fire today, boss. Make your call."

"Behave, Lieutenant," the Lieutenant Major said absently as he drew lines on the map in his implant. "We're going for the command center. *Don't* die on me."

"Wouldn't dream of it," she said breathlessly, a moment before gunfire echoed at a volume that had to be *her* shooting at somebody.

"Good luck," he told her, gesturing Ramirez and the squad Sergeant over to him. "We're heading for the command center; I'm flipping you a map. Let's move."

"I can see at least one point where they're going to make trouble for us," the Gunny told him, highlighting the choke point in front of the command center.

"The command center is going to be fortified," Edvard agreed. "Let's just be glad it's not surrounded by vacuum this time, shall we?"

The last Terran space station Edvard had assaulted had been a prison, with a hundred-meter "moat" of hard vacuum to secure the prison component. Since they'd had such a nice security barrier, they'd used it to protect one side of their command center.

Carefully keeping himself in the middle of the squad, Edvard watched his Marines follow his carefully laid-out path through the station, running into surprisingly little in the way of resistance. No Marines, no sealed internal bulkheads, nothing.

Until they reached the chokepoint outside the bridge, where the point fire teams rounded a corner—and then immediately dove back for cover.

"Security bulkhead is closed and auto-turrets are active," the Lance Corporal reported. "No Marines, though. Just automatic defenses."

"How long to hack them?" he asked.

Ramirez shrugged.

"Bravo's EW expert is with Third Squad," he noted. "Unless we want Poulson to extract the shuttle and ram another hole in the station to pick up Alpha or Charlie Platoon's EW guys?"

"…I don't think that shuttle is flying anywhere ever again," Edvard replied. "But if it's just auto-turrets…grenades on the bounce, people; download the point team's visuals and blow those turrets to hell in five!"

Moments later, twenty high-explosive grenades went around the corner with carefully calculated bounces. They didn't hit together, tiny differences in response time between different Marines spreading the attack over about half a second, but they turned the antechamber of the station's command center into a concentrated inferno.

"On the bounce, MOVE!" Ramirez bellowed, the Gunny leading the point teams back around the corner.

One auto-turret was still active, spitting high-velocity penetrators at the Marines. One of the point team Marines took a round to the leg, going down in a crashing heap of ceramic and alloy as his comrades took out the turret.

"I'm fine," she ground out a moment later. "Suit sealed the wound. Not walking anywhere."

"Move her into cover. Demo team, blow the bulkhead," Edvard ordered.

The wounded out of the way, the rest of the platoon followed as the two demolition troops set charges.

"With me, on the blast," Edvard ordered. "Remember—we need them to *surrender*. No one dies who doesn't pull a gun!"

Affirmatives responded—and then the explosives blew and they were moving. The suits had built-in stunners for circumstances just like this, and Edvard armed them as he charged through the debris.

There were two Marines in the control room, neither in battle armor but both behind bipod-mounted anti-armor rifles. They were expecting an attack, but his people had the advantage regardless. Electron lasers pulsed in the smoke and both men went down before they could fire.

Edvard ignored them, striding forward and hunting the man he knew had to be there—the older man in the Navy uniform at the center of the room.

"Commodore Arkwright," he said flatly, leveling his rifle at the unarmored man. "The time for games is up. Order your people to stand down."

"And if I refuse?" the Terran replied contemptuously, staring down the barrel of the gun. He certainly had *fortitude*, for all that Edvard wanted to hate the old man's guts.

"You die and I find someone who is willing to order them to surrender," the Marine said coldly. "*Vae victis*, Commodore. You are defeated."

27

Aurelius System
14:10 June 5, 2736 Earth Standard Meridian Date/Time
Cataphract-D Command Starfighter

THE TWO GAS giants exchanged atmosphere in an immense funnel cloud linking the two worlds, creating one of the single largest natural obstacles Russell had ever seen in his years as a pilot. The chaotic mess of the Aurelius Pair meant that none of the starfighters could safely accelerate at their full capability.

Of course, that didn't mean they couldn't do so *dangerously*, and Wing Commander Russell Rokos took his four understrength squadrons into the heart of the storm at five hundred gravities. With ten minutes' headway, the Katanas were almost a million kilometers ahead of him, around the far side of the gas giant and closing on Echo.

The Terrans had reduced acceleration to a more sedate three hundred gravities, and his people had brought *Chameleon*'s almost-two-thousand-kilometer-a-second velocity with them.

"This is Tomacino," Echo Squadron's commander reported in. "We lost Tatiana and her crew, but the rest of us are still here. They fired two full salvos of missiles at us to get her too.

"We're looping lower than they're willing to get, but they've got us cut off," the young man said grimly. "I don't think these fighters can take going deeper. We're stuck unless you can relieve us."

"Understood," Russell transmitted back. "Can you launch on them?"

"That last salvo of theirs got lost on its way down. I'm not sure our missiles will do any better heading up," the other pilot admitted. "I can engage, but not without coming under fire myself."

"Link networks with us through the Q-Com; prep for a time-on-target salvo," the CAG ordered.

"Yes, sir."

Russell felt as much as saw his fifth squadron link in. With the loss of another of Echo Squadron's starfighters to the Katanas' missiles, he was down to thirty-four starfighters from his original forty—and facing the Commonwealth's best hardware.

"They'll launch a full minute before we do, boss," Alvarado pointed out quietly. With the Terrans accelerating away from him, his missiles had to play catch-up—but *their* missiles were flying right down his people's throats.

"I know," he said gruffly. "We'll still launch before they *hit* us. Have everyone prep for a full-launch cycle. I know Alpha and Bravo only have one launch left, but Charlie and Delta have two. If the Terrans fired twice at Echo, they've only got one launch left in the tubes."

That "one launch" was still going to be *eighty missiles*.

"Designate that entire first launch, except for Echo's birds, for a defensive intercept," Russell continued. "These Sarissas aren't much better at that than our Starfires are, but every bird they take down is one we don't have to shoot down."

"Setting it up," his gunner confirmed. "Sixty seconds to their range of us, one twenty-five to our range of them. They're still pulling three hundred gees away from us."

Russell grunted acknowledgement. The people he was chasing were paying more attention to keeping Echo corralled then they were to trying to evade him. They knew as well as he did that they had him as badly outclassed as he had them outnumbered.

"Should we ask them to surrender?" Alvarado asked softly.

"That's the boss's shtick," Russell replied. "If they want to live, they can surrender on their own. I'm perfectly willing to send a few more Terrans to the Void than necessary."

Neither of his flight crew said anything. He doubted they disagreed; they'd lost as many friends in the last year of declared and undeclared war as he had. The pilots they faced today might be rookies, but they were of the same ilk that had killed thousands of Alliance pilots by now.

"Katanas are launching missiles."

The words were quiet, drawing attention to what the computers were already reporting. All twenty Katanas had flipped for a few fractions of a second and fired. Eighty Javelin fighter attack missiles flashed across space, accelerating toward Russell's people at a thousand gravities.

"Prepare counter-salvo," he said calmly. "Flight Lieutenant Alvarado has the call."

In the back of his mind, he was aware of Echo Squadron rising out of the lower depths of the gas giant, carving an arcing course that would carry them into missile range of the Katanas but not lance range.

"Missiles...launched," Alvarado announced softly into the silence of the cockpit. Twenty-eight starfighters each launched two missiles, sending fifty-six missiles into the teeth of the Terran salvo. "Second salvo in ten seconds. Coordinating antimissile fire, laser suites active."

Russell exhaled slowly, taking over control of the positron lance and studying the sensor sweeps of the mess in front of him carefully. The upper reaches of the gas giant's atmosphere barely qualified as such, but they certainly made for a denser combat environment than he was used to.

"Missile intercept...*now*."

The sky lit up with explosions, dozens of antimatter warheads going off simultaneously as their happily suicidal brains drove them to collisions and near misses that wiped missile after missile from reality.

Russell had sacrificed his own heaviest shot to gut the Terrans' *only* shot, and over half of their salvo vanished in the eye-searing blast wave.

That still left a missile per Federation fighter and then some, and Russell turned his attention to the deadly dance of maneuver, lance, and laser that would decide if he lived through the next ninety seconds.

Each blip of a potential missile earned a pulse of positrons. Only a handful of the pulses triggered the massive explosion marking an actual hit, but he wove his starfighter through a series of tight spirals, enough to throw off the targeting systems of any incoming missile.

A final crescendo of explosions swept over his starfighters and it was over. Three more of his starfighters—and twelve of Russell's people, including his Charlie Squadron commander—were gone.

The Terrans, however, had shot their bolt. Now they were turning back toward Russell's squadrons, trying to close to lance range. Their lances were heavier than his, and if they made it to range, they could rip his fighters apart with impunity before his people closed the range.

Sixty seconds after their missiles blew apart around him, though, Echo Squadron's salvo slammed home. Twelve missiles rose out of the depths of the gas giant, screaming in on the Katanas at a thousand gravities.

With twenty starfighters, the Terrans took them all down—but only at the cost of focusing their defenses toward the gas giant. Ten seconds later, over thirty missiles came screaming down on them from Russell's force—and twelve more rose up from Echo.

They tried, but it was in moments of stress like these where experience made all of the difference. The combat experience most of the Terran pilots didn't have.

Russell's face was harsh as the explosions worked their way through the Katanas, shredding starfighter after starfighter—and leaving their broken formation vulnerable as Echo's third and final salvo arrived.

28

Aurelius System
16:00 June 5, 2736 Earth Standard Meridian Date/Time
TCN Logistics Depot Aurelius

LIEUTENANT MAJOR HANSEN met Kyle and Glass in the landing bay as the third wave of shuttles disgorged more of Federation Intelligence's professional looters. With over a quarter of *Chameleon*'s crew tearing apart the entire depot, the whole affair was making him nervous.

"Are we sure we have the entire crew contained?" he asked the Marine CO.

"No," Hansen admitted. "We *do* have the Marines and MPs accounted for, as well as all of the armories. We've killed surveillance throughout the station, and my troops are accompanying our search parties.

"The main threat at this point is discovery, not a holed-up sensor tech with a pistol," the Marine noted. "There's no way they didn't call for help."

"And the nearest warship is four days away," Glass reminded them both, the old man glancing around the shuttle bay as crates of *something* were loaded onto the shuttle. "We can fill our holds before then, so long as we're efficient and choose what we steal carefully."

"Munitions first," Kyle said firmly. "The next time we go up against the TCN, I want to have more than one salvo of capital-ship missiles."

"Our computer techs are ripping into their systems as we speak," Hansen promised. "They expect to have at least a basic inventory of the external cargo containers by twenty hundred hours."

"Those are where we'll find the real prizes," Glass said. "There'll be some munitions and so forth in ready transfer bays on the main station, but it's the cargo containers that will have the main stockpiles."

"I also understand there's a vault in this station?" Kyle asked.

"We've located seven so far, actually," Hansen reported. "Not entirely sure what's going to be in them beyond high-value, low-volume stuff. I'm hesitant to blast them open.'

"Cut them out and bring them with us," Kyle suggested. "That will give us time to work over their systems and get into them at our leisure. We get the value and we don't distract ourselves inside our timeline."

Hansen nodded slowly.

"We can do that," he confirmed. "We'll probably want to run secondary power lines, make sure their emergency systems don't destroy whatever's in them. Still a lot of work."

"Missiles and munitions are handy, but no one should turn down loot, either," Kyle told him. The surveillance might be shut down, but he still didn't want to get too explicit while aboard the station.

The pirates they were pretending to be wouldn't leave the vaults, so they wouldn't. Anything of value would be turned over to the Federation, but the crew would split about a five-percent chunk of that value between them. Across some four thousand people, it wasn't likely to add up to *much*, but it would still likely be a nice bonus for the people he'd dragged hundreds of light-years from home.

"What have we done with the prisoners?" he asked.

"Shoved them in a hold half-full of food and followed them with enough bedrolls and portable toilets for everyone," Hansen replied.

"We're watching them carefully, but Arkwright got them sorted out surprisingly quickly."

"That is one terrifying old man," Kyle observed. *"Watch him."*

"Like a hawk, Captain," the Marine promised. "Like a fucking *hawk.*"

———

"What am I looking at?" Edvard demanded, ducking past a door that had miraculously acquired a pair of Marine guards—both dressed in a haphazard mix of gear and armor that belied the precision of their stance.

"You'll see," Ramirez promised, leading the officer past a chattering swarm of Navy techs. "When the hacker boys opened up the files, they found something I figured we wanted to bounce all the way up the chain ASAP."

"Then we should be bouncing it, not playing twenty questions," the Lieutenant Major pointed out. "Why the mystery?"

"Take a look," his Gunny replied, switching the lights in one of the ready cargo bays—the bays on the exterior of the station designed to be linked up with the equivalent bays on warship and have their entire contents transferred over.

The lights flickered up on rows upon rows of starfighters. Sets of five ships had been locked together with girders for ease of transport, cables linking from emergency ports to the carrying cases showing how the thrusters and mass manipulators were sent up to run in tandem.

The Terran Commonwealth Starfighter Corps organized its ships into ten-fighter squadrons. Unless Edvard missed his count, he was looking at a minimum of *six* such squadrons, neatly boxed for transport—about the only state in which Alliance hackers had a snowball's chance of taking control of them.

———

"So, we have munitions of every type we could possibly desire, parts to manufacture *more* munitions if we get the other raw materials, and a pile of vaults and high-value goods that will make the crew *very* happy when we get home." Kyle summarized the essence of the presentation Glass's people had just given on the contents of the inventory files.

"What's our transfer timeline look like?" he asked, glancing at Chownyk.

"Assuming the inventory records are correct, I want to prioritize hard munitions over anything else," the XO said. "We should have our Stormwind magazines full by oh nine hundred hours tomorrow, at which point we can move on to starfighter missiles, general supplies, and the high-value items.

"Complete loading should take no more than forty-eight hours," Chownyk concluded. "At any point after nine hundred hours, we should be sufficiently supplied as to carry out the next stage of operations."

Even aboard *Chameleon*, surrounded by the officers who would be planning the attack, none of them were quite comfortable talking about attacking Tau Ceti yet. It was a Commonwealth *Core System*, after all.

"So, if someone shows up for lunch tomorrow, we can flip them the engines and be out of here without worrying about it," Kyle said with satisfaction. "I like it.

"I've got a wrench, unfortunately," he continued. "One that's going to come down on Mister Rokos's shoulders."

The CAG hadn't *quite* been asleep in the corner, though he'd clearly been feeling the adrenaline and other effects of the earlier battle. At the mention of his name, however, the burly man straightened and started paying more attention.

"Sir?" he said questioningly.

"The hackers found something that *wasn't* in the inventory," Kyle told them. "It seems that they were only partway through the transfer of the Katanas." He held up a hand to curb any excess of enthusiasm. "There's good news and bad news here.

"The bad news is that while we've *found* Katanas in the station, all of them have been, quite sensibly, broken free of their transport matrices and restored to full systems security," he warned them. "I'll leave it to Glass if those are likely to be useful to us—we'll be bringing at least two squadrons worth with us as *cargo*, but if we can actually man and deploy some of them, we will.

"The *good* news is that someone was being nice and ahead of the ball dealing with their *old* fighters. Major Edvard's people found *fifty* Scimitars in transport matrices, with their systems unlocked for ease of transport.

"Now, this doesn't give us access to weapons control or their electronic warfare software, but it does give us the ability to *overwrite* that code. Mister Glass, I don't suppose we have *copies* of the software for the Scimitar?"

The spy chuckled.

"As a matter of fact, we do," he allowed. "It's not a perfect match, much more generic—and they'll suffer for the lack of Q-Coms after we gut their Terran Q-blocks—but we can make it up with dirty tricks packages 'borrowed' from the League *condottieri*."

"The Scimitar, honestly, isn't really a superior fighter to the Cataphract-D," Kyle warned Rokos. "But it *is* a better missile platform, with twice as many launchers—and one that our Commonwealth friends are going to assume is *theirs* until it's too late."

"We'll take them," Rokos said flatly. "That's an edge I won't throw away without a *damn* good reason. What about the Katanas, sir?"

"We don't have a software suite we can force in over the old code," Glass admitted. "We'll need to actually crack open and take control of their existing software. It'll take time and… Well, it's not something pirates would be able to do.'

"But it's not out of the capability of the better *condottieri* units?" Kyle asked.

"No," the spy confirmed.

"It doesn't hurt our cause if we make the Commonwealth think we're actual League mercs instead of League-based pirates," *Chameleon*'s Captain pointed out. "We'll take them for R&D to rip apart anyway, so if we get any of them set up for our use, Rokos can use them.

"I can see some…*sneaky* uses for having the same starfighters the Terrans do."

29

Aurelius System
23:00 June 5, 2736 Earth Standard Meridian Date/Time
Chameleon

ONCE THE AFTERMATH, planning and discussions were over, it was late by the ship's clock.

Kyle found himself pacing his office, unable to even consider sleep. A beer—one of his microbrews from Castle, probably mind-bogglingly expensive at this end of the galaxy—sat on his desk, open but untouched.

In the middle of the battle, he hadn't had time to doubt himself. When things had gone sideways, he'd done what he'd always done: gone for the throat while making the enemy look somewhere else. Despite his fear, he apparently still *was* the Stellar Fox.

He sighed.

Tatiana Nazarov, Levon Kevorkian and Norman Costa had died because they'd gone with a different plan. He wasn't sure about the other pilots they'd lost, and he could convince himself they would have lost the Marines either way, but Nazarov's flight crew had died because Echo Squadron had been off on their stealthy own.

A clever plan, a sneaky plan...but not the aggressive one he'd conceived of, sitting in that briefing room. It had been a risky plan, but not an all-or-nothing throw of the dice. Until, of course, everything had gone wrong and an all-or-nothing plan had been the only way to *win*.

To his surprise, a buzz at his door announced the presence of Wing Commander Rokos. His last CAG, Michael Stanford—killed at Huī Xing when Kyle had messed up—had spent many evenings drinking with him, but they'd been friends as well as coworkers. He was too senior to Rokos to have the same relationship, though that required distance could cause problems as well.

"Come in," he ordered.

Rokos stepped through the door, looking like a train had run over him.

"Couldn't sleep," the CAG said gruffly. "System said you were still up, figured I'd check if you needed company."

"You're more than welcome," Kyle said with a grin. "Beer?"

"Sure. Just one," Rokos insisted. "Still got work to do in the morning."

"You're in command, CAG," the Captain pointed out, pulling a second bottle from the fridge. "When do you ever not?"

"When I'm not aboard ship," the CAG admitted, taking the beer. "Still have letters to write before I sleep. With Flight Commander Zitnick dead, I'm due the letter to her mother—and the letters for her squadron's dead."

"Do you need help?" Kyle asked. That was part of his job, if needed.

"Not with the writing," Rokos replied. "Just...moral support. This is gonna be worth it, right?"

Kyle sighed.

"You saw Intel's projections," he said. It wasn't a question—Kyle had fought hard to make sure his senior officers had access to that report. "Walkingstick is going to see reinforcements of over a *hundred* capital ships in the next year. With the Reserve going into commission, we'll launch fifty.

"The numbers don't get any better going forward. We *need* to change the parameters of this war, no matter what the cost."

"So we drag an innocent nation into a war with the Commonwealth," Rokos pointed out. "Is that a cost we're prepared to accept?"

"The truth," Kyle sighed. "The truth is that if the Commonwealth stops to *talk* to the League, this whole thing comes apart. We're counting on them to do what they've always done—and on Periklos to respond in a way the League has never responded before.

"There are diplomatic moves in play as well," he reminded Rokos. "If the League goes to war with the Commonwealth, we'll offer them an alliance. Starting a second front has value all on its own, but if we can *coordinate* with the League, suddenly we can face the Commonwealth on something approaching an even footing.

"That's worth a lot, Rokos."

"Can't argue," the CAG said, shaking his head. "Still seems…dirty."

"It's a black op we can never admit we were involved in," Kyle agreed. "It's dirty, all right. Using their own starfighters against them? Stolen munitions, stolen birds, Gods—*Chameleon* was theirs, not that *we* stole it from them."

"We didn't start this war," Rokos said quietly. "I don't even *like* Terrans, sir. But this is a mess."

"It is. But it's *our* job and *our* mess. Someone was going to do it, Wing Commander. Who better?"

Rokos laughed.

"They might have found a better CAG," he pointed out, "but they sure as hell couldn't have found a better Captain. Not sure anyone else would have had the nerve to pull off what you did today. Most would have written Echo off and run."

"Wasn't going to happen, Rokos," Kyle said with a cheerful grin as the other officer's confidence finished filling a hole he'd barely even realized he'd been struggling with. "Just…was *not* going to happen."

———

EDVARD WAS DRUNK. It was a state he generally tried to avoid on deployment, but a second circle of empty chairs at the heart of a second wake in a week was a bit much for him. He'd joined a peacetime military, though everyone had known war was coming. He'd lost more Marines under his command in the last seven *days* than in the first seven *years* of his career.

They'd been lucky, too. They'd run up against equal numbers of Terran Marines, and if the Terran commander hadn't fed them into his people piecemeal, he'd have lost more than the dozen men and women he had.

With thirty-six fatalities, Edvard was down almost a fifth of his company. He'd gone a little too far into a whiskey bottle when that realization had hit—and Riley had gently steered him out of the wake before it became necessary for him to trigger the implant override that would flush the alcohol from his system.

They'd travelled far from the party, not heading anywhere in particular, when he stumbled and fell into her. She tried to catch him, but that only resulted in them both going down in a tangled heap of limbs and uniforms.

Lieutenant Sandra Riley was, quite literally, a killing machine, her body augmented with various systems that made her extremely dangerous despite her slim build. Hearing her *giggle* was an unexpected pleasure.

Sharing her laughter, Edvard tried to disentangle himself from his subordinate, only to suddenly find them face to face, still sprawled along the floor and with *far* more of their bodies touching than the Articles would ever find acceptable.

They both froze then; ever so slightly, Riley's lips parted and she leaned toward him.

And then an emergency alert hit both their implants, causing them to scramble apart as Edvard *finally* engaged the override that cut the effect of alcohol on his brain.

"Hansen, what's happening?" he demanded.

"Sir, um…we have a problem," the Sergeant running the security detail on the Terran prisoners said hesitantly.

"So I'm assuming," Edvard snapped. "What's happened?"

"It seems Commodore Arkwright found the guy running the Marine defense of the station. He's, ah, he's kicking the shit out of the man. Should we intervene?"

Edvard had to think about that for a longer moment than he was really comfortable with. The pirates they were pretending to be were only somewhat likely to care...but neither the *condottieri* they were *also* pretending to be or the Marines they were could really let that stand.

Even *if* the Terran Marines' CO had managed to kill off most of his own people with incompetence.

"Yes," he ordered. "Break it up, and see if we can sort out somewhere to throw them both to cool off."

"Will do, sir," the Marine replied.

The mental image of Arkwright, the calmly collected old man who'd almost refused to surrender at *gunpoint*, beating up a presumably much younger and likely much healthier man still amused Edvard, enough to keep him smiling until he turned to meet Riley's gaze and remembered what had been happening when he'd received the message.

There was an unfamiliar pallor to her face that told him that she'd also triggered the override to flush the alcohol from her brain and the rest of her body. She met his gaze and smiled shyly.

He shook his head wryly, both acknowledging what had almost happened—they both knew it wouldn't have ended at a kiss—and warning her that it *couldn't* happen.

"We're adults, sir," she said quietly. "We can behave."

"So we can," he agreed with a sigh. "May I walk you to your quarters, Lieutenant Riley?"

———

By the time Russell finished his beer and headed back to his quarters, the fatigue of the day had finally caught up with him. The burly pilot wasn't really having *problems*, per se, but he was definitely looking forward to his bed.

Passing the flight lounge, however, he caught a flicker of light. *Flickering* wasn't generally a good sign on starship—it usually meant there was a problem with the power feed to an entire section of the ship. Flickering *lights* often meant that section of the ship wasn't far away from flickering *life support*.

He turned toward the lounge, concern overcoming fatigue for at least a few moments, only to stop as he reached the entrance to the room and realized he was seeing *candlelight*.

Candles were discouraged outside the handful of religious shrines aboard Federation warships, but they weren't exactly *forbidden*. He paused at the door, outside of sight from most of the room, and looked to see what was happening.

Cavendish was sitting at a table off to the side of the lounge, a set of lit candles laid out in front of her. Five others that he recognized as flight crew from her black-ops squadron sat around the table with her, each with three candles in front of them.

One for each of Echo Squadron's people who'd died today.

It wasn't something he was familiar with, but he could also see how a unit that operated as insularly as Cavendish's had before being assigned to *Chameleon* would have its own rituals and traditions.

He stayed in the corner for a moment, watching the black-ops flight crew and their candles. Despite his inability to hear their quiet conversation, he still felt like he was intruding.

He slowly withdrew, making sure to make his way past the lounge without coming into their view. The candles were a minor fire hazard but not enough to be worth commenting on.

Everyone had the right to mourn in their own way.

30

Aurelius System
12:00 June 6, 2736 Earth Standard Meridian Date/Time
Chameleon

"*WATCH IT!* Those are *missiles,* for Stars' sake!"

"Why? It's not loaded with antimatter yet."

"Maybe not," the Chief agreed with her heckler, "but if you *damage* the containment fields, when we *fill* it with antimatter, the whole shebang will *explode.* And then *you* don't get the lunch you're rushing to, because the whole *ship* will be gone!"

Kyle smiled slightly at the perennial sound of senior noncoms explaining their subordinates' failings to them, watching as another cell of twelve Stormwind capital-ship missiles drifted through the zero gravity connection between the logistics depot and the Q-ship.

"Our ready magazines are now full," Chownyk reported crisply, the two men standing in an observation bay watching the loading process. "That's one hundred and twenty missiles. As a reserve, we're loading another four hundred and eighty in the cargo holds like that."

The cyborg gestured toward the packaged missiles with one plastic-and-chrome finger. "We can't transfer them into the magazines *quickly*, but even a ten-minute load cycle is better than no reloads at all."

"Agreed," Kyle confirmed. "The starfighter missiles?"

"A twentieth the size, so the numbers are bigger but the story's the same," his XO replied. "When the Terrans designed her, they gave us twenty-missile magazines for each Stormwind launcher—and *eighty*-missile magazines for the Javelin launchers. We've loaded the best part of a thousand missiles into the magazines, and since the Scimitars need them as well, we're stacking *ten* thousand spares into one of the holds."

"That must have made Rokos happy."

"Like a kid at Christmas," Chownyk agreed. "We've also loaded in an entire company's worth of battle armor and weapons for the Marines, plus enough munitions to fight a good-sized war." He shrugged. "We can manufacture most of that, given time, but it seems handy to have around.

"I did make the call to leave behind the combat vehicles, though," the XO told Kyle. "While I'm sure imaginative-enough officers could find a use for a main battle tank aboard a space station, carrying them didn't seem…cost-effective."

"Did Hansen even complain?" Kyle asked.

"I'm not sure the Lieutenant Major even noticed the tanks were an *option*. Or cared. He was busy gloating over the container of anti-armor carbines we found."

"The starfighters?"

"We're moving the Cataphracts into the cargo hold with the Katanas we brought over," Chownyk noted. "Once that's done, we'll begin moving the Scimitars into the main flight deck. Rokos has two squadrons flying combat space patrol until the transfer is complete.

"My understanding is that the software work is already done and Rokos's people will be able to fly the birds as soon as they're fuelled and armed."

"Good work, Chownyk," Kyle concluded. "Anything else going on I need to be aware of?"

"Something is going to break," his XO pointed out pessimistically.

"I expected it to be with the missiles, but the catastrophic failure point *now* is the starfighter loading. For about six hours, those twelve birds Rokos has up are it for our defenses. We're attached to the station, and the rest of the Cataphracts are in cold storage."

Kyle had signed off on the plan recognizing the risk. That was why they *had* the CSP, but he understood his XO's concern. This was the most vulnerable stage of the whole operation.

———

RUSSELL WATCHED UNCOMFORTABLY as the last of his undeployed Cataphracts slotted neatly into the frameworks that carried them through deep space. While there were connections between the cargo bays and the flight deck, they weren't large enough—aboard *Chameleon*, at least—to move the starfighters themselves.

So he was going to have most of his remaining fighters moved *out* of the flight deck and into the cargo bay, a relatively straightforward process that would unfortunately tell anyone watching that he didn't currently have any more starfighters to deploy.

Then they would move the Scimitars in in similar frameworks, break them down, adjust the hangars to fit the *completely different* style of spacecraft, check that the systems were all working as Glass had promised...and only then fuel them and load them with missiles.

Six hours, Hanz told him. He hated to call his Deck Chief a liar, but he doubted they'd do it in less than twelve. He had Echo and Bravo squadrons, his most intact formations at this point with six fighters apiece, flying CSP.

"That's it," Hanz said sharply from behind him. "We'll move them out and have the new birds in here in a jiffy, boss."

"Should have done this in deep space," Rokos told her. "We could have waited."

"Could we?" she asked. "I'm not in the operations briefings, CAG. Are we going to have six hours to stop in deep space and make the switch like this?"

He snorted. The plan was to head straight to Tau Ceti.

"Probably not," he admitted. "It just makes me twitchy."

"You're just grouchy you couldn't justify flying the CSP yourself."

"Fair," he agreed. "But if you'll excuse me, Chief Hanz, I'm going to go baby the tactical plot in PriFly until this is over."

———

THE FIGHTER FRAMES were making their final ungainly way back into *Chameleon* as Russell entered the Q-Ship's primary flight control center. With as much local traffic as there was, the room was a hub of activity, with the techs providing safe courses and corrections to the twelve starfighters and almost sixty assorted other small craft swarming around *Chameleon* and the depot.

One screen was showing footage from one of those shuttles, hanging back to provide assistance if something went wrong, watching another shuttle winch in the cables linked to a vault the size of a starfighter. None of the vaults had contents listed in the inventories their hackers had yet accessed, but it was unlikely something with that level of protection *wouldn't* be worth the effort to haul it out of the station.

Bravo Squadron was flying a high overwatch, orbiting above the depot in a position to intercept an approach from any attack. Echo Squadron was doing the opposite, orbiting below the chaotic space of the depot, where the engines and energy of the station helped conceal the already stealthy starfighters.

The hope was that if someone attacked, Echo's intervention would come as a surprise. It was a pretty frail hope, in Russell's opinion—as the man who'd drafted the plan—but the truth was that any surprise was unnecessary. At most, there was a loose patrol of Katanas in the system somewhere. A dozen Cataphracts *should* be able to deal with that without any games.

"How are we doing, Flight Commander?" he quietly asked Shine, the Space Force officer running the shift.

Shine was one of exactly two officers in the Space Force contingent who lacked the necessary implant bandwidth to fly a starfighter—and the black-eyed woman lacked it for the same reason as Kyle Roberts did: neural scarification induced implant degradation.

Shine, like Captain Roberts, had been *just* too close to an antimatter warhead going off. She'd lived, but she'd been grounded and offered an Article Seventeen medical discharge. Instead, she'd taken a support role normally assigned to officers who'd pissed off their CAGs.

Running PriFly was a job she was sharing with Cavendish, for example. Unlike Cavendish, she'd *volunteered* for it so she could still contribute.

"It's a hornet's nest out there, but it's *our* hornet's nest," Shine said cheerfully. "Scanners are clear of anything we don't know about."

She pointed at one corner of the holographic plot as she spoke, though. Aurelius 4A was finishing its spin around 4B and approaching the depot. All three were orbiting the shared center of gravity, so at different times, different planets would be closest to the station—more driven by the station's orbit than the planets' rotation around each other.

"Cosner, you said you were going to dig into that sensor blotch you spotted," she called to one of her techs. "Why is it still showing as an unknown on my plot?"

"Haven't seen anything since," the tech replied. "It *could* have been an engine flare, but nothing's shown up since." He shrugged. "It *might* be a platform or a Q-probe they had in orbit down there. Or it could be a sensor glitch."

"Is there any way to be sure?" Russell asked.

"We *could* pulse the entire area with the main radar array," Cosner said slowly. "We're using it for local sweeps, but we could do a high-power pulse along the line of the ghost. But it's just a ghost."

"I don't believe in ghosts," the CAG told him. "I *do* believe in sneaky Terrans. Run the radar pulse, Specialist."

"Yes, sir!"

It took a few seconds to redirect the several emitters that made up the main radar array. Russell waited impatiently as the immensely powerful beams of radiation were charged and then unleashed toward Aurelius 4A.

More seconds ticked by, the speed of light having its own piece to say in the timing of their data, and then the "sensor ghost" lit up again and started to resolve.

"*Damn*," Shine whispered. "Vampire!" she shouted, getting the attention of everyone in the PriFly center. "We have vampires—five Katanas on approach.

"Come on, people," she snapped as some of her crew stared at her blankly while others leapt to work. "You know the drill! Check your sectors and responsibilities. Get the shuttles to safe zones and clear attack vectors for the starfighters. We have sixty unarmed ships out there and it's *our* job to make sure we don't lose any!"

Russell left her to it and stepped up behind Cosner.

"Get me details, son," he said quietly.

"They're at five hundred thousand kilometers, closing at two thousand kilometers per second," the scanner tech reported.

"They're *in* missile range," Russell realized. "Get me Tomacino!"

"Too late," the tech whispered, gesturing at the screen.

The five starfighters had just brought their drives up at full power and were pushing up from the gas giant they'd hidden their acceleration behind. They'd approached from wherever they'd been patrolling in the system and used Aurelius 4A to set up a slingshot maneuver and "sneak" up on the depot with their engines down.

All five fighters launched, sending twenty missiles blasting toward the collection of shuttles and small transport ships Shine was attempting to coordinate. Only some of them had any kind of antimissile defenses at all, and *Chameleon*'s defenses couldn't cover them all.

"CAG, this is Tomacino," Echo Squadron's acting commander's voice sounded in his ear. "I see them. We are vectoring to intercept the missiles."

"Bravo is on their way to reinforce you," Russell told the younger man, as if that made a difference. Even as they spoke, a second salvo of twenty missiles launched into space. Bravo Squadron would be able to drop missiles on the Terrans, make sure that none of the Katanas survived their suicide strike, but they wouldn't be able to intervene in the missile strike.

The only way to save the shuttles was to put Echo Squadron's six starfighters between them and the missiles—and then use their ECM to lure the missiles to them.

"We will do our duty, sir," Tomacino said calmly, far more calmly than Russell would have felt in his place.

The only way to save the shuttles was to make the missiles try to kill Echo Squadron.

———

"Missiles away," Taylor announced grimly.

Kyle nodded absently, studying the tactical plot as he tried to see a way out of the situation for the squadron trapped between the oncoming Terrans and the defenseless small craft now swarming to try and hide behind *Chameleon*.

The Q-ship was locked to the station but, unlike in New Edmonton, they had missiles to spend this time. Six Stormwinds flashed into space toward the attacking starfighters, and a dozen Javelins followed them.

More Javelins followed in rapid succession, Taylor putting salvo after salvo of the smaller missiles into space in a counter-missile pattern that would cover the space shuttles…eventually.

"Their third salvo doesn't stand a chance," she told him. "Their second… we'll only get one salvo in space in time to intercept. That's twelve missiles against twenty."

He nodded again, more grimly. On a good day, a Javelin had a thirty percent success rate as a counter-missile, which meant most of that second salvo would get through.

Worse, there was *nothing* they could do about the first twenty missiles.

"Bravo Squadron has launched on the Katanas," Chownyk reported. The XO was on the bridge for once, but had readily taken up his normal role relaying information from the CIC crew. "We're assessing a zero percent survival chance—those bastards are done."

"They knew that going in," Kyle said quietly. "They were hoping to get to lance range, but they launched as soon as they were seen."

He crunched the numbers in his implant, but it didn't change anything. They'd disabled Aurelius Station's antimissile defenses to stop any loose Terrans from turning them on the shuttles. *Chameleon's* own defenses provided a safe zone that covered many of the unarmed craft, but those first two salvos would reach the ships outside that zone before they could evade.

"There's nothing else we can do," he told his bridge crew, his voice calm and confident. Somehow. "It's up to Tomacino's people."

———

RUSSELL WRACKED his brain as the Terrans closed, trying to find *some* way that they could intervene from there, but it all boiled down to hard math. The Katanas had launched sixty missiles and Echo Squadron had six starfighters.

Any missiles from the first two salvos that got through would kill shuttles. About a third of the spacecraft under threat had the same crew as the starfighters—a Navy pilot, copilot, and engineer. The rest…had more. Bigger crews on larger craft. Shuttles with passengers.

"Cosner," he snapped. "Keep those arrays on the Terrans. At this range, *Chameleon* should be able to read the damn *serial numbers* on the missiles. Feed the data back to Echo."

"On it!" the tech replied.

It was all he could give Flight Lieutenant Tomacino, but it wasn't nothing. At this range, focusing *Chameleon*'s main radar arrays would overwhelm any attempt to jam scanners or otherwise obfuscate the missiles' location.

Normally, that kind of focus was dangerous, but anything that *hadn't* been hiding in Aurelius 4A's shadow would be seen coming—and anything following the Katanas would be caught in the same focused scans.

"We've got them dialed in," Shine said quietly at his shoulder. "Will it be enough?"

"It has to be," Russell replied harshly.

More icons flashed onto the screen as Tomacino's people launched their own Javelins, emptying their magazines in less than twenty seconds to send thirty-six missiles into the teeth of the Terrans' twenty.

Explosions rippled through space as the salvos intersected, three sets of explosions lighting the sky as each of the Federation salvos struck home.

Even with the radar hammering the entire area, the explosions from the last missile intercept faded to reveal *far* too many surviving missiles. There were a few seconds of silence, then Echo Squadron's lasers and positron lances ripped into the remaining missiles and lit up a new series of explosions.

The series of fireballs reached a crescendo and then faded away to show only four starfighters remaining—but none of the missiles had made it through.

"*Chameleon*'s missiles intercepting," Cosner reported softly.

There were a lot fewer missiles to intercept the incoming weapons this time, though they did better than the Federation crews had any right to expect. Fully half of the second salvo disappeared in the massive fireballs of mutual annihilation.

The last ten missiles bore down on Echo Squadron's four remaining starfighters and Russell held his breath in horror as their defensive suites reached out and met the incoming.

He waited.

"Breakthrough!" Cosner snapped. "We have two missiles running in—they're heading for the station!"

That wasn't a possibility that had occurred to Rokos. Destroying the depot station would kill several thousand TCN personnel—but it would also prevent *Chameleon* from stealing any more of the vast quantities of munitions and other resources aboard the platform.

It wasn't the call he would have made, but he could see the logic of the Terran commander. They'd committed to a suicide mission and apparently had decided everyone *else* got to die as well.

"There has to be *something*," he whispered. "*Chameleon*'s defenses cover the station, right?"

"They should," Shine agreed. "It depends on… *Son of a bitch!*"

Both missiles blew apart as *something* blurred back around.

"Report!" the shift supervisor demanded.

"One of our assault shuttles," Cosner said slowly. "Navy Chief Poulson piloting. She…got one with the lasers."

"They're both gone," Shine replied, then paused as what Cosner had said caught up. "My Gods."

"She rammed the other," the tech said quietly. "There was no one else aboard."

"What about Echo Squadron?" Russell demanded, his attention turning back to his people as he confirmed the station was safe—the last salvo had run into the solid wall of *Chameleon*'s missiles, and the Katanas were running from the missiles Taylor had earmarked for them.

"I have...one fighter on the screens," Cosner reported after a moment of silence. "Flight Lieutenant Volger's Echo Three, sir. No one else."

"Please tell me those bastards aren't getting away," Russell said, his voice feeling carved from stone.

31

20:00 June 6, 2736 Earth Standard Meridian Date/Time
Chameleon

"THERE WAS a four-person flight crew on assault shuttle nine when Chief Poulson realized what was going on," Chownyk reported quietly to the rest of *Chameleon*'s senior officers. "There wasn't even enough time for her to explain what was happening; the gap between the missiles breaking past Echo Squadron and her interception zone was twenty-two seconds.

"Assault shuttles are designed for hostile environments and have seat-by-seat ejection mechanisms for an emergency. Chief Poulson triggered all of them but hers and then went after the missiles."

The briefing room was silent for a long moment.

"Aurelius Station is not designed for combat," the XO noted. "While most warships can take several near misses or even a direct hit and stay in action, the depot could not. A single gigaton-range warhead would have vaporized approximately forty percent of the station and killed at least five hundred of our people and most of the Terran prisoners aboard."

"We lost sixteen people today," Kyle said grimly. "They sacrificed themselves to save over three thousand. Lieutenant Tomacino knew exactly what he was doing when he put his squadron in front of those missiles. Chief Poulson could have followed orders, evaded action exactly as she was supposed to."

But she'd had the only armed spacecraft with an interception profile. She'd made the same choice Kyle would have in her place, and he saluted her for it.

"While the files and details will be classified and buried, I've recommended all of Tomacino's flight crew for Stars of Heroism and recommended the Senatorial Medal of Valor for Chief Becca Poulson."

Flight Lieutenant Vogel and his two crew members would receive the only awards on that list that *weren't* posthumous. They were heroes, but the records would be sealed. No one would ever know why those pilots and crew had never come home.

"With the destruction of that patrol, I believe we have accounted for any remaining loose starfighters," Kyle noted, "but we do have three of our Q-probes sweeping the system for further stragglers. Their vectors will bring them back aboard in twenty-four hours.

"That will guard our back while we finish loading—and when they return, we are leaving this system," he finished firmly. "Is that going to be a problem?"

"The Scimitars are aboard and being checked out," Rokos reported. "The last of the Cataphracts were heading into storage as I came over here, and we have two squadrons of the Scimitars ready to deploy. Flight Ops will be ready to go in twenty-four hours."

"I'd prefer longer," Chownyk admitted, "but we already have the munitions we needed aboard. We're loading food and spare parts at this point. *Chameleon* still has a lot more cargo capacity than any warship, so it would take us longer to fill her cargo holds than we've *got*." He shrugged. "We can make twenty-four hours work."

"Anyone else?" Kyle asked, glancing around at Taylor, Lau and Glass.

"Good," he concluded. "We are a little over thirteen days from Tau

Ceti. We'll engage in a little bit of deception as we leave, which will bring us up to approximately fourteen days.

"We will not be stopping for long along the way. If there is *anything* you need to do in real space, it needs to be done in the next twenty-four hours."

"What about memorial services, sir?" Chownyk asked.

"We don't have an obelisk aboard," Kyle replied sadly. Any Castle Federation warship carried a white stone obelisk with the names of every human being who'd died aboard her engraved in it. Having one for *Chameleon*, however, would have risked betraying her true origins should she fall into Commonwealth hands.

"I'll talk to the crew come morning," he promised. "It's been a rough few days, so I think it's time we told them our final destination. They need to know—Gods, we *all* need to know—that this is going to be worth it."

————

EDVARD HADN'T QUITE fallen asleep when the door to his quarters buzzed for admittance. It was late at night and anything *truly* urgent should be arriving via implant message with a priority code.

He was seriously considering ignoring it when it buzzed again.

With a sigh, he pulled up the hallway footage and saw Riley standing outside his door, glancing back and forth around the hallway. Sighing again, he pinged the door to let her in and got out of bed.

"What is it, Sandra?" he asked as he stepped out of the sleeping cubicle.

She paused on seeing him and carefully looked him up and down, a gesture that made him remember that he slept in shorts.

"Lieutenant?" he said sharply.

"Sorry, sir. Yes, sir," she replied, yanking her gaze back to his face. "We may have a problem, sir."

"I'm noticing," Edvard told her.

"*Not* that," Riley replied. To his surprise, he realized she was *blushing*—and that his own face was growing warm.

"What kind of problem, Sandra?" he asked, throwing his uniform jacket on to cover his torso and reduce the awkwardness of the situation.

"I'm worried one of my friends is about to go off the deep end," she admitted. "If I'm *wrong*, even suggesting this could wreck their career. But if I'm right…"

"Last I checked, all of your friends on this ship were covert operators," Edvard said quietly. "That's *not* my idea of people we want 'going off the deep end'."

"Well, *you're* not a covert operator," she pointed out, then sighed. "Look, boss…Edvard. I have no illusions here. *Lieutenant* Riley has a legal and moral obligation to report my suspicions and have my friend arrested.

"But that would destroy them. Completely."

"So you're hoping for a compromise of some kind," he replied. "What do you want from me, Sandra? I am not in the habit of making special cases for my subordinates," he warned her.

With her in his quarters late at night, he was currently quite aware of how attractive he found her. He still wasn't going to let that influence his decisions if he possible could.

"I'd hope not," Riley said. "I want… I need authorization to put together a contingency plan." She swallowed, then nodded firmly. "MP override access to the ship's sensor suites and having at least a few of my people on standby at all times."

Those were relatively small requests. Edvard could guess who Riley was concerned about, and she was right—if they had a serious concern, they *did* have a legal obligation to detain them. But…

"All right," he told her. "On one condition."

"Name it."

"The instant you have *anything* beyond a bad feeling, *any* evidence that anything is actually being planned, we shut her down hard. No second chances, Sandra. Not even *first* chances. Understand?"

"Yes, sir," she said crisply. "And…thank you, Edvard."

He flashed her a smile that he knew was not entirely appropriate for their professional relationship.

"Get out of my quarters, Lieutenant Riley."

KYLE SAT in the center of the hive of activity that filled *Chameleon*'s bridge in the morning, watching his crew go about their tasks. Everyone was busy, but there was a subdued tone to the affair as well. It was always harder, he knew, to lose people *after* the battle was supposed to be won.

He tapped a command, linking him into the ship's PA system.

"This is the Captain speaking," he announced, pausing a moment to let people slow down and pay attention.

"This trip has been a series of gut-punches for us all," he admitted. "We've lost a lot of Space Force people and Marines. We lost people aboard *Chameleon* to the near miss when we took this system, and now Poulson and more fighter crews to the stragglers.

"You all know we're on a black operation. There will be no obelisk here to carry the names of our lost forward in the memory of the fleet. No records of their heroism. The citations for their awards will be classified until long after we're all dead.

"Worse, because it's a black op, you don't know what's happening. You're not sure *what* Poulson and Tomacino and the others died for.

"We've all had our small memorial services for our own immediate comrades, but without the obelisk, we haven't gathered as a *crew* to mourn our dead. And that hurts. We've lost brothers and sisters, but haven't stood together as a family to remember them.

"Today, we're buried in work, making sure *Chameleon* is ready for what's to come. Once we're under way once again, we'll hold that memorial service, I promise."

He sighed.

"We'll hold it because we may not get another chance, people," he warned them. "From here we are going to the heart of the Commonwealth, to challenge the defenses of the Tau Ceti Naval Yards.

"The Terrans are developing a new type of starfighter weapon, one that could leave us outclassed as well as outnumbered," he said grimly. "If Walkingstick gets these weapons without us knowing what we're facing, he may cut all the way to Castle before we can stop him.

"No other ship can do this, and I'd have no other crew aboard her when we strike at the heart of the Commonwealth," Kyle continued fiercely. "The Federation and the Alliance are relying on us to learn everything we can—and to put the fear of the night in the Commonwealth.

"Today, their leaders look to the stars and are confident that all humanity will be unified and kneel to Terra—to them! When we're done, they'll look to the stars and wonder where the next attack is coming from!"

32

Aurelius System
21:00 June 7, 2736 Earth Standard Meridian Date/Time
Chameleon

KYLE LEANED back in his seat and tried not to openly heave a sigh of relief as *Chameleon* pulled away from the Aurelius Depot. He'd been *reasonably* confident there were no more straggler patrols hanging around the system, but the five starfighters they *had* missed had extracted far too high a toll.

As the Q-ship passed the one-light-second mark, Kyle gave Taylor a silent nod.

Several seconds later, the light from a series of massive explosions reached them. They had rigged every single one of the ancillary stations and cargo pods to detonate—after carefully evacuating them.

The primary depot station remained intact, though it had deep wounds carved into its hull where Kyle's people had removed the vaults of valuables—and later destroyed its weapons to make sure there were no clever ideas as *Chameleon* withdrew.

The rest of the depot, still containing billions of Federation stellars' worth of supplies, came apart in a blaze of multi-gigaton antimatter warheads that almost certainly flash-blinded any sensors they'd missed when they'd crippled the station.

"What a waste," Kyle said aloud. "We could have rearmed an entire *fleet* from those supplies."

"So could the Commonwealth," Glass noted.

"The plan was mine, Mister Glass," the Q-ship's Captain reminded him with a smile. "I don't regret it for a moment. It's still a waste."

"Indeed. If Trickster's forces hadn't been crippled by betrayal, I would have suggested inviting them to come take their pick," the spy said. "It would have had risks, of course, but the backup might have been useful."

"The risks would have outweighed the benefits," Kyle replied. "And that was *before* their organization decided to start shooting at itself."

Turning away from the spy, he studied their course outsystem.

"Commander Lau," he barked. "Do you have our course?"

"Yes," the navigator replied. "Twelve-hour detour. Thirteen-day, ten-hour flight to Tau Ceti."

Lau's terseness technically bordered on insubordination, though Kyle was *mostly* used to it by now.

"Take us out, Commander Lau," Kyle ordered. "Warp space at your discretion once we're clear of the gravity wells."

———

WHEN THEY WENT FTL an hour later, Kyle was in his office and *did* allow himself to sigh in relief.

Aurelius had turned out well, but it had been a near-run thing. Their plan had been predicated on potential cut-outs and risk reduction...and had promptly blown up in their face when they'd run into an unexpected patrol.

"I see you're as pleased to see the end of that system as I am," Glass noted. The spy had his feet propped up on the second chair in front of Kyle's desk as he sipped at one of the Captain's beers. "I have to apologize, Captain—not knowing they had Katanas falls on me, not you."

"Given that we didn't know the Katana *existed* until Ostrowski sold us that data, I'd say we have a bigger intelligence failure than that," Kyle pointed out. "What I'm hearing from the front is that if we hadn't sent in that warning, Walkingstick would have jumped our fleets with the Katana before anyone expected it."

"We did know the Katana existed," Glass corrected. "But it was supposed to be six months from deployment. Part of the original plan for this operation was to find and destroy the first few production lines to delay that further." He shrugged. "We gave up on that before you were recruited for this op," he noted dryly. "You're right that we should have known they were being deployed, though," he admitted. "I raised the same point to Admiral O'Neill rather, ah, forcefully. We have agents and spy ships in the Commonwealth, and so do our allies. We should *not* have been surprised by a mass deployment of new starfighters."

Admiral Jacqueline O'Neill was the uniformed commander of the Federation's Joint Department of Intelligence or JD-Intel. If Glass was directly talking to her—and with enough comfort to do so "forcefully" —that placed him higher in JD-Intel's hierarchy than his usual presentation suggested.

It wasn't the first such clue and Kyle filed it away in the back of his mind.

"So, what happened?" he asked.

"We're not sure, but we think the TCN's weapons development team pulled a fast one on us," Glass said after a long swallow of beer. "They've been running both starfighter and starship development in the Monroe system for fifteen years. They kept up enough of a show of starfighter prototypes and tests to keep our attention focused, while actually completing the Katana project and starting this *new* starfighter project somewhere else.

"We don't know where," he admitted. "We're not even sure *when* they made the shift, but we have people trying to backtrack it all now.

"Without knowing where they're carrying on the research, we have no idea how far along they are with the starfighters and their new missiles," he said grimly. "We *need* the data at that Tau Ceti R&D facility—they may be hiding the development, but any mass production will be authorized at that station, which means that full data *must* be there."

"What if it isn't?" Kyle asked, a thought bringing up a map of the galaxy on the wallscreen. "Monroe is forty-two light-years from Tau Ceti. Forty-four from Sol. It's not exactly convenient to anywhere, so they could have picked somewhere just as inconvenient for their new project site.

"Why run hardware and schematics through Tau Ceti at all? If the Navy HQ in Sol approves it, they can disperse it via Q-Com."

"Navy HQ won't even *look* at anything the R&D base at Tau Ceti hasn't vetted," Glass replied. "They got burned during the last war when a friend of a member of the Committee got a starfighter design rushed into deployment that proved... Well, it was the Dagger type."

Kyle winced. The Dagger type had been one of the first starfighter designs the Commonwealth had deployed—and on at least ten different occasions had blown *itself* to pieces when firing its positron lance.

"So TCN has a team of engineers and scientists whose sole job is to make sure everything the Commonwealth puts into full production is actually worth the resources," Glass continued. "At this point, they're actually the people who draw up the final manufacturing schematics.

"If those new ships are anywhere *near* ready to fly, the schematics are at the Tau Ceti R&D Station. Ostrowski's data suggests they'll be delivered in three days.

"So long as they're there, we need to steal them."

"That's a tall order," Kyle noted. "I'm guessing the place is surrounded by no-fly zones and starfighters and warships?"

"Exactly. Every detail we have is the file I'm flipping you right now," Glass told him. "The system is busy enough that we can get close, but we're going to have to board the station by force and defend ourselves while Hansen finds the data we need.

"We'll need a distraction. The shipyards make the best target, but they're all solidly defended."

"I'll go over it with my staff," Kyle promised. "We have two weeks."

"If anyone can work it out, it's you," the spy allowed. "This deep a smash-and-grab wasn't in the original cards."

Kyle grinned broadly, a confidence that had grown unfamiliar warming him as he studied the spy's data.

"Then you picked the right Captain." He thought for a moment. "I don't suppose we actually have *Chameleon*'s original *Christopher Lee* IFF codes on file?"

——————

MORNING SAW Kyle standing in a mostly clear spot in one of the cargo holds, watching a significant portion of his crew find their seats in the chairs set up amidst the crates of food. One end of the cleared zone was now filled with a set of tables holding an array of the higher-quality foods they'd acquired courtesy of the Terran Commonwealth Navy.

Aboard a main-line Federation warship, he would be standing next to the stone obelisk, reading off the names of the dead while robots laser-etched the names into the plinth. With no plinth and no robot, they were improvising.

Castle's traditional wake informed the traditions of the Federation's military. They'd managed to improvise the braziers to burn incense, and the traditional paper lanterns drifted above. Most importantly, they still had *food*.

"Spacers of the Castle Federation," Kyle said after he was sure most of the people present were paying attention. "My brothers- and sisters-in-arms.

"It is never easy to lose friends and comrades. Never easy to say goodbye. This memorial remembers for us, as if we would ever forget."

The words were formal, as much part of the tradition as the food and the lantern. Kyle had only heard them once before the lead-up to the war, in the aftermath of the *Ansem Gulf* incident that had earned him his first Star of Heroism.

Now he could recite the words from memory without even using his implant.

"We remember," he told his people, letting the formal words echo into the silence.

"We remember Flight Commander Andrea Zitnick," he began, listing off the dead in decreasing order of rank.

———

EDVARD STOOD SILENTLY at the edge of the wake. He'd released his company from the training schedule to allow them to attend the ship's memorial service, another layer of shared relief to salve his company's painful losses.

Today, though, he wasn't joining his Marines in drinking the sorrows away. If nothing else, it was still too early for an official ship function to include alcohol—though he assumed it was out there.

He had taken a coffee and a plate of food, but today he was watching the crowd. Without an official ship's marshal or MP detachment, *Chameleon*'s law-enforcement needs ran through him. So far, the pressure of being this far out and being under the command of the Stellar Fox himself had kept those needs to a slow burn, on the low end for the number of crew they had aboard.

The shock of their losses at New Edmonton and Aurelius could easily change that. He was more concerned about his own people than anything else, but they'd also lost Navy personnel when the near miss had washed over *Chameleon*.

The Space Force losses had been even worse than his own. The black-ops squadron was basically *gone,* and the others were all down a flight crew or two. From forty crews, he understood Rokos's wing to be down to *twenty-six*, with almost fifty dead along the way due to the Cataphracts' lack of escape pods.

Chameleon's crew had been hammered and they were a *long* way from home. They'd been buried in work in Aurelius, but he'd already had three fights reported this morning. The tension aboard the ship was starting to ratchet up.

So far, he had no evidence—other than Riley's concern over her "friend"—that anything serious was being planned. Fistfights weren't even worth bothering the Captain with, but if someone was planning real violence, it would be *stopped*.

Which left Edvard Hansen standing on the edge of the party, watching his fellow crewmates, and wondering if any of them were close enough to cracking to be a problem.

Today, he hated his job.

33

Deep Space, Under Alcubierre Drive
10:00 June 9, 2736 Earth Standard Meridian Date/Time
Chameleon

RUSSELL LOOKED around his remaining squadron commanders' faces with a heavy feeling in his chest. With Cavendish grounded and only one flight crew left of the entire squadron, he'd dissolved Echo Squadron. Flight Lieutenant Vogel and his crew were now part of Alpha Squadron.

That left only four faces in the room. Four faces who represented only twenty-six flight crew, few enough that he could easily have reorganized into *three* squadrons.

"All right, people," he told them. "We've had a full day in deep space to start sorting out our teething difficulties and get the squadrons in order. Where are we at?"

Flight Commander Churchill, CO of Alpha Squadron, shook his head.

"We're flying enemy fighters with shit for guns two hundred

light-years from home on a suicide mission, and we're down almost half the damn wing," he said flatly. "I mean, my people have spines and they're *up* for it, but we're a ways past 'teething difficulties', CAG."

Russell grunted.

"Fair," he allowed. "Your people are up for it. Are *you*?"

Churchill straightened in his chair and glared back at him.

"Yes," he said, his tone still flat. "But damn it, CAG, we can't fly into a *Core System* with twenty-six starfighters and expect to live."

"The Captain has a plan," Russell told him, hoping that was true. He had to *get* said plan out of Roberts shortly. If it didn't exist, they'd need to *make* it. "Lucky for *you*, Churchill, you're going to get to hand those Scimitars back.

"Wait, what?" his Alpha leader asked, finally losing the stone in his voice.

"Glass's people have cracked the security on two of the Katanas," Rokos told his people. "They're prepared to guarantee us an eight-ship squadron by the thirteenth. That gives Alpha Squadron a week to get used to the birds, which is the *minimum* I'm willing to see anyone go into combat with a new starfighter with."

"Okay, so eight of our crews—meaning I'm poaching people from one of these guys"—Churchill gestured at the other squadron commanders—"have fighters worth the antimatter to blow them away. It'll take a few more seconds for us all to die."

"I have no intention of dying at Tau Ceti," Russell replied. "If that's where the Void takes me, fine, but I'm sure as Stars not planning on it. I don't think the Captain is planning on dying there either, or on *spending* us with no chance of survival.

"But you're right," he conceded. "So long as we're down to barely *three* squadrons, the odds are worse than they are with five."

"To be honest, I'm not sure three squadrons versus five makes that much difference," Churchill said slowly. "It's going to be a game of smoke and mirrors anyway."

"But having five squadrons we can deploy gives us a few more mirrors, doesn't it?" Russell asked with a grin. "We have the birds. What we don't have is flight crew. So what I need from all of you is a list of the fourteen gunners and flight engineers with the most simulator and live flight hours."

His Flight Commanders looked at him in shock as what he was asking for sank in.

"We can borrow engineers and gunners from the Navy," he continued. "They'll likely be borderline for implant capacity and their skill sets won't line up perfectly, but if we have people who are close to their wings to *fly* the damn things, I can live with less efficient repairs and potentially needing to coordinate salvos at the squadron level.

"Can we do that, people?"

Russell swept his gaze across his leaders. One was a brevet promotion, bumped to replace Flight Commander Zitnick. He'd have to reinstate Cavendish to flight status to command the fifth squadron, but he figured he could find her a mission that didn't have her in range of *him* with gigaton-range weapons.

"Wilco," Churchill said after a long moment. "We'll make it happen."

"Good. Because if we don't, the Commonwealth may just spring a surprise on the Alliance we're *not* ready for," the CAG warned them. "I won't tell you the entire fate of the war turns on this mission—there will be other chances to turn the tide, I'm sure.

"But if we pull this together and we carry this off, well." He smiled grimly. "It's a shame this will all be classified, because that story would be worth free beer for *life!*"

———

KYLE WAITED as the steward finished pouring the coffee, watching as his three senior officers settled in at the small table in his dining room. With the Commander Air Group, Executive Officer, and Tactical Officer in the room, everyone with a stake in how *Chameleon* was run and fought sat around the table with steaming plates of spaghetti in front of them.

"Sir, I…"

"Eat, Rokos," Kyle ordered as the CAG tried to bring up business. "You being here convinced the cooks not to try anything complicated tonight, which I wish I could convince them of *every* night," he observed with a chuckle. "There'll be time for business."

The CAG shrugged and dug into the food, following the Captain's example. Taylor and Chownyk, used to Kyle's foibles by now, were equally prompt.

"How's your wife, CAG?" Kyle asked as the pace of chewing slowed slightly.

"She managed to get herself promoted again," Rokos replied after a moment. "If she keeps this up, she'll be running the precinct by Christmas!"

The CAG's wife was a ranking police officer on New Amazon. Kyle wasn't entirely familiar with her rank or even the rank structure of the municipal police force she worked for, but he was *reasonably* certain Rokos was exaggerating.

"She felt she needed to catch up, did she?" he asked. Rokos, like most of the old *Avalon*'s crew, had been promoted after the Battle of Tranquility. They didn't stand out as much now, as war was having its usual impact on the Federation's neat tables of 'required time in grade'. Kyle himself had been one of the youngest officers the Federation had ever promoted to O-7.

"She can break me with one hand tied behind her back," the CAG replied. "I wouldn't *dare* imply anything of the sort!"

"How's Captain Solace?" Rokos continued after a moment. "I heard Seventh Fleet got jumped."

"Mira remains as unflappable as usual," Kyle allowed, remembering her tired video in the aftermath of the battle. "Thanks to our warning about the Katanas, they turned the Commonwealth back." He laughed softly. "From the sounds of it, she may end up with a star before I do. Reversing our initial problem would be…irritating, if ironic."

"That was a shock to the entire crew," Rokos pointed out. "I don't think most of us even realized something was a *possibility* until she was on *Camerone* and you two were openly together."

"Even in wartime, the Articles come down like a ton of bricks on something like that," Chownyk pointed out. "I saw my first Captain drummed out of the service for it, though reading between the lines, the JAG running the hearing figured he'd been doing more than asking nicely to get his XO into bed."

Kyle tried not to visibly shiver at Chownyk's comment. He'd done a decent job of convincing *himself* he hadn't noticed his old XO's attractiveness, but he could see ways that the intimate but hierarchical relationship between Captain and XO could be abused.

He'd been celibate the entire time between abandoning his pregnant high-school girlfriend to join the Space Force and reconciling with her after the Battle of Tranquility, so he trusted *his* restraint—if not necessarily his relationship judgment.

He *hoped* that no one would end up in command of a warship without a similar level of restraint, but the fact that the rules existed and had been enforced in the memory of the four officers in the room suggested otherwise.

"How do you make it work?" Taylor asked. "There was…a pilot aboard *Sunset*. She and I hit it off, but with the war…" The young Commander shrugged. "Now I'm *two* ranks senior to her, and one of us could die, and… I just don't know, sir."

"Your last two points are key," Kyle said quietly. "One of you could die. And you don't know." That realization was what had led him to reconcile with his son and the boy's mother. It was also why, despite the habits of a dozen years, he hadn't pushed Mira away when she'd, well, jumped him.

"We might not come back from Tau Ceti. *Sunset* could be sent to the front. Your friend could be transferred to one of the new ships heading to the front. Gods, Castle could be attacked again.

"Military personnel since the dawn of time have dealt with long spells apart and not knowing who may or may not come home," he said gently. "It's not easy. But…it's part of the job, and if we can't take the joke…"

"We shouldn't have signed up," she agreed, smiling slightly. "That…actually helps, sir. Thank you."

"Whatever you do," he warned her, "don't rely solely on *my* relationship advice! I just follow Captain Solace's lead and pretend I have a clue what's going on!"

That seemed to break whatever tension Taylor's question had

raised. He gave her a reassuring nod and she returned it, her smile broadening. Hopefully, that had helped—and he suspected a certain pilot aboard *Sunset* was going to have at least one *very* good evening when *Chameleon* made it home.

If *Chameleon* made it home.

"CAG, you had something you wanted to talk to us about?" he asked Rokos. That request was what had triggered this dinner invitation, after all, and everyone was clearly done eating. He could probably allow business to start now.

Rokos paused, clearly marshaling his thoughts as the steward cleared away the plates and refilled the coffee cups again.

"We've lost thirty-five percent of the fighter wing so far," he began, his voice low. "Normally, we'd have retrieved at least a third and more likely half of the flight crews aboard those starfighters. Acquiring the Scimitars and Katanas we picked up at Aurelius would allow us to put those crews back into space, and we'd be down less than a single squadron."

The dinner table was silent. The lack of escape pods aboard the League starfighters was a disturbing sign of how highly the *condottieri* carrier commanders regarded the flight crews that actually did the fighting and dying in the League's semi-formalized internal wars.

"Having lost every one of those flight crews as KIA, the fighter wing has lost a lot of capability," he concluded. "I don't know what the plan is for Tau Ceti, but I can't imagine that loss of capability is going to do us any favors."

"I have only the barest skeleton of a plan so far," Kyle admitted. And since *his* plan depended on Glass coming up with the original TCN IFF codes for the ship, he wasn't pulling his officers in to build on that skeleton yet. "But I'm guessing you have an idea for making up that capacity?"

Rokos nodded.

"I have three gunners and a flight engineer who have completed the sim and live flight hours to qualify for their wings," he explained. "There's formalities and procedures, but I can arrange those. Those four I can make pilots without hesitation.

"I have ten *more* gunners and engineers who have at least half of the flight hours to qualify," Rokos continued grimly. "Regs say the Captain has to sign off on my putting *them* in cockpits."

"And that will still leave you short over forty engineers and gunners," Kyle concluded aloud, thinking. With "only" about three thousand people aboard, the odds were that they didn't even have forty people with enough implant bandwidth to properly link into the starfighter.

"We might have enough people aboard with the bandwidth capacity, but only a few would have appropriate training," Chownyk noted, echoing Kyle's own thoughts. "They'd slow you down...but I guess better slow fighters than no fighters."

"Exactly," Rokos told them. "If I can't get people with both the training and the implant bandwidth, I'll take people with the training: missileers and engineers trained in drone and nanotech work."

"Taylor, Chownyk?" Kyle asked.

"I'll have to talk to my Chiefs," Taylor said swiftly, suggesting that she'd clearly learned the *key* rule of how to run a department aboard a Navy warship. "But I *think* we can pull people out of the launcher crews who are rated to target and run a missile launch. They won't be able to do much *else* aboard your fighters, but we made sure everyone aboard *Chameleon* was rated for both capital and fighter missiles."

She paused, considering. "They'll all be enlisted, though," she pointed out. "Possibly not even Petty Officers."

"If any of my people has a problem with an enlisted running their missiles, I'll set them damn straight," Rokos growled. "We put three people on a starfighter for a *reason*."

"I'll have to check with Ajam and *his* Chiefs, but I'd guess the engineers will be the same," Chownyk concluded. "They'll have the skills but not the implant bandwidth or the commission."

"If they can run the nano-repair and the drones at *all*, we need them. We won't be at a hundred percent efficiency, but better forty fighters at eighty percent than twenty-six at one hundred."

"Run it through the Chiefs, people," Kyle told them, "but *make it work*. We have few enough resources for this mission as it is. If we can get the Wing back up to strength, that gives us options."

He glanced back at Rokos.

"You'll need me to sign off on another promotion to Flight Commander?" he asked.

"A bunch of Junior Lieutenants to Flight Lieutenants," Rokos replied, "but I don't need a Flight Commander. I'm going to have to unground Cavendish—I don't know if I can *trust* her, but I *do* know she can do the job."

"It's your call," Kyle told him. Reinstating the black-ops pilot would make Glass happier, he knew, but he also had no hesitation backing Rokos's decision to ground her.

"She can fight," the CAG said grimly. "I just don't want her *behind* me."

———

IN THE INVIOLABLE sanctuary of Alcubierre-Stetson drive, it was an open question amongst military theoreticians and actual officers just *what* the best use of the crew's time was. Most agreed that maintaining the ship—primarily the drive itself—was a key priority, but that was hardly enough to fully occupy the thousands-strong crew needed to run the ship safely in real space.

Exercises, training, paperwork—these were the things that kept the crew occupied in FTL. This worked most efficiently when the entire crew was on the same day cycle, resulting in the "FTL dark watch" by the middle of any long flight—a watch where only the minimum crew were on duty.

They were over an hour into that watch when Russell stepped into PriFly. Given that flight operations were impossible in FTL, it was a truly skeleton crew holding down the dark watch here—two Petty Officers, a Chief Petty Officer, and Flight Commander Laura Cavendish.

She sat on the central command chair like it was a throne, her eyes darting from screen to screen in silence. Despite the appearance of rigid control and utter coldness, however, Russell could see from the *door* that one of the Petty Officers was playing a video game and the other was reading a novel, both on their work consoles.

Perhaps she wasn't as much of a lost cause as he thought.

Smiling to himself, he stepped into the control center.

"Good evening, people," he rumbled, attracting everyone's attention and ignoring the not-particularly-surreptitious activation of "boss programs" to switch screens away from their technically illicit uses.

"Chief Lipskold, if you could take the Commander's watch, please?" he asked. "I'm sure you're up to the many and varied challenges."

His airy hand wave covered the mostly blank screens of the room.

"Commander Cavendish, my office, please," he instructed.

He turned on his heel, taking an admittedly somewhat childish pleasure in upending everyone's evening, and walked the exactly fifteen steps to his office. Swinging behind his desk and taking a seat, he waited for Cavendish as he dug through his desk.

"What do you need, sir?" Cavendish asked. The appropriateness of her words was more than a little undermined by the impatience and disgust *dripping* off her tone.

He sighed. Unfortunately, he *needed* her more than he needed to *like* her.

"Here." He slid her wings across the table. "I'm un-grounding you and placing you back in command of Echo Squadron."

"You dissolved Echo Squadron after you got almost all of my people *killed*," she snapped. "What exactly am I assuming command of?"

"The same hodgepodge of qualified crews, unqualified pilots, and co-opted Navy personnel the rest of us will be leading," he said flatly. "We're pulling together forty flight crews that *probably* won't accidentally blow themselves to bits when they launch. We have ten days to train them on Scimitars and Katanas, and then we will take them into action against impossible odds to try and turn the tide of this war.

"You're a hothead and I can't trust you, but you're also one of the only experienced squadron commanders I have," he told her. "I need you."

"A little late to be admitting that, isn't it?" she snapped.

"*Don't* assume I can't promote someone else," Russell warned you. "This is a second chance—but a lot of people died at New Edmonton because of you. Fuck up again and I will end your *career*. Do you understand me, Commander Cavendish?"

She nodded sharply.

"I understand that you're desperate," she said. "Make no mistake, *Commander*; there will be a reckoning for my people's deaths. But I'll take your squadron. I've trained worse."

"Good," he said after a moment's silence, more shaken by her implied threat than he could let her see. "I'll see you at the squadron commander's briefing in the morning.

"Good night, Commander."

34

Deep Space, Under Alcubierre Drive
15:00 June 10, 2736 Earth Standard Meridian Date/Time
Chameleon

"Do you think it will work?"

Kyle considered Chownyk's comment as he and his XO stood on one corner of the flight briefing, currently packed with the mix of Navy and Space Force personnel who were going to be taking his ship's fighters into combat.

"It doesn't have to work perfectly," he said quietly. The five Flight Commanders were moving through the crowds, passing out flight crew assignments. "It just has to work well enough to get every one of those starfighters into space.

"They'll do well enough for that," he concluded. It wouldn't be the first time a star nation had put people into starfighters who didn't have enough implant bandwidth to enter the full immersion network normally used to fly the smaller ships. You couldn't *pilot* a starfighter effectively without it, not in a combat environment, but it wasn't *as* necessary to have the gunner and flight engineer able to join the network.

"Even if they were only going to be flying at half capability—which they're not—just having the birds in the air makes a huge difference," Kyle continued. They would arrive late in the day on June Twenty-First, which gave him almost eleven days to percolate his plan.

The first planning sessions were tomorrow. However this mess broke down, it wasn't going to be pretty—but having five full squadrons of Commonwealth starfighters was going to help.

"A third of the people flying them have never even set foot in a starfighter before," Chownyk noted aloud. "I can't help but worry."

"Rokos has ten days to get them in order. A hundred hours of sim time isn't enough to fully qualify someone for the jobs we're asking them to do," Kyle admitted, "but it isn't nothing, either. We've given him the best people we can; now it's down to him."

His careful study of the crowd suggested it was time for him, and he gave Chownyk a reassuring nod and a bright grin as he walked up to the briefing podium.

"All right, people," he barked, drawing the attention of everyone in the room.

"First, I want to thank the Navy people in the room," he told them. "We've asked you to do the impossible and we gave you six hours to decide. In the finest tradition of the Castle Federation Space Navy, you all volunteered.

"I'm sure the fact that this is going to look *fantastic* on your next promotion review had nothing to do with it." He gave them all a grin, one met by chuckles from around the room. "But I want you to know that *I*, personally, appreciate you being willing to step up.

"You know what we're up against. We're going to have to be sneaky and we're going to have to be smart. We're going to be up against some of the Commonwealth's best. Listen to Wing Commander Rokos and the Space Force people you've been assigned to; these squadrons are veterans of some of the toughest fighting of this war so far.

"What would you expect, after all?" he asked them. "They've been flying for *me*."

Kyle gestured Rokos up to the podium.

"Now Wing Commander Rokos will let you know just *how* busy your next ten days are going to be," he said wickedly.

"Good luck, people."

———

Russell replaced the Captain on the stage, trading nods with the more massive man as Roberts disappeared back to the multitude of tasks involved in running a warship, even one eleven days from emerging from the sanctuary of FTL.

"All right, people," he echoed Roberts. "The Flight Commanders have, by now, made sure everyone knows who their flight crews are and, perhaps most importantly, who your *pilot* is.

"Get to know these people and the rest of your squadron," he instructed. "When the shit hits the fan, your pilot is going to be the first person keeping you alive—but remember, pilots, your engineers are going to be making sure you have power for your fancy maneuvers, and your gunners will be running your antimissile suites.

"You're going to be relying on your flight crew. After them, you're going to be relying on your squadron, and then on the rest of the Wing and on *Chameleon*," he reminded them. "Get to know each other, because how well you work together may well decide whether you live out the month."

The room was very quiet, and Russell scanned his gaze across the faces in front of him. He met Cavendish's eyes as the Flight Commander glared at him, and his own words made him wonder if reinstating her was a mistake.

"The rest of you: our Space Force veterans, I have two key tasks for you," he continued. "Firstly, back up your new people. Most of our Navy seconds have never set foot in a real starfighter before. You need them as much as they need you. Don't hold back your experience and knowledge, even from somebody else's crew—avoiding the mistake you warn of today may allow them to save your life in Tau Ceti.

"Second, I need you to study Commonwealth doctrine. Hard. The one big advantage we have going into this is that we're flying starfighters they're not going to register as hostile. The better we can fake being Commonwealth, the more confused they're going to be!"

The thought of what they were going to try and pull on the Terrans was going to feature in his nightmares for a long time, he knew. Friendly starfighters suddenly opening fire? They had no choice, but he didn't have to like it, either.

"You have an hour to get to know your new crews," he warned them, "then we're going to lock you all into starfighters in simulator mode. We have ten days for me to put you through the wringer, and I warn you now: don't expect to be doing much other than sleeping and training.

"We have too much ground to make up to do anything else."

———

"WELL?" Russell asked.

"Moving starfighters around without the ability to take them outside the hull is excruciatingly difficult on this ship, sir," Master Chief Petty Officer Hanz said flatly, the squat woman studying the crude solution they'd come up with.

"So you cut a hole in the side of the flight deck," he noted. "I *agreed* to that, Chief. Please tell me it worked."

Thankfully, Terran starfighters were cylindrical instead of the wedges favored by the Federation, so they'd "only" had to cut a circular ten-meter hole in the interior end of his flight deck. Then through the thankfully empty set of quarters there, followed by a water storage tank that they'd needed to install a tunnel through, and *then* a final ten-meter hole into the cargo hold they'd stored the Katanas in.

Ugly as the hole was, he was watching the rounded eight-meter-wide and twenty-meter-long shape of a Katana starfighter emerge from it like it was laying a giant metal egg.

"The Scimitars are all out," Hanz reported. "We… Well, we broke one."

"You broke a *starfighter*? How?" Russell demanded. While starfighters were unarmored tin cans by the standards of their threat environment, they were still armored against the demands of relativistic velocity in open space and hardly fragile.

"With another starfighter," she said sadly. "We mucked up an angle and a speed and rammed one Scimitar into another. The movement cradles kept the *first* one intact, but it went four meters *into* the other one."

She shrugged. "That was part of why we moved the Scimitars first. This way, we've found the likely glitches and lost one of the ships we were putting in storage."

The Katana Russell had been watching finished inching its way out of the hole and the flight deck's machinery went to work. Once it was inside the zone where the deck's robots could handle it, the odds of damage were almost infinitesimal as it was picked up and slotted neatly into the stall designated for it.

"That's number four," Hanz noted. "Intel did us proud and we have six more moving in over the next hour. That will give us a full Commonwealth-standard squadron of the beasts. Which one did you want?"

He shook his head.

"I'm keeping the Scimitar," he told her. "Unlike most of the Wing, *I* have my full regular flight crew, which means we can handle being in an older bird with lighter weapons." He held up a hand. "And I've already argued that out with Churchill *and* Roberts. My Wing, my call. Rank hath its privileges."

"Usually when we say *rank hath its privileges*, it's the privilege of the *better* ship," she pointed out.

"The circumstances aren't normal," he replied. "How long until they're all locked in and we can set up for sims?"

"Two hours," Hanz promised. "Call it nineteen hundred to give me some leeway?"

"I'll hold you to that," Russell said with a grin. "These new crews need every hour in simulation we can give them."

"It'll happen," she said. "I want them to have every minute of sim time I can buy them too, boss."

35

Deep Space, Under Alcubierre Drive
20:10 June 10, 2736 Earth Standard Meridian Date/Time
Chameleon

WING COMMANDER RUSSELL ROKOS had trained new pilots and crews from scratch before, but normally they came in smaller batches. Two or three entirely new flight crews in a squadron of eight. Scratch-built squadrons assembled from the wrecks of previous groups, veterans who'd never worked together but veterans nonetheless.

Working up an entire Wing where almost every flight crew had at least one person who'd never set foot on a starfighter was worse. They'd been at it for three hours, well into the ship's "night", and every one of the exercises they'd run had suffered some kind of misstep.

He sighed aloud as the latest exercise disintegrated as a miscue sent a spray of starfighter missiles into the heart of Charlie Squadron. Two virtual starfighters disintegrated as the friendly fire slammed home, arriving *far* too quickly for the antimissile suites to engage.

The entire Wing net went silent and he froze the simulation.

"Okay," he said over the general channel. "Arguing over what just happened isn't going to help anyone. We've hit the limit of what we're going to usefully achieve tonight. Everyone is officially off duty until eight hundred hours tomorrow, when you should all be *right* back here."

He cut the channel and dropped his face into his hands.

"Hopefully *not* shooting each other in the back," he muttered aloud.

"To be fair, CPO Wong was fed an incorrect IFF sequence for targeting.," Alvarado pointed out, his gunner looking equally tired. *"That was from Junior Lieutenant Meissner aboard Flight Commander Ramada's bird. Meissner was at Huī Xing with us. He should know better!"*

"I know," Russell admitted. "We start again in the morning and dig *upwards*."

"Sounds like a plan," his subordinate agreed, rising from his chair and then stopping in place, staring at the exit from the cockpit.

"Sir, can you order the door to open?" he asked slowly. Their flight engineer, Junior Lieutenant Gianna Cavalcante, was buried in the rear half of the ship. The two men were alone in the small cockpit at the front of the starfighter. "It's ignoring my implant."

That was strange, but Russell gave the order with a wave of his hand at the offending portal. His mind was focused on his plans for the morning's exercise and it took him a moment to realize that the door still hadn't opened.

"That's *very* strange," he said slowly, his attention finally on the here and now. Rising from his chair, he strode back to the door and tapped the command pad that acted as a secondary control. Nothing happened, and it remained stubbornly closed as he triggered a command override that would allow him to turn the fighter's engines on inside the ship, let alone open a door.

Nothing.

He reached out to the ship's network to call for help and found…nothing.

"We're being jammed," he said aloud, a sudden chill sinking in.

"What?" Alvarado asked.

"Try and link to the ship," Russell ordered. "I can't find the network."

The gaunt gunner paled.

"I can't even link to the fighter," he reported.

"Jammed," Russell confirmed. "Help me with this panel; there's an emergency physical lever to force the door open."

Now that he was paying attention, the air was starting to seem stale. The air circulators *should* have been switching it out, but the room was *far* quieter than it should have been. Linked into the full immersion net, he wouldn't have noticed them turning off—there were supposed to be *alarms* for that.

With Alvarado's aid, he ripped the emergency panel off to find the door lever. Somehow, he was unsurprised to find that someone had used a cutting laser to remove it, leaving a sliced-off stump—a stump that had been *welded* into place.

He tried to link back into the fighter's systems—how long they'd been without air was important; the cockpit *should* contain enough for several hours, but if the circulation had been cut off during the exercises, they could be running short. He couldn't even form the connection.

"The jammer is probably mounted on the outside of the hull," Alvarado said, his voice high-pitched with fear. "We can't link to anything at all." The gunner swallowed. "My implant just triggered an air quality alert. I don't think we have much time."

Russell's in-head computer pinged the same warning. Low oxygen. High carbon dioxide. He was already starting to feel sleepy, something he'd put up to a long stressful day before.

"We can't link to anything by radio," he told Alvarado as the man started to hyperventilate. "Check your damn console, Rauol!"

That only got them so far. At some point after Russell ordering the end of the exercise, *something* had cut off power to the consoles. No touch screens, no implant controls, nothing to do except hope someone realized they'd been trapped before they suffocated.

"Help me take this off," Russell ordered as he stepped over to another panel, near the door but not part of its systems. Most of the repair work aboard the starfighter would be done by nanites and drones directed by the flight engineer—and the fact that Cavalcante hadn't fixed this already said something was *very* wrong—but the provision was made for *some* manual repair.

Ripping off the panel exposed a collection of wiring, including the dense crystalline cording that carried the data streams of the ship's computer network. And, tucked away in the corner of the panel, an emergency item almost never used anymore—a narrow cable with a connector designed to link into a tablet.

"You have a tablet?" Alvarado asked.

"No," the Wing Commander admitted, pulling the cable out. "But I'm going to owe my grandfather an apology."

While most of the Wing Commander's hair was buzz-cut to fit under his shipsuit's helmet, he had a small patch behind each ear that he grew out a bit longer. Pulling aside the hair behind his right ear, he exposed an old-fashioned physical data port for his implant.

It had been decades since implants installed in the Federation came with the physical port as default, but the eldest living Rokos was alive because he'd had that port one day when everything *else* had gone wrong on his ship—and he'd insisted on paying for it to be added to his grandchildren's implants.

Russell had never used it until today, but he slid the emergency connector into the port and inhaled in a moment of almost-pain as the unfamiliar link formed.

"Cavalcante, report!" he barked over the network. Even as he was trying to reach her, he was confirming that the door was completely nonfunctional. All of the machinery around it was slagged.

Silence was his only answer and he slammed a command override into the system, taking control of the ship's self-repair system and flagging the cockpit as emergency priority.

"Cavalcante's not answering," he told Alvarado. "I have everything swarming the door; get ready to grab it open on my command."

He was running through menus on the repair remotes, checking their capabilities—he was trained on the Federation's version, and the Terran one was noticeably different, even including...

"Never mind, get back from the door," he ordered, pulling the cable from behind his ear so he could move.

"What?"

"*Do it!*"

Russell yanked Alvarado away from the door and behind the crash couches as the three remotes he'd set to suicide hammered into the other side, each destabilizing and detonating its high-density battery as a shaped charge in sequence.

Any cockpit door, even aboard a starfighter, was an armored monstrosity. The explosions weren't enough to destroy the door—but they did punch a head-sized hole through the door and spray shrapnel across the cockpit.

Russell *felt* something hit the crash couch he was hiding behind and fail to penetrate—and could almost immediately feel the change in the air as fresher atmosphere poured in.

"Come on," he told Alvarado, moving back to the half-wrecked door. "Grab the top… On three. One. Two. THREE."

They pulled and the door ever so slightly slid open. Two more solid attempts and it was open enough for Alvarado to squeeze through and find the manual override lever on the other side, pulling the door open for Russell.

"Still nothing on the network," the gunner said worriedly.

"I know," Russell agreed. "Even the starfighter couldn't talk to anyone."

He stopped in the corridor, flipping open a panel he never thought he'd use on *any* starfighter and typing in his override code. The panel popped open, revealing the starfighter's weapons locker.

He passed a harness with a pistol and carbine on it to Alvarado, who looked at him like he was crazy.

"Sir?"

"Someone just tried to kill us, Rauol," Russell pointed out grimly. "I don't plan on letting them succeed.

"Let's check on Gianna."

————

THE STARFIGHTER DIDN'T HAVE an engineering section the same way a starship did, but it did have a workspace and console attached to the primary zero-point cell that powered the ship and fueled her engines. In a battle, an engineer would be all over the ship, running the ECM and repair systems through her implant while backing up her remotes with the spark of intuition and insight that the artificial intelligences lacked.

In a simulation, though, Cavalcante spent her time at the console, so that was where she'd died. It *looked* like a minor system failure had freakishly blown debris across the room and into the back of her skull, but Russell wasn't buying that for a second.

"What the *fuck?!*" Alvarado shouted at the sight of her body.

"Someone is *very* determined to kill us," Russell said grimly, "but also to make it look like an accident. Everything except the jamming *could* have been a system malfunction, and if they removed the jammer before anyone came looking for us, no one would ever know it had been there."

"*Why?*"

"Probably to kill me," the CAG said, his voice far calmer than he felt. He even had a good idea *who*, though he'd expected that pulling her back into the fight would have helped her find *some* balance.

"I *object* to that plan, so let's see if we can short-circuit it. Come on."

"Shouldn't we do something for Gianna?" his gunner asked faintly.

"We will," Russell promised as he headed for the fighter's exit. "Later. Right now, we need to stay *alive*, which means getting away from this ship and out of range of that jammer."

Swallowing hard, the junior officer followed him away from their comrade's body.

Reaching the exit, Russell gestured the younger man to the other side of the door while he tapped an override code into the control panel.

"Watch yourself," he ordered, his finger hovering over the last button. "If what I think is going on is, there'll be a backup plan and it'll probably involve shooters."

They'd been trapped for long enough that he was sadly certain the deck had emptied. With a sigh, he hit the last button and triggered the door, the metal panel moving swiftly aside to allow them back onto the flight deck.

The first thing he noticed was that the lights were down. Faint red emergency lighting cast the entire deck in an ominous bloody wash—but the lights on the flight deck shouldn't have been off.

The color and tone of the emergency lighting was carefully chosen. It was more than enough for anyone with a military-grade implant to see. It *wasn't* enough for someone with said implant to see *distances,* and Russell knew he was in trouble.

He yanked Alvarado back as the junior officer started to exit the starfighter, pulling him behind the hull just in time for a bullet to smash into the floor past where he'd been standing.

"Stay *down,*" he hissed. He hadn't heard the shot—he was guessing low-velocity bullets from a suppressed weapon. That didn't change his guess of who was trying to kill him.

More bullets walked their way across the deck, keeping them trapped in the starfighter. That didn't make sense…unless!

He *threw* Alvarado back into the starfighter, the lighter man sprawling across the floor as a *second* shooter's bullets sprayed over his own collapse.

Russell, however, had collapsed toward the door with the carbine in his hand. His ground combat training was almost nonexistent, but his kinesthetic sense was off the charts. When the second salvo slammed into the ground where he'd originally landed, he had his attacker dialed in.

Of course, he wasn't as good a *shot* without a starfighter. He emptied the entire carbine clip, walking the bullets all over the entire area where he'd located the shooter. If there was any audible response, he couldn't hear it over the gunfire—but the shooting stopped.

A moment later, the suppressive fire began again, one round skipping off the deck and slicing a burning furrow up the side of his face.

He recoiled, trying to take cover and hoping his emptied clip had bought *some* notice from the ship's sensors. Ejecting the empty, he pulled the only spare mag from the harness and tried to load the weapon.

Sweaty with stress, he slipped. The mag went scattering across the floor and skidded to a halt barely two meters away—and was promptly obliterated by a single perfectly placed bullet.

"Alvarado," he snapped, "pass me your weapon."

Silence answered him and he contorted to look back at his subordinate. The gunner *appeared* to still be breathing but had hit his head when Russell had thrown him out of the way of the bullets. He was unconscious, possibly badly injured.

And that left Russell with a *pistol* as at least one and probably more shooters—almost certainly Cavendish and one or more friends, probably also black-ops cyborgs—were starting to close in on his position.

He swallowed, preparing to try and make a move anyway—and then the pistol was blown out of his hand along with at least two fingers as a perfectly placed bullet smashed through him.

Diving back toward Alvarado and the other man's weapon, he collided with an iron arm that flung him back onto the Q-ship's flight deck.

Laura Cavendish loomed over him, an ugly black-looking carbine in her hands.

"The plan called for you to choke to death," she told him. "But this is better. This way, you know why you're dying, you son of a bitch."

She jerked away as a gunshot suddenly echoed through the empty void, a single shot from an unsuppressed weapon more powerful than the carbine in the pilot's hands. Despite her surprise, the weapon remained trained on Russell's head, and he was deathly certain he wouldn't survive attempting to knock aside the weapon.

"Let him go, Laura," a soft female voice said aloud. "Assam is dead. So's Carlisle. How many more people need to die?"

"Just the son of a bitch who killed my people!"

"The Commonwealth killed your people. And they went willingly, doing their duty. What are *you* doing?"

Russell could now see the slim form of the commander of the black-ops ground troops—Riley, he thought her name was?

"Getting rev—"

Cavendish's hand and head exploded away as she tried to jerk the trigger on her carbine, heavy fragmenting rounds *slamming* into her with brutal force.

Riley stepped forward again, kicking the carbine away from Russell and offering her hand.

"Dammit, sir, I'm sorry," she said quietly, looking into the starfighter and seeing Alvarado's still form. "I didn't think she was this far gone."

"He's just unconscious," Russell choked out, putting pressure on his wounded hand. "Need a medic, but we're jammed."

"Tourville, check him," Riley ordered. "Dirkse, find the jammer. She wasn't *just* running her people's implants."

She turned back to the CAG.

"We'll sort it out, sir," she promised.

36

Deep Space, Under Alcubierre Drive
08:40 June 11, 2736 Earth Standard Meridian Date/Time
Chameleon

KYLE'S HEAD hurt as he leaned back in his chair, studying the collection filling his office. Rokos's face was half-covered in a bandage, nanites working away beneath it to reknit the flesh. A regeneration cup covered the stumps of two fingers on his right hand, rebuilding bone and flesh in a process Kyle *knew* was uncomfortable.

Riley sat next to him. She wasn't injured, but the black-ops Lieutenant looked even more pissed than the Wing Commander did.

Glass looked as imperturbable as always, the bald old man silently sitting at one end of the row of chairs. Hansen and Chownyk held down the other end, giving the impression that Riley and Rokos were surrounded.

"So, now I know what *happened*," Kyle said, as calmly as he could, "would someone please explain *how* the hell it happened?"

"My platoon has worked with Cavendish's squadron before," Riley replied. "Staff Sergeant Sabah Assam and Commander Cavendish apparently go even further back, which I was *not* aware of. He was able to acquire weapons from *my* armory without anyone else knowing."

She sighed.

"The weapons used were properly signed out and the system would have alerted myself or Lieutenant Major Hansen if they'd been signed out for more than ten hours. With both simulator and live-fire training going on, we're not set up to require officer approval on weapon sign-outs. Any E-5 or above, like Assam, can sign out weapons for their squad basically at will.

"I had people keeping an eye on Cavendish, but Staff Sergeant Assam was one of mine," she concluded quietly. "Junior Lieutenant Carlisle was Flight Lieutenant Vogel's engineer, the last one left of her squadron.

"Tracing back his steps, he logged a maintenance ticket on Commander Rokos's starfighter at ten hundred hours this morning. I presume he removed the safety lever then and had the rest of the sabotage as a coded virus in the starfighter's systems."

"Carlisle wasn't supposed to be doing maintenance on my starfighter," Rokos pointed out.

"The system wouldn't care, CAG," Kyle told him. "Not unless we're at a higher security level than we currently are. It makes it easier when we're transferring people around, exactly as you're doing right now."

"My surveillance tech warned me that Cavendish hadn't left the flight deck and something weird was going on," Riley said with a shrug. "We didn't realize the fighter had been sabotaged, but I pulled a fire team of my guys and came to check.

"We arrived just after Commander Rokos shot Carlisle," she finished.

And Rokos had already told them all what happened then.

"You had enough suspicion to have someone *watch* Cavendish," Kyle noted. "But not, I take it, enough suspicion to inform anyone"— he gestured at the row of superior officers surrounding Riley—"of your fears?"

"She told me," Hansen admitted. "She didn't tell me *who* she suspected, but it wasn't hard to guess. I..." The Lieutenant Major sighed. "I trusted her judgment over whether or not Cavendish was a threat—I figured she would do something to show her hand before it got this far."

"She guessed she was being watched," Riley said quietly.

"And because all of your people have built-in *jammers*, none of this showed up on the ship's security systems," Kyle snapped. "And now four *more* people are dead. Is that about right?"

The room was silent for ten seconds. Fifteen.

"Your actions saved Rokos and Alvarado's lives," he finally allowed. "But had you told the rest of us what you suspected, the others—including Cavendish—would still be alive."

"I didn't know for sure," the Lieutenant replied, her emotions vanishing behind the flat mask of a threatened operative now. "And she was my *friend*, Captain."

"We all thought that her being restored to flight status would reduce her threat level," Chownyk said levelly.

"We did," Kyle admitted, holding Riley's gaze. "And I doubt any of us actually expected her to try to *kill* Commander Rokos. We all had our suspicions, and you did more than the rest of us to minimize the damage. It might have been done better, but you did well regardless."

"Thank you, sir."

"Rokos, most of the fallout from this is going to land on you," he continued. "How's your hand?"

"Well, I now know what having fingers shot off feels like, which I could have lived without," the CAG replied. "It'll heal. The Wing's morale did *not* need this latest kick in the ass, but we'll recover. I still have ten days to run them ragged and make them forget.

"Churchill's running them through the scheduled exercises right now," he added. "We'll make it work, Captain."

"If you need backup, let me know," Kyle told him. "I *want* you in the planning sessions this afternoon, but having your Wing combat-ready is more important."

"We'll see," the CAG replied.

"Let Chownyk know." Kyle glanced around the room. "Dismissed, people. Glass, if you could stick around for a moment?"

————

KYLE WAITED PATIENTLY for the last of his subordinates to leave the room and sealed the door to block sound behind them. Then he turned to Glass waiting calmly in his chair and released *some* of the self-control he'd been holding.

"What kind of fucking *monsters* did you bring aboard my ship?" he demanded. "One of your 'operators' apparently thought she could get away with *murdering my CAG*—and the other would rather carry out a questionably legal surveillance than report that she thinks someone is about to *do* so?"

"You just admitted that Sandra wasn't the problem," the old spy replied. "We all had our concerns about Laura and *none* of us actually expected her to attempt to murder Commander Rokos. Sandra was worried about her friend—and I'll point out, had to *shoot* her friend last night."

"Do not mistake letting a junior officer off the hook because I don't expect her to know better for her *not having fucked up*," Kyle snarled. "Your people were supposed to bring skills and expertise to this mission that regular Navy and Space Force personnel couldn't. I haven't seen much evidence of that yet!"

"Despite my best efforts, we have yet to end up in a circumstance where Riley's people's skills would be of value," Glass admitted. "I will also confess that I expected better from both the stealth coatings on Cavendish's fighter and from her crews."

"Those crews stood and died at Aurelius to protect their comrades," Kyle admitted slowly. "They fought like soldiers, I could have expected no better from the Space Force."

"Indeed, but I will freely call myself their partisan and I saw no special skill, no unusual experience, present in my black-ops crews," the spy replied. "They were veterans, yes, but hardly the unstoppable juggernauts of skill and violence Cavendish and her superiors paint Federation Intelligence's black fighter group as."

"No one is unstoppable in a starfighter," the ex-starfighter pilot in the room said. "Modern weapons do not respect skill or violence. How did someone *that* on the edge end in command of a squadron in the first place?"

Glass coughed delicately.

"The criteria to command a black-ops squadron are not the same as those for a regular squadron," he pointed out. "We ask people to sign on for long tours, far away from home—often deep into enemy territory. They must wear personas that allow them to mix with mercenaries and strangers, but be ready to kill those around them in an instant if the order comes down.

"It's not a job many are good at and it's a job fewer want," he concluded. "Officers are selected to command those squadrons based on skill and charisma and, bluntly, the willingness to do whatever is asked of them.

"Cavendish had carried out missions that could not have been asked of Space Force squadrons. Not necessarily war crimes but gray areas—the kind of mission you don't ask a *soldier* to complete.

"Is it any surprise, Captain, knowing that, that Cavendish and our other squadron commanders are not *stable* individuals in the main?" Glass asked with a shrug. "She was a specific type of tool, one we know can turn on us. I didn't expect quite so...dramatic an action on her part."

"Unstable," Kyle questioned. "You mean you put starfighters, with weapons that can devastate *continents* if not worlds, in the hands of psychopaths?"

"Basically," the older man admitted. "But be honest, Captain; we both know there are psychopaths in any organization. Modern mental health and nanite chemical rebalancing do wonderful things. We just... found them in the ranks of the Space Force's pilots and...nurtured them.

"Intel's black-ops forces are shadowy and vicious tools, never meant to see the light of day. But they weren't enough for *this* mission —that's why you're here. Why Rokos and the rest of your crew are here."

"And Riley?" Kyle asked. "Is she...'unstable'?"

"No more than you, Captain," Glass told him. "Like you, she compartmentalizes the violence in her life away from her ethics and sense of being a 'good person'.

"We all tell ourselves lies about what kind of people we are. Riley is good at believing hers."

"You are *not* making me comfortable with this," Kyle replied.

"You are a soldier, Captain. Do you *expect* to be comfortable with your job?"

———

RUSSELL STOOD at the edge of the flight deck, watching his people exit the starfighters after another grueling round of exercises—exercises that would not have been made easier by wondering just what the *hell* had happened last night.

It only took a few seconds for the crews close enough to him to see him and start crowding toward him, a cacophony of questions following only moments behind.

"Please," he told them, raising his hands, "give me a moment for everyone to get here."

The sound had served the purpose of attracting everyone's attention, and Russell hopped up onto a nearby pile of sturdy-looking hardware as the rest of the Wing gathered around. The muttering only increased as his people gathered around and got a look at the bandages covering half of his face and hand.

"I'm sure the rumor mill has done its usual job of attempting to turn simple facts into grand conspiracies and dramatic tales," he said loudly as the last few men and women trickled in. "It's relatively obvious, though, that something *did* happen, as this is a little big for cutting myself shaving!

"The sad truth is that Flight Commander Cavendish attempted to murder me last night," he explained, his words cutting the last few muttered conversations to silence. "She *succeeded* in murdering Junior Lieutenant Gianna Cavalcante and badly injuring Junior Lieutenant Rauol Alvarado."

He felt absolutely no qualms at blaming Cavendish for Alvarado's injuries. It had been *her* bullets he'd thrown the younger man aside to protect him from.

"Rauol will recover in time to fly and fight at Tau Ceti," he promised everyone. "But Commander Cavendish refused to surrender when Marines intervened and was killed.

"So were a Marine she'd co-opted and Junior Lieutenant Carlisle," he told them. "Four people died aboard *Chameleon* last night. *Our* people, killed by our people."

He paused to let that sink in.

"Half of you were with me and the Captain on *Avalon* at Alizon and Barsoom," he said softly. "This isn't the first time we've seen someone turn on our own for reasons we don't understand. It's not easy to deal with and it's not something we should *have* to deal with, but we'll do it.

"In less than ten days, this starfighter wing goes into battle," Russell reminded his people. "We can't afford to get hung up on the whys and wherefores. We have to do our *job*."

The message wasn't sinking *entirely* home, he could tell, but he had good people. They'd step up.

"First off, it's looking like our plan in Tau Ceti is going to involve the starfighters pretending to be Commonwealth birds until the rocket goes up. The Commonwealth's Starfighter Corps uses a ten-ship squadron.

"To fake *being* them, we're going to do the same."

That it was also helpful in making up for his suddenly lacking squadron commander went unspoken but understood.

"We're also going to start running through some *Terran* scenarios we've acquired," he warned them. "Their policies, procedures, and default tactics are different than ours—and the last thing *I'm* going to put up with is blowing the Captain's nice shiny plan because one of us answered the radio 'Roger' when Terran pilots use 'Understood'.

"Do you get me?!"

37

Deep Space, Under Alcubierre Drive
13:00 June 12, 2736 Earth Standard Meridian Date/Time
Chameleon

"YOU REALLY DO SEEM to pick up the crazy women who want to kill your CAG, don't you?" Mira Solace said with a grin Kyle could tell was forced. "Is Rokos okay?"

"I think he's more shaken than he's letting on," Kyle admitted, glad that Mira's ship was sufficiently clear of active operations—for the moment! —for them to have a live conversation. "His wound was pretty significant. It'll regenerate quickly, at least, but he also lost one of his flight crew. That's…that's hard for starfighter people. Our crew are family."

"I can think of a certain ex-starfighter officer who didn't lose that attitude when they picked up a much bigger ship," the elegant black woman teased. "How are *you* holding up?"

"Pissed," he answered. "Not much I can do about it, though. She's dead and we're going into action."

Chameleon was only about twenty-four hours from going into full communication lockdown herself. This would be the last time they spoke before he reached Tau Ceti, and there was so much he couldn't say. He couldn't, for that matter, even tell her *when* he was going in communications lockdown.

"Things are quiet here," she told him, clearly following some of his thoughts. "Intel says Walkingstick is playing at keeping us busy all along the front until he gets the reinforcements they figure he's been promised."

"I don't trust that man to be doing what it appears he's doing," Kyle told her. The last time they'd thought they'd known what Walkingstick was doing, the Terran Admiral's local commander had sucker-punched an entire system's defenses out behind them.

"Neither do I," his lover agreed. "And neither does Alstairs, which is why I'm spending six hours a day making sure *Camerone* is ready for war and another six in strategy-planning meetings."

"At least I get to talk to my sister and occasionally you to break the monotony," she said with a smile.

"How's your sister?" he asked.

"She is very bright, very enthusiastic, and very fifteen," Mira replied. "She *mostly* understands what being on deployment means, but she still keeps asking when I can bring you home to meet her. She has a bad case of hero worship going on for the Stellar Fox."

Kyle sighed.

"I keep revisiting the potential plan of beating journalists up in dark alleys until they stop using that name," he noted.

"It's entered the popular mind now; you're doomed," she told him. "What about your family?"

"I can talk to *you* because you're a Navy Captain and are presumed to have a sense of discretion," he said quietly. "The Navy is not so generous in its assumptions when it comes to neural physicians and twelve-year-old boys. We get to trade letters when I'm this deep.

"That said, they're doing fine. Like most of his generation now, Jacob is Navy-mad and wants me to sign his models of every ship from Seventh Fleet when I get home." Kyle shook his head, the thought bringing up something of a smile.

"I can't quite get myself past just how inaccurate the 'official licensed models' are," he told Mira. "Proportions are off, numbers of visible weapons are off; Gods, I don't think they gave the *Ursine*-class carriers *flight decks*."

"You, my dear Captain, are a purist."

"And you clearly don't understand how bad a portrayal of our poor ships these models are," Kyle pointed out. "I mean, I understand it's for security, but they could have at least *tried*."

She was laughing aloud at him now and he gave her as big a grin as he could manage.

"I look forward to introducing you to them," he told her. His was a strange life, where not introducing his new girlfriend to his ex was basically impossible. Unless he wanted to remove Jacob from his life again—which he did *not*—Lisa Kerensky was also going to be a part of his life.

"I look forward to it," Mira told him. "Even meeting Lisa. From the sounds of it, I'm in more trouble if I don't live up to *her* standards for you than if I missed *yours*."

"*She* went and found herself a Member of the Federation Assembly to date," Kyle pointed out. "What's a 'mere' Navy Captain?"

She shook her head, glancing away as she did.

"My next meeting is rushing up on me," she admitted. "Kyle…take care of yourself. *I'll* be pissed if you don't come back."

"Orders received and understood, ma'am," he told her with a crisp salute. With that and a blown kiss, he let the channel close and considered his desk.

Time to work on making sure *everyone* came back.

———

EDVARD GESTURED Riley to a seat across from his desk, trying to assess his subordinate's mood as she sat. Her face was locked down again, hiding her thoughts from everyone.

"How's your platoon?" he asked. Ostensibly, this was the same check-in meeting he was having with his other two platoon commanders, but they both knew it was more than that. After rearranging things, all of his platoons were down half a squad—and his twenty-trooper headquarters section was only thirteen strong.

"Pissed at Assam," Riley said flatly. "But they're on the job. This kind of shit is…" She sighed. "I'd say a lot more common in black-ops units than regular Marines, but let's be honest: it *happens* in black-ops units and doesn't in the Marines.

"The kind of guys and gals you put in a unit like mine are *not* good people, Edvard," she warned him. "My job is as much to keep these idiots from stabbing everyone *else* in the back as it is training or pointing them at the enemy."

Edvard shook his head, trying to envisage any unit that was that…difficult.

"How do your units even function?" he asked.

"They keep it out of the unit, in the main," she replied. "They work together in action, follow orders, do what they're ordered. And then, when we're off duty, they turn into a bunch of prima donnas who'll stab anyone outside the unit who looks at them cross-eyed."

"Like Cavendish," Edvard noted. "How are you holding up?"

"I fucked up and had to kill one of my few actual friends because of it," Riley snapped. "How do you *expect* me to be holding up?"

"Like shit," he said frankly. "It's not your fault."

"Bullshit. The Captain said what a Captain says when he's letting a junior officer who shouldn't know better off the hook," Riley replied. "I was pulled from the Corps for black-ops when you were in boot, Hansen. I *know* what kind of psychopaths we have in unmarked uniforms.

"I knew what Cavendish was. Chilling sign of how used you are to people who kill at the drop of a hat when most of your close friends fit that bill, isn't it?

"I knew what she was. I knew she wouldn't let it lie at complaints, but I said *nothing* because she was a friend," Riley said bitterly. "I let my personal feelings compromise my professional judgment and I should have known better."

"So did I," Edvard snapped. "You *told* me you had suspicions. It was *my* job to yank you up short and order you to act on them. I didn't because of our frankly *dangerous* feelings toward each other."

That admission shut her up. It was the first time either of them had admitted anything aloud to the other, but he knew and he knew she knew, and so on and so forth.

"Yes, you fucked up," he told her gently. "But if I'd assessed the risk differently, I would have pressured you to come clean. I didn't. A lot of people had to misjudge Cavendish's limits for it to go this far.

"I need you on point, on duty, and one hundred percent, so that we all get to come home alive. I do *not* need you beating yourself up for your failures. Can you do that for me, Sandra? Can you let this go and do the job?"

She inhaled sharply, the mask cracking into unshed tears for a long moment before she nodded and inhaled again.

"I think so. Just…promise me one thing, sir."

"This isn't a negotiation, Lieutenant," Edvard pointed out.

"Not that kind of promise, Edvard," she replied. "Promise me *you'll* live through this too."

"I have no intention of dying this far from home, Sandra. It's war, and we won't all make it home, but I plan on bringing as many of my people home as possible."

———

"Our target in the Tau Ceti System is threefold," Kyle summarized to the gathered officers in the planning room. A massive hologram filled the center of the room, showing the two habitable worlds and heavy spaceborne industry of Tau Ceti.

"Firstly, we need to board the TCN Central Research Station here." An icon flashed in orbit of the second gas giant. There was *slightly* less traffic around the ninth planet than around the larger eighth, but it was a relative matter. The massive Navy facilities orbiting Tau Ceti H more than made up for the much-reduced civilian traffic.

Tau Ceti H was the quietest part of the system. It was still busier than anywhere Kyle had ever seen except the Castle System itself. Dozens of cloudscoops provided a constant stream of fuel for the slightly safer fusion plants that fueled the massive shipyards and the civilian support infrastructure.

"The Central Research Station is now our primary objective," he told his people. "We will do our best to insert Riley's people *without* compromising our cover. Every minute we can give them to operate on the station without triggering a system-wide security alert increases our chances of retrieving the data we're after.

"To help distract everyone from Riley's attack, we will be using Rokos's starfighters to launch as covert a strike as we can manage at Shipyard Alpha."

A second station, this one a massive agglomeration of yard slips, construction gantries, and half-assembled ships, highlighted in the hologram. It formed a rough spindle shape, a wide circular top hosting the shipyards and their incomplete children, with a sharp spike "hanging" down to link to the pontoon-like hexagon of pods with stabilizer thrusters that held the whole structure up against Tau Ceti H's gravity.

The scale on the hologram happily informed everyone that Shipyard Alpha was over fifty kilometers across and seventy high, the single largest manmade structure in the star system.

"Shipyard Alpha single-handedly represents forty percent of the construction capacity in this system and roughly one point two percent of the military construction capacity of the Commonwealth," he explained. "It also has a *lot* of noncombatant personnel aboard and is a massive target. A direct assault on the facility would be an arguable war crime, one I am not prepared to countenance regardless of the level of secrecy cloaking this operation."

Despite the size of the station, such an assault would be far from futile. He'd run the numbers in private: if the estimate on the defenses was correct, a full salvo from all forty of their starfighters would punch through the defensive suites and deliver more than enough firepower on target to vaporize the entire station.

Along with about a hundred and twenty thousand people, less than ten percent of whom were even uniformed Navy personnel, let alone combatants.

"Depending on where in their approach we trigger the system alarm, the Wing will use their missiles to destroy the orbiting defense platforms and close with the station to launch precision positron-lance strikes," Kyle continued. "There are twelve capital ships in various stages of construction, including two *Volcano*-class supercarriers that our intelligence suggests are mere months from deployment."

Twelve capital ships was more than all but four members of the Alliance fielded. They could destroy an entire Navy's worth of ships in a single strike...and they would only mildly inconvenience the Commonwealth.

"Our third objective is to *terrify* the Commonwealth," he said calmly. "We want them looking over their shoulders for the monsters in the night. We want them blaming the League for pirates and *condottieri* breaking down their doors.

"We are striking at the very heart of the Commonwealth's military machine." One of several such hearts, but that was beside the point. "We want them to be afraid, in a way the Commonwealth has never known fear."

He smiled coldly at his people.

"That's the plan, ladies and gentlemen. We have nine days until we have to execute it. By then, I want us to have gone over every way we can think of it breaking. We're going to test and wargame every scenario we can think of.

"We're pretending to be *condottieri*, after all, which means we need to be thinking about our return on investment."

38

Deep Space, Under Alcubierre Drive
20:30 June 14, 2736 Earth Standard Meridian Date/Time
Chameleon

WING COMMANDER RUSSELL ROKOS watched his exhausted flight crews shuffle slowly off the flight deck, keeping his face utterly impassive as he watched them go. It would never do, after all, for them to realize the taskmaster whipping them along was actually extremely pleased with their progress!

He was planning a break for them, giving them a half-day off and some positive words. It would be a surprise to most of them—he *tried* to be constructively critical, but they were still doing a *lot* wrong.

"So, CAG, have they stopped blowing each other up in simulations yet?" the Captain asked cheerfully from behind him.

"We managed to progress past that stage relatively quickly," Russell told him. "Though I'll admit I was expecting it to take us longer to get there. Your Navy people have set to with a will, and their skill sets transfer better than we were afraid they would."

"Shall we chat in your office?" the Captain replied, revealing the inevitable pair of beers in his other massive hand. "Catch me up."

Russell grabbed the beer and gestured for his superior to proceed him. His office was only slightly farther from his starfighter's flight deck hangar than it was from PriFly, a sensible design choice in his admittedly biased opinion—and one that was shared between both Terran and Castle warship design.

Collapsing into his chair, he popped the beer on his desk and regarded Roberts levelly.

"We're not doing great just yet," he told the Captain. "If we put together a single squadron of my Space Force people and gave them Falcons, they'd eat this entire Wing alive. But..." He held up a hand. "They are improving. Rapidly.

"I think we've underestimated just how cross-compatible our drones and nano-repair systems are between the Navy versions and the Space Force version. It's the same hardware, software, *everything*. But we have ourselves half-convinced that it's a different skill set.

"It certainly helps, though, that all of the missileers were cross-trained on fighter missiles because of *Chameleon*'s armament," Russell admitted. "We're not building skills from the ground up in either case, just teaching people how to apply them in new circumstances.

"Our biggest weakness is going to be ECM. I've kept it to one Navy crew per fighter, and all of our people have *some* training in ECM, but the only birds that are going to be running jammers and decoys at full power are the ones with Space Force flight engineers."

"But they'll be ready?"

"They'll be ready," Russell said in a rush of breath. It was the first time he'd dared say that aloud. "I was hoping for seventy percent effectiveness, and I'm thinking we might be as high as eighty-five. Your people sent me *good* techs."

"Good," the Captain rumbled. "I'd hoped so, but it shows solid judgment from them both. Speaking of my people, though, Taylor's thrown a new wrinkle in the plan."

"And what's that?"

"She thinks we should keep a squadron in *Chameleon*'s tubes for a

CSP," Roberts explained. "It gives us more flexibility for a *lot* of our scenarios, but it cuts your strike force by a quarter."

"It does," Russell said, thinking it over. "It depends on which squadron, really. If I leave you ten Scimitars, that has less of an impact than if I leave the Katanas."

"And yet," the Captain said, letting the sentence hang in the air.

"I intentionally put my least-qualified flight teams on the Katanas," the CAG admitted. "They're solid fighters, easily the equal of Falcons in a lot of ways. The less-experienced crews weaken that squadron, but using the better fighters to offset the weaker crews gives me the strongest *wing*."

"What are you thinking, CAG?"

"If I leave you the Katanas, that gives you the most flexibility possible in defending *Chameleon*, which is, I may point out, our only ride home," Russell said thoughtfully. "It will also likely be easier to hide a three-squadron task force in the background of system traffic if they're a homogenous force: I doubt the Commonwealth deploys mixed groups for in-system patrols."

"And you can complete the mission with the Scimitars?"

"The mission becomes impossible to complete if Shipyard Alpha goes to full alert," Russell replied. "It's not going to matter whether or nor I have an extra ten fighters when that happens. If we can't close to use lances, our options are to run or commit a *war crime*."

"That is not on the table," Roberts said flatly.

"Then I suspect the Katanas will be more valuable as our ace in the hole than as another set of positron lances to rip up Shipyard Alpha."

The Captain took a giant swallow of beer.

"I wasn't going to argue if you said you needed them," he noted with a grin, "but I know *I'm* going to be happier with that hole card than without it."

14:00 June 18, 2736 ESMDT

RUSSELL WAS one of the first people out of the starfighters this time as they broke for lunch, making sure he was in position to watch his flight crews' reaction as they exited their ships to find the center of the flight deck turned into a banquet hall.

While his people had been immersed in their virtual realities for the last six hours, as they'd done for the first half of every day in the eight days since the fighter wing had been reorganized, Master Chief Hanz had marshaled a small legion of the ship's stewards. A dozen long tables had been laid out, as had chairs and massive piles of food and drink.

At the front of the whole ensemble was a small dais with a podium, and Russell walked over to it as his people stumbled to a halt, staring at the meal laid out for them.

"It's real, people," he told them as he stepped onto the platform. "Please, grab a seat, grab a plate and dig in."

The crowd obeyed, slowly at first, then with alacrity as they started to catch on. Drinks and plates started to be passed around as the crews fell on the food like ravenous wolves.

"So, as any of the veterans can tell you, I'm a hard man to get praise out of," Russell told them once they were seated and eating. "You've done well. Better than I expected, even. So I'm giving you all the rest of the day off.

"We've been beating our heads against this wall for a week. We can't do twelve-hour days forever and *then* go into action, not and expect victory. Report back to your starfighter at oh eight hundred tomorrow and do *not* get in trouble until then.

"Enjoy the food and get some rest. You've earned it."

Stepping down from the platform, he grabbed a plate of food of his own and slid into a chair next to Churchill.

"Ready to be wrapped in a silk glove?" he asked the squadron commander quietly.

"Is *that* what you call handing me every green pilot we have?" Churchill replied, his voice equally quiet as he glanced around to be sure no one could hear them.

"*Chameleon* needs a punch no one is expecting, a mailed gauntlet in a silk glove," Russell pointed out. "That's going to be your Alpha

Squadron. And you got the Katanas out of the deal; don't complain about your pilots."

"I'm not complaining about my pilots; they're good people," the other man objected. "But no pilot in my squadron except *me* actually has their wings, CAG."

"And that's the other reason I'm willing to leave you as the back-up," Russell admitted. "The Katanas give you the punch if you're needed, but if you're not, we don't have to risk your people."

"Do we *really* think we're going to get through this mess without needing backup?" Churchill asked.

"No. Which is why I want you to drill your people even harder than everyone else. When everything inevitably goes to shit, *you'll* be the ones the Fox has to hand for whatever crazy idea will pull us out of the fire.

"I need your people able to pull that idea off. Think you can manage that?"

"Wilco," Churchill said grimly, glancing around at his crews. "We'll make it happen."

39

Tau Ceti System
18:00 June 21, 2736 Earth Standard Meridian Date/Time
Chameleon, *approaching Tau Ceti H*

THE LAST OF the uniforms had been packed away—destroyed in case the worst came to pass, in fact—and Kyle's bridge was filled with officers and enlisted in unmarked black shipsuits. There were no Merchant Marine hats this time: the deception to come would be played out with computers and avatars, not his own theatrical abilities.

The room was utterly silent, unusual even in this era of neural networks and in-head displays. Everyone was focused on the main holographic display as Lau guided them in the last few seconds of Alcubierre drive...and then collapsed the space warp.

"Arrival," the taciturn navigator announced into the silence.

Kyle refrained, by dint of great effort, from demanding an instant sitrep. Taylor's people would have been working the instant the warp dropped and they started to receive current light from the system.

Live data began to propagate on the holo-display, rippling out in a spherical pattern around *Chameleon* as Taylor's people focused on the closest potential threats first.

"Chownyk, how's our IFF?" he asked, watching the display carefully as manmade objects began to appear on the display. Even in a system as rich as Tau Ceti, there were only a small number of warships —just one in Tau Ceti H orbit, in fact, though he presumed there were more over the two habitable worlds—but he could see multiple squadron-strength-or-more starfighter patrols and dozens of the in-system clippers that would fuel an industrialized system's economy.

Any one of those could doom the entire operation if they saw *Chameleon* as anything except a Commonwealth Navy vessel.

"Everything is checking out from here," his XO replied. "We are TCNS *Christopher Lee* to everyone looking. If there's some trick to their IFF codes, though…"

"We're running their code on their hardware," Kyle pointed out. "If that won't work, this whole operation was doomed from the beginning."

"The good Lieutenant is ready to go," Glass told him, the spy having taken over the communications console on the bridge to allow him to run the simulacrum that would hopefully get them close *enough* to finish the mission.

"Thank you," Kyle replied, then turned back to Taylor. "All right. Tactical: what do we see?"

"Shipyard Alpha and the Central Research Station are exactly where they should be," she replied. "We have a *Saint*-class battleship orbiting Shipyard Charlie, roughly forty light-seconds from the area of operations.

"Defenses for both Alpha and the Research Station match up to our intel. I've got just over three hundred starfighters running security patrol through the Tau Ceti H planetary system and local space, but none of them are within two million kilometers of us at this moment."

"Any other warships?"

"Two *Lexington*-class carriers and two *Assassin*-class battlecruisers are attached to a resupply station halfway between the two habitable planets," she reported. "They're the main system defense force, but they're also over a day from H."

Though with the various defenses around the gas giant, the *battleship*, and the thousand-plus starfighters swanning around the system, the main system fleet arriving a day late to the party wasn't going to change the odds.

"We're looking as clear as we're going to get," Kyle said aloud. "Commander Rokos?"

"I'm seeing it," Rokos replied. "Your orders?"

"You have a go to drop ten minutes before we hit turnover," the Captain ordered. That was still just over an hour away, and they'd still be almost ten million kilometers from the research station, thirteen million from Shipyard Alpha.

"All right," Rokos confirmed. "Plenty of time for us to get dropped off like garbage. See you on the other side, skipper. Good luck."

"Good luck to you too. Happy hunting."

"Not the moment of truth just yet," Kyle said cheerfully as the channel cut. "Any reaction to our presence in general?"

"Tau Ceti Traffic Control just sent out a handshake request from an automated sensor platform," Chownyk reported from CIC. "We fed it into the old software and it sent back a response. I give it a few minutes before anyone realizes the Q-Com address doesn't work anymore."

The pirates who'd stolen what had then been *Christopher Lee* had destroyed her original quantum-entangled particle blocks within hours of seizing her. Inconvenient to Kyle now, though the current mix of League, Alliance, and "black" quantum blocks she carried was certainly *secure* enough. He *had* Commonwealth quantum blocks, but they weren't *Christopher Lee*'s, which made them useless today.

"Your friend is going to be up in a few minutes," Kyle told Glass, considering. How long would depend on *who* made the call to reach out by radio—and who actually did the reaching out.

"That's what we have him for," the spy said confidently.

The seconds ticked away, each carrying the Q-ship thousands of kilometers closer to her destination, accelerating towards their turnover point at a sedate one hundred gravities.

Kyle could imagine the consternation going on Tau Ceti Space Traffic Control. They were flying a Navy IFF, though the STC *might* have it listed as "lost in action". They were doing nothing offensive. They had correctly replied to the radio handshake, but the Q-Com connection they preferred to use for final setup was *valid* but coming up blank.

"We have an incoming radio transmission," Chownyk reported.

"Throw it on the holotank; do not record for reply," Kyle ordered.

The big system display in the holographic tank flickered and a flat video image appeared off to one side. The sole occupant of the image was a middle-aged woman in the black-and-red uniform of the Terran Commonwealth Navy.

"This is Captain Alice Nguyen, TCN," she said harshly. "Tau Ceti System Control has flagged you as a potential threat. *Christopher Lee*, you are on our records as lost in action, details classified, and your Q-Com blocks are not functional.

"Identify and explain or I will be forced to deploy starfighters to destroy you."

Nguyen's image froze as the transmission ended, and Kyle waved airily at Glass.

"You're up, Mister Glass. How's the good Lieutenant feeling?"

"Mister Adelaide's come a long way at great cost and is almost home," the spy replied brightly. "He's stressed but relieved. Let's see what he has to say."

Lieutenant Pierre Adelaide was a young man with pitch-black skin and hair from the Proxima Centauri colony. He had also been the Assistant Tactical Officer aboard *Christopher Lee* when she'd been captured by pirates—and had still been *alive* when Federation Marines had stormed the Q-ship.

Adelaide was a loyal son of the Commonwealth, but he was also *very* grateful to no longer be the personal sex slave of a woman who was the poster child for "psychopathic slaver." Regardless of whether or not he'd knowingly given the Alliance any classified information, Federation Intelligence had a *lot* of video footage of the young man.

The image that appeared on a new video screen on the holographic display was a digital simulacrum assembled from that footage, one that would say and do exactly what Glass instructed in exactly the way that young Adelaide would.

He stood on a bridge that was in much worse shape than the one Kyle sat on. The command chair was gone, and many of the consoles had been replaced by jury-rigged stopgaps. The space was the painstaking kind of clean that only happened in the mess after true disasters, where "real" clean was impossible.

Those stopgap consoles just happened to be facing away from the camera Adelaide was looking into, and none of the half-dozen people in shabby shipsuits on the young officer's bridge had faces visible in the transmission.

"This is Lieutenant Pierre Adelaide, Acting Captain of *Christopher Lee*," the simulacrum said in a voice that mixed exhaustion and relief.

"As you yourself said, Captain Nguyen, exact details of *Lee*'s mission are classified, but we were captured by pirates and my superiors were all killed. The pirates destroyed the Q-Com blocks and flew *Christopher Lee* as a pirate for some weeks before I and the remaining crew managed to escape and retake the ship.

"I owe my life to the brave Specialists and Marines who risked *everything* to break out," he continued. "We've managed enough repairs to get the ship flying, but without the Q-blocks, we had no ability to call home. We..." Adelaide swallowed. "Our orders were not to reveal *Christopher Lee*'s existence to anyone unnecessarily and to return to Tau Ceti.

"We are not in need of medical assistance," he said carefully, "but I am not confident of *Lee*'s ability to sustain acceleration or to create another Alcubierre bubble. We have a package to be hand-delivered to the Central Research Station, but then I must request a slip at one of the shipyards for major repairs."

The image froze.

"Message sent," Glass reported. "Any idea on turnaround time?"

"Captain Nguyen is on one of the defensive platforms around Shipyard Alpha," Chownyk reported. "We're still a full light-minute away, so a minimum two-minute turnaround even if she's authorized to make the call on her own."

Two minutes passed in silence. Kyle kept up his usual cheery appearance, though he doubted he was the only one on the bridge who wanted to hold their breath. This was the first moment of truth, one of the points where the entire plan would come apart if the Commonwealth didn't buy it.

Five minutes passed.

"We are at emergence plus twenty minutes," Taylor announced quietly. "We are forty-five minutes from starfighter deployment, ninety from closest approach to the research station."

Kyle didn't say anything in response, waiting and watching. None of the fighter squadrons patrolling the star system were moving toward them, which was a positive sign, but without some kind of response…

"Incoming transmission," Chownyk reported, almost fifteen minutes after they'd sent their message. "This one is coming from the Research Station itself."

A different Terran officer appeared on the screen, this one a tall man with darkly tanned skin and a short black braid hanging down over his right ear. He wore the same uniform as Captain Nguyen—except with the two gold stars of a Commonwealth Rear Admiral.

"This is Admiral Alec Cornsilk," he said. "Captain Nguyen relayed your transmission to me and I apologize for the delay, Lieutenant Adelaide. I cannot *imagine* what it cost for you to retake your ship and return all this way. Welcome home!"

The Admiral's clear, honest enthusiasm and warmth left Kyle feeling guilty. Everything they had told the Terrans was a lie—less than fifty of *Christopher Lee*'s crew had still been aboard when she'd been recaptured. The "brave Specialists and Marines" their simulacrum had praised were, in the main, *dead*.

"Continue on your course for Shipyard Alpha," Cornsilk ordered. "I'm informed we should have a slip free for *Christopher Lee* to slot into for repairs. You said you had a package to deliver to my station. If you have a shuttle you can send over, I'll have someone waiting to meet you.

"Once you've docked, get in touch with my staff," the Admiral instructed. "We will need to debrief you, and after the kind of trip you've just had, I'll want to do that over the best meal I can find!"

The image froze and Kyle smiled.

"Much as it pains me to do a disservice to such a kind Admiral," he said aloud, "he seems to have given us the open door we need. Let's have the good Lieutenant deliver the appropriate kind of thanks.

"Then let's get ready to drop Rokos's fighters. We are now at launch minus thirty-three minutes."

———

RUSSELL WATCHED through his starfighter's sensors as the massive cargo hatches at the end of the flight bay slid open. Normally, the two doors were sequenced to open and close one after the other, in a time lapse so short humans barely registered it, to allow starfighters to leave or board the ship with the minimum loss of atmosphere.

Now, with every loose object secured and the support staff evacuated, both doors slid open at Chief Hanz's command. The starfighter handling systems, designed to operate in vacuum as an emergency measure, gently removed the Scimitars from their hangar bays four at a time and set them loose, letting them drift out into deep space with the escaping air.

The Wing Commander tried not to hold his breath. This wasn't necessarily the most *dangerous* part of the operation, but it was the one where everything could go wrong. There were enough different fighter groups and commands in the star system, he agreed with the assessment that once they were in and flying, everyone would assume they belonged to everyone else.

The most likely failure point was when they brought their engines online, but the Scimitars weren't the stealth fighters Cavendish had brought along. They had no way to hide their internal heat, no smart hulls to blend them into the background. If anyone was looking with a telescope, what they were doing would be obvious.

"Your turn, sir," Hanz told him as the robotic waldos locked onto his ship. "While I have to confess I'm not overly fond of these Terran birds, I do quite like their crews. Do try and bring everyone home, sir."

They both knew that wasn't going to happen. Starfighter wings always took losses—often brutal ones. Even with the limited population fit to fly starfighters, any star system could replace pilots and fighters far more easily than the astronomically expensive starships they launched from.

And this mission was going to be hell.

"I'll just have a quick chat with the Terrans, explain that we just need to steal some data and blow a fleet's worth of warships to the Void, and then we can all go home," he told her dryly. "I'm sure they'll be completely on board with just letting us get things done."

She snorted.

"I've never met anyone whose tongue was *that* silver, sir. Shoot straight."

The waldos released him, and his Scimitar drifted down the deck. A few seconds later and his ship was in space, drifting along with the rest of his Wing.

The last pair of fighters followed him out, and he had a thirty-strong strike force drifting through space at the same velocity as their mothership.

Chameleon was heading toward turnover on a straightforward and obvious vector toward Shipyard Alpha. She'd pass by the Research Station on the way at a perfectly safe thousand kilometers a second… about ten minutes before the starfighters, which would *not* decelerate, reached Shipyard Alpha itself three million kilometers farther on.

───────

TURNOVER.

Chameleon flipped in space, the spherical ship rotating to bring her massive antimatter thrusters to bear in the opposite direction. Super-heated energetic particles washed forward, creating a powerful wake of radiation that preceded the Q-ship at lightspeed.

The perfect shield to hide behind. Moments after the Q-ship started throwing drive fumes out toward every sensor in orbit of Tau Ceti H, the thirty Scimitars behind her lit off their own engines and began to accelerate toward Shipyard Alpha.

This time, Kyle *was* holding his breath. They'd fooled the Terrans with their electronic simulacrum, and it appeared the deployment of the starfighters, now sixty thousand kilometers behind them as

Chameleon continued to accelerate towards turnover, had gone unnoticed.

If anyone was feeling suspicious, the sudden appearance of a three-squadron patrol behind the new ship would set alarm bells ringing. While those alarm bells should only trigger a query initially, they still needed over thirty-five minutes—and answering that query would only buy them a handful.

This was the single biggest risk of the plan, and Kyle was relying on an error that had been repeated hundreds of times since its most famous occurrence at Pearl Harbor on Earth: since the only fighters that could possibly *be* in Tau Ceti were Commonwealth, any fighter seen *had* to be Commonwealth.

That they were flying Terran-designed starfighters would help, though the whole deception would come crashing down if they tried to interrogate more than Rokos's fighter by Q-Com. The presence of a legitimate Terran Q-block was too risky for them to leave them in place on more than one ship.

Seconds ticked by.

"This is Strike Actual," Rokos reported. "We are online and headed for Shipyard Alpha. No challenges detected as yet. Keeping the Q-Com online and watching for new friends."

Kyle glanced over at Taylor, who gave him a slow, hesitant nod.

"We show you clear as well, Strike Actual," he replied. "Radio silence until the rocket goes up now. *Chameleon* out."

There was, quite appropriately, no response.

Kyle opened another link.

"Major Hansen, we have official approval to send over a shuttle," he told the Marine. "Are your people ready?"

"I'll be going over with Lieutenant Riley's platoon, and the remainder of the company is standing by for heavy assault if we can launch in time."

"Numbers say you have barely five minutes after landing till Rokos raises hell," Kyle warned him. "Are you up for it?"

"*Vae victis*, Captain." Hansen threw the *condottieri's* motto at him. "We will overcome, no matter who you ask us to pretend to be."

"We have no margin, Lieutenant Major," Kyle said quietly. "We *need* the plans for those new starfighters."

"There's only so much I can do with five minutes, boss," Hansen replied, his tone equally quiet. "And we're more likely to trigger alarms than anyone else now."

"We'll have your heavy assault right behind you when you do," *Chameleon's* Captain promised. "If we can steal it quietly, I'm not complaining—but once it goes hot, it's smash-and-grab. We need those plans—at all costs."

"Understood," Hansen acknowledged grimly.

40

Tau Ceti System
19:45 June 21, 2736 Earth Standard Meridian Date/Time
Chameleon *Assault Shuttle Three*

EDVARD HAD his eyes closed as the assault shuttle decelerated hard toward the Terran space station. While he had the high implant bandwidth compatibility necessary to be a military officer in the twenty-eighth century—though not enough to be starfighter crew by any stretch—he found that having his eyes closed helped deal with multiple implant stimuli.

Right now, he was watching the entire star system through the shuttle's sensors. Without data they intentionally didn't have on the shuttle, he wasn't certain which of the patrols swanning around Tau Ceti H was their own strike team.

"Contact in four minutes," the pilot announced over the PA.

"Check your gear," Riley snapped.

Even with his eyes closed, Edvard knew what the scene in the shuttle's main compartment would look like. The black-ops platoon was in low-profile body armor that could pass for shipsuits except under close inspection. It wouldn't stop a battle-armor penetrator but would stand off a few regular rounds.

The second wave was packing anti-armor carbines, just in case, but the first squad carried the kind of light arms that *might* pass without too much comment. Riley and her computer specialists carried only sidearms, as did Edvard himself.

"I don't actually need a babysitter, you know," Riley told him over a private implant link. "This is my ballgame now. I know the plays better than you do."

"I know," he admitted, "but it's *my* responsibility—and I'm the one who has to make the call on the follow-up assault. I'll try not to jog your elbow."

"I appreciate it," she said. "But if you get yourself *killed* on this damn fool endeavor, I will never forgive you."

Opening his eyes to avoid visibly shaking his head, Edvard drew and checked the safety and magazine on his sidearm while he arched an eyebrow at her.

"We both have a job to do," he told her as he slid the mag back in with a sharp click. "Let's leave…anything else until afterwards."

Riley chuckled, the first part of the conversation audible to anyone else around them.

"I'm taking that as a promise…boss."

———

THE ASSAULT SHUTTLE settled calmly to the deck of the space station's landing bay, a far cry from many of Edvard's recent experiences with landing the small spacecraft. Rising, the Marine checked his intentionally haphazardly fabricated Terran Commonwealth Navy Petty Officer chevrons and picked up the courier case at his feet.

Riley and three of her electronic-specialist troopers, wearing the equally crudely made insignia of a Terran Commonwealth Marine Corps Corporal and Privates, fell in around him as they exited the shuttle. The carefully shielded hull of the assault craft would prevent the station's sensors from realizing just how packed full it was with the *rest* of Riley's platoon.

The landing bay was surprisingly small and spartan, with only one other shuttle and a single exit deeper into the station. The walls presumably held compartments with refueling gear and so forth, but the only visible break was a window allowing a flight control officer to overlook the bay.

Edvard presumed the three people standing next to the exit were the welcoming party and made a beeline for them.

The leader of the party, a tall pale-skinned woman with the single gold bar of a Commonwealth Marine Corps Major, met him halfway with a crisp salute that Edvard's assumed rank did *not* deserve. The story of Adelaide's "brave escape" had clearly spread.

"Major Armstrong," she introduced herself. "I understand you have a package for us, PO."

"I do," Edvard confirmed, lifting the courier case. "I have no idea what it contains," he admitted cheerfully, "but the Skipper said the orders he found on the old Captain's computers said to deliver it to the starfighter research department here."

"I can deliver it for you," Armstrong said calmly. "You're not cleared to go farther into the station."

"People died for us to get this back," Edvard said quietly. "Adelaide ordered me to see it delivered myself."

The data chips in the case were actually full of garbage data, but that was hidden under one of the Commonwealth's top-level ciphers—from a year earlier, but that was reasonable, given when the then–*Christopher Lee* had left.

"I appreciate both Lieutenant Adelaide's concern and your orders," the Terran Marine said gently, "but I have no authority to allow you on the station. I need you to give me the case and return to *Christopher Lee*."

There went *that* part of the plan, though Edvard had never put *that* much faith in it.

"Can we at least grab a bite to eat?" he asked plaintively. "We've been on reprocessed ration bars for *weeks*."

The recycling systems on a warship were fantastically efficient things, but *no* crew voluntarily went onto reprocessed ration bars. The taste was surprisingly tolerable, but no one could get out of their minds just where the bars came from.

Armstrong winced but shook her head.

"I can recommend a place on Shipyard Alpha," she said apologetically, holding her hand out for the case, "But this is a Class One facility; I *can't* let you aboard."

Edvard mentally checked the time. Still four minutes before the fighters were in range, but he'd run this conversation out as long as he could.

"That's unfortunate," he told Armstrong aloud—and sent the "go" signal to Riley and his people through the implant.

He didn't even see Riley *move*. There was a flash of motion and Armstrong was down, her trachea crushed by an iron-hard fist to the throat and her legs swept out from underneath her. The Terran officer likely didn't even realize she was under attack before Riley had killed her.

Her escorts didn't last any longer, their life-spans extended by fractions of a second only because they'd been hanging back and it had taken the black-ops cyborgs slightly longer to reach them.

"Go! Go! Go!" Edvard shouted aloud, shoving his shock at the speed and brutality of the deaths aside—he'd seen sudden death before, if not like this.

The rest of the platoon heard the order and came boiling out of the shuttle—but even as they did so, the emergency shutters on the flight control booth slammed shut.

Edvard was already linking into the Q-Com aboard the shuttle.

"Rocket, Rocket, Rocket," he announced to *Chameleon* and Commander Rokos. "Station Security didn't buy the story. Launch the second wave; we're moving on the bay flight control to locate a data center."

He paused.

"Good luck."

———

HEAVY SECURITY SHUTTERS had slammed shut over the exit as well, but while Edvard had been letting everyone *else* know the shooting had started, the black-ops troopers had been pulling out a bipod-mounted rocket launcher.

One of the troopers slammed a long box magazine into the top and stepped away to clear the space behind it, waving aside a trooper who'd misjudged the danger zone. A second soldier braced the launcher's bipod against his torso and aimed the weapon. A moment later, the whole assemblage spewed fire as it salvoed four rockets in under a second.

The smart weapons slammed into the shutter covering the bay flight control window in a neatly calculated pattern and detonated their shaped charges—reducing the entire security shutter and a significant chunk of the surrounding metal wall to shards of debris that swept the control center.

By the time *those* explosions had ceased, a second salvo rippled out of the launcher. These four fragmented into submunitions at a precalculated distance, each rocket delivering five magnetically tipped grapples to the intact wall above the shattered window.

Each grapple then spun out twenty meters of cable, dropping the less than ten meters to the ground where Charlie Platoon's first squad was waiting.

They swarmed up the ropes and through the massive hole into the control center. There was no gunfire—if anyone had survived the first salvo of rockets, they weren't crazy enough to get into a fight with the black-ops cyborgs.

"Here," one of the troopers exiting the shuttle shouted to Edvard before tossing him an anti-armor carbine. "Going up, sir?"

"Yes," he replied, gesturing for the third squad sergeant to come to him as the second squad went up the ropes. "Alpha and Bravo platoons are two minutes out at top speed," he told that worthy in command of a squad half made up of black-ops troops and half of Edvard's headquarters-section Marines. "Hold this launch bay. It's our main way home."

"Yes, sir!"

With a firm nod to the man, Edvard joined Riley and scaled the rope after the black-ops squads—only slightly more sedately. He might lack their hardware, but he was still one of Castle's damned Marines!

"We're in control," one of the data specialists told him. Somewhere between killing Armstrong's guards and arriving there, she'd produced a forearm-mounted slab of circuitry he recognized as a hacking module, and that module was linked into the wreckage of the center's systems.

"Can you access the station's systems?"

"Negative," the hacker replied. "It looks like each research department has their own secured data center, sir."

"Oh, *Void*," Edvard spat. "Find me the fighter research data center, Kismet," he ordered the Lance Corporal. "Riley!" he shouted, gesturing his platoon commander over. "Get ready for a breakout. We're going to have to punch through to the data center."

"Let's do it," she agreed with a cold smile. "Bunch of research pukes? Not a problem."

"Alpha, Bravo," he barked, linking into his oncoming platoon shuttles. "Charlie is moving on deep assault; we're leaving one squad to secure the landing bay. Follow in, force a beachhead, and then move out by squads to meet up with us.

"We have to let the door slam shut behind us," he told them, looking around at the forty people he had to punch through a fortified, secured facility in the heart of enemy space.

"I'm going to need you to kick it open again."

41

Tau Ceti System
19:55 June 21, 2736 Earth Standard Meridian Date/Time
Chameleon

"ROCKET, ROCKET, ROCKET."

"Damn," Kyle said mildly, watching the security alert wash across the system. With Q-Coms tying everything together, the various stations and deployments were reacting within moments of each other, but lightspeed delays meant it seemed as if the reaction rippled out from the Central Research Station.

"Incoming transmission!" Glass reported. The spy threw it up on the main display instantly, revealing yet *another* new face.

"*Christopher Lee,*" the blond man in the Starfighter Corps uniform drawled, "this is Wing Colonel John Oklahoma. We have a security alert where your shuttle touched down. You will abort your approach to Shipyard Alpha, vectoring ninety degrees to galactic north at your maximum acceleration.

"You will stand by to receive a Marine inspection party and you will provide all possible assistance to that party," Oklahoma ordered. "If you do not vector as ordered immediately, we will have no choice but to destroy you if you continue on approach to Shipyard Alpha.

"If you are who you say you are," the officer drawled, "this is an unnecessary precaution—but I am responsible for the security of Shipyard Alpha and I will *not* put it at risk. You *will* comply."

The bridge was silent for a fraction of a second, then Kyle shook his head.

"Wouldn't buy us enough time, people," he said aloud. "Besides, look."

Shipyard Alpha's immense height was now lit up with dozens —*hundreds*—of smaller, more intense energy signatures as the stations defenses came online. The orbiting platforms, only semi-somnolent to begin with, now awoke to their full fury.

Rokos was going to fly into a hornet's nest no matter what *Chameleon* did.

"Launch Hansen's shuttles," Kyle barked. "Churchill—prep your people to deploy. We're going to keep you in the tubes for a few moments longer, but we're *going* to need you. Taylor—get me Q-probe coverage; I don't care if they see it now."

His bridge crew leapt into action and Kyle watched the entire *system* explode into action around him.

Charlie Platoon had landed sixty people in one assault shuttle, but none had been in battle armor. Even understrength, the other two platoons of Marines *were* in battle armor—half were in the even more massive *boarding* battle armor, at that—and filled *five* assault shuttles— shuttles that blasted directly at the Central Research Station at five hundred gravities.

They were going to have *rough* landings, but that was what assault shuttles and battle armor were built for.

A new transmission from Oklahoma arrived unsurprisingly a moment later.

"What the *hell* do you think you're *doing,* Adelaide?" the Terran officer demanded. "Recall your shuttles or I have no choice but to shoot them—and *you*—out of my sky!"

"Taylor?" Kyle asked cheerfully.

"They have nothing in place to intercept the shuttles," she responded. "They're clear to the station."

"Let Mister Oklahoma stew in his own sweat," the Captain said calmly. "Keep our vector on Shipyard Alpha. Watch that battleship and all approaching fighters; this might get hairy."

"*Hairy* is right," Glass said. He'd apparently risen from the com station and was now standing right behind Kyle's command chair. "Rokos can't make it to lance range, Roberts," the spy said. "You *know* it. You also know he'll try to complete the mission, but he'll *die* and achieve *nothing*."

Glass was right. Rokos had about another thirty seconds in which he could abort—he was decelerating toward the station, but if he broke and accelerated away from the station at ninety degrees from his current course, he would pass it at a thousand kilometers a second well over a hundred thousand kilometers clear.

That was inside the station's range against his ships, but the distance would mean most of his people would survive. If they closed to the forty thousand kilometers necessary for them to precisely target the ships, the defenses would annihilate them.

"We have to destroy the station," Glass continued. "If they fire all of their missiles, they can take it out. It's a *fleet's* worth of warships, Roberts. A full percent of the Commonwealth's shipbuilding."

"Abort Rokos's strike," Kyle ordered sharply, ignoring the spy.

"*Dammit*, Roberts, we *can't* let this opportunity pass us by!" the spy snapped, his voice rising in volume now as he realized Kyle wasn't going to instantly obey. "Yes, there's civilians aboard, but it's still a legitimate military target—and forcing them to do search and rescue is the only way this ship is getting out of this system alive!"

Kyle stared at the hologram and, for a moment he would forever regret, *almost* gave the order.

"No," he finally said with a deep breath. "We are *not* the Commonwealth. We will *not* embrace the slaughter of civilians in a moment of expediency or fanaticism."

"No one would ever know," Glass objected. "This is a black op for a reason!"

"They would find out," Kyle said flatly. "Hypocritical of them or not, they would hunt those who killed their people until the end of time. No deception would last. No lie would hold them off. I will not answer atrocity with atrocity."

"I *order* you!" Glass shouted, every scrap of relationship and rapport they'd built over the last months shattering in the face of what he clearly saw as failure.

"Sergeant at arms!" Kyle bellowed, attracting the attention of the two Marines guarding the bridge door. "Remove Mister Glass to his quarters. He is not permitted to leave until I authorize it!"

"Damn it, Roberts—you'll doom us all."

"No," Captain Kyle Roberts said calmly. "I am the *Stellar fucking Fox*. I will find another way."

The argument had cost precious seconds, but thankfully, Rokos had already begun his abort. It couldn't help but draw attention to him, but the elevated alert level would rapidly involve calling in all fighter squadrons—and if they hadn't realized yet that they had thirty starfighters who weren't supposed to be there, they would shortly.

Glass was right about one thing, Kyle knew. The *Saint*-class battleship was already heading their way. It wasn't *fast*—as a capital ship, it was designed for Tier Two accelerations, less than half that of a starfighter—but it would catch *Chameleon* before she could flee.

Unless that ship was distracted, the best they could hope for was to retrieve the starfighter plans and transmit them by Q-Com before they died.

Destroying the station outright might not even achieve that, he admitted grimly to himself. In the place of the *Saint*'s Captain, *he'd* risk missing some civilians by dropping his small craft for search and rescue while he took the battleship after the person who'd killed them.

He needed a job they'd *have* to use the battleship for. Something where mere starfighters and search-and-rescue spacecraft just wouldn't cut it...

The sheer scale of Shipyard Alpha tugged at his eye and a cold smile spread across his face.

"Get me a live link to Rokos," he ordered.

———

"WE HAVE A PROBLEM," Taylor announced grimly as Kyle cut the channel to the Wing Commander. "The Research Station just launched starfighters—and they're like *nothing* I've ever seen."

"Show me," he ordered.

The holographic display zoomed in, providing a surprising quality of detail. One of the Q-probes had to be close to the station, keeping an eye on their assault shuttles.

Ten strange-looking spacecraft had left one of the station's bays. Their vector wasn't a pursuit of *Chameleon*, but they were definitely angling in the direction of Kyle's ship, and he did not like the look of the ships.

They consisted of a central spike reminiscent of the very first starfighters the Federation had deployed, with scaffolding-like structures extending out on all four sides...and each of those scaffolding-like structures carried a missile half the size of the central hull.

"Those are torpedo bombers," he said grimly. "Churchill—emergency launch, *now!* Taylor—full defensive missile launch; I want salvos of everything in the air as counter-fire. If I'm guessing right, at this range, they may as well be capital-ship missiles."

They were barely three hundred thousand kilometers away from the station, though their two-thousand-plus-kilometer-a-second velocity meant they were well out of range of anything *short* of capital ship missiles...or, potentially, whatever the Terrans had mounted on their new bombers.

Ten more icons flashed into existence on the screen, Churchill's Katanas blasting into space to protect the Q-ship. They immediately lit off their engines, accelerating toward the Terran bombers at five hundred gravities.

Moments later, the icons of *Chameleon's* missiles appeared as well, as Taylor flushed the launchers. Six Stormwinds and a dozen Javelins lanced out at the bombers.

"Bombers are not accelerating toward us; they are maintaining distance," Taylor reported. "I have missile launch—four birds per starfighter, total forty inbound."

"Lau, Taylor, coordinate with Churchill," Kyle said quietly. "It seems we get to play guinea pig for the new toy we wanted specs for, people. Save *everything*, track *everything*."

The first thing he noted was that the missiles were *fast*. The interaction between mass manipulators and antimatter engines had "tiers" of efficiency, plateaus where the fuel consumption for a given power-to-weight ratio was predictable and stable. Missiles used the fourth of those tiers, fuel-sucking compared to even the consumption a starfighter could afford, but capable of accelerating at a thousand gravities.

Except these new missiles were pulling a thousand and *fifty* gravities.

"They've cracked the top band of the Tier Four accelerations," Chownyk said from CIC, echoing Kyle's thoughts. "Estimated impact in nine minutes. Katanas will reach lance range in sixteen minutes."

The geometry and *Chameleon*'s existing velocity meant there was no point in Churchill's people launching their own missiles—they'd be in lance range well before the birds struck home.

Kyle studied his tactical feed of the system. The bombers were the most immediate threat to the Q-ship, but that was a threat measured in long minutes. Hansen's people were on a similar time frame, though the assault shuttles would hit home before Rokos made his firing pass on Shipyard Alpha.

Whether or not *Chameleon* completed her mission was up to Hansen and Rokos.

Kyle's job now was to make sure there was a way for everyone to go home afterward.

42

"THEY'VE DEFINITELY SEEN US NOW," Alvarado reported.

The gunner was thankfully no worse off, despite having been knocked unconscious in the earlier mess. His nanites and the ship's doctors had had a rough few hours controlling and repairing a moderately severe concussion, but Russell was glad to have him back.

"I see them," the Wing Commander agreed aloud, watching the vector change of the fighters around them. There were twelve squadrons—a hundred and twenty starfighters—close enough to intervene in the chaos the "pirates" were causing.

All of them were now accelerating toward his thirty ships. It was an intimidating display of firepower—and that was before one counted the kilometer-long battleship also heading their way.

"Earliest intercept is ninety seconds after the launch point," the gunner said quietly. "Missiles only; no one will be able to force us to lance range."

Russell smiled grimly. The routes of in-system patrols like this were designed carefully so a significant chunk of them could always generate an intercept vector on an incoming force—but his strike force was *inside* that zone, far closer than the people designing those routes had accounted for.

"Launch in twenty seconds," he said firmly. "Downloading target coordinates to Strike Force."

A few seconds of silence followed.

"Sir, that's Shipyard Alpha," Alvarado said quietly. "It's…"

"The coordinates are *very* specific," Russell said sharply, intentionally sharing his comments with the entire strike force. "Trust me. And trust Roberts."

He *heard* Alvarado swallow hard, but he could also see the gunner setting up the salvo.

At the same time, Russell started the carefully random dance of a starfighter near the enemy as the defensive platforms around Shipyard Alpha opened fire. Hundred-kiloton-per-second lance beams sparkled on his neural feed, the computer drawing in the invisible beams for him.

They weren't *quite* in range, but a single lucky hit now would save the station from four missiles.

"Missiles away," Alvarado announced as the icons populated Russell's display.

Each of their thirty fighters put four Javelins into space, totaling a hundred and twenty missiles charging toward Shipyard Alpha. Russell found himself praying that they'd got the target coordinates right, or he'd just launched the worst atrocity ever committed by Castle Federation forces.

Before he'd even finished the thought, two of his starfighters flashed into vapor, the station's defenders scoring their lucky hits a few seconds too late to make any difference.

"Watch your evasives," he snapped. "Prep your second salvo, stand by on prior target coordinates and target those incoming starfighters."

He flashed a highlight on the closest starfighter formation, marking them as the target for his people's missiles once they entered range—in time to watch all thirty starfighters change course. They had seen his people's missiles.

"Alpha bogeys are going after the missiles. Bravo, Charlie and Delta are still on an intercept course for us," Alvarado reported.

That didn't remove Alpha from the engagement, but it did reduce their threat level. Russell's people were still outnumbered three to one by the starfighters coming after them, so he agreed completely with the Terran commander's decision.

"Do we...fire again on those coordinates?" Alvarado asked slowly.

"Negative," Russell replied. "Hold prior target on standby," he repeated to the all-ship net. "Set your course for a return to *Chameleon* and your missile targets will be Bogey Formation Delta."

"Why Delta?" Alvarado said quietly. Formation Delta was a four-squadron patrol sweeping back in from the outer system. They *could* reach the strike force, but they were also the enemy they were most likely to evade.

"They're the only ones who can catch *Chameleon*," the CAG said grimly. "Missile status?"

"Thirty seconds to impact."

Bogey Alpha had launched their Javelins in counter-missile mode. The angle *barely* allowed them to do so, but it was an awful shot. The defensive platforms' lasers and lances were taking their toll, with dozens of missiles already destroyed.

Russell watched, half-holding his breath now as the missiles charged toward Shipyard Alpha, their path marked by the antimatter explosions of the ones that didn't make it.

Ten seconds and still fifteen thousand kilometers short of the immense space station, Bogey Alpha's hundred and twenty missiles caught up with the surviving missiles of the Federation salvo. They blazed through each other in a deadly intercept that incinerated half of the Commonwealth missiles...and left only fourteen of Russell's missiles to close the final distance.

The last-ditch defenses flared to life, lasers on the station itself and its inner security platforms opening up—and missing as the missiles' course went ever so slightly differently from what the defenders had been expecting.

The Terrans adapted in the seconds they had, and more missiles blasted into vapor...but three made it through, slamming into the massive stabilizer ring at the base of the immense station and obliterating it in a tripled blast of antimatter fire.

"We hit the stabilizers!" Alvarado announced, his voice shocked. "The station is... *Starless Void*, the station is *spinning*."

"And destabilized," Russell said with satisfaction. "And...falling."

Slowly. The big station was rotating at a rate that would have it upside down in a little under a minute, and falling at less than a kilometer per second. Russell didn't have the data to guess its crush depth in the gas giant, but he figured the locals had hours to save it.

Probably not days.

"Let them deal with that," the Wing Commander said calmly. "We have a ride to catch."

————

"First missile intercept in thirty seconds," Taylor announced grimly, the words cutting through the jubilation on *Chameleon*'s bridge like ice. They had three waves of missiles out to cover the torpedoes, but with no data on the weapons' capabilities, they were almost shooting blind.

The damage to Shipyard Alpha bought them time—it was *exactly* the distraction Kyle's people needed to live through today, and achieved with minimum loss of civilian life. While Taylor's focus was on the missiles bearing down on the Q-ship itself, he was watching the wider scope.

The battleship had already changed course, accelerating rapidly toward the falling space station. They were still ten minutes away from their zero-zero intercept, but the big warship was the only ship in range that might be able to save the platform.

Three of the closer formations of starfighters had changed course toward the station as well, though what exactly the relatively tiny spaceships intended to do, Kyle wasn't sure—cover the swarm of shuttles already starting to evacuate the facility from Rokos's people, he guessed.

"Jamming is up," his tactical officer declared, pulling his attention back to the immediate threat.

Kyle whistled silently as he studied the power readings they were getting on the ECM emitters the torpedoes mounted.

"I've got chaff and complex electronic warfare running as well," Taylor said softly. "Sir...without more data, I'm not going to make much of a dent."

"Do what you can," he ordered. "And record everything. We need to *get* that 'more data', Commander."

There was no time for acknowledgement as the first salvo of their missiles charged into the incoming torpedoes. Six capital-ship missiles and a dozen fighter missiles sliced in simultaneously. The fighter missiles, lacking the heavier computers and sensors of their big brothers, failed completely, detonating too far away from the incoming weapons to achieve even near-miss kills.

The six Stormwind capital missiles, however, took out three torpedoes. A fifty-percent kill ratio in defensive mode was impressive—except that they had less than four minutes to impact. Even with the salvos already in the air, Taylor would only have ten more salvos.

That would leave almost a quarter of the torpedoes for the Q-ship's close in defenses, and Kyle was grimly certain that would be *far* too many.

"Second intercept in fifteen seconds."

"XO—collate everything we can pull from the intercepts and dump it to Churchill," Kyle ordered. Alpha Squadron would interpenetrate with the torpedoes just after the third salvo of missiles intercepted. Every ounce of data they could extract from the earlier intercepts might give the starfighters a better chance of killing missiles.

And every missile they killed was one fewer to rip into *Chameleon*.

Two more series of explosions lit up the neural feeds as the next two intercepts passed, wiped five more incoming torpedoes out of existence. One of those kills, Kyle noted absently, was from the *Chameleon*-launched Javelins.

Churchill didn't waste missiles he was unlikely to hit with. For a few precious seconds, his squadron went to full deceleration, extended the time they were in range of the missiles. Lances and lasers flashed out, targeted by the power of ten starfighters' radar arrays at point-blank instead of the still-distant Q-ship's arrays and the minimal scanners of the missiles themselves.

Explosions flared around the starfighters, and Kyle cringed as one of the starfighters lost all power and spun off into space. The crew were almost certainly dead—but *surviving* that kind of near miss was what had cost him his own pilot's wings.

"Twelve remaining inbound," Taylor said quietly. "Fourth intercept in fifteen seconds. Torpedo impact two minutes after that."

Kyle waited silently. He was out of tricks to influence this. Missiles at this range came down to math, and these torpedoes were new. They didn't *know* the math. They didn't know exactly how much chaff they'd deployed, how much power was in the jammers, what cues would suggest a sensor return was a false image versus a change of course.

Taylor kept firing missiles into the teeth of the incoming torpedoes, eighteen missiles every thirty seconds, spending the magazines like water.

It wasn't enough. Kyle *knew* it couldn't be enough. It wouldn't have been against forty capital ship missiles at this range, and it wasn't against forty of the torpedoes at this range, not without more of a fighter screen.

"Lances and lasers online," Chownyk reported from CIC. "CIC assuming control of inner defense perimeter. Taylor, handle the missiles. We'll run the beams."

The young woman at the console didn't even acknowledge, still running her missiles with ice-cold concentration. She was back to fifty percent kills with the Stormwinds, Kyle noted absently—she was as brilliant as Mason had suggested she might be.

Six missiles hit the inner perimeter, throwing their extra fifty gravities of acceleration into defensive maneuvers the Q-ship's computers could *track* but hadn't *expected.*

The inner defense caught four. Taylor fired Javelins into the teeth of the last pair, a desperation move that sent the entire *ship* lurching as twelve *gigatons* of antimatter detonated barely two kilometers from the hull.

Then the entire half-kilometer-wide starship *jerked* as a final missile slammed home with crippling force. Lights on the bridge flickered as the zero-point cells fuelling the ship's primary power locked down to prevent catastrophic failure.

Then it was over. The lights returned to full brightness. The zero-point cells unlocked—most of them, at least.

"Status report," Kyle ordered.

"They hit us right on the weapons array," Taylor said after a long moment of silence. "All of our missile launchers and a third of our lances are gone. Half my people went with them," she finished, her voice choked.

"Engines damaged but functional," Lau reported. "Eighty gees safe, no more."

"That near miss wiped our entire surface sensor array," Chownyk reported, the CIC link still stable. "One of the primary zero-point cells is in full automatic shutdown. The others are fully online."

With the sensors gone, the world outside *Chameleon* was black. Kyle had no idea what was going on.

"I thought we had Q-probes out," he demanded. The FTL com–equipped probes were designed to provide real-time data across the system, but they'd also back up the capital ship now that she had no sensors of her own.

"We lost power to the Q-Com section when ZPC Four went down," Chownyk replied. "We're rebooting, but we have no quantum communications until then—and everything we'd receive a *radio* message with is melted."

"So we're blind, we're defenseless, and we can't even talk to anyone," Kyle concluded grimly. "Get me my coms back, people. We're not out of this yet!"

———

"*Chameleon* has been hit hard," Russell concluded aloud to his people. "We're going to have to assume she's still capable of Alcubierre and of picking us up, but it doesn't look like she's in position to defend herself.

"Which means she's in trouble," he told them grimly. "Our Delta bogeys are ignoring us and changing course to pursue her—whoever is in command figures we can't escape without the ship we arrived on...and he's right.

"He's also probably figuring he's got us outnumbered almost two to one and we're going to play it safe." Russell chuckled. "But he doesn't know who we fly for or who I learned tactics from, or he'd think again!"

He'd lost five fighters and fifteen people looping Shipyard Alpha, but he didn't have time to mourn yet. That four-squadron flight of Terran starfighters was already vectoring toward *Chameleon*. They were still over ten minutes and a million kilometers away, but unless the Q-ship started maneuvering or at least sending out active radar signals sometime soon, she was a sitting duck.

The angles meant *he* would close the range on them in under eight minutes, if he was willing to throw twenty-five starfighters at forty. The Commonwealth wing had the same Scimitars he did. Their crews almost certainly didn't have Navy petty officers running engines and guns.

But their crews also didn't have the hardened veterans that made up the *rest* of his crews.

"Set your course for intercept," he ordered. "We've still got a dozen missiles apiece, and if we can wipe Delta, everyone else who can intercept *Chameleon* before she can warp space is busy running for Shipyard Alpha."

Assuming, of course, that the Q-ship started moving again sometime soon. Russell stared at the battered warship and caught himself praying under his breath.

The Eternal Stars weren't out to change much in this life. They left that to humanity.

———

THE BIG HOLO-DISPLAY flickered and came alive a moment before Kyle's neural feed did.

The quality of the image was lower, closer to what he was used to at long range—a key sign that they were feeding their sensor data from a nearby Q-probe.

Part of what the probe showed them was the exterior of their own ship, and Kyle hid a wince as he studied *Chameleon*. Her cheery paint job had been vaporized and a massive crater marred her once nearly spherical hull.

"Engines functional," Lau reported. "Orders?"

"Hold for now," Kyle said quietly, still studying his ship. "How are we for weapons?"

"I have one half-megaton lance and twelve secondaries," Taylor said quietly. "We should be able to target them via the Q-probe, but we will suffer a loss of accuracy—and I'm picking up a four-squadron formation headed our way."

"Play dead," he ordered. "Let's see if we can lure them in and set them up for Rokos. How's Churchill?"

"Seventy seconds from lance range," Chownyk reported. "Bombers are evading, but they started late. They can't escape now."

A moment later, it became clear that they hadn't *planned* to. At a quarter-million kilometers, the bombers flipped back and opened fire —each of the gangly spacecraft blasting four Javelins into space before resuming their course.

Churchill didn't even blink. His own salvo was in space a second later and his people continued on course.

"They were trying to make us think they'd panicked," Kyle said quietly. "But...they got the timing wrong. Someone tried to be clever."

The Terrans had tried to take Churchill by surprise, but the same geometry that had caused the veteran squadron commander not to bother launching his own missiles meant their missile salvo couldn't save them.

The Javelins were almost thirty seconds away from impact when Alpha Squadron reached lance range of the bombers, and the Katana had been built to do one thing very, *very* well: kill starfighters.

Ten sixty-kiloton-per-second positron lances sliced into space and the bombers never stood a chance. Without their own starfighters to protect them, they were sitting ducks for enemy starfighters.

Without the launching starfighters to trigger the ECM, their missiles were no luckier. Churchill's counter-salvo gutted the attack and not one of the survivors connected as the Katanas began to decelerate, looping around the Central Research Station toward *Chameleon*.

"If Rokos can stop the outsystem patrol, we are clear all the way out," Taylor reported.

"Lau, bring up the engines at whatever they'll take," Kyle ordered. "Link in to everyone's Q-Coms; let them know our status. Can we retrieve starfighters?"

With the more immediate threats, he'd barely checked the status of the flight deck.

"We will be able to retrieve but not launch," Chownyk reported. "Half the launch tubes are just...gone. The other half are warped beyond safe use. The flight deck itself is intact, though I understand the doors are currently flash-welded shut. Hanz is working on that."

"Tell her she's authorized to blow them off," Kyle said grimly.

"I...believe that to be her plan at this point, yes," the XO confirmed.

"It won't be a first for me," Kyle told him. "Warn Rokos we aren't able to provide fire support—and see if we can get an update from Hansen.

"This whole damn affair is a half-pointless sideshow if the Marines haven't found that data yet."

43

Tau Ceti System
20:10 June 21, 2736 Earth Standard Meridian Date/Time
Terran Commonwealth Navy Central Research Station

"DOWN!"

One of the troopers unceremoniously grabbed Edvard by the shoulder, yanking him out of the path of a spray of bullets and calmly returning fire. There was a scream of pain and the shooting stopped.

"Thanks," the Marine told the other man. "Didn't see him."

"These are *not* clear fields of fire, sir," his rescuer replied.

They had *finally* reached the data center for the fighter research section of the station, only to find their communications completely jammed and an entire company of Terran Marines trying to corral them in. Unfortunately for both sides, the area around the data center was a mess of cubicles, private offices, and winding corridors of the kind only the people regularly there could find their way around.

And the data center itself was, quite sensibly, in security lockdown. Massive metal shutters had closed over the accesses and Riley's people were busy hacking security instead of hacking the data center's storage drives.

The molecular-circuitry computers that filled a center like that were tough, but blasting the door open would still risk damaging or destroying them. Worse, if they even damaged one, it would make their attempt to find the *right* data even more difficult.

"Here they come again!"

Wishing that they'd brought battle armor with them—not for the first time since this had become a defensive fight—Edvard swept the area with his anti-armor carbine, watching for the next wave.

One squad came down the corridor most of the assaults had arrived down, but something tickled at Edvard's paranoia as he opened fire. The carbine fired the same penetrators as his main battle rifle, though its recoil management systems were getting uncomfortably warm even through his armored shipsuit.

The Terrans knew that his people had enough anti-armor weaponry to make a direct assault suicide, and it wasn't in the Terran Marines' lexicon to try and run his people out of bullets with bodies, which meant…

"Danger left!" he bellowed, pivoting in his cover to target the nearest visible section of clear metal wall. Even as he did so, the wall disintegrated as *another* squad, this one in heavy boarding armor, burst through the wall at what was supposed to be his exposed flank.

The lead Marine took a three-round burst from his carbine and went down in a massive heap. The cyborg who'd rescued Edvard a moment before joined him in covering the new angle, and two more Marines went down.

Now *their* fire responded and the black-ops trooper next to Edvard grunted and fell backward as a heavy round crashed through his chest. Another trooper charged into his place with a grenade launcher, spraying down the new opening with anti-armor grenades.

At least two more Marines went down, and then the shooting stopped again, for the moment.

"Are we through the door yet?" Edvard asked Riley grimly. "We are *completely* pinned down."

"Yes!" Kismet announced as the specialists' hack module made an audible beeping noise. One set of shutters slid up, revealing a door the black-ops trooper calmly kicked open without even taking a breath.

"Fall back into the center," Edvard ordered. "It's got better cover than these damn offices!"

The data specialists went first, then Edvard and Riley—no one was going to let the company commander hold down the last line—and then the remaining troopers. They'd lost over half of the two squads they'd started with, and without the ability to contact the shuttle by radio to use its Q-Com, they couldn't relay the data home.

"Download *everything*," he ordered the hackers. "Don't bother decrypting it, just…download everything. We have the storage, right?"

Kismet and the other techs were already on it, hooking their hacking modules up to the data center's computers with direct cables and getting to work.

"These," Kismet told him, gesturing around, "are mostly for processing and backup. But…we don't have enough storage. We'll have to steal theirs."

"Do it," he ordered. "We can't contact our backup and we're running out of time!"

———

By the time Kismet yanked a pair of molecular-circuitry storage crystals out of the data center's systems, it was very clear they were not leaving the way they came.

The Terrans were no more willing to wreck the data center than the raiders had been, and with only one door, it was easy to keep them away from the one door—but the door also limited Edvard's people's field of fire and was allowing the Terrans to sneak right up to the entrance.

"Each of these crystals has everything," the tech told Edvard, handing him one. "One of us gets out of here, El-Maj, or all of this was for nothing." She glanced around. "What do we do now?"

"We go down," Edvard replied. "Since we have what we need—blastcord on the floor and take cover!"

A circle of blastcord—a length of preshaped high-explosive charges designed for basically this purpose—was thrown on the floor and the Federation troops took cover behind the crystalline stalagmites of the data center's molecular computers.

"Fire in the hole!"

The room shook as the explosives went off and Edvard found himself dragged forward by iron-hard hands and all but thrown down the hole. Kismet was the only one in front of him, carefully balancing herself as she gestured at a map only she could see.

"This way, sir," she announced as the rest of the black-ops troopers dropped down behind them.

"Any chance of linking up with the Marines?"

"Still jammed," Riley told him. "We need to meet up physically—hell, we don't even know where they *are*."

And so long as they were jammed, they couldn't relay their data back to *Chameleon* or the Federation. Until they reached the shuttles and their Q-Coms, this all remained for nothing.

"Then let's move," he ordered.

———

THEY MADE it almost halfway back to the shuttle bay before they ran into the Terrans again. Despite the overwhelming jamming, the station defenders clearly had their own communications working as the raiders ran headlong into a barricade—with emplaced heavy weapons.

Their entire front team went down in a spray of fire as three tripod-mounted machine guns opened up, filling the corridor with streams of high-velocity penetrators. Overkill against the light armor they were wearing—enough to not merely go through Kismet's armor but also through the storage crystal she was carrying.

Edvard found himself slammed bodily into a wall by a cursing Riley, out of the line of fire as her people ducked backward to safety.

"Stay *down*, sir," she snapped. "You're now carrying the only copy of that data we have. Do *not* get shot."

He spent a second reviewing what he had seen of the barricade. Portable neutronium-coated barriers—with built-in mass manipulators to make them easier to carry and harder to move when placed—

blocked the entire corridor. Slits in the barriers showed little more than the barrels of the machine guns.

"We are not going that way," he said quietly. "Give me a moment."

He pulled up the map Kismet had hacked out of the systems in the flight bay control room, looking for another way back to the bay. This was the *fastest* route, but there were other ways.

"We need to go back," Edvard ordered. "About twenty meters, then if we swing right, there are three other ways we can get back to the shuttle bay."

"Make it happen, people," Riley barked, gesturing for their rear guard to about-face.

They'd barely started moving before their *original* pursuers arrived. Battle-armor rifles spat *more* penetrators.

"We're trapped," Riley said grimly. "Close up, everyone! Shoot anything that moves and isn't us!"

Edvard studied their situation grimly. They had about four meters of corridor in which they weren't going to come under fire, but if they went either way, they ran into enemies with heavier armor and heavier gear.

They'd started the assault with forty of Riley's black-ops cyborgs.

Including the two officers, they had sixteen people left. Presumably, the cyborgs intended for covert ops couldn't be traced back to the Federation, but the losses hurt.

"We're out of options, Edvard," Riley said quietly. "You have to get back with that data crystal. We're going to have to blow a hole in that forward barricade."

"That's a frontal assault," he hissed. "It would be *suicide.*"

"Yes," she said flatly. "But we can break them open and get you through to where the Marines have hopefully set up their beachhead. My people have to be the rear guard anyway, Edvard. You *know* what we have to do."

Edvard spent several precious seconds staring at her in horror. She was right, but he couldn't—*couldn't* let her do it.

Except…

"I cannot let my personal feelings compromise my professional judgment," he whispered.

"No," she agreed, holding his gaze. Everything they both wanted to say was in their eyes, but this wasn't the place or time.

"Do it," he ordered, his voice harsh.

"Form up, people," Riley snapped loudly. "We're going forward and punching a hole! Last of our smoke grenades first, then follow them up with real grenades. We know where they left the holes in that neutronium bullshit, so put grenades through them.

"You can do this," she said softly after a pause. "We knew what we'd signed on for." She glanced around, probably realizing that there was *some* kind of recording most likely going on, and replaced whatever she'd been ready to finish her little speech with: *"Vae victis!"*

Two of the troopers stayed with Edvard, following some unseen signal from Riley to keep him out of trouble. The rest threw their grenades and charged.

Without the eye implants the cyborgs possessed, he couldn't see through the smoke—but neither could the Terrans. There was a reason Riley's people were down to their last set of smoke grenades.

He heard the grenade explosions, followed by one long, ear-tearing burst of fire from a single heavy machine gun and a chaotic flurry of gunshots from rifles and carbines. He *itched* to lunge forward, but Riley was right: this was her job.

"All right, move up!" he heard her bark.

He and his two escorts charged through the dispersing smoke toward the mobile barricade. One of the barriers was completely wrecked, thrown forward onto the ground when its mass manipulators had been shredded and shorted out.

There was no way that super-heavy panel of compressed matter was moving, but the remaining barricades still covered over half of the corridor. Riley and her people were behind them, waiting for Edvard and his escorts.

He was only halfway to the barrier when the floor started the distinct rumble of charging troops in battle armor. He was being pursued.

One of the heavy machine guns was still intact, however, and opened fire as the pursuing Marines rounded the corner into range.

"Get in here!"

Edvard wasn't going to argue. He charged forward, keeping his head down as the machine gun fired several more times, suppressive bursts to keep the Terrans back.

There were a lot fewer people on the other side of the barricade than he'd hoped. Including Riley, only four of the fourteen black-ops troopers who'd charged the barricade were still up.

The full twenty-man squad of Marines, with battle armor, fixed defenses and heavy weapons that had tried to stop them was shredded, bodies tossed where they'd fallen. Some had even gone down to close-range monomolecular blades—and Edvard tried not to notice that *Riley* was the only one with the shortsword–like weapon out.

"They're not going to slow down," she said grimly. "You're not making it back without a rear guard."

"They have numbers, battle armor, and heavy weapons," he objected. The only way Riley could slow the Commonwealth Marines down was by making them take the time to kill her, an option he was unwilling to accept.

"I have neutronium barricades, plenty of ammunition, and a heavy machine gun," Riley said with a smile that didn't reach her eyes.

"Taylor, Madison, escort the El-Maj back to the launch bay," she continued sharply. "We're out of time and out of options, boss. *Go.*"

"I'm sorry," he said softly. He wasn't apologizing for leaving her behind.

"Make it back, Edvard. Make it worth it."

"I will," he promised.

"Good. Now go!"

———

THE TWO BLACK-OPS troopers clearly thought they were going to have to physically hustle Edvard along. Once he'd made the decision to leave Riley behind, however, he almost left *them* behind.

They were physically augmented—but he was in better *shape* than they were around the implants. They caught up quickly enough, but he found a tiny amount of amusement in leaving them behind even for that instant—and anything remotely positive was hard to find right now.

The machine gun opened fire again moments after they left, now with rifles and carbines adding to the chaos as the last handful of men and women from the two squads they'd launched the assault with did their best to hold the line.

The sound faded as they pushed toward the outside of the station, and Edvard could only hope it had faded due to distance. He kept expecting to run into the forward elements of the beachhead his Marines were supposed to be putting up—the silence and empty corridors as they drew closer to the shuttle bay were worrying.

When they turned a corner and ran headlong into a trio of Terran Marines, it was almost a relief to see *anyone*. He and his escorts opened fire first, dropping two of the Marines before they could react—but the third's armor held against even the anti-armor rounds, and they returned fire.

Madison went down before Edvard and Taylor's fire punched through the Marine's armor, the short exchange of violence sending adrenaline pumping through the Lieutenant Major's veins—enough to allow him to drop to the floor as *another* fire team of Terrans swept into the corridor, following the sound of the guns.

One went down under Edvard's fire—but Taylor went down under theirs. Edvard twisted his weapon, trying to get it to bear on the two remaining Marines, only to run out of ammunition as he dropped a bead.

He didn't have time to grab another magazine, and for a moment, he *knew* he was going to die and render Riley's sacrifice worthless.

Then the resounding noise of a series of full battle rifles opening up echoed down the corridor. Both of the Marines about to shoot Edvard spasmed as heavy penetrators punched in through the back of their armor and failed to leave through the front.

"Sir, is that you?" Rothwell bellowed. The demoted Sergeant was leading a fire team forward—something Edvard suspected was above the rank he'd left the bully, but he wasn't complaining at the moment.

"Looking for my armored beachhead," Edvard told the big man as he rose to his feet and checked the integrity of the data crystal. To his uneducated eye, it looked intact. It *had* to be intact.

"You found us," the Marine replied. "Communications suck; we're having problems holding an intact perimeter."

"I have what we came for," Edvard told him. "We're falling back to the shuttles; I'll need your team to escort me and pass the word as we go."

"Yessir!" Rothwell answered, crisp and professional on the battle-field, his commander noted. He paused. "Where's the rest of Charlie Platoon?" he asked.

"They aren't coming."

44

Tau Ceti System
20:15 June 21, 2736 Earth Standard Meridian Date/Time
Scimitar-Type Starfighter "Strike Actual"

CHAMELEON'S REDUCED acceleration would have been blood in the water to any nearby enemy or pirate within half a star system, normally. With Shipyard Alpha spinning slowly toward annihilation, however, only the one formation of starfighters was chasing the Q-ship.

"They do see us coming, right?" Alvarado asked.

"Oh, they see us," Russell agreed. "And they're not going to let us shoot at them unopposed, but their target is *Chameleon*. They know that if they take her out, we're trapped here for the *rest* of the squadrons to chase down."

"So we stop them," the gunner said with a confidence Russell hoped he actually felt.

"Exactly," he agreed. "Range in forty seconds, Rauol. Punch every missile we have down their throats, no reserves, no games. This play's for the ride home."

Churchill's Katanas had settled into a defensive shield between *Chameleon* and the approaching Scimitars. They'd stop *some* missiles if Russell's strike force couldn't knock out the entirety of Bogey Delta, but they couldn't stop a full salvo from forty Scimitars.

"Our third salvo will hit after they launch," Alvarado warned him. "Should we redirect it after their missiles?"

Russell ran the numbers in his implant, studying the geography as the three groups of ships approached each other.

"No," he finally said. "Our intercept chances would be atrocious; we're better off making sure Delta doesn't get a second salvo into space."

Alvarado didn't respond, but the firing plan he transferred to Russell for review a few moments later had all of their remaining missiles targeted at the fighters in front of him.

With a thought, the Wing Commander approved it and flashed it out to the other twenty-four fighters remaining in his flight.

"Launch in fifteen seconds," his gunner confirmed.

Russell nodded silently, his mind linked into the starfighter as he studied the threat environment. While it wouldn't make any difference to the survivability of his fighters, Delta would be a rare commander if he didn't take a shot *back* at the Federation force.

"Launching," Alvarado announced. A moment later: "Enemy has also launched."

"How crippled do you think *Chameleon* is, I wonder?" Russell murmured. If Delta thought *Chameleon* was out of the fight—a frankly accurate assessment—he'd fire three of his available salvos at Russell's people, use his last to overwhelm Churchill's squadron, and take the Q-ship with lances. If he thought *Chameleon* was capable of defending herself, he wouldn't spend more than one salvo on Russell.

"Second salvo," the gunner announced. "No enemy response."

Russell breathed a sigh of relief. A single salvo could *hurt* his force but couldn't wipe them out. Even one follow-up wave, in the teeth of defenses weakened by the first salvo, would seriously threaten his command with annihilation.

"Third salvo in space," Alvarado announced. "First salvoes are one hundred twenty-six seconds from impact. Bogey Delta is one hundred forty-five seconds from launch range on *Chameleon*."

If everything broke right, they would never make it to that range.

A link flickered to life from *Chameleon* over the Q-Com link.

"We have a status change on the Marines, CAG," Chownyk reported. "Shuttles are breaking free and beginning their return flight. We show them as clear of Delta's firing arc until after Delta can fire on us, but watch their vectors, Rokos."

"Understood," Russell replied, watching the new data filter into his feed—and spotting the shift in Delta's formation.

"Delta is splitting off a flight team to go after the shuttles," he warned.

"Do we redesignate as primary targets?" Alvarado asked.

"No," Russell replied. "We can't."

If his missiles took out the starfighters aiming for the shuttles, that was a win. If he took them out but *failed* to take out the ones firing at *Chameleon*, that was an instant loss.

"Churchill," he pinged Alpha Squadron's commander. "Watch that breakaway flight team. You should be able to put a salvo on them before they can range on the shuttles."

He considered for a long moment. "Equal priority to defending *Chameleon*," he said softly. "The Marines deserve that much."

"Wilco," Churchill replied. "I won't mind if you make all of this irrelevant, boss. Killing them all would be *real* handy."

"I'll see what I can do!" Russell replied, shaking his head. The counters ticked down inside his implants, and time was running out.

Waves of jamming flashed out from groups of starfighters, trying to confuse and overwhelm the relatively simple minds of the small missiles. Russell led his people into the swirling, spiraling mess of a "formation" mastered long before by his veteran pilots, one that made the ECM even more effective by crossing courses and engine streams to confuse the targeting sensors again.

Then the lasers reached out and Russell activated his lance, sweeping the weapon across chunks of space and firing pulses of anti-matter through space at the incoming missiles.

Both missile salvos were lit up in space now by the fiery sparks of gigaton explosions as the leading weapons came apart under the fire. Every second saw a dozen missiles die—and the survivors draw closer, flying faster and faster toward their prey.

Russell could *feel* the inexperience of the gunners and engineers running his defenses—and was prayerfully grateful he'd left most of the new pilots with Churchill. They danced around the jammers, the decoys and the chaff, a swarm of deception and overwhelming radiation that was *almost* enough.

Almost.

The last explosions tore through his formation, each marking the final resting place of another trio of his people.

The Terrans had sent a hundred and twenty missiles at twenty-five starfighters and killed nine of his ships. A painful toll, one Russell knew he was going to feel later, but one that still left him with sixteen ships' worth of people to shepherd home.

The Terrans were more familiar with their ships. All of their engineers and gunners were fully linked in. They were facing fewer missiles each—only a hundred missiles against forty starfighters. They had every advantage over Russell's people…except the hard-forged experience of the veterans that still made up two thirds of his crew.

They only lost eight ships to his nine, but that was more than they *should* have. Russell's second wave crashed down on them with their squadron networks fragmented, their brothers bloodied for the first time in battle.

They lost sixteen more ships to the second salvo—but that left sixteen to launch on *Chameleon,* hurling over sixty missiles at the crippled Q-ship.

None of those sixteen survived the last salvo. With no Terran starfighters left around them, the only question was whether Churchill's Katanas could save *Chameleon.*

———

KYLE WATCHED the missiles boring in on his starship and felt helpless. The plan had come together about as well as could be expected, and his people had performed above and beyond anything he could have reasonably asked of them.

And now there was a good chance none of them would get to go home.

"Vector Q-probe Three to cut it through that swarm," he ordered aloud, his voice projecting the same confidence he always had, a confidence that was still fragile after Huī Xing. "If we can time it right, we can feed Churchill's people live data. Even a quarter-second less delay may make a difference."

"On it," Taylor confirmed.

He focused on his link to CIC and Chownyk. "Do we have *any* ECM?"

"Every surface emitter is gone," his XO admitted. "The repair drones can fabricate much of it in place and we have spares for what they can't, but we haven't had time. I've got nothing, sir."

"Alpha Squadron is launching missiles," Taylor announced. "I'm linking Churchill's gunners to Q-probe Three. That *should* give us a decent intercept chance."

That…was clever. Using Q-probes to feed telemetry for *capital ship* missiles was an old-game, both on the offensive and the defensive. Fighter missiles were fired at ranges where it wouldn't be relevant… except in the case of the counter-missile role, where fractions of a second were everything.

Making a mental note to be *very* sure Taylor got credit for that in his report on this mess, Kyle almost held his breath as the two missile salvos intersected… and vanished in a cascading ball of fire.

"Twenty-eight kills," Taylor breathed a moment later. "That's almost a seventy-five percent intercept rate!" She paused. "Q-probe Three won't be close enough to provide the same value for the next salvo," she warned.

"Every little bit helps," Kyle told her gently, keeping the pleased awe out of his voice. The second salvo from Churchill's ships had a more ordinary thirty percent intercept ratio, wiping a "mere" twelve missiles out of space.

But that meant that instead of facing sixty-four missiles intent on murdering everyone, Churchill's Katanas had to defend against *twenty*-four missiles. Missiles that weren't aimed at them and that had to show their vulnerable aspects as they flashed through the starfighter formation.

Taylor's handful of remaining lasers nailed the single pair of survivors ten thousand kilometers clear of *Chameleon*'s hull, and Kyle finally, *finally* allowed himself to breathe.

"Get everyone back aboard," he ordered. "Lau, time to Alcubierre?"

"Thirty-two minutes," the navigator replied.

"Chownyk?"

"Everyone who *could* intercept us is headed for Shipyard Alpha," his XO replied. "More concerned about saving a hundred thousand souls from being crushed than catching us."

Kyle hesitated for a moment.

"They're going to succeed, right?" he asked softly, his conscience twinging at him.

"If nothing else, they've the shipping to evacuate everyone before it hits crush depth for the in-system clippers," Chownyk replied.

"Good," Kyle said softly, eyeing the still-spinning immense station on his screen. "Get me Hansen on the link."

"Captain," the Marine answered a moment later, exhaustion tingeing his voice.

"Did we get what we were after?"

"We did. It's already being uploaded to *Chameleon* and JD-Intel," the Lieutenant Major confirmed.

"I expected no less," Kyle told the younger man. "Well done."

"We paid too much for it," Hansen said quietly.

"That, too, was expected," Kyle admitted with a wince. "We're clear all the way out; get your shuttles aboard."

―――――

No one stood down even a fraction for the rest of the flight. Kyle and his crew remained on the bridge, their eyes and neural feeds poring over every scrap of data from the Q-probes, looking for the tiniest hint that someone was moving toward them.

Rokos and his starfighter pilots remained in their ships. With the flight deck half-trashed, they had no easy way to deploy them, and rearming them was impossible, but their lances and remaining handful of missiles were the only real defense the Q-ship had.

"That gunship is tracking our vector," Taylor warned as they approached the safe zone where they could warp space without ripping the ship apart.

"That's why we're not going straight home," Kyle noted. "Lau?"

"Sixty seconds."

"Are we clear?" Kyle asked Taylor and Chownyk.

"We're clear," the XO reported. "There's nothing within a million klicks of us. That gunship is going to know where we went, but we wanted that, didn't we?"

"We did. Taylor, blow the Q-probes."

Their screens went dark as the three probes orbiting around the starship self-destructed.

"Thirty seconds," Lau reported.

"Establish Stetson fields," Kyle ordered.

"Up. Singularities forming. Seem clean."

Without the sensors, they couldn't even be sure of that—they'd had to spend what repair time they had rebuilding the Stetson emitters on the hull, not repairing radar emitters and receivers. It was a risk, but none of the mass manipulators were damaged.

They should be okay.

"Warping space."

Kyle held his breath for a long moment, letting the indescribable sensation of the reality around compressing and twisting to propel the ship forward.

"Bubble formed. Stable."

The Captain exhaled.

"All right, people," he said quietly. "Hanz—run out tunnels and get Rokos's people off their fighters. Everybody else—stand down to skeleton crew. Send everyone we can possibly spare to bed. We're safe under Alcubierre and we're not seeing anything except deep space until we're home."

45

Deep Space
16:00 June 22, 2736 Earth Standard Meridian Date/Time
Chameleon

KYLE KNOCKED on the door in the guest quarters of the ship, gesturing for the guard standing outside Glass's quarters to stand down.

"Take off for a meal," he told the Marine. "I don't think we'll need a guard from here on out."

"Enter!" Glass's voice echoed over the intercom. "It's not like I can say no, is it?"

Kyle stepped through the door and shook his head reprovingly at the spy.

"You're not actually under arrest, you know," he pointed out cheerfully. "Restricted to quarters, though I see no reason to keep that up unless you *want* to be a problem. I'm not going to barge in without permission."

The elderly spy stood by his wall screen, looking frail in the light of the images and feeds he was studying flickering in and out of existence.

"I figured from the fact you left me Q-Com access," he noted. He gestured at the wall. "You were right."

"Just...right out there, huh?" Kyle asked, somewhat surprised.

"Captain Roberts, I have spent *ten years*, on and off, preparing for this mission," Glass told him. "I considered every option, every variable, and long ago steeled my heart to commit the massacre I saw as a worst-case scenario.

"Faced with apparent failure, I leapt to that option without thinking. I was prepared for the worst case, so I *saw* the worst case," the spy admitted. "You saw...something else."

"It's always about angle and force," the Captain said softly. "Shipyard Alpha was a bit more literal than usual, that's all."

Glass made a gesture and a video started playing. A *Saint*-class battleship approached the Shipyard Alpha station at surprisingly high speed, presumably trying to match the rotational velocity of the spinning platform.

Kyle winced as the jagged end of the station that *had* been linked to the stabilizer ring *hit* the battleship, crunching through armor and baffles to wedge itself in the warship's hull.

"Commodore Kayla Lougheed decided that salvaging Shipyard Alpha was more important than preserving *Saint Andrew* as a combat-capable unit," Glass said calmly as the video continued, showing the station's spin slowing and stopping as the battleship's engines flared. Vapor *exploded* out of the ship after a moment, and Kyle winced again as he recognized the source.

"I was not aware," the spy continued, "that it was *possible* to overload a Class One mass manipulator."

"It's not easy," Kyle said quietly.

"She burned out three," Glass concluded. "Replacement value is half the cost of her ship and *Saint Andrew* is no longer capable of FTL or high-speed maneuvers. But she saved the station, and if the Commonwealth are smart, they'll give her a medal."

"What about the rest of the ships at the station?" Kyle asked. Apparently, his resident spy had more data on the mess they'd left behind than he did, though his focus had been on *Chameleon*. "The slips were not designed for that kind of rotation."

"Not at all," Glass agreed. "*Vesuvius* was six weeks from deployment. She had four missile launcher assemblies in position for install but not attached to anything, simply floating in zero gee. She *now* has four sixty-meter holes down most of her length."

"It'll be cheaper for them to build a new ship," Kyle said after a moment, considering that level of damage.

"They haven't even *begun* their damage surveys yet, but that's my estimate as well. Two capital ships effectively destroyed. The other eleven under construction damaged to various degrees, extending their build time by periods from months to years.

"Your 'angle and force', Captain, did almost as much damage to the Commonwealth's construction program as my plan to vaporize the station," the spy said. "With, according to their current estimates, under one percent of the civilian casualties.

"You were right," he repeated. "I brought in an expert and I should have listened to him."

"We'd have done better all along if you'd thought that way," Kyle pointed out.

Glass winced but nodded.

"And I apologize, Captain Roberts. This operation has been my... obsession, for a very long time. What's *Chameleon*'s status?"

"We're en route to New Edmonton right now. We'll drop out of FTL in four more days and redirect to Castle." Kyle shrugged. "We're thirty-two days from home. Once we get there..." He sighed. "*Chameleon* will never fight again, Mister Glass. I'm not even sure she'll be safe to fly again. We got hit hard."

"Was it worth it?"

"Yes," Glass told him. "Hansen's people got us *everything* on Project Longbow. Also on the Katanas' development and half a dozen *other* fighter-development projects in various stages from rejected to just starting.

"Void, he got us construction schematics, Captain," the spy concluded, his voice awed. "By the time we make it home, we'll probably have built our own samples of the Longbow for testing. The odds are our own first-generation bomber is basically just going to be a straight copy."

"Won't that make our involvement here obvious?" Kyle asked.

"Trust me to have done my part of this as well as you did your part, Captain," Glass replied. "By the time we're done, *everyone's* first-generation bomber will be a copy of the Longbow. We've already sold the design to the League through a broker who asks no questions...and leaks like a sieve.

"As for the rest...they've traced our exit and entrance vectors, and their relief force at Aurelius has now launched a major investigation," he said. "I believe the Committee on Human Unification and the rest of the Star Chamber will reach the desired conclusions in a week or two."

"So we just dragged an innocent star nation into a war they didn't want," Kyle said sadly.

"Yes," the spy agreed bluntly. "And in so doing, may have *saved* our own. The harsh calculus of war allows nothing else. You did well, Captain."

"Thank you," Kyle said. "I have one question, though."

He'd been wondering since the beginning, but he hadn't *wanted* to know the answer. It would have tied his hands when he needed them free.

"I owe you answers at this point, I think."

"How many stars?" Kyle said frankly. "Gods know you're no civilian, 'Mister' Glass."

Glass laughed and shook his head.

"This op is over, and I'll be stunned if I ever see the field again," he allowed. "Plus, I do owe you answers and I trust your discretion."

He bowed melodramatically.

"Vice Admiral Nicholas Voyager, at your service," he introduced himself. "Head of the Commonwealth branch of Covert Ops for Castle Federation Joint Department of Intelligence, if you were wondering.

"At this point, Captain, if there is anything Intelligence can do for you, ask. We owe you."

"I want a command. A real command," Kyle admitted.

"If it wasn't for your political enemies, this stunt would have earned you a damned star of your own," Voyager said calmly. "It's probably for the best, though. We both know you still need more seasoning for that."

Kyle breathed a sigh of relief at that. Even *he* didn't think he was ready to be an Admiral!

"What about those enemies?"

"The word is already out to the...shadowy sections of the Federation's economy that if anyone *fucks* with the Stellar Fox, JD-Intel is going to *fuck* with them," Voyager said calmly. "And we don't need such normally positive things as 'warrants' and 'evidence beyond reasonable doubt'. I can't control your friend we won't name, but I can make sure he can't use cat's-paws to hunt you or your family.

"Beyond that...we'll see when we get home," he finished. "A lot will depend on how the Commonwealth jumps."

Niagara System—Commonwealth Space
08:00 July 3, 2736 ESMDT
BB-285 Saint Michael*—Marshal Walkingstick's Office*

"I'M SORRY, JAMES," Senator Michael Burns said bluntly from his screen. The head of the Committee on Human Unification was a heavyset man with space-dark skin and shockingly white hair. Age hadn't slowed him down, and more than any other man or woman alive, Michael Burns ran the inevitable expansion of the Commonwealth.

"I managed to mostly talk the *Committee* out of this stupidity, but it ended up in front of Congress, and the damned Star Chamber voted for a punitive expedition against the New Edmonton System. I figured we may as well bake brick if they hand us clay.

"The expeditionary force has orders to take and hold. New Edmonton is worth the expenditure, and it will make the point the Star Chamber wants about letting the *condottieri* go pirate in our space."

Fleet Admiral James Calvin Walkingstick, Marshal of the Rimward

Marches and the man charged with conquering the Alliance of Free Stars, sighed.

"We both know damn well that Tau Ceti was almost certainly an Alliance covert op, not *condottieri*," he noted calmly. There was no *proof*, but a League attack simply made no sense. "We also both know that the situation in the League is not normal. Periklos is seriously trying to take permanent control of that mess and pass it to his heirs.

"He can't stand by and let us chop off systems at our leisure, regardless of apparent provocation."

"I know," Burns agreed. "Which is the rest of the bad news I have for you. I'm short-stopping most of your reinforcements and sending them in the direction of the League. We don't have an official Marshal for spinward, but we will if—when!—Periklos strikes back.

"Admiral Amandine's expeditionary force isn't enough to fight the massed *condottieri* even if they weren't likely to have their own bombers by then. I'm ordering new fleets formed to back him up, but that means *your* reinforcements are going to be a quarter of what we promised."

"I need those ships, Senator," Walkingstick warned. "Katanas and Longbows increase my striking power, but regardless of whether Project Longbow designs were stolen by the Alliance or the League, New Athens Armaments leaks like a sieve. If Periklos starts building bombers, the Alliance will have the designs inside a week.

"I need carriers, cruisers, battleships, Marine divisions—everything I was promised."

"You told us you could take the Alliance with the resources you had," Burns reminded him. "I'm afraid you may have to prove that."

"I can," the Fleet Admiral said flatly, yanking gently on his long black braid. "But it will take time. Years, not months."

"You will have it," the Senator told him. "And more ships as I can scrape them up. We both know how this ends, James. Unification is inevitable."

"It is," Walkingstick agreed with a sigh. "Let me know final numbers on what I'll be getting as soon as you can. We'll work with it."

A few more pleasantries and the channel closed. Walkingstick stalked across his office, studying his strategic plot.

He was *certain* the Tau Ceti Raid had been an Alliance operation—and he knew Burns agreed with him. They'd been too clean, too precise. Too *self-sacrificing*, not something he would expect of mercenaries like the *condottieri*.

In one move, they'd cut the force he'd planned to crush their systems with in half. He would adapt. That was what he did.

The answers often lay in what one's enemies had already done, and his gaze settled on the rimward side of the Alliance, the scattered systems where Castle and Coral still politely struggled for economic and political dominance among systems that hadn't been worth recruiting for the Alliance.

"Jessica," he raised his senior aide on his implant. "Get me... Commodore Tecumseh. And see if you can dig up which ships here in Niagara are fully fueled and supplied for long-term operations before he gets here.

"I have a job more suited for the good Commodore's talents than logistics."

———

JOIN THE MAILING LIST

Love Glynn Stewart's books? Join the mailing list at

GLYNNSTEWART.COM/MAILING-LIST/

to know as soon as new books are released, special announcements, and a chance to win free paperbacks.

ABOUT THE AUTHOR

Glynn Stewart is the author of *Starship's Mage*, a bestselling science fiction and fantasy series where faster-than-light travel is possible–but only because of magic. His other works include science fiction series *Duchy of Terra, Castle Federation* and *Vigilante,* as well as the urban fantasy series *ONSET* and *Changeling Blood*.

Writing managed to liberate Glynn from a bleak future as an accountant. With his personality and hope for a high-tech future intact, he lives in Kitchener, Ontario with his partner, their cats, and an unstoppable writing habit.

VISIT GLYNNSTEWART.COM FOR NEW RELEASE UPDATES

facebook.com/glynnstewartauthor

OTHER BOOKS
BY GLYNN STEWART

For release announcements join the
mailing list or visit **GlynnStewart.com**

STARSHIP'S MAGE
Starship's Mage
Hand of Mars
Voice of Mars
Alien Arcana
Judgment of Mars
UnArcana Stars
Sword of Mars
Mountain of Mars
The Service of Mars
A Darker Magic
Mage-Commander (upcoming)

Starship's Mage: Red Falcon
Interstellar Mage
Mage-Provocateur
Agents of Mars

Pulsar Race: A Starship's Mage Universe Novella

DUCHY OF TERRA
The Terran Privateer
Duchess of Terra
Terra and Imperium
Darkness Beyond
Shield of Terra
Imperium Defiant
Relics of Eternity
Shadows of the Fall
Eyes of Tomorrow

SCATTERED STARS
Scattered Stars: Conviction
Conviction
Deception
Equilibrium
Fortitude (upcoming)

PEACEKEEPERS OF SOL
Raven's Peace
The Peacekeeper Initiative
Raven's Course
Drifter's Folly (upcoming)

EXILE
Exile
Refuge
Crusade
Ashen Stars: An Exile Novella

CASTLE FEDERATION
Space Carrier Avalon
Stellar Fox
Battle Group Avalon
Q-Ship Chameleon
Rimward Stars
Operation Medusa
A Question of Faith: A Castle Federation Novella

SCIENCE FICTION STAND ALONE NOVELLA
Excalibur Lost

VIGILANTE
(WITH TERRY MIXON)
Heart of Vengeance
Oath of Vengeance

Bound By Stars: A Vigilante Series
(With Terry Mixon)
Bound By Law
Bound by Honor
Bound by Blood

TEER AND KARD
Wardtown
Blood Ward

CHANGELING BLOOD
Changeling's Fealty
Hunter's Oath
Noble's Honor
Fae, Flames & Fedoras: A Changeling Blood Novella

ONSET
ONSET: To Serve and Protect
ONSET: My Enemy's Enemy
ONSET: Blood of the Innocent
ONSET: Stay of Execution
Murder by Magic: An ONSET Novella

FANTASY STAND ALONE NOVELS
Children of Prophecy
City in the Sky

Printed in Great Britain
by Amazon

31782177R00200